THE MACEDONIAN HAZARD

ERIC FLINT
GORG HUFF
PAULA GOODLETT

THE MACEDONIAN HAZARD

This is a work of fiction. All the characters and events portrayed in this book are fictional, and any resemblance to real people or incidents is purely coincidental.

A Baen Books Original

Baen Publishing Enterprises
P.O. Box 1403
Riverdale, NY 10471
www.baen.com

ISBN: 978-1-9821-2586-8

Cover art by Tom Kidd
Maps by Michael Knopp

First printing, January 2021
First mass market printing, January 2022

Distributed by Simon & Schuster
1230 Avenue of the Americas
New York, NY 10020

Library of Congress Control Number: 2020044429

Pages by Joy Freeman (www.pagesbyjoy.com)
Printed in the United States of America
10 9 8 7 6 5 4 3 2 1

ONE FOR THE ROAD...

"How they hanging, Dag?" Travis asked.

"Same as always," Dag said. He handed a bottle to Travis. "It's not coffee, but it's bitter as an old girlfriend's heart."

"What would you know about that, kid?" Travis complained with gusto, and got up to go to the cabinet. Travis got down two mugs and poured the dark green mixture of cocoa and yerba maté that was the most potent coffee substitute available. When the microwave pinged he pulled the mugs out and passed one to Dag, who filled the mug the rest of the way with cream. This stuff was in severe need of softening and sweetening, so after the cream he added two spoonfuls of granulated honey, then sipped cautiously.

Travis emptied his mug with three chugs in quick succession. "That's the stuff," he said as Dag shuddered. He was starting to feel strange. His stomach was upset and his vision was getting blurry, with halos around the lights.

...vis rubbed his head and muttered about caffeine ...rawal headaches. Then Travis poured another ...nd drank it cold. As soon as he finished, he ...ed his chest—and Dag knew something was ... Travis having a heart attack was bad enough, ...im having a heart attack while Dag was seeing ... was too much of a coincidence.

...g pulled his phone from the case on his belt and ... 9-1-1. It was the same number on the *Queen* ...had been back in the twenty-first century before ...vent.

...ison!" Dag got out.

THE RING OF FIRE SERIES

1632 by Eric Flint • *1633* with David Weber • *1634: The Baltic War* with David Weber • *1634: The Galileo Affair* with Andrew Dennis • *1634: The Bavarian Crisis* with Virginia DeMarce • *1634: The Ram Rebellion* with Virginia DeMarce et al. • *1635: The Cannon Law* with Andrew Dennis • *1635: The Dreeson Incident* with Virginia DeMarce • *1635: The Eastern Front* • *1635: The Papal Stakes* with Charles E. Gannon • *1636: The Saxon Uprising* • *1636: The Kremlin Games* with Gorg Huff & Paula Goodlett • *1636: The Devil's Opera* with David Carrico • *1636: Commander Cantrell in the West Indies* with Charles E. Gannon • *1636: The Viennese Waltz* with Gorg Huff & Paula Goodlett • *1636: The Cardinal Virtues* with Walter H. Hunt • *1635: A Parcel of Rogues* with Andrew Dennis • *1636: The Ottoman Onslaught* • *1636: Mission to the Mughals* with Griffin Barber • *1636: The Vatican Sanction* with Charles E. Gannon • *1637: The Volga Rules* with Gorg Huff & Paula Goodlett • *1637: The Polish Maelstrom* • *1636: The China Venture* with Iver P. Cooper • *1636: The Atlantic Encounter* with Walter H. Hunt • *1637: No Peace Beyond the Line* with Charles E. Gannon

1635: The Tangled Web by Virginia DeMarce • *1635: The Wars for the Rhine* by Anette Pedersen • *1636: Seas of Fortune* by Iver P. Cooper • *1636: The Chronicles of Doctor Gribbleflotz* by Kerryn Offord & Rick Boatright • *1636: Flight of the Nightingale* by David Carrico

Time Spike with Marilyn Kosmatka • *The Alexander Inheritance* with Gorg Huff & Paula Goodlett • *The Macedonian Hazard* with Gorg Huff & Paula Goodlett

Grantville Gazette I–VIII, ed. by Eric Flint • *Ring of Fire I–IV*, ed. Eric Flint

To purchase any of these titles in e-book form, please go to www.baen.com.

To my daughter, BJ Matthews,
because I love you beyond all reason.
—Paula Goodlett

To my father, Harold D. Huff,
inventor, writer, and generalist,
who taught me that a rear axle is a lathe
and a tool is whatever you use to do a job.
—Gorg Huff

To my mother, Mary Flint,
who was an Alexander the Great fangirl.
—Eric Flint

CONTENTS

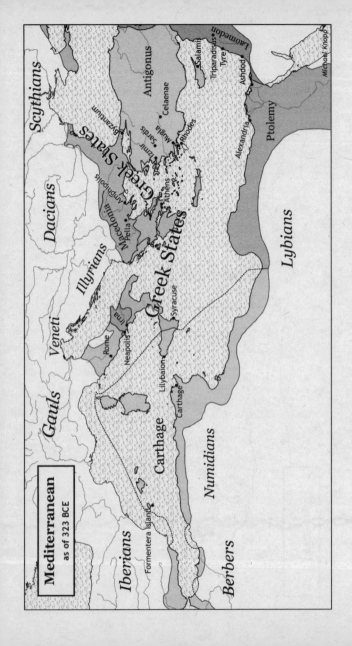

Mediterranean
as of 323 BCE

Scythians

Dacians

Gauls

Veneti

Illyrians

Iberians

Rome

Neapolis

Formentera Islands

Carthage

Lilybaion

Carthage

Numidians

Berbers

Syracuse

Greek States

Macedonia

Pella

Amphipolis

Byzantium

Athens

Smyrna

Sardis

Celaenae

Rhodes

Antigonus

Salamis

Triparadisus

Tyre

Ashdod

Laomedon

Alexandria

Ptolemy

Lybians

Michael Knopp

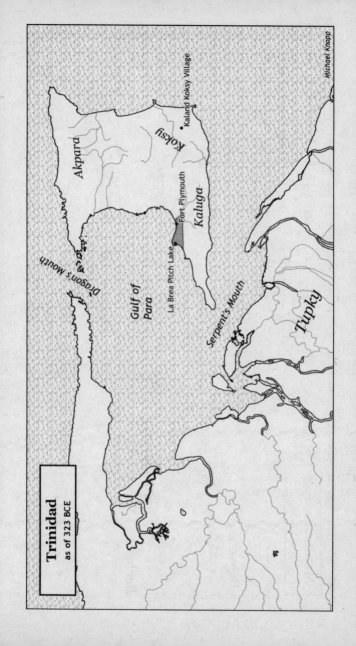

Trinidad
as of 323 BCE

Akpara

Koksy

Kaland Koksy Village

Fort Plymouth

Kaluga

La Brea Pitch Lake

Gulf of Para

Dragon's Mouth

Serpent's Mouth

Tupky

Michael Knapp

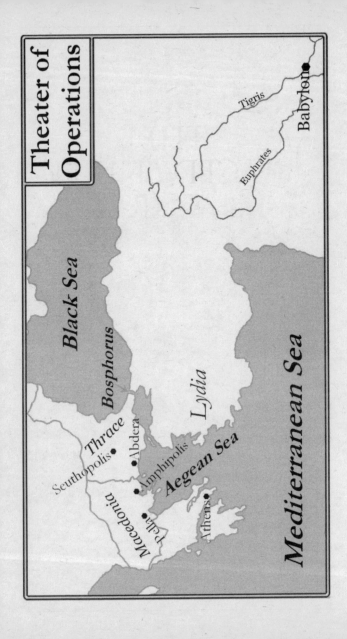

Theater of Operations

THE MACEDONIAN HAZARD

PROLOGUE

BUILD, SELL, OR DIE

Queen of the Sea, *off the coast of Trinidad*
November 28, 321 BCE

Stella Matthews lay on the bed in her cabin on the *Queen of the Sea* and watched TV. Stella was fifty-two years old, a bit overweight, recently divorced, with two adult children left behind by The Event, and was on the *Queen of the Sea* to, as the movie said, "get her groove back."

Being dropped into the fourth century Before the Common Era was not helping Stella get her groove back. The fact that she was going to be dumped off the *Queen of the Sea* with nothing but her luggage and some so-called "money" that was sucked out of Eleanor Kinney's thumb wasn't doing anything for her groove either.

So she wasn't goofing off watching TV. She was studying. There were recorded programs that could be watched on demand. The one she was watching was a discussion including Allen Wiley, who was the

President of New America, his assistant Amanda Miller, Eleanor Kinney, and a few others.

"As you all must know by now," Kinney was saying, "there is no way that the *Queen of the Sea* can support the passengers indefinitely. That, as much as the oil, is why we're here."

Allen Wiley nodded his politician's head with his face a picture of grave concern. "We will need to build ourselves a new nation here in the past. Grow our own food—"

"There is no way that the colony on Trinidad will be able to grow its own food this year and probably not next year either," Kinney interrupted. "With all the hard work and goodwill in the world, it takes time for plants to grow. The colony—"

"New America," Wiley interrupted in turn.

"New America," Kinney agreed with a nod at Wiley, then looked back at the camera. "New America is going to have to buy all, or almost all, its food for at least the next year. Probably the next three to five years. Some of that will come from oil, but not all. There are only two ways that New America can support itself: manufacturing and trade. This is different from previous colonies because this is the largest initial colony that we have been able to find, not that we've looked that hard." She smiled at the camera. "But the *Mayflower* carried one hundred and two passengers and about thirty crew to the New World. We will be more than two thousand..."

They kept talking, but Stella, a legal secretary, didn't have a clue what she might build or sell. There probably weren't going to be a lot of lawsuits for her to type up and file.

They went on talking about who owned the oil well and, for that matter, the oil field. The oil field was owned by the colony, and the oil rig was owned by the investors, which included the *Queen of the Sea*, some of the crew from the *Reliance*, the colony, and the roughnecks working on it. There would be a dividend, but Stella could do math. Especially financial math. It was unlikely that she was going to be able to live off the annual dividend. *I'm going to need a job.*

Fort Plymouth, Trinidad
December 8, 321 BCE

Stella looked at the lot marked by sticks in the grass-covered sandy soil and silently raged. She knew perfectly well that her rage was fueled by terror, but there was a lot of terror to fuel it. Her hunt for a job wasn't going well. It wasn't that there wasn't work for secretaries. It was that there were a lot of secretaries on the *Queen of the Sea* when The Event happened. And several of them had better ins with the new government than Stella did. All Stella had was her buyout from her room on the *Queen of the Sea*.

The money she got as the buyout of her share of the *Queen of the Sea*, along with a mortgage, was paying for this piece of land and the "townhouse" to be built on it here in Fort Plymouth. The deal was that fifty percent of the combined cost of the land and construction was covered by the buyout, and the rest was a loan at three percent annual interest. The total cost was forty thousand New America dollars, and she would pay out the other half over ten years, along with paying for her food and drink at the community center. She would be eating at the community center because her house wasn't going to have a kitchen for the foreseeable future. Very few of the houses in Fort Plymouth were going to have kitchens. Having a kitchen of your own upped the cost of a townhouse by over ten grand. She had no idea how she was going to get the money to make the payments on the basic townhouse. For the moment she had five grand in the bank from the sale of her cell phone to the ship, and that was going to go away in about ten months' worth of payments.

That was what the stakes were for, marking out her part of the block of townhouses that were to be built together. It wasn't much of a townhouse. Seven hundred and fifty square feet, one bedroom, one workroom, a closet that was supposed to be a bathroom once they got running water, no kitchen.

They claimed that it would have electricity and plumbing as soon as they could manage it. For now, it was to be built with a place for the wires and pipes.

She looked over to her left to see an old white guy with a walker. He was looking at the lot next to hers. After a moment, she recognized him. He had been in the cabin next to hers on the *Queen of the Sea*. Two internal cabins with no windows translated into two apartments in Fort Plymouth.

"You weren't using a walker on the *Queen*."

He looked at her and started to bristle, which Stella welcomed. She could really use a yelling match right now. Someone, anyone, to have a fight with would help.

But then the cowardly bastard deflated. Just looking sad and old. "The *Queen* had elevators and carpeted halls. Besides, I didn't have to go very far at any given time. There was always some place to sit."

Stella nodded and introduced herself.

He was Donald "call me Don" Carnegie. Seventy-seven years old and a retired plumber who smoked for fifty years and was about to take it up again because, with his diabetes, he was going to die soon anyway.

The natives used tobacco in pipes, had for who knew how long. Don figured why the hell not. At least he'd die happy.

Work area, Fort Plymouth, Trinidad
December 15, 321 BCE

The half tent—roof, no walls—was part of the gear from the *Queen*. Now it was filled with benches as Stella joined the work crew. A man waved her over and directed her to a chair. The crude bench table in front of her had a rough wooden framework for slats with strips of thin wood crisscrossed between them. And a bucket of gray-brown-looking goop. There was also a flat piece of wood with a handle sticking into the goop in the bucket.

Once everyone was seated, the man held up one of the frameworks and said, "This is wattle. It's just a thin framework of just about anything and its only purpose is to provide a place to put the daub." He set down the wattle framework and picked up a bucket. "This is daub. It's basically mud. A little more complicated than that, but not much. It's pretty similar to the stuff you would use to make mud bricks. Your job is to use the trowel"—he held up a flat piece of wood with a handle like the one in Stella's bucket of mud—"and use it to spread the daub on the wattle in a smooth even coat. And have a care, folks. This is liable to be part of the wall of your house. And if it's not yours, it will be one of your neighbors."

They got to work, and it was hard work. The daub was thick and spreading it evenly over the wattle took effort. You had to pick up the wattle and rotate it to reach the far end. It took ten to fifteen minutes to finish a panel. Then you would raise a hand and an inspector would come around with a cart, look at it, and either point to places where the daub was uneven or didn't cover everything, or put it on the cart to be taken to the drying shed.

It was hard work, but it paid fifteen bucks an hour in ship credit and Stella was going to need every dime of that.

214 12th Street, Fort Plymouth, Trinidad
December 28, 321 BCE

Stella climbed the short bamboo ladder to the ground floor that was four feet above the ground. President Wiley promised that they would get plumbing using bamboo as soon as possible, but for now there were composting toilets that amounted to honey buckets that would be picked up by carts that would come around daily. The flooring was rough planking with gaps. You wouldn't fall through, but it was obvious that speed was the controlling factor in construction. No time was spent on fitting or finishing.

The names of the streets were, for now at least, based on a grid of numbers and letters, and your place in town was based on your room on the ship. Twelfth Street was populated with passengers from Deck 6 aft inboard. It wasn't a law. If you had the money, you could buy any plot of land you wanted in Fort Plymouth or outside it. But there was a discount for taking what was offered, and Stella was not flush.

The "townhouses" were two-story post-and-daub buildings made of wood post panels. The panels consisted of a network of twigs that were then filled in with daub, the same stuff used to make mud bricks. They were made in standard frames in a central location and then carted to the townhouses to be installed. The second story was more of a loft than an actual second story, six feet high at the back and ten at the front.

The floors were wood, split logs. The locals—one of the native tribes—built their houses on stilts, so they had logs. The *Queen of the Sea* fabricated a bunch of log splitters to turn logs into rough planking. But the labor involved made that expensive, so they only used it for the flooring. The walls were the mud daub. That was also the reason for townhouses. They were easier to build them in a batch than as individual houses. It also saved room, which the wall around Fort Plymouth put at a premium.

Her townhouse now had a shape, but was still weeks away from livable. She went next door to look at Donald Carnegie's place. He wasn't up to making the visit himself, but he did know about plumbing, so he was working on the *Queen* with the five other plumbers who happened to be on the ship when The Event occurred. Not that she, or Don, were going to get indoor plumbing anytime soon.

January 17, 320 BCE

Moving day. Stella walked behind Donald as he lifted the walker with each step. He was on a limited diet now, to try to help with the diabetes, but it wasn't working, not really. He was shaky and had trouble walking. When they got to the stairs up to the ground floor, she took the walker and lifted it to the front walk, while he held the railing. Then she helped him up the four steps to the wooden sidewalk, or front porch, depending on how you thought of it. Once up, she helped him into his front room where there was a chair and a bed, both of which were pulled from the *Queen* as the interior rooms on the ship were converted to workshops rather than sleeping places. Stella, without the income from helping design the plumbing system for Fort Plymouth that Don earned, was making do with a locally made bed, reeds in a sack on rope supports in a wood frame.

Stella wasn't trained to be an old man's helper. She'd been a legal secretary who had spent her entire working life in a lawyer's office. She knew how to punctuate a tort, not how to take care of a sick old man.

Once she got Don situated, she went back to her house, got her laptop, then headed to the computer center. The computer center was five blocks away on 7th Street, near the center of town, a larger building with a steam-powered generator to charge batteries and power computers.

Stella used her ship ID card as her credit card to clock in. Use of the computers wasn't free. Neither was use of the charging station and the network link that let her hook her laptop up to the larger computers and drives that held copies of Wikipedia and the *Encyclopedia Britannica*, but it was cheaper than using one of the computers for rent. Still, even using the charging station to charge her computer's batteries was another reason for making do with locally made furniture. She was researching glassmaking, because Lisa Hammonds from Deck 8, Cabin 8235, said that it was simple. Stella didn't believe it, but she was going to find out.

While her computer was downloading the Wikipedia and *Britannica* articles on glassmaking, Stella thought back a few days to the discussion.

Queen of the Sea, *Lido Deck*
January 14, 320 BCE

"Isn't glassmaking complicated?" Stella had asked.

"Nope. Glass is sand, potash, and if you want clear glass, you flavor it with a little lead oxide. It's also the first industry started in the New Plymouth colony in like 1620."

"And where are you going to get lead oxide and potash?" Stella didn't mention sand, because she pretty much knew that Lisa would point at the beach if she did. But she was almost sure that just any sand wouldn't do. You needed some special sort of sand.

"They call it pot *ash* because it's ashes that you mix with water in a pot to leach out the stuff you want. It comes from the ashes of plants, especially water plants. Seaweed." She pointed at the beach where there was a line of seaweed at the high-tide line. "As for the lead oxide, that might be harder, at least here. But it's just lead ground into powder because lead rusts really fast. That's why lead isn't shiny."

"So why aren't you planning on glassmaking?" Stella asked.

"Because I've got a degree in electrical engineering. That's not as good as a mechanical engineer in this time, but somebody needs to design the electrical systems for Fort Plymouth and figure out how to make radios for when the ones we have wear out. And, if I live long enough, build computers." Lisa Hammonds was thirty-three, on vacation with her husband Richard, who taught English Lit at the University of Tennessee. They shared an outboard cabin with a balcony before The Event. Between that and what Lisa was making helping to design Fort Plymouth's electrical grid and the larger payout for the bigger room, they would have over fifteen hundred square feet and be nearer the computer building and capitol building. Once those got built.

Computer center, Fort Plymouth, Trinidad
January 18, 320 BCE

The download finished. Stella started reading the articles while her computer's battery charged. Glassmaking was more complicated than Lisa implied. For one thing, you didn't make glass in a Crock-Pot or a smoker. You needed heat. The sort of heat you needed to make pottery, 2,450 degrees Fahrenheit. Not much less than the melting point of steel. That, in turn, meant you needed a kiln. Then you needed a different kiln to anneal the glass after you made it, or it would shatter. At least, that was the impression that the mishmash of articles was giving her.

As soon as her computer was fully charged, Stella put it carefully in its carrying case, and with the strap over her shoulder, headed home. It started to rain while she was in the computer center, so at the corner of every block she walked down steps onto a street that had turned to mud, slogged through the mud to the next block of townhouses, went back up four steps to the wooden walkway, then the same again for seven blocks. Fortunately, because of the way the townhouses were made, the walkway was covered by the second-story balcony.

"Little boxes, little boxes," she half muttered. Then she couldn't remember some of the song, and continued, "And they're all made out of ticky-tacky, and they all look just the same." She knew why that was. It was because standardization made for faster, cheaper construction. And building housing for three thousand people wasn't cheap, no matter how you did it.

☆   ☆   ☆

Once Stella got home, she dried off using a dirty towel because laundry was expensive now too. Then, using the same towel, she dried her computer case and pulled out her computer. Then she knocked on Donald Carnegie's door and tried to interest him in glassmaking as a business.

214 12th Street, Fort Plymouth, Trinidad
March 12, 320 BCE

The kiln design was mostly out of Wikipedia, but Donald had helped. It turned out that plumbing helps with preheating air to make the fire hotter. Something called reverse flow. The air came in right next to where the burned air went out, so the flue preheated the air. Stella was the one who wrote up the variance request that let them put the kiln behind the house in the fifty-foot field that went between the houses and the town wall. Stella had never in her worst nightmare imagined that she would be living in a walled fort. The wall was going to be eighteen feet tall when it was finished.

April 14, 320 BCE

Stella helped Donald up the stairs to the second floor, then out onto the balcony, so they could watch the *Queen of the Sea* sail out. The second floor was fourteen feet above the ground after adding the four-foot crawl space below the first floor. That put Donald and her eyes a touch above the wall, so out in the bay she could see the *Queen* clearly.

She looked over at Donald and saw a tear leaking onto his cheek, and Stella wanted to cry too. Because she knew as well as Donald did that he would probably not live to see the *Queen of the Sea* return to Fort Plymouth.

She helped him back inside and they sat for a while as she waited for him to get enough energy to make it down the stairs. The stairs were sort of actual stairs, though they were like the stairs on a warship. They had flat rungs, but the angle was closer to a ladder than what Stella thought of as stairs. They did have extra steps, so Donald didn't need to lift his feet that far to reach the next step.

Once Stella got Donald situated, she went out to the "hardware" store near the center of town to buy tar. The "hardware" store did indeed have hardware. It had hammers, though it had more wooden hammers than steel hammers, and the wooden mallets were quite a bit cheaper. It had brushes and buckets, mostly handmade. The tar she was here to buy came in chunks. It was a waste product of the "oil refinery," a still located near the oil well a few miles out of town. The tar was the crud that collected on the bottom of the still, and was mucked out by hand.

It was also the best sealant for cracks in the roof, floor, and walls in the "townhouses" of Fort Plymouth. And Stella and Donald's townhouses had a lot of cracks to be filled.

One good thing was that Stella was losing weight. She was doing quite a bit of hard manual labor every day, between emptying the chamber pots, sweeping the floors, building the kiln, and, today, using a pot stove on the balcony to melt the tar. It stank, and would stink even after it cooled for days. It was a tar-paper shack, without the paper. Once she had the tar melted, it went up onto the roof by buckets as local tribesmen painted the roof with it, to give her and Donald, for the first time since they moved in, roofs that didn't leak.

The back of Stella's townhouse was up against the fifty-foot field, a fifty-foot stretch of open ground between the town and the town's wall. The field was designed to let defenders move from one point on the wall to another easily, but Stella got a ten-foot variance to build her kiln out back. The kiln was brick two layers thick, and it had a preheating chamber and was oil powered. Why not? She lived only a few miles from an oil well. It was also, after months of her work and the occasional labor of the locals, not quite completed yet.

Community center, Fort Plymouth, Trinidad
April 19, 320 BCE

The community center was a combination restaurant, general grocery, half open-air gaming area, and live theater. There was even a big-screen TV from the *Queen* in one room that played movies from back in the world. At the moment, Stella was sitting at a table, eating cornbread and chili beans with enough super turkey meat to make it almost real chili. The peppers were as local as the super turkey. They grew all over this part of South America and the Tupky were selling them to the colony by the canoe load. Everything from fresh to smoked and dried. Chili was almost like home. Well, except for the people who insisted that chili wasn't supposed to have beans in it.

Next to Stella on the bench was Carol Knight Harvell. Carol was forty-five and worked as a domestic before The Event. The trip on the *Queen* was her second honeymoon, and her husband John Harvell had been a truck driver in Chicago. They had three adult kids who had not made the trip, and were committed Christians before The Event. They were both working at other businesses now. John was working on one of the steam generators. His job was to watch the dials, control the crude oil that the steam engine burned for fuel, and make sure the steam engine ran at a consistent speed. The sole function of his steam engine generator was to charge a bank of lead acid batteries that were then used to power electrical devices. That system was in use because here in New America they lacked the control systems to avoid power spikes.

Carol, on the other hand, worked in the condom factory. "You have nothing to complain about," Carol told Stella. "I spend my whole day with a wooden dildo in my hand, dipping it into a pot of hot latex, then sticking it under a blow-dryer, then dipping it again until the condom is thick enough not to rip. Then I turn it over to Tess Panay while I grab another dildo and do it all again. I've handled more woodies since we got here than in my whole family for generations back."

Stella didn't want to talk about the utter and complete lack of woodies of any sort in her life since The Event, so she changed the subject and they talked about some of the new industries that were starting up in Fort Plymouth. They were all kitchen industries, wood shops and leather workers, manufacturers of latex water bottles and some guy trying to make a sewing machine. Another guy was trying to get a Jacquard loom built, and someone actually had a pedal-powered carding machine up and running.

After lunch, Stella went back to the counter and got a salad to go for Donald, which she carried back.

☆   ☆   ☆

Donald Carnegie was sitting on the wooden sidewalk in front of his "townhouse." His head was lolling to the side and his mouth was open. There was some drool leaking and Stella tried to wake him. He wouldn't wake up. She checked his heartbeat. It was still beating, but he was barely breathing at all. She shouted to William McIan, their next door neighbor on the other side. "Donald is unconscious! Run get the medics."

The medics arrived about fifteen minutes later, and took him away in a two-wheeled cart pulled by two men.

Fort Plymouth Hospital, Trinidad
April 21, 320 BCE

President Allen Wiley stepped into the ward and looked around. This was the experimental ward. There were twelve cots, six on each side of the room, and about half the beds were filled. These patients were the ones with terminal illnesses that would have been merely chronic back in the world. The beds emptied and were refilled on a regular basis as the healers tried to do what they could, and in the process did human experiments.

Al went over to the doctor, Ronald Kemper, who had been a registered nurse back before The Event.

Ronald looked up from the patient he was injecting. "It's fish-derived insulin, Mr. President, and not nearly as pure as I would like. But this guy is in a diabetic coma and headed to the grave if we don't do something."

"Did you have his permission?" Al asked.

Ronald nodded. "It's on the chart. We can try anything we want." It was a standard question that all the citizens of New America were asked to fill out even before they moved off the ship.

Donald's eyes flickered. The insulin was working.

May 15, 320 BCE

Ronald Kemper pulled the sheet up over Donald Carnegie's head. The allergic reaction to the insulin contributed to a chest infection, which in Donald's weakened state proved fatal. Other patients were doing fine, at least for now, on the fish-derived insulin that was only purified by centrifuge. But there were too damned many who died from allergy to the non-insulin element that the poor purification methods left in the juice, and even for those it did work for, there were often side effects. Gradual damage to the fatty tissue around the injection points. Other things.

He got up and scratched his head. He was a nurse, a surgical nurse, and a good one. Not a doctor, much less an expert in experimental medicine, which was what they needed.

214 12th Street, Fort Plymouth, Trinidad
May 16, 320 BCE

Stella looked around Donald's room in the double townhouse that was now hers. Donald's will left her everything he had. She lived upstairs in her side, and there was another room just like hers in Donald's side that he never occupied. She would move the bed and the chair up to her room and happily get rid of the sack full of reeds.

This floor, the ground floor, was designed to be a workshop. She spent two hours cleaning and packing everything Donald had. It wasn't much. Some clothes and a book reader. Donald spent most of his time reading after The Event. He told her that he was never much of a reader before, but he was so weak after that he couldn't do much else, and the nearest TV was in the community center.

Once she was done with his room, Stella went next door to look at her latest failure to make glass. She used a pry bar to break open the mold and looked at the roughly lens-shaped piece of flint.

The glass kiln in the back was up and operational, although the firebricks weren't of the quality she wanted. But as the dark gray object indicated, the real problem was that in spite of having all the equipment and reading up on it, she had no clue how to make glass. She needed an expert, and though there was one guy who blew glass as a hobby for a while when he was younger, he used premade glass ingots for his glassblowing. Besides, he wasn't interested in "helping the competition." The asshole.

She had to find someone who could make glass.

Community center, Fort Plymouth, Trinidad
May 17, 320 BCE

Stella plugged her computer into the ethernet port. There was a row of them with bench seats and little wooden half walls between them. It was where Stella did all her research, and after much consideration she called up not Wikipedia nor *Encyclopedia Britannica*, but instead the post-Event news feed and did a search for glassmaking. What came up first on the search was glass baubles made in Carthage and Alexandria, and there bought by the *Queen* and available for sale on their next landing at Fort Plymouth. Apparently, the Carthaginians were competent glassmakers. One thing that Stella knew from her reading was that glassmaking was easier if at least part of your mix was already made glass. She put in an order, but then she had a thought. She needed someone who knew how to make glass. Why not try to hire someone from Carthage or, for that matter, anywhere in Europe where they made glass? She sat at her computer and wrote out an ad to hire a glassmaker. Then she called up the translation app for Phoenician.

> *Wanted: Skilled glassmaker to move to*
> *Fort Plymouth, Trinidad, New America.*

Then she added her name and how to get in touch with her. After translating it into Phoenician, she translated it into Greek, Egyptian, and Latin. Then she checked the price for sending a message to the *Queen* and cursed for two minutes straight. The price, even for text, was twenty bucks.

Queen of the Sea, *Port of Izmir*
May 17, 320 BCE

Joshua Varner pulled the next message from the queue. It was an ad for a glassmaker. It wasn't the first of that sort of message. Over the last month since they left Trinidad, they'd gotten several requests for skilled craftsmen of one sort or another. This one, though, wasn't from the government. It was a private individual. Joshua forwarded it to Eleanor Kinney.

☆   ☆   ☆

Eleanor Kinney sat in her office, checking her email. They were going to be shipping craftsmen to the new world if they could find them. The "Indians"—everyone knew the term was inappropriate but it was still the one they wound up using because it was handy—mostly lacked the skills that they needed in Fort Plymouth, and the ship people certainly lacked them, skill being a completely different thing than knowledge.

The question was how to get the people they needed. In the here and now, a lot of the skilled craftspeople were slaves. Not all of them, but the majority. Eleanor would have liked to start up an underground railroad, but that wasn't practical. A thought rose up in her mind and she slapped the disgusting thing back down to the evils of her subconscious where it belonged. But it wouldn't stay slapped down.

We might have to buy slaves.

May 18, 320 BCE

Lars Floden listened to Eleanor's proposal and turned to Marie Easley. First, because this really wasn't his thing. And second, because it wasn't really a proposal so much as a plea for him to tell her it was all a bad dream and she didn't actually have to consider paying the bastards who kept slaves so that they could profit even more from their barbarity. He couldn't tell her that, and he couldn't quite bring himself to say, "Yes, pay the bastards."

Marie looked at Eleanor. "I think that we may have to do so, but first we need to talk to Roxane. And, for that matter, Eumenes. And if she is available, Cleopatra. They, especially Cleopatra, will be more conversant with the local laws and customs."

Queen of the Sea, *en route to Amphipolis* May 17, 320 BCE

Roxane looked around the private conference room where Cleopatra, Marie Easley, Lars Floden, Eleanor Kinney, and Dag Jakobsen sat. There was wine on the table and Cleopatra was sipping hers, clearly to buy time. Of course she was confused. She didn't have Roxane's time with the ship people. She didn't understand how anyone could be as rabidly antislavery as they were.

Cleopatra put down her wineglass and said, "Well, certainly you can buy slaves. I had understood that you forbade slavery on the *Queen* and in New America."

"They do," Roxane said. "They will be freeing the slaves once they buy them."

"Then why buy them?" Cleopatra asked. "Wait. Do you imagine that slaves will be so grateful that they will work for you after being freed? Slaves are the most ungrateful people in the world. It's well known."

"Gee." Eleanor's voice dripped sarcasm. "Why wouldn't they work for free just because they didn't have to?"

Cleopatra looked at Eleanor, and Roxane decided she should interrupt before things got heated.

"I told you, my friend"—she waved at the ship people—"on this they are fanatics beyond reason."

"And apparently beyond courtesy as well," Cleopatra agreed, but her tone was more observant than harsh. She turned back to Eleanor and continued. "However good you feel their reasons are, once freed they will run off to their own endeavors. Buying a slave to ship to New America to work in one of your shops will get you no work if you free the slave. In fact, if you free the slave the moment it boards your ship, it will turn around and walk right back off."

"What about contracts?" Dag asked. "I know I may be being corrupted by the locals, but crew on the *Queen of the Sea* signed on for at least a full voyage. They couldn't get to Port-au-Prince and quit their job without being in breach of their contract."

"A contract made under duress is invalid. And anyone signing a contract while a slave is, by definition, under duress. But you do bring up an interesting point, Dag. There were contracts of indenture. They were outlawed by the Thirteenth Amendment to the Constitution of the United States, at least as the Supreme Court has interpreted it. And the UN also had rules against it. But there are still binding employment contracts. It could be done. A person could, as part of the deal to gain their freedom, sign an employment contract, with some part of their wages garnished to pay off the debt they incurred in borrowing the money to buy their freedom. But I guarantee it's going to end up in front of New America's Supreme Court, all three of the judges. And I can't guarantee that it will pass their muster."

"I doubt it will pass mine," Lars Floden said.

"I hate to say it," Eleanor Kinney said, "but you may have to reconsider if you want Fort Plymouth to survive, and even more if you want us to have any real role in the emancipation of slaves. Absent at least some acceptance"—she paused, clearly trying to find words that didn't make her feel like Nathan Bedford Forrest—"of a right to recompense, there is no motive for the people in New America to buy the freedom of slaves. It's wrong. I *know* it's wrong. But is it as wrong as just leaving them in slavery?"

☆   ☆   ☆

Over the next few weeks, the radio was full of back-and-forth discussions, some public and some private, between the *Queen of the Sea*, the *Reliance*, and Fort Plymouth. It also included the personnel at the newly placed radio stations that the *Queen* was installing from Carthage to Babylon. And so, indirectly, involved the governments of the lands around the Med.

Fort Plymouth, New America
June 20, 320 BCE

Another bad batch. Stella Matthews was getting closer, though. The broken glass shards she had added to the mix lowered the heat needed and got her something that was almost glass. It was gray and cloudy, but almost translucent. It was even smooth on one surface. But it was also full of bubbles. Just knowing the theory wasn't cutting it. She needed a professional, and so far as she knew the only real glassmaking professionals in the world were in Europe and North Africa. She put her stuff away and dressed in her clothes from the cruise that were by now approaching the status of rags, and headed for the community center.

☆   ☆   ☆

Stella plugged in her computer and logged on to the email server. She had responses to her ad, but they weren't applicants. They were slaves—slave owners, rather—offering to sell her qualified craftsman for *Queen of the Sea* dollars. For now, *Queen of the Sea* dollars and New American dollars were effectively the same thing. They were worth exactly the same amount of silver. There were several offers. Two Carthaginians, three Egyptians, and a Phoenician from Tyre. For just a moment she wanted to get ready to stage a march on Al Wiley's office, and not a Martin Luther King Junior–style peaceful protest. No. She was going to start the revolution.

It wasn't news exactly. The New America Congress had passed a law saying that for the next twenty years contracts of employment made with the express purpose of buying a slave out of bondage would be enforceable. And the three Justices of the New America Supreme Court had approved the law by a two-to-one major-ity, and one of the guys voting yes was black, Justice Keith Robertson. The practice of buying and freeing slaves with "Advance on Wages Contracts" was legal.

The advance on wages weren't paid to the slave, but the slave owner. The Advance on Wages contracts were way too close to a contract of indenture to survive any American court back in the world. That type of deal was all over the news last week, including the fact that the slave had to agree for the sale to take place. Surprisingly, not all of them did. The thing she hadn't known about—or at least hadn't realized—was that the radio stations being installed all around the Mediterranean were used by the locals to buy and sell in advance. Everything from linen to slaves, back and forth between city-states and nations, whether the trades involved ship people or not.

There were also Advance on Wages contracts where the "contract employee" was just getting the transport cost to Trinidad paid.

Transportees could become citizens just like any other immigrant, if the person lived here for the two years needed and could recite the Bill of Rights in English and showed a basic knowledge of how the government worked through a standardized test.

What Stella didn't understand was why anyone would want to come live in a town that was mostly a housing project, where the plumbing was nonexistent and the only roads that were paved even with just tar sand were 7th Street and Garnet Avenue. And that had been done only after two people died because the ambulance carts got stuck in the mud.

She went back to the ads. One of the Carthaginians had agreed to a contract for a ten-year period. The cost was high: five thousand New American dollars, plus transport costs. The only way she would be able to afford it was to sell her laptop. She had already sold her cell phone to the *Queen of the Sea*. Donald Carnegie's book reader was now owned by the community center and Stella's mortgage on both townhouses was paid for the next year, along with the community dues that paid for her meals and the use of the center.

☆   ☆   ☆

Stella was a decisive woman when she had to be, and now she had to be. The truth was that the chickens hadn't come home to roost yet, but they would if she didn't do something. She checked the prices being offered by the *Queen of the Sea*, the government, and individuals for laptops, and pulled up the specs on her laptop to compare. She should be able to get around eleven thousand three hundred dollars for her computer.

She unplugged her computer and headed up to the counter. Here in the computer center was a lock room, constantly manned, where items from back in the world and very expensive local items were stored for resale after being examined. Among the items was a two-foot-tall solid-gold wall hanging in the shape of the sun. It weighed twenty-two pounds. And was worth rather less than any of the hundred fifty plus computers stored there.

It took them two hours to check out her laptop and do the paperwork, but by the end of the day her account in the Bank of New America had an available balance of ten thousand two hundred dollars and ninety-eight cents. That would change once the computer was put up for auction and actually sold.

Then, using one of the publicly available computers, she bought the contract of indenture for Carthalo, a man owned by the Barca clan. The *Reliance* would pick him up on their way back. Carthalo was the cheapest on offer.

Radio room, Carthage
June 20, 320 BCE

Tina Johnson read the notice off the computer screen and shook her head in disgust. Part of the deal was that she had to transmit and receive messages.

Even messages that involved human trafficking. It was disgusting enough when the locals did it, but ship people ought to know better. Even as she thought it, she knew that she wasn't being completely fair, but she didn't care. Sure, she walked the streets of Carthage every day among slaves and slave owners. She had dinner prepared by slaves at least three days a week, but that didn't matter. She didn't *own* slaves.

Put whatever face you wanted on Stella's Advance on Wages contract; it was buying a slave. And as agent for the station, Tina was going to have to go pay the present owner and pick up the slave.

☆   ☆   ☆

Carthalo woke up when the bucket of water was thrown onto him. No, not water. It was piss. He came up ready to fight and the overseer laughed. It wasn't like he could reach the man. He was chained to the wall. The iron chain went from a bolt in the wall to a manacle around his ankle. He couldn't go after the bastard anyway, because his ankle was rubbed raw and infected, and none of it was his fault.

What happened was an accident, pure and simple. Carthalo didn't push his owner's nephew into the furnace. The nephew bumped him. Carthalo was just trying to keep his balance.

"You are a lucky bastard, Carthalo. You've been sold."

☆   ☆   ☆

Ten minutes later, sluiced down, but still wet and limping, Carthalo was led into one of the master's rooms. Not any slave quarters this. And a woman was seated on a chair at a table. There was another chair, and Carthalo was motioned to it. He sat cautiously, and the woman began to talk. She would say a few words, then the little box she carried would speak. It was not like anything he had ever heard of. He was to get his freedom, but not until he had worked for ten years. There was a provision for him to buy himself free early by paying back the money she was paying for him.

Carthalo figured he could do that. Before Padus Boca fell into the furnace mouth, Carthalo had several drachmas stashed away for work he did on the side.

Maybe he was lucky. Besides, the woman who was buying him was attractive. He might be able to seduce her. Then he learned that he wasn't being bought by this woman. She was just acting as agent.

He was going to sail on the *Reliance*. To New America.

214–216 12th Street, Fort Plymouth, Trinidad
June 30, 320 BCE

Stella woke to a siren that lasted for almost a minute before it was shut off. Then the public address system reported native attacks on the outlying farmsteads. It also warned everyone to stay inside the walls, and included a request for emergency housing.

Stella got up, got dressed, and headed to the community center. She had extra room. In the community center, she was introduced to a farm family, Mrs. Banner, and two kids, and four natives were assigned to her. They were especially worried about Brad Banner, who had stayed at the farm to try to protect their super turkeys.

For the next two days the town of Fort Plymouth was cut off from its outlying territories and invested by a force of locals from the river Orinoco.

July 2, 320 BCE

They couldn't see the Indians, not even from the second-floor balcony. But they could see the arrows that the Indians were shooting and they could see the troops on the parapet with their crossbows and occasional guns. Fort Plymouth was crowded now, not only with all the passengers, but with the allied tribes. That was most of the tribes that lived on Trinidad. All of them who were close enough to get here before the Tupky and their allies invested the fort.

Stella was watching the battle as best she could when the public address system announced that the *Reliance* was in the Gulf of Paria.

Reliance, *Gulf of Paria* July 3, 320 BCE

Carthalo limped over to the side of the barge portion of the *Reliance* and helped hand bullets up to the steam cannon crews. He wasn't the only one. The *Reliance* had twenty passengers. About half of them were transportees like Carthalo. The others were immigrants who wanted to go to New America, but couldn't afford passage on the *Queen*, often people who signed employment contracts to raise the fare.

Still, Carthalo was worried what would happen to him if the ship person who owned his contract died in the battle. They said he was a free man now, just one with an employment contract. But Carthalo didn't really believe that.

Trinidad Docks
July 4, 320 BCE

Carthalo walked across the gangplank to the long wooden dock that the *Reliance* was tied up to and was met by a ship person. He thought he could tell ship people by now. This one was a man who said his name was George Grosskopf. For the rest of the day, the transportees were herded from here to there, dropped off at various locations, until a local dressed in a loincloth and body paint led him to a house.

☆   ☆   ☆

Stella looked up from an argument between the two Banner kids to see a man limping along with one of the Indians. *He looks like a Tupky but apparently one of the Tupky on our side.* In very broken English, the Tupky said, "Your slave."

"He's not a slave," Stella insisted, and the Tupky shrugged and turned away, leaving a man with short-cropped hair and a beard that was just starting to grow out standing there.

Stella introduced herself, and best she could tell, the only words he understood were her name. She called Mrs. Banner to take care of her kids, and using gestures, she led Carthalo through her townhouse to the kiln in back. It was better than walking around the block to get there. By now her house had some furnishing, mostly local work. A table, some camp chairs. A chest with gourd mugs and wooden plates. Even some wall hangings. All locally made. Stella wasn't spending her dwindling cash supply on things like glass cups or plastic trays.

She noticed that Carthalo was looking around curiously, and once they got out the back to the kiln and he was sure she didn't object, he examined it carefully.

214–216 12th Street, Fort Plymouth, Trinidad
July 23, 320 BCE

Carthalo turned the knob that increased the amount of heated oil that was fed to the burner. This was the third day of the melt. One of the big things that Stella didn't know was how you could tell that you were melting the glass long enough and hot enough. You got them both by looking and seeing what it looked like. The trick Carthalo used for heat was one he had learned back in Carthage. You took a wooden plank with a small hole in it, then as the light of the melt shone through it onto another piece of whitewashed wood, you looked at the color. You needed to do that at night or you needed your kiln in a room, because daylight washed it out so you couldn't tell the color well. For time, you stuck a rod into the glass and pulled out a blob. If there were unmelted bits or too many bubbles, you needed to keep it melting longer. He needed the glass to glow a yellow closer to white at this part of the melt, so that the bubbles would be able to escape.

Another day at the increased heat should do it, he thought. The idea of using oil to control the flame struck him as brilliant. At least it did now. His first reaction was that they should be using wood like they did in Carthage.

He put the iron plate back over the opening in the kiln using tongs, then left the kiln and went back into the house. He had a room at the back of the house next to the back door. The whole place stank of tar.

He thought of running away. He had thought of running away almost every day since he was sold into slavery at age six. But usually only a passing thought. There was nowhere to run. Now, well, there was still nowhere to run. No one spoke his language except a few other transportees and, as was amply demonstrated by the battle being fought as he arrived, the Indians were dangerous.

Besides, he had his own space, even if it stank of tar. He had meals and access to the community center. He could move on his own. He wore no chains or any mark that he was a slave. And he got paid. Most of his pay went to the debt he owed Stella for buying him, but he got some money every week. Not a lot, but enough to buy an extra glass of wine when he wanted one, or new clothing if he saved up.

July 25, 320 BCE

Stella watched as Carthalo shoved the big spoon into the melt. The spoon was a brass bowl with a long wooden handle and must weigh twenty pounds empty.

Full, it was closer to forty, and as he walked with it, Carthalo jiggled it, tossing the glass blob up out of the bowl with every step until he got to the stone table, where he plopped it down. It was glowing red orange and still very flexible as he used a pair of shears to cut off a smaller blob, and put it in a ceramic mold. Then he pressed the other half of the mold onto it. If this worked, they would get a lens-shaped piece of clear glass.

Carthalo then took a handpress made of iron and pressed the rest of the blob into a roughly flat sheet about two feet across. He used a knife to cut the glass into a square about a foot across.

☆　　☆　　☆

It didn't work. The glass was Coke-bottle green. The lens shape was rough and the lens had a dozen little bubbles in it. Carthalo was quite happy with it, though, insisting that with reheating and smoothing it would make a lovely ornament that would fetch a good price.

They weren't where they wanted to be, but they were in the glassmaking business.

CHAPTER 1

A WAR TO FIGHT

Queen of the Sea, *forward radio room*
November 2, 320 BCE

The radio printer clacked and Joshua Varner jerked in his office chair. He couldn't get used to it. The *Queen* had arrived in this time equipped with top-of-the-line laser printers, and they still had them. But to keep that happy state as long as possible, they had, over the past year, built printers, using chips from anything they could scavenge. Dot matrix printers, which were slow and noisy. The radios sent digitally. That meant they could send anything from picture to voice to text, but text used the least bandwidth, and so was the most common. He was from the twenty-first century and here he was in the fourth century BCE, using mid-twentieth-century tech to receive what amounted to radio teletype from Rome about the Senate's response to Antigonus holding Babylon against Attalus.

He rotated in his chair and scooted over to the printer. The roll of paper was held on the rubber cylinder with a serrated blade. He tore off the sheet. It was locally made rag paper. The words were in Latin and Joshua couldn't read Latin. But the address was clear. He folded it, sealed it with wax and a stamp made by the machine shop, then called a new hire. "Delivery for the Romans. Titus Venturis Calvinus."

☆   ☆   ☆

Titus took the sheet from the messenger and gave him a ship people dollar as a tip. Once the door to his cabin was closed, he used a fingernail to pop the wax seal and opened the letter.

He sat at the small desk in his room and read.

From the Office of the Consuls
Rome will take no action regarding the conflict of the diadochi.
Make no promises to either side.

"Any side, they should say," Titus muttered.

You will endeavor to obtain the designs for an electrical battery.

"A battery of cannons would be easier." Titus tossed the cable on the desk and picked up the phone. "Who do I see about a battery?" he muttered to himself again. Then, making up his mind, dialed a number.

When the phone was answered, he said, "Capot, I have some scoop for you and I need a favor."

"What sort of a favor?"

"Rome wants batteries. The electrical kind. Who do you know and what are your suggestions?"

"Hm," Capot Barca said, and Titus could imagine him playing with his fancy beard. "I think lead acid is probably your best bet. I'll have some names for you by lunch. Meanwhile, I'm going to send Carthage Rome's plans, once you give me the scoop."

☆   ☆   ☆

Two hours later, Capot lay on his bed and read the Carthaginian response to his message. It was longer and more detailed, but amounted to much the same thing Titus got from Rome. The people back home were confident that with Alexander dead and the generals fighting each other, Carthage remained safe.

Then Capot got to the next section.

> *Do all in your power to prevent the Romans from seeing the work going on in the military harbor. In this history, Carthage will not wait for the Romans to sow our city with salt.*

Insane, Capot thought. Rome wouldn't be a threat for another hundred years, and by that time the world would have changed beyond all recognition. Capot stopped himself. No, that wasn't right. Rome had read the butterfly book too. They would know about the three Punic wars, and would see Carthage as a threat, no matter what Carthage did or didn't do. As much as he hated the thought, the government might well be right. The effect of the butterfly book was to rush things, to push the world in decades into wars that would have happened over centuries.

Had it not been for the *Queen of the Sea*.

Queen of the Sea, *Piraeus, Port of Athens*
November 3, 320 BCE

Marie Easley looked around the conference room. Eumenes, Dag Jakobsen, and Daniel Lang were talking together, pointing at a map on the table. Eleanor Kinney, the chief purser for the ship, and Roxane and Eurydice, the queens-regent of Alexander the Great's empire, were a couple of seats away. And all the way across the room, Olympias was scowling at all and sundry. She was greatly displeased that her stock of hallucinogens and other drugs had been taken. They were under lock and key in the pharmacy. Captain Lars Floden wasn't going to let the fourth century BCE's most famous poisoner keep her stock of poison while she was on the *Queen*, even if she was the mother of Alexander the Great.

For the past few days, Eumenes had attempted to get the *Queen of the Sea* to take a force of his soldiers around the Horn of Africa, because he had two fires to put out: Cassander in Macedon, and Antigonus in Babylon.

There were radios in Rome, Carthage, Alexandria and other places around the Mediterranean and Aegean Seas. But they didn't have any radios in Babylon or anywhere in the eastern stretches of the empire.

Eumenes couldn't let Cassander consolidate in Macedonia, because Macedonia was the tail that wagged the dog of Alexander the Great's empire. But if Eumenes concentrated on Cassander, it would give Antigonus One-eye time to cut the empire in half. To counter that threat, he wanted to remind the eastern satraps that they weren't safe, even if Antigonus held Babylon, for the *Queen of the Sea* could reach them anyway.

Eumenes wasn't going to get what he wanted.

The delegates from Antigonus One-eye were lobbying just as hard against Eumenes, insisting that it was an internal matter. And, for that matter, that Attalus' attack on Antigonus in Babylon had not been an authorized action, but little more than an act of banditry. They also argued that even if the queens-regent Roxane and Eurydice were to rule against Antigonus, it was still an internal matter, and for the *Queen of the Sea* to interfere would destroy its neutrality.

It was a good argument, as much as Marie might sympathize with Roxane and Eurydice. Lars wasn't going to let the *Queen* be dragged into the politics of the *diadochi*, Alexander the Great's surviving generals, any more than could be avoided.

Lars came in with Staff Captain Anders Dahl, and took the seat at the head of the long oval table right next to Marie's seat. Anders took the next seat over. The position of staff captain was analogous to that of executive officer on a navy ship or a cargo ship. But the way it was working out since the twenty-first-century cruise ship *Queen of the Sea* arrived in the year 321 BCE, "staff captain" was going to be the title for executive officer in the future and "exec" was going to be ignored except by dusty old scholars like Marie. Marie felt her lips twitch at the thought.

Lars gave Anders a look, and Anders said, "If everyone will be seated, we'll get started."

Eumenes, Dag, and Daniel took their seats quickly, as did Eleanor, Roxane and Eurydice as well. Olympias went around the table to take the seat opposite to Lars, as though that were the head of the table. It was an obvious powerplay, and Marie looked at Lars.

Lars let it pass. Whatever the changes over the last year and a bit, Lars had been a cruise ship captain for almost ten years and an officer on a cruise ship for even longer. He was a polite man and willing to let others appear to score points...as long as they didn't actually interfere with the running of the *Queen*. That was one of the things Marie liked about Lars, even though she occasionally found herself wishing he would rip someone's head off—metaphorically speaking—when the situation required it. Lars had proven his willingness to do it literally. He had washed the decks of the *Reliance* in blood when pirates seized her, and used the *Queen* to turn a fleet of triremes into kindling.

Once everyone was in the proper place, or close enough, Lars again let Anders say it.

"I'm sorry, General Eumenes, but the *Queen of the Sea* can't involve itself in the internal politics of the United Satrapies and States of the Empire. Quite aside from logistical concerns, which are real and serious, we have to maintain our neutrality... at least officially."

"Officially?" Roxane asked, lifting a sculpted eyebrow. She very much reminded Marie of Sophia Loren. Since the arrival of the *Queen*, she had added golden highlights to her black hair and now wore artfully applied makeup. Roxane's lush but athletic figure was much the same as before her arrival, save perhaps a bit healthier. Roxane liked to listen to audiobooks while she worked out in the cruise ship gymnasium.

"Officially," Lars agreed. "I've been in contact with President Wiley by radio, and New America expresses a willingness to ally with the USSE. On the basis of that, we will help where we can, within the limits of our situation. That doesn't mean using the *Queen* very much, I'm afraid, but we should be able to supply you with some gunpowder."

"Gunpowder," Eumenes said studiously, "is a flash in the pan."

Marie Easley looked at the general in something partaking of both disgust and admiration. Disgust because the statement was patently ridiculous. Admiration because the expression "flash in the pan" was utterly unknown in 321 BCE, since it was based on a gunpowder misfire—the priming powder flashing in the pan but not igniting the charge. A bright flash, then gone with no effect. For Eumenes to use it here indicated that the man had managed to understand and internalize the concepts involved in a very short time.

"It will remain so till we get pans for it to flash in." Eumenes shook his head. "And barrels to hold the charge and shot with touch holes to transfer the fire from the pan to the charge. It's like so much of what you brought—of great potential use but needing an industry built before it can be used effectively. For now what we can build will make a great display, but no real difference. We don't have cannons and we don't have the means to make cannons in any numbers."

The *Queen of the Sea* was the only facility that was yet able to make the sort of cannons that were used in their time. Also the only facility that could make cannons of any sort quickly. But aside from the steam cannons on the *Queen* and the *Reliance* and some black powder cannons for Fort Plymouth, the *Queen* wasn't making cannons. It was making the tools to make the tools to make cannon. And most of those were made for and sold to New America. Cannons for

Eumenes' army would be made by Greek craftsmen, hand-carved from bronze. Neither cheap nor fast.

"What about rockets?" Dag asked.

"A flash in the pan, as I said. Pretty fireworks, signifying nothing."

"Not necessarily," said Daniel Lang. "First, because we can make good rockets using venturi and fins to provide spin. We know how and we have the basic technology here on the *Queen*. We even have a stock of venturi, though a limited one. That will give you rockets almost as good as you might have found in World War I, or even World War II."

Eumenes was looking interested, but Olympias interrupted. "What is world war? The only world-spanning war was my son's. There—"

"Olympias," Roxane said, "you insisted on being here and promised to listen, not interrupt."

"I will have my say. I am Alexander's mother, and Philip's wife."

"No," said Marie, as pedantically as she could manage. "You *were* Alexander's mother and Philip's wife. But *your* Philip and *your* Alexander are gone. Now, Roxane is Alexander's mother and regent, and Eurydice is Philip's wife and regent. You have paid your fare, but you are simply a passenger on the *Queen of the Sea. Not* a ruling monarch."

Olympias stood and spoke in a version of Greek that was even more archaic than that spoken in the fourth century BCE, something that went back to Agamemnon or maybe Hercules. Assuming that there had at some point been actual men that Agamemnon and Hercules were based upon. She also waved her hands in obscure and spooky gestures.

Marie stared at her. Then, quite unable to help herself, she started to laugh.

Olympias stopped gesturing and speaking. She sat back down, not as though she had intended to, but simply as though shock left her legs unable to hold her up.

"I'm sorry," Marie said, trying to get her laughter under control. "Your error is in assuming that everyone shares your mythology. In the time we come from, essentially no one shares it. We have our own. I didn't mean to denigrate your beliefs, honestly I didn't. But the gestures you were making looked like something that a carnival fortune-teller might use."

Marie snapped her mouth closed about a paragraph too late, as she finally realized just how demeaning and infuriating her response would seem to Olympias. She looked into the woman's eyes and knew that she had just made a mortal enemy.

Considering Olympias' history, mortal enemy wasn't hyperbole. Not in the least.

"To get back to the point," Anders said, "we can provide you some black powder rockets and you have the formula and techniques to make black powder."

Anders didn't sound thrilled about that last. The secret of black powder hadn't stayed a secret. It was listed in Wikipedia and by now copies of the formula were available from Venezuela to Babylon. Nor was black powder the only ship people secret that was no longer secret.

"What about cargo?" Eumenes asked.

"What do you mean?" Anders asked.

"I mean I would like to buy wheat and rye here and have it delivered to Iskenderun, so that Pharnabazus can keep the pressure on Antigonus while I go after Cassander."

"The *Queen* is not a cargo ship, and we have a schedule we need to get back to," Lars said before Anders could.

"Also, if we deliver fifty tons or so of provender to the Mediterranean coast when your army isn't there to protect it, it's likely not going to be there by the time your army gets there," Dag said. "You'd be better off hiring a local ship and maybe seeing if you can get a steam engine to move it. That way Pharnabazus can move his cavalry to meet the provision ship. It still means going to Izmir first."

The discussion continued and Eumenes didn't get what he wanted, but did get considerably more than Antigonus' representatives would have approved. Arrhidaeus would be livid if he knew how much Eumenes was getting in terms of ship credit. The *Queen of the Sea* had a great deal of silver and gold by this time. Part of it from trading in Europe, but much of it from South America, where the locals used it as decoration. Gold was a soft, malleable metal, often with a pleasing color, and it was shiny, unlike lead. So masks and bracelets were made from it in South and Central America. The natives were happy to trade the yellow metal for steel knives on a pound-for-pound basis . . . at least at first.

Eumenes would be getting some of that gold, but he would also be getting a drawing account that would be recognized throughout the Mediterranean. That was half of what the radio teams that the *Queen* was sending about the Med were for.

"The amount in the account will be known?" Eumenes asked as he looked at the paper.

"Not unless someone gets bribed," Eleanor Kinney said. "Which could happen."

"How much is it?" Olympias asked.

Eleanor looked at Eumenes, Eumenes looked at Roxane, and so did Eurydice.

"It's a drawing account and it takes Eumenes to access it," Roxane said.

"How much is in the drawing account?" Olympias asked, not to be put off.

"That," Eurydice said coldly, "is a government matter and you are not a member of the government." She turned to Roxane. "I told you it was a mistake to let her in here."

"Please, everyone, calm down," Roxane said. But from the looks Olympias and Eurydice gave each other, it was too late.

Roxane's suite
One hour later

Roxane sat on the couch and said, "That was a mistake."

"It doesn't matter." Eurydice shrugged. "You know what happened in that other history and you know how Olympias felt about Philip's mother. There is nothing I can do to keep safe from her, not as long as we are both on this ship." She glanced at Philip.

Philip and Alexander were across the room. Philip was writing out equations in a combination of Greek and ship people English notation, while little Alexander sat across from him, drawing nonsense on a small chalkboard.

Roxane leaned back. "You have decided then?"

"There was never any choice. Not once Captain Floden let that woman on the ship. I will go with Eumenes."

"I will go too," said Philip.

"No. You stay on the ship," Eurydice said, "where you'll be safe."

"If it's not safe for you, it's not safe for me."

"But the treatments!" Eurydice complained. "You're much better than before and I don't want you to lose that."

Philip considered. "I will miss the computers more. We can take the squeeze box with us and I can do maths for the army. I won't have the drugs, but the doctor says that she wants to wean me off those as soon as possible." The drugs were anti-anxiety drugs, basically low-dose morphine, designed to let Philip interact with the world without going into hysterics. "Besides, we can get weed if I need it. The doctor says it's been in use in Egypt for centuries and made its way to Greece as well."

Eurydice laughed because she knew perfectly well that Greek soldiers had been using cannabis for recreational purposes since they first passed through Egypt over a decade ago.

Captain's suite, Queen of the Sea

"I don't trust that woman," Lars Floden said to Marie Easley as they sat on his couch.

"I know. And I shouldn't have laughed." Marie took a sip of wine. "But she looked ridiculous."

"I don't disagree, but that doesn't change the fact that we have a mass murderess on board."

By now word had reached them about the sack of Amphipolis and what Olympias had done. It fit together all too well with her previous reputation. Whether she had used drugs, magic, or the power of suggestion, her slaves and servants had run amok and died to the last man, all the while setting the city on fire even before Cassander breached the walls.

"Mass murderers are not uncommon in this time, Lars," Marie said. "I think I've mentioned that before. In fact, I'm almost sure I have."

"It may have come up in the occasional offhand comment," Lars agreed. Then muttered, "About a million times."

"The problem is, Lars, that you too are a mass murderer now. Remember the steam guns turned on the *Reliance* and running over the galleys in Alexandria Harbor?"

"That was war—" Lars stopped.

"Yes, it was. And you were right to do it, in both cases. But by Olympias' standards, she was right too."

"Oh, nonsense," Lars said. "I'm as willing to accept cultural differences as the next screaming liberal, but drugging your slaves to go on a rampage is not the same thing as shooting people who are engaged in an act of piracy."

"No, it's not. Not to you and not to me. But to Olympias, it was simply a tactical maneuver to cover her escape and the slaves were collateral damage." Marie held up the wineglass in a "wait" gesture. "I'm not justifying it, or approving of it, or excusing it. None of those things. All I am saying is that it's the way most of the people we are going to be dealing with think, here and in Trinidad. All around the world. And just calling someone like Olympias a nut job is not nearly precise enough. And that will lead us into tactical errors in dealing with her and the others like her."

"So what am I missing?"

"She is an incredibly smart nut job. One who has survived a snake pit for decades by being the most venomous snake in the pit. The question is: can she adapt to a world that isn't all a snake pit? If she can, she could be very useful. And even if she can't, she has connections and alliances enough that killing her would be incredibly dangerous. Not to mention wrong in the same way her poisoning all those people was wrong."

"She hates you now. I want you to promise me that you'll be careful around her." Lars hugged Marie tightly. "I don't want to be without you."

"Oh, I will. I think I'll see about borrowing one of Roxane's Silver Shields."

Queen of the Sea, *Port of Izmir/Smyrna*
Nursery in Roxane's suite
Dawn, November 5, 320 BCE

Eumenes reached down and tickled his son Sardisius in his crib. "Daddy has to go away for awhile, but you get to stay on the ship with the ship people and learn their magic. And you will have baby Alexander to play with and all the other children. Not bad for the grandson of a wagoneer. Grow well, my son, grow strong."

Then, not letting himself cry, Eumenes turned away and went to board the lifeboat, now used as a ship's boat, that would take him to shore.

☆   ☆   ☆

Eumenes, Eurydice, Philip, a small company of personal guards, and the radio crew boarded the ship's boat for the trip into shore. The bay of Izmir was not nearly deep enough for the *Queen* to navigate safely.

It took only five minutes for the boat to get to the dock, but an hour to unload. Erica Mirzadeh was supervising the unloading with the help of several Silver Shields, the veteran elite infantry of Alexander's army. With them was another ship person named Tacaran Bayot. Tacaran was five foot seven, thin faced, with a goatee and curly black hair, black eyes, and skin that fell between olive and light brown. He had straight white teeth and an engaging smile. He wore khaki pants with pockets on the sides of the legs and a khaki shirt with big button-down pockets, all of which were full. There was the radio system and the generator to charge the batteries that ran it. The system was owned by the ship people, but assigned to Eumenes' army under the direct control of Erica.

However, the rest belonged to Eumenes. Five hundred steel crossbows and a thousand venturi. They would build the rockets later, on the road, using designs worked out on the *Queen*. They would also be making black powder, which wasn't a mystery to Eumenes anymore. They could do ninety percent of making goods that the ship people made, but the ten percent they couldn't was often the crucial ten percent. Like the venturi, which needed to be an exact shape and of good metal. But the rest of the black powder rocket was well within their means. They could use rocks or small cast-iron shards for the shrapnel. They knew sulfur, saltpeter, and charcoal, and they knew now how to mix them. They could make the rockets from light wood turned on a lathe. So far they were pedal-powered lathes, but they were still lathes. They had designs for steam-powered lathes, as well, although they hadn't been able to make any yet.

The thing that increasingly bothered Eumenes was that even now Ptolemy's agents on the *Queen* were getting ready to give him the same knowledge, and the Carthaginians would have it in another week, if they didn't have it already. Even the barbarous Romans would have it soon. It wouldn't be long before Cassander and Antigonus got hold of it. Likely as not, Ptolemy would sell it to them.

Warfare was about to change in this part of the world and all their experience as generals was going to be almost useless. Sometimes worse than useless. A phalanx of Greek hoplites facing a rocket barrage was dead meat. At least, that's what Daniel Lang said, and Eumenes didn't doubt him.

Suddenly, Eumenes felt a smile twitch his lips. That was all true, but Antigonus wouldn't believe it any more than he would believe that a wagoneer's son could be an effective general. Antigonus knew what he knew, and even if he realized that tactics had to change—which was by no means certain—that didn't mean that he would be able to change himself.

Eumenes' smile died as his mind turned to Cassander. Cassander was no general, but he was smart and had a flexible mind, and that might well be more important in this new sort of warfare than personal courage.

Finally the unloading was finished, and another ship's boat pulled in and started unloading supplies and equipment. The *Queen* would be heading for Alexandria as soon as the boats were back aboard.

Queen of the Sea, *Alexandria Harbor*
November 10, 320 BCE

Ptolemy sat in the Royal Lounge, reading the constitution of the United Satrapies and States of the Empire. The USSE constitution was interesting, and it was going to require him to reconsider his options. He looked up at Thaïs and waved the document. "What do you think?"

Thaïs tilted her head in a gesture that Ptolemy knew well. It wasn't quite a nod nor a head shake. Thaïs wasn't sure or, more exactly, liked part of it and disliked other parts. "What do you like about it?"

"It's a good framework," Thaïs said. "For the most part, it will leave you as ruler of Egypt and give you a level of legitimacy that even the agreements at Babylon didn't."

"And what part of it do you dislike?"

"You are probably going to have to give back Syria, Israel and Judea. And you may well be called on to contribute troops to Eumenes. If the constitution is valid, so is the appointment of Eumenes as *strategos* for the empire."

"Frankly, that bothers me less than giving up Syria. I bought that territory with good silver and quite a lot of it. What bothers me isn't the specific of having to send troops to Eumenes. It's the general principle of placing the defense of the realm under the over-government that they establish."

"Federal government," Thaïs said, using a ship people word. "You will be able to appoint a representative to the upper house, the one they are calling the House of States."

"What about the elections?"

"That's mostly ship people influence, but the Greek city-states piled on in a hurry. Especially Athens. Representation will be allocated by population and elected by the citizenry. That includes free women as well as all free men, no matter their wealth. But not slaves. We went round and round on that and I am not sure we made the right choice. The compromise that we finally agreed on was that slaves didn't count for representatives. Not even war captives, much less two-footed livestock. That at least encourages manumission in order to increase a state's or satrapy's representatives, in the House of the People."

Thaïs used the Greek words. The world of fourth century BCE had lots of types of slaves and each had their own word, most of which didn't translate to twenty-first-century English. Not directly. They had words for chattel, slaves, serfs, and war captives—who were in some ways more like chattel, but had higher status.

Ptolemy looked at his longtime lover and—given the new situation—possible future wife, with a sardonic lift of an eyebrow. He knew her background. Born a slave, she'd been sold to a school for hetaera as a child and then required to work off her debt. She had every reason in the world to dislike the institution of slavery. But at the same time, she had managed to go from slave to only one short step down from a queen through her abilities. "What do you really think? Are the ship people right about slavery?"

Thaïs stood up and walked to the window, then turned back to face him. "No, but they will be."

"What does that mean?"

"The way the world is now, we couldn't survive the abolition of slavery. There isn't enough wealth to pay all the freed slaves for their labor and with everyone weeding their own garden, we would fall into barbarism. But that's right now. It will change as the ship people's machines magnify the productivity of individual workers. In a hundred years, perhaps less, they will be right about slavery. We need to be ready for that day, or our children and grandchildren will live in a world even more soaked in blood than this one."

"So, do you think I should sign it? Commit to this new nation?"

"No." Thaïs frowned. "Not yet. Don't commit either way. See how Eumenes does against Cassander, at least. Perhaps even wait to see how he does against Antigonus and the eastern satraps. Don't tie yourself to this new ship of state until you know whether it will float. Stay neutral as long as you can."

Ptolemy nodded. One of the things he liked best about Thaïs was that she gave good advice. Even when it wasn't entirely in her best interest. "You're right, as usual, my very dear. And I have missed you."

When the *Queen of the Sea* left again, it would leave Thaïs and the children here.

"I do want to send someone to keep an eye on the ship people. Whom do you recommend? I considered Dinocrates or Crates or one of the fellows of the library, but I am concerned that they will be seduced by ship people knowledge."

"It's not just the ship people on the *Queen of the Sea* that matter. We need relations with New America too. You would be shocked at how much they accomplished in a year and I suspect they are just getting started. We will be able to buy impossible devices from them soon." She paused a moment in thought. "The *Queen* will visit New America regularly and we will have the radio to keep in contact so perhaps we only need one watcher. Menelaus?" Thaïs' voice made the name a question. She wasn't fond of Ptolemy's little brother and aide.

Ptolemy grinned at her. "It will get him out of the palace, but he's not going to like giving up his slaves."

"My heart bleeds for him," Thaïs said, using a ship people expression directly translated into Greek.

224–226 12th Street, Fort Plymouth, New America
November 10, 320 BCE

Crack! The sound jerked Daoud Khoury around. He looked at the red-hot door of the furnace. He moved up and, using a long, heavy wooden pole, opened the small door. Holding up his hand, he tried to look into the fire. He couldn't. It was much too bright to see anything, and it made him feel like his eyeballs were going to boil.

He went back to the table and got the tinted glasses from the *Queen of the Sea* and looked again. The cracking sound was what he was afraid of. The crucible was cracked, and the molten iron was pouring down into the bottom of the furnace.

Quickly he went to the shutoff valve and shut the oil feed. It took five minutes for the fire to go out and an hour for the furnace to cool to merely scorching hot.

Cool enough for him, using tongs, to lift out what was left of the crucible. It took another day for the furnace to cool enough for him and his crew of locals to remove bricks to make an opening to pry out the melted iron. Then it was brick the whole thing up and start over with a new crucible, as his money got lower and lower and he got deeper and deeper in debt to the Bank of New America.

It didn't help that he couldn't keep a trained crew. The locals came and worked long enough to get the money to buy what they wanted. Then they went back home. Some few locals stayed, but far more of them just wanted what they wanted, then back to their own ways. Daoud couldn't really blame them either. He'd give anything on this earth or another if only he could go back to his own ways. Accounting might have been boring except at tax time, but trying to make steel with primitive tools was one hell of a lot worse. He wondered when the *Queen* would get back. At least somewhere still had air-conditioning.

CHAPTER 2

NEGOTIATIONS

Queen of the Sea, *Alexandria Harbor*
November 12, 320 BCE

Menelaus looked around the small stateroom. There was a door to his left and next to it two drawings, each captioned in Greek, Punic, and Latin, as well as the ship people English. "Shower for Bathing," and the picture was of a man with little lines coming down on him. The other said "Toilet for Elimination," and the same man was seated on the toilet with his robe up. That one was obvious and the shower almost made sense. He opened the door and stepped inside. He looked at the shower and saw knobs with the words HOT and COLD. He turned the hot, and water came out in a fine spray, making sense of the drawing. Menelaus snorted. He much preferred a proper bath with a slave to oil him up and scrape his body down afterward.

After examining the "bathroom," he walked across the room to another door and opened it. It led out to a balcony with a painted iron railing. He stepped out onto the balcony and looked down . . . and down, and down. The water was far below him. He'd never liked heights. He gripped the iron railing and squeezed his eyes shut.

Gradually, the world stopped spinning and his stomach settled a little. He tried to open his eyes and couldn't do it. He knew what he would see. With an effort of will, he removed his right hand from the railing and reached behind him until he found the door. Found the handle, and grasped it, then he turned his head and, being very careful not to look at the water, he squinted his eyes open. He focused his attention on the door with all the concentrated will of a drowning man focusing on the log that might save him. He got the door opened and almost fell into his room.

It was a very nice room with a big bed and a desk and chair. It had a peculiar thick piece of glass that they called a "television" and even a closet of sorts. Compared to any ship he had ever been on, this was magical luxury. But it was luxury that was too many feet above the sea.

Finally, after his breathing was back under control, he looked out the window afraid that the terror would assault him again. But it didn't, as long as he wasn't close to the edge. As long as he didn't look down, he was fine.

Menelaus took a deep breath and another, then he went back out the door of his stateroom. He took the lifting box up still farther, to the Royal Buffet restaurant. He would get something to eat and settle his stomach. After discussing the situation with Thaïs and Epicurus, Menelaus decided not to bring any of his slaves with him. On the upside, however, one of his favorite hetaera, Bethania, had booked passage. He didn't have to be lonely, depending on her other engagements.

He reach the Royal Buffet on the deck with the swimming pools and went through the line. That was another irritating thing. He had to wait in line as though he were some minor scholar, not the brother of Ptolemy. There was a tuna steak, cooked rare, with a mustard sauce. It looked good and he took a plate to put it on the tray. Then he got a serving of the tuber that was labeled in Latin as well as Greek script as "nut potatoes." And something called "squash in butter sauce." He took it to a table away from the large window that looked out and down on the ocean, sat, and then realized that he had not gotten anything to drink.

He went back to the line and looked at the strange device that delivered liquids. It was interesting. There was a wire frame and when you set the plastic drinking vessels on the grate and pushed it against the frame, liquid came out and filled the drinking vessel. He read the labels as he watched a Carthaginian filling his drinking vessel. There was Egyptian beer, yerba maté, wine, and pasteurized milk.

The Carthaginian was getting the pasteurized milk. "What is that?" Menelaus asked.

"It's processed cow's milk," the Carthaginian said. "They boil it in a special way to keep it from going bad. It's quite good, but it doesn't mix well with wine. I am Capot Barca. And you are?"

"Menelaus, brother of Ptolemy."

"We have similar roles then. I am here to watch

the ship people for Carthage and you are here to watch them for the satrapy of Egypt."

Menelaus wasn't convinced, by any means, that a Carthaginian merchant was of the same class as a Macedonian noble and the brother of the satrap of Egypt, but Thaïs warned him that he should not try to stand on social rank with the ship people, so he nodded as politely as he could.

It turned out to be a good choice. Capot was fairly knowledgeable about the ship and the ship people, and directed Menelaus to the carrot cake, a sweet breadlike substance that was made without yeast, yet wasn't a flatbread, as well as offering other tidbits of knowledge and suggestions about food and drink.

Queen of the Sea, *Carthage Harbor*
November 16, 320 BCE

Standing back from the railing, Menelaus watched as Capot waved at Carthage Harbor. It was much the same shape as the images he remembered from the *Queen of the Sea*'s computers, but smaller, nowhere near the thousand feet across it was supposed to be. It had the circular inner harbor, but it was smaller, only about three hundred feet across, and the long commercial harbor was both shorter and narrower than it would be a hundred years from now.

"Well," Capot asked, "what do you think of our harbor?"

"It's impressive," Menelaus said. And it was, sort of.

Capot laughed. "A bit of a letdown after seeing the pictures in the computer, but we may be able to speed up the new harbor this time, since we have the designs."

"Not if you're going to have to dig it out to a depth of ten meters rather than two."

"The steam engines will help."

"How are you doing with those?"

Capot grimaced. "Not well. Another boiler blew up and there is talk of a large sacrifice to persuade the gods to be more generous."

Menelaus looked at him and Capot shrugged. "I am not involved. I just got it over the radio."

The city-state of Carthage had received a radio on the *Queen*'s last stop here, just under two months ago. Each radio station was a small team of ship people and at least one Greek who spoke some English, often a retiring Silver Shield. The Greek was there mostly as a translator and spoke Greek, some English, and the local language, whether it was Latin, Phoenician, Egyptian, or whatever. They also dropped a computer with a translator app and the ability to manage the band hopping necessary to bounce ham radio signals off the ionosphere consistently. It meant that as long as the team members were not molested, they could keep that city in touch with the other cities on and around the Mediterranean, and they could keep the city in touch with the *Queen of the Sea*, no matter where she was. Even in Trinidad. The translation app, combined with someone who spoke both Greek and the local tongue, meant that they could communicate even if it took some effort.

Alexandria had a station, as did Athens, Ashdod, Sardis, Rhodes, Tyre and more. Often the embassy was staffed by passengers from the *Queen*, usually older passengers. Carthage, for instance, was manned by

Colonel James Godfrey, his wife Ila, and their widowed daughter, Tina Johnson. James was appointed colonel in the armed forces of New America before he and his family were seconded back to the *Queen* to be the radio operators for Carthage. James handled the computer, but he was hard of hearing and therefore spoke loudly. His wife and daughter handled most of the voice contact and were learning Phoenician, although their Alabama accents added some difficulty.

Capot's smile developed a bitter twist. "Look over there." He pointed and Menelaus, who was still standing back from the railing, followed his pointing finger. "That is where they made their demonstration." As part of the procedure for dropping off the radio teams, the *Queen of the Sea* demonstrated the ship's guns and made it clear that if anything happened to the radio team, the guns would be turned on the city that failed to protect them.

"I know how you feel, but be happy, my friend. I saw the *Queen* run over Gorgias' fleet in Alexandria Harbor. Granted, it was a stupid thing for the general to do, to try and take this ship, but a whole fleet! And in some ways what they did at Rhodes was even worse. All that happened to you was a few grapevines got trashed and they paid for them."

"Yes, but they were my family's grapevines," Capot said. "And last I heard, the government is still holding onto the money."

Carthage
November 17, 320 BCE

Allison Gouch sat in the house of the Barca clan and

sipped the wine. She looked over at Tina Johnson.

Who shrugged indifference. "I like margaritas, with lime and salt."

Allison smiled. "This is actually quite good." It was a red wine, fruity, with overtones of oak. Not quite like anything that she had tasted in the twenty-first century. Two thousand plus years had changed viniculture in a number of ways. The yeast was different, even the grapes were a little different. Most of all, the techniques were different. Mostly, from her experience in this century, worse.

But here in Carthage, she was tasting something that she hadn't tasted before. There was a mix of flavors that was new. She swished the wine around in her mouth, then swallowed. This was not a twenty-first-century wine tasting, where she was trying five hundred wines. She would, today, try only sixteen wines, three from the Barca wineries, and two each from the Manipua wineries and some others. Capot was here to translate for his mother and sister.

One thing that she had learned about Carthage was that women had a distinct role from men, but it wasn't a lesser role. The women owned virtually all of what a twenty-first-century person would call real property. At least in Carthage proper and those places under its direct control. So she sat here on an inlaid terrace, drinking some excellent wine from silver chalices, while chatting with three women in gowns that exposed their breasts. It was surreal, but not offensive. These women were not property. They were property owners.

Then the servant brought in the next amphora, and Allison hid a grimace. *This* woman was property. Quite literally property, a Gallic slave from what would in a future world be Spain. She had reddish-blond hair and a very self-effacing manner.

Again, Allison looked over at Tina and saw a carefully hidden headshake. One thing that Allison did know, because she was there when it was decided, was that Tina was the chief of station, the chief spy, for the ship people and New America here in Carthage.

Allison made notes on the vintage on her slate. The handwritten notes were translated to text and sent to the *Queen* even as she wrote. She would have a record when she got back.

Queen of the Sea, *Carthage Harbor* *November 20, 320 BCE*

The supplies were loaded and the *Queen* left for Formentera Island, which would be the next stop on their itinerary. At Formentera Island, they stopped for several days while the owners of that island provided guided tours of the under-construction hotel complex. They also got goods from that set of tribal lands that wasn't yet Gaul, much less France, Spain, or Germany: sturgeon and caviar, beef and barley, amber, and everything else anyone could think of that the ship people might want.

The ship people didn't actually want most of these items, because they had better goods that were made cheaper. Things like combs and brushes were of great value and tremendous cost to make for the locals but not for the ship people. On the other hand, the concentration of goods was in itself a draw for other traders.

That was rapidly turning the small town on Formentera Island into a hub for international trade. It was nominally Carthaginian, but not in Carthage, so it traded with anyone that put in. That anyone probably included the occasional pirate. But then, in the fourth century BCE, almost any ship—military or civilian—would turn temporarily pirate if the opportunity arose.

Fort Plymouth, Trinidad
December 5, 320 BCE

"It's good to have you back, Captain," President Al Wiley said, shaking Lars Floden's hand with all the appearance of genuine friendship.

Lars was not completely convinced. Not because President Wiley didn't sound sincere. He did. Not even because they had had conflicts in the past. They had. But at the same time they had worked together well enough. No, the reason that Lars was less than confident was because Al was a twenty-first-century American politician, and such people made swindlers seem honest and straightforward in comparison.

"I really am, Captain," Wiley assured him as he guided Lars to a chair in a corner of his office. It was hand-carved of native wood and the cushions were native-dyed llama wool. It was no doubt bought from one of the native tribes dotting the coast of northern Venezuela. They were good at woodworking because many of their houses were built on stilts. Wiley took another at right angles to it, with a coffee table between them. The table looked more modern. In fact, Lars was pretty sure it had been made in the *Queen's* carpentry shop during the months that the

Queen had sat in the harbor helping build the tools that Fort Plymouth was using to build the tools to build a twenty-first-century world out of a Stone Age starter kit.

President Wiley saw him looking and seemed to read his mind. "We've had to rejigger our notion of what 'Stone Age' actually means quite a bit since we landed among them. And we have the whole range from hunter gatherers to not-quite-Mayans within a few hundred miles."

Lars nodded. He got regular reports and the *Queen* visited Fort Plymouth monthly. The "not-quite-Mayans" were several tribes that failed to fully enter the archaeological record because they built their cities out of wood, not stone, and built them on stilts, often in floodplains.

Apparently this was going to be a friendly meeting. "For all sorts of practical reasons. The factories on the *Queen* have a new load of cylinders and steam piping. The presence of the *Queen*, even more than the *Reliance*, acts as a warning to the locals."

That much was true. Even though it was the *Reliance* that had performed the punitive expedition against the Tupky alliance a few months ago, the *Queen* was larger and just more visually impressive.

"As well as a promise," Wiley continued, "because we have been touting the university you are establishing on the *Queen* all up and down the Venezuelan coast. We have a group of young people anxious to board the *Queen* and begin their studies. And most important of all, Captain Floden, we need to talk. And we need to do it face-to-face, not over the radio."

Lars felt a sudden apprehension that he was about

to buy a lemon at an outlandish price. As well as a strong urge to retreat back to the *Queen* and never return to the port at Fort Plymouth.

Just then a native woman came in, pushing a cart of snacks and tea. The cart was wood with simple leather bearings made in Fort Plymouth. The rubber on the wooded wheels was locally produced, one of the products of the high-end Stone Age culture that existed in central and northern South America when they landed. The woman pushing it was dressed in a calf-length skirt, sandals, and not much else. Nothing at all covering her chest. Lars lifted an eyebrow at Wiley.

"Wasn't my idea." Wiley shrugged. "The locals, from hunter-gatherer types to city dwellers, don't have much of a nudity taboo and they took offense when some of our old biddies, of both sexes, suggested that their lack of attire was immoral. It became quite a political issue in our legislature. And even if we ship people have a prominent position in the new nation we are forging here, we are outnumbered by the locals by a large margin. And that's only going to get worse as the proto-citizens of the coastal tribes get the vote over the next couple of years. A lot of our politicians recognized the demographics and flip-flopped on public nudity as soon as the backlash developed. Looking to the next election, when a lot of those nekkid people will be voters." Wiley didn't sound thrilled about the situation.

Lars had a relaxed Scandinavian view on the subject; nudity didn't particularly bother him. He put that aside with a shake of his head. "What was it you wanted to speak to me in person about?"

"We want to buy two of your lifeboats, Captain Floden. The big ones. They will become the basis of our navy until we can get ships built."

"I have a responsibility to my passengers and crew, Mr. President, and it's not one I can or will abandon."

"I know that, Captain, and I would never ask you to. But with the conversion, the *Queen* only carries three thousand passengers, including the factory workers who work in the *Queen*'s shops, and six hundred crew. I would never ask you to sell us more than you can do without. Two of the three-hundred-passenger mega-lifeboats would provide us with coastal defense and the ability to reach the coast of Venezuela in force, and not endanger your passengers at all. Especially when you consider that you have all the inflatable life rafts."

"Those inflatables are a backup system. They have no engines and are not designed for long-term use."

"True. But they can be towed by your lifeboats and they are covered against weather. They represent a real capacity that means you're safe even if you lose some of the 'real' lifeboats. Besides, Captain, you've been using the lifeboats as ship's boats since The Event put us all here."

"That's one of the problems, Mr. President. We are putting more strain on the engines than we ever intended. We are having to use the machine shops on the *Queen* to fabricate new parts for the engines just to keep them running. Should the worst happen, I don't want my people stuck in the middle of the Atlantic with a busted engine and no way to get to shore."

They kept arguing, but Lars knew that Al Wiley was correct. Besides, the *Queen* needed the silver and gold that Al Wiley was offering. Not everyone in Europe trusted ship money. There were gold and silver mines in Central and South America, and the locals provided the precious metals to the ship people on Trinidad on a pound-for-pound basis in exchange for good steel knives and other tools.

The iron was mostly bought in Europe, transported to Trinidad by the *Reliance*, then remelted and converted to steel here in Trinidad, using oil-burning furnaces in a crucible process that was slow, tedious, and expensive, compared to back in the world, but produced good steel.

☆　　☆　　☆

After lunch, they got back to it.

"I want to convince you to change the schedule of the *Queen of the Sea*," Wiley told Lars bluntly. Almost belligerently. "We are working on steam sailing ships that will run to five hundred tons of carrying capacity. They will have a sailing rig and steam engines. The sailing rig will be the main power source, with the engine as a backup for when the winds are blowing the wrong way, or not blowing at all. But it's going to take us upwards of two years, maybe three or four years, before the first ship comes off the quays. And that's using all the steam-powered heavy equipment that we have been able to put together."

"That seems a good reason for us to stay on the route we're on now. With all respect, Mr. President, your colony here probably can't survive if the *Queen* isn't bringing goods and colonists from Europe on a regular basis," Lars said. "We have a schedule that is quite profitable for the *Queen*, between the university and the paying passengers, not to mention the cargo we can manage. And it's a capacity you desperately need if you are going to survive, much less prosper."

Al Wiley shook his head. "Don't you think I know that, Captain? I have nightmares about the Roanoke colony, and wake up to worse. I watched a man die yesterday, from complications due to the improperly purified bovine insulin we are using. I held the hand of a man who had actually built a homebuilt airplane back in the world. The only person on the *Queen*, so the only person in the *world*, to have actually built an airplane is dead. All his real-world experience is lost. Because we can't make decent insulin yet. And he's not the only one. Half the reason that Fort Plymouth is so crowded together is because we are desperately trying to keep walking distance down for our more elderly passengers. Every time one of them dies—and we've lost over five hundred of the over-sixty-five crowd since The Event—we lose a treasure trove of experience.

"Still, Captain, if we are going to spread civilization—and even more, if we are going to develop trading partners—we need to get started on it sooner rather than later. Also, to be blunt, the *Queen of the Sea* is the most impressive thing on the oceans of this world and will remain so for the foreseeable future. We are going to need that sense of awe and the tacit threat it represents to keep our trade ships safe."

Lars considered. Wiley wasn't the first person to suggest that they run a more flexible route. Eumenes wanted them in the Persian Gulf. Any number of ship people wanted them to go find coffee plants. Others wanted them to go find real tea and other goods in China, like silk, and cotton from India, Peru, or Mexico.

No one was really sure which, though Wikipedia said there was wild cotton in Peru.

In truth, there was a very great deal that improved trade around the world would do for the world, and Lars was inclined to do it. But he wasn't going to do it for nothing. He started negotiating.

214–216 12th Street, Fort Plymouth, Trinidad
December 7, 320 BCE

Carthalo sat on the wooden bench with a cloth in his hand and a bowl of emery mud next to him. He dipped the cloth in the mud and started rubbing the lens that was locked into the wood-and-wire rack. It was slow, tedious work. The finer the finish, the better the lens. But while he had to get rid of the rough bits, he couldn't change the shape without distorting the lens. So it was rub, rinse clean, check, rub, rinse clean, check. Over and over and over again.

Stella Matthews was working on a machine to grind lenses, but Carthalo was doing it the way his people and the Greeks had been doing it for the last century and more. It was a slow process, but you could make a lens that would start a fire, and as he had learned since his arrival in this strange land, a lens that would project an image on a screen or, in combination with other lenses, make a telescope.

Queen of the Sea, *off Fort Plymouth*
December 10, 320 BCE

"We'll be going to Mexico first," Eleanor Kinney said. "Or at least that part of the world that will become

Mexico in a few hundred more years." She lifted a spoon full of chocolate ice cream. "It's this that ultimately decided the matter. We can get chocolate here, but we think we will be able to get it cheaper up north."

Roxane nodded. She didn't have chocolate ice cream. She was eating apple pie with whipped cream for dessert. They were in the Royal Buffet. "After that?"

"It depends on how long it takes, but back here, then if we can be sure that Ptolemy will have oil for us, we may head directly for the Horn of Africa and up to the Red Sea."

"What's the rush?"

"Sugar cane. It's probably to be found in India or New Guinea, and a load of cuttings that we could plant here or in the Caribbean could develop into a lucrative industry."

Roxane looked at Eleanor with a raised eyebrow, and Eleanor tried not to bristle. "The production of sugar doesn't need to involve slavery. We can create processing machines. And if cutting cane is going to be a labor-intensive chore, it can be done by sugarcane farmers who own their own land."

"But will it?" Roxane asked, then held up a hand that was still holding a fork full of apple pie to stop Eleanor's response. "I'm not condemning you." Then, with a sardonic twist of her lips, she added, "I'm honestly starting to think you are right about slavery, at least in the long term. But the circumstances that led to your history's extensive use of slavery in sugar production are present in the here and now."

Eleanor nodded, even as she noted the strange accent that Roxane's English had developed through her extensive use of text-to-speech software. She sounded a bit mechanical and mispronounced certain words. Roxane spent at least an hour every day on the exercise machines in the gym, and for all of that time she was listening to Wikipedia articles that Dag had used text-to-speech software to turn into audio files. It wasn't that Roxane couldn't read. She could get by quite well reading Greek, but reading English in Latin script was going to take a bit longer. However, she did have an excellent ear for languages and in the past months had learned to understand English quite well. Even to speak it well, if with a computer accent. The computer accent wasn't unique to Roxane. It was becoming quite common among the people from this time.

"It's not only sugar," Eleanor said. "There is also Indian cotton, which may be different in fiber length or color, as well as a host of other products." Eleanor stopped, because cotton, like sugar, had made extensive use of slavery in its history. "Darn it. Is there anything that didn't use slavery to produce?"

Roxane laughed. "Well, furs from hunters, but other than that, I can't think of anything off the top of my head. What honestly concerns me more is that these delays mean that Eumenes, as well as Eurydice and Philip, are going to be on their own longer."

"What have you heard?"

"Not much. It takes time to set up the radio and Eumenes seems to be moving fast."

CHAPTER 3

THE WAR IN EUROPE

Lydia, east of the Bosphorus Straits
December 10, 320 BCE

Eumenes looked west across the Bosphorus. In theory, he owned this side as satrap of Lydia, and Lysimachus owned Thrace on the other. Lydia was south of the Black Sea and east of the Sea of Marmara and the Aegean Sea. Thrace was north of the Aegean and the Marmara and west of the Black Sea. The Bosphorus ran north to south from the Black Sea to the Marmara. Given his preferences, Eumenes would move his army across the Bosphorus, pass through Thrace doing as little harm as possible, and march on Cassander in Macedonia with his army in good order.

Eumenes still hoped that might happen, but Lysimachus wasn't a fan of Eumenes. He had been cordial when Alexander was alive, but that had been out of personal loyalty to Alexander. With Alexander dead, that cordiality was getting a little frayed, especially since the queen with Eumenes was Eurydice, not

Roxane. And the emperor with Eumenes was Philip, not Alexander IV.

"What do you think?" Eurydice asked.

"I think he doesn't want to get in the middle of a war between a wagoneer's son and the son of Antipater who never killed a boar."

"A plague on both our houses," Eurydice said.

Eumenes wondered where she'd heard the phrase she'd just rendered in Greek. Probably from the ship people, he imagined, but he put the question aside and agreed. "Something very much like that. However, from our point of view, he might as well be on Cassander's side. Because to get our army into Macedonia, we are going to have to cross the Bosphorus and travel through Thrace."

"If we get a message from Roxane, would that help?"

"It just might. I think Lysimachus was a little in love with Roxane from the beginning."

Eurydice sniffed and Eumenes stifled a smile. In spite of the reconciliation, and even the start of a friendship between the two queens of Alexander's heirs, mention of Roxane's beauty was still sure to get a sniff from Eurydice, if not a comment on the stupidity of men.

"What about Seuthes?" Eurydice asked, and Eumenes lost his urge to smile.

Thrace had been conquered by Macedonia in Philip II's time and rebelled at Philip II's death, and again at Alexander's. The last Eumenes had heard, Seuthes III, the present king of Thrace, was in a military stalemate with Lysimachus. "I would rather not support a rebellion in your husband's empire, Your Majesty."

"If you don't, Cassander will!" Eurydice shook her

head. "If Lysimachus will see reason, fine. If not, we should form an alliance with Seuthes and use him to guard a section of the Bosphorus while we build a pontoon bridge like Darius the Great did."

"What would you offer him?" Eumenes asked.

"Statehood for Thrace," Eurydice said quickly. "Thrace would switch from a satrapy to a state. Seuthes would have the title of king of Thrace, and be able to appoint the representative to the House of States." The biggest difference between the status of state and that of satrapy in the new Alexandrian Empire was that the government of a state got to choose the heir. But the government of a satrapy was chosen by the central government and could, at least in theory, be recalled and removed by the central government at its whim.

Eumenes looked across the Bosphorus again. This was one of the three narrowest sections of the Bosphorus and it was still more than a *hippikon*, four *stadia*, wide. An idle thought struck him and he waved over the ship person who was in charge of the radio. Her name was Erica Mirzadeh and like so many of the ship people she had hair that was dark brown nearly half its length and the other half blond like a Gaul.

"How far is it to the far shore in your ship people's measurements?"

"Just by eye, I'd say around a half a mile. Let me see. Tacaran!" she shouted. "You want to bring me the rangefinder?"

She turned back to Eumenes. "The ship didn't have that many rangefinders, but the machine shop worked up an old-fashioned substitute so we could do surveying if you folks needed it."

It took a few minutes and Eumenes would have called a halt, but he was interested in how they would do the measuring.

Tacaran, who—if Eumenes understood correctly—had been a Muslim before The Event and was now "reconsidering his options," brought over a large case, long and made of stiffened leather. From that he pulled a tripod and a rod. The rod was attached to a rotating section atop the tripod and a weight attached to the bottom of the rod. Clever. They now had a rod sticking straight up and it would be straight up, even if the ground was uneven.

Another rod was attached to the first at a right angle, balanced over the first rod. And then another device, one with a bubble of air in a glass tube of liquid, was laid on top of the first. Tacaran Bayot examined it and said, "Good." Then he tightened some knobs.

Erica Mirzadeh explained. "What Tacaran Bayot did first was use the weighted rod to level the crosspiece. Then he used a bubble level to be sure. Once he confirmed it, he tightened the screw clamps to lock it in place. And now we have a level rod. Now we rotate the rod so that we can see a terrain feature on the other side of the channel."

Erica Mirzadeh took over, rotating the rod so that it was almost perfectly parallel to the Bosphorus and the eyepiece looked directly across the channel. She looked into the eyepiece. "Yep." She muttered and mumbled in the ship people's tongue.

One of the Silver Shields translated. "A funny-shaped rock. That'll do for a reference point."

She tightened another knob, then she started to twist another one delicately, still talking in their language.

The Silver Shield said, "What she's doing now is adjusting the angle of a mirror on the far end of the rod. When the angle is right, she will be able to see the rock, both directly and through the mirror. Then—"

"Thar she blows," Erica said. She lifted her eye from the eyepiece. She looked at a dial that was painted white, with little black lines and numbers on it. Then she pulled out her phone and opened the wooden case that held it. She used it for a minute, then said, "I make it seven hundred and thirty-seven point three meters. About three quarters of a klick. We could hit the far side with rockets if we needed to."

Eumenes looked across the Bosphorus yet again. He wasn't entirely sure what a meter was, but if seven hundred of them took you to the far shore, then they were about the length of a pace, perhaps a bit more. And that meant that over a distance that long, the ship people could measure to half a pace and less. *And that's an old-fashioned device.* "Is it the rod or the phone?" Eumenes knew what a phone was. He had used one. They were, in subtle ways, some of the most powerful magic of the ship people. That was why Erica kept hers in a padded wooden box except when she was using it.

"Mostly, it's the rod-and-mirrors rig. The calculations are nothing you couldn't do. Well, nothing that Philip couldn't do. There are some sines and cosines in there. But if you had a reference book, which is for sale in the *Queen of the Sea* bookstore, you could do the calculations."

"Perhaps we should buy the book you mentioned and another of those devices, then," Eumenes offered, mostly because he wanted to see how Erica would respond.

"That would be a good idea," she said. "Once we get the radio set up, we can put in the order and it will be on the *Queen* the next time she gets to a local port."

Eumenes gave her a slow nod as he thought about the implications of the ship people's willingness to share their magic. What they called science or technology.

Byzantium, Thrace
December 14, 320 BCE

Lysimachus read the letter. It was written in Greek and was purportedly from Roxane. But Lysimachus wasn't convinced. Maybe things would have been different if he was sure, but no. He had read the book of future history and in a world without Alexander, a man had to look after himself. Besides, he had another letter, this one from Cassander. Cassander called him king of Thrace and offered him alliance against the traitor, Eumenes.

He called a scribe over and began to dictate.

Eumenes may cross with his army, but only after I have received documentation of my owner-ship as an independent king of both Thrace and Lydia.

He scratched his jaw, and continued.

The age of Alexander has passed away, and the age of the successors is upon us, whether we would have it so or not. So much we can see from the ship people book of the future, no matter what

*they claim of the effect of butterflies on future
events.*

Look to your own fortunes, Eumenes.

*No. I guess you are already doing so. Just hid-
ing behind the supposed heirs and their queens.*

                    Lysimachus, King of Thrace

Lydia, east of the Bosphorus Straits
December 16, 320 BCE

Sitting at a table in the inn they were using as headquarters, Eumenes read the letter and passed it to
Eurydice. Then with a sigh, he said, "I thought better
of him but it doesn't matter now. It is Seuthes. It
must be."

"If Seuthes hasn't gone crazy too," Eurydice said
bitterly.

Eumenes looked at her and she looked back. "I
didn't want it to be this way, Eumenes. I was just
afraid it would be."

Eumenes nodded sadly. "Cassander must have offered
him kingship."

Fortress of Pydna, Macedonia
December 17, 320 BCE

Cassander looked at the young woman, Thessalonike.
She was healthy, he had to give her that. Thessalonike
spent at least an hour a day swimming in the tile-
lined artificial pond. Unfortunately, she also had her
father's nose, which looked well enough on a Greek
king, but not well at all on a woman. "Do you agree
then, Queen of Macedonia?"

"I don't know, Cassander. My nephew, Alexander IV, is still alive. I don't think Olympias would like it If I tried to displace her grandson."

"Olympias is on the ship with the ship people. Granted, we cannot reach her there, or Alexander's brat, but the truth is there is little they can do to affect things. We face Eumenes the Carter's son, and that's all."

Seuthopolis, Northern Thrace
December 20, 320 BCE

Seuthes III, king of Thrace, sat in the private chamber of his new-built palace and read the letter. It was a respectful letter, but at the same time it did not offer him what he truly wanted. Freedom for Thrace, his kingdom independent of the Macedonians.

> *To Seuthes III, king of Thrace, if you accept this proposal, Thrace will be a kingdom within the Macedonian Empire. It will have all the rights accorded to a state by the constitution of the United Satrapies and States of the Empire. See attached.*

Seuthes had seen the attachment. It was widely published. He didn't think such a ramshackle system could work, with some parts of government placed in the hands of the empire and other parts placed under the control of the states and satrapies. With rights given to citizens of the empire, as though the empire was Athens.

But he wasn't sure it would fail, either.

He leaned back in the chair and considered, staring blindly at the wall hangings. What if it did fail? Would he be worse off? No. He would have the legitimacy that the USSE could bestow. But what if it didn't fail? He would be locked in, a lesser king who must bow to a babe and a lunatic. He tossed the letter on the table and stood. He had other work to do.

He thought it over for two more days as he did the rites, saw petitioners, and settled disputes among his people, but he finally decided to ally with Eumenes. Eumenes, who, according to the ship people's future history, was the only one of Alexander's generals to remain loyal. Perhaps Eumenes would be honorable.

That left the very large issue of whether he could do it or not. He and Lysimachus had fought each other to a standstill, but that was before Eumenes and Eurydice entered the game.

Two and a half days after receiving the letter, he stood. Decision made. Beard bristling, he bellowed, "Bring me a horse! And arrange a boat! I travel to Lydia!"

Thrace, north of the Sea of Marmara
December 30, 320 BCE

The scout slipped quietly into the camp, and waved to King Seuthes. The camp was about four miles from the coast, near a fishing village. He walked over and squatted down next to where the king was sitting cross-legged on the ground. "Lysimachus, or at least raiders claiming to be Lysimachus' men, came through the village a few weeks ago and took their catch. But nothing since then."

"Good. Do they have a boat?"

"If you can call them that. Tie six of them together and a man has room to stand up."

"Telos, you're a snob." Seuthes laughed quietly.

"I have been on triremes in battle, my king. These things are emptied-out washtubs."

"Then let us go wash." King Seuthes held out a hand. Telos took it and pulled his king to his feet.

☆   ☆   ☆

Two hours later, King Seuthes was less scornful of Telos' pronouncements. The boats were round, about five feet across, with no sail and not much in the way of oars, just enough room to give a man a place to sit while he cast nets into the sea in hopes of catching a meal for his family.

It meant that Seuthes had a decision to make. Lydia, across the Bosphorus, was a hundred miles from here. A hundred and fifty if they hugged the coast. There was no way that the horses could make the trip in those boats. He'd been expecting that, but these boats weren't safe for men more than a mile or so from shore.

He turned to the village headman, Banyous, who was bowing like an idiot, more in fear than out of respect. It gave Seuthes pause. This was one of the people that the ship people would make citizens of the USSE?

"I need to get to Lydia to talk with Eurydice and gain the support of the ship people."

"Are they real?" Banyous asked, surprise for a moment overriding his fear.

Seuthes nodded his bearded head gravely. "Yes. There is ample evidence from many sources." In a way, the man's doubt was reassuring. Seuthes was more than a little skeptical when he first heard about the ship people, but since then he had talked to merchants who had actually seen the great ship. "They are quite real and have powerful magic."

"They say they know the future?"

Seuthes tried to answer the man honestly, but he wasn't entirely sure how it worked. "They know the broad strokes of history, but not the details." Seuthes was beginning to wonder just a little bit if perhaps the ship people might have a point. As the village headman got more comfortable around Seuthes, he seemed to gain in understanding of the world.

"What do the ship people say of Thrace?"

Seuthes felt his lips twist. "Stalemate between Lysimachus and me, but I am forced to yield over time as the rest of the Macedonians support him." That wasn't exactly how the ship people book had put it, but close enough.

Banyous looked at Seuthes carefully. "But you are not yielding. Do you think you can change even the broad outlines then?"

"They say that their very presence changes them. And I believe it. For in the history that was in their past Antipater lived and took both queens back to Macedonia. In this world, Roxane is on the ship people ship, and Eurydice is with Eumenes in Lydia."

"That's why you're going, to make a deal with Eumenes and the girl," Banyous said, and it wasn't a question. "Our little boats won't get you there, but I know a man in Perinthos, up the coast a way. They have a large boat. It won't carry very many, but you and a few of your men . . . perhaps five."

"That's not a lot. I don't want to appear weak."

Again, Seuthes was surprised by the level of under-standing that the headman of a small fishing village had, once he got over his fright.

"Not weak, my king. Trusting, and therefore trust-worthy."

"Perhaps you're right. Perhaps. Where is this village with the large boat?"

Perinthos was half a day by horse, and two days by the little round boats of the village. They rode.

Perinthos was also a hotbed of rebellion against the Macedonians, and so had a garrison of Lysimachus' troops.

Small grove of olive trees, about a mile outside Perinthos

Banyous climbed—almost fell—off the small old mare that he had ridden. Rianus, one of Seuthes' lieutenants, caught the fisherman before he landed on his arse. Which, Seuthes thought, was probably an especially good thing, considering the probable state of that portion of Banyous' anatomy after the first ride of his life took them some twenty-five miles.

"How do you survive, my king?"

"You get used to it. Walk around a little."

"Yes, Your Majesty. But since I am walking anyway, I might as well walk into town."

They stopped outside the town because they didn't want the garrison to see them. Seuthes looked down at the smallish man. He was bent over, with his hands on his knees, making him seem even smaller. But he was ready to serve the gods and Thrace, even if he could barely walk.

It made Seuthes almost ashamed. He was a big man who rarely missed meals. He was dressed in fine cloth decorated with fine needlework. He rode well and fought well. As priest king of Thrace, he was educated in the mysteries and had all the advantages that implied.

But Banyous had a kind of courage that he had rarely seen. It was the slow, steady courage that kept going through pain and privation.

Suddenly Seuthes decided. He got down from his horse and looked around. His men, they were all better dressed than the village headman. Still, Seluca was about Seuthes' size and was in need of a new tunic. "Seluca. Trade tunics with me."

"Sire?"

"I'll be going with Banyous."

"Not a good idea, Sire. You might be recognized."

"No. I have an idea." He reached into his saddle-bag and pulled out a length of twine. Then he tied his beard into a tight bundle hanging from his chin.

"Sire, that looks ridiculous."

"But does it look like me?"

"No, Sire, it doesn't. Someone looks at you, all they are going to see is that silly knot of beard."

Seuthes went to a nearby stream, collected some mud and rubbed it through his hair, not failing to dab a little on the side of his nose. "Now?"

"You look like a madman," Banyous said. "Very clever. Who would ever expect King Seuthes to look so?"

"I certainly wouldn't," said Cotys, Seuthes' son, who was sixteen and a good lad, if a little too impressed with their status as the true royal house of Thrace. Seuthes looked at his son's expression and started laughing.

Cotys' face got red, then he started laughing as well. Then they were all laughing, even Banyous.

"Well, Father, if you're going to look like a madman, I can look like a peasant." He looked at Banyous and gave a proper bow. One that as prince of Thrace he might give to another prince. "Headman Banyous, would you trade tunics with me?"

Cotys was quite attached to that tunic. Clothing, cloth of any sort, was exceedingly expensive, and the sort of fine cloth that was worn by princes was the labor of months to produce. And here he was, willing to give it up to go with his father into danger. Seuthes felt his chest swell with pride in his son.

Perinthos
Sunset, December 30, 320 BCE

Neales, captain of the fishing trawler *Mermaid*, heard a knock at his door and went to answer it. There, in his doorway, was Banyous, dressed in a muddy tunic. That was wrong. Banyous was a fastidious man in Neales' experience. That thought caused him to look more closely at the muddy tunic, and two things became apparent. The tunic was of better quality than any Neales had ever owned, and the mud wasn't the accidental acquisition of a careless man. It was intentionally applied. All this had taken Neales only a few moments to realize, but apparently it was more than Banyous was willing to wait.

"Are you going to let us in?"

"Us?" Neales looked past Banyous for the first time, to see four other men. A lad in what Neales recognized as Banyous' tunic. A big man with his beard tied in a knot and his hair in muddy spikes, wearing a muddy tunic that was of too good a quality...

"Neales," Banyous said again, with impatience clear in his voice.

"Come in then, all of you." Neales said. It was a nice house by the standards of the time. It was one room, but a large one, with mudbrick walls and a roof held up by heavy wooden beams. There was a raised firepit in the center of the room and a hole in the roof for the smoke to escape. His wife was there, and his daughter, Persephe.

The men trooped in, and the lad was looking at Persephe with a look that, as her father, Neales wasn't any too fond of. But Persephe was looking at him the way she might look at a dead mouse in her shoe.

"All right, my friend, what's this all about? Why have you brought a troop of madmen to my house and where did you get that tunic and cloak?"

"Did I not tell you, my king?"

"You did." The madman grinned, and Neales looked again. *No! It can't be!*

"We need to rent your boat."

Pendik, Lydia
January 1, 319 BCE

King Seuthes walked down the gangplank at dawn on the first day of the year 319 BCE by the ship people's measure. At least, he thought it was January 1 as they counted things. He wasn't entirely sure, not because he was unsure of the date, but because he was unsure of how the dates matched up. He thought it might be a good omen if it was. Starting a new life on the first day of a new year. He was washed and his beard was again a beard rather than a tied-up mass, but he was still wearing the lesser tunic of his guard. And if the mud had been rinsed off, it was still a very dirty tunic. But he walked down the gangplank as a king, not hiding his presence in any way. He had talked it over with Banyous and his son Cotys, and decided that as a show of good faith he should not sneak now that he was in Lydia. A man in armor was walking down the quay. Seuthes turned to face him.

"Who are you?" the soldier asked. "And what are you doing at this dock? This is a military—"

"I am King Seuthes III of Thrace, here to see *Strategos* Eumenes and Queen Regent Eurydice."

The man stopped, looked, and looked again. His face got a little pale, then he turned without a word and shouted back down the pier. "Sergeant of the guard! Sergeant of the guard!"

Seuthes turned back to Banyous and Neales. "Thank you, my friends, for your aid." He gave them each a small gold ring and added, "There will be a new government, I think, one way or the other. And I hope you will find it good."

CHAPTER 4

BUILDING THE TOOLS

Queen of the Sea, *Hoi Polloi Lounge*
January 2, 319 BCE

Travis Siegel leaned over the table and whispered in his horribly accented Greek. "It's the piss of a redheaded boy." No one was listening, but it added to the feeling of secrecy and secret knowledge. Travis sat back and looked at the Macedonian's face. Calix didn't seem to be convinced, so Travis explained. "It's not the way *we* do it because we have spectrographs that let us determine the amount of carbon in the steel by color. But it was used successfully for centuries in places like Damascus. It's genetics. Pheomelanin, the same chemical that makes redheads' hair red, acts as an additional flux in the making of steel."

Travis didn't laugh. The reason he was on the *Queen* was because of the poker games in the casino. He could do a poker face.

"And that's all it is?" Calix asked.

"No, of course not. I'll write you up a full report on

the history and techniques involved once your check clears." He leaned back in his chair and grinned. *Hey, the techniques won't actually hurt the steel.* He excused his actions. *The carbon content will be unaffected and the temperature drop between piss and any warm water won't change at all. Besides, these fucks have been conning people with their phony baloney cults for centuries.*

Lydia
January 3, 319 BCE

Eumenes watched the still rather dirty "king" of Thrace come into the tent.

Eurydice nodded regally. "Welcome, King Seuthes." Philip sat beside her, but he was not looking at Seuthes. His eyes were focused on a spider spinning its web in the corner of the tent.

The king bowed a real bow, inferior to superior, which took Eumenes by surprise. He was expecting more haggling. Actually, he was expecting a lot more haggling before Seuthes bowed, and he wasn't at all sure that the haggling would come to an acceptable conclusion. He shifted his eyes over to Eurydice and she was looking surprised and pleased. There was a short pause, then Eurydice said, "Bring a chair for the king of Thrace. Now is not a time to stand on ceremony."

"Probabilities shift," Philip III said. Which made no sense to Eumenes, but much of what Philip said made no sense.

Seuthes looked at the king, who was still watching the spider, then looked back. "The curse of Olympias still troubles him?"

"It's not a curse," Eurydice said with surprising heat. "He has a spectrum disorder."

The words were Greek, but it was clear that they made no sense to Seuthes. They didn't make that much sense to Eumenes either, but by now they made some. He looked at Eurydice.

It was Philip who said, "Spectrum disorder is a grab-bag term for people who think in different ways. We see things others don't and miss things others see."

"Just as you say, Your Majesty," said Seuthes, and Philip nodded once, sharply, and went back to watching the spider. Actually, he had never stopped watching the spider, even while he was speaking.

Then they got down to business.

It was surprisingly cordial. Seuthes was willing enough to see to elections in Thrace, as long as his status and those of his nobles were respected. He would give aid to Eumenes as the *strategos* of the empire, but he wanted to make sure that Eumenes would remove Lysimachus and his army from Thrace. More, he needed to be sure that they really meant it when he was promised local autonomy. They went over the constitution, then started talking about the crossing of the Bosphorus, where and when.

"It can't be soon. We don't have the pontoons."

"Air weighs .0807 pounds per square foot, water weighs 62.426 pounds per square foot. It will take 3.6 square feet of displacement to lift one average man," Philip said.

Seuthes looked at Philip, then said, "Those are heavy men."

"Weight of pontoons included." Philip still stared at the spider.

"Oh," Seuthes said, staring at Philip. Then he looked at Eumenes.

"I have known Emperor Philip III since we were both children. I have never known him to be wrong in any calculation."

Seuthes nodded.

"The point is, it's going to take us some time to make the pontoons and the rest of the bridges. We don't have that many ships," Eurydice said. "Also, we want to assemble the bridge in sections on this side of the Bosphorus, as quickly as we can assemble them. But we are going to need a force to keep Lysimachus from attacking us while we are on the bridge."

"How long to make the pontoons?"

"Less time than you probably fear," Eumenes said. "We will use tarred cloth for the skin of the pontoons." Eumenes winced even as he said it. That much cloth was the total output of some of the states of the empire for a year. That was changing as the new spinning wheels, carding machines, and automated looms of the ship people came into use.

Even now the ship people machines made cloth much faster. Still, the price of that much cloth soaked in tar and olive oil made Eumenes a bit queasy. And from Seuthes' expression, it shocked him.

The truth was that the cloth design for the pontoons weighed less than wooden boat hulls would, so would hold up more weight for the same amount of displacement. Erica Mirzadeh and Philip III had worked it out together.

The discussion of tactics continued as Eumenes wondered how things were going on the *Reliance*.

Reliance, *Mid-Atlantic*
January 4, 319 BCE

Captain Adrian Scott looked out at the wooden ware-
houses that were now sitting on the deck of his ship
with a mixture of pride and annoyance. The *Reliance*
was a fuel barge, or at least it had been before The
Event shifted them all back in time. Now, well, it was
still a fuel barge. As could be told by how low they
were in the water. They had a full load of oil from the
oilfields of Trinidad. They also had fourteen tons of
cloth, twenty-four tons of processed cassava root and
lots of other goods, including sixty-four super turkey
eggs in an incubator. The super turkeys had red meat
and were about twice the size of a normal turkey, and
there were several people in Alexandria who wanted
to start flocks. According to Bob Jones, they ought to
hatch about the time he got to Alexandria.

"Well, Skipper," said Dan Neely, "at least we got
to spend Christmas at home."

Adrian looked over at his radio man and lifted an
eyebrow.

"Well, it is. At least now. Fort Plymouth, New
America, is our home. I have my ranch there and
now Lasli." Lasli was Dan's pronunciation of his new
girlfriend/mistress/wife's name. She was a native and
by now was mostly running his ranch when he was
on the *Reliance*, which was most of the time.

"Frankly, Dan, it's not home to me, at least not
yet. Home to me is still back in twenty-first-century
Bristol. Or maybe on the *Queen*." Adrian shrugged.
"Hell, maybe it's here on this overloaded steel barge."

"We're not that overloaded, Skipper," Dan said,

which was just plain crazy. The *Reliance* was an oil tanker with a full load of oil. And that was all it ought to be carrying. If they hit heavy weather on this trip, they were liable to turn submarine. They probably wouldn't sink because the sealed tanks were lighter than the surrounding water, but they could go under long enough to lose all the goods stacked on the hull. Not to mention drowning the crew.

"Get on the horn, Dan. I want to know what the *Queen* is seeing, weather-wise."

Dan rolled his eyes, but got on the horn.

Queen of the Sea, *approaching Gibraltar*

"The *Reliance* is wondering about the weather again, Skipper," Doug Warren said, a grin on his chubby face.

"Well, tell them." Lars Floden leaned forward in the captain's chair. He understood Doug's amusement, but he didn't share it. "Mr. Warren, the *Reliance* is overloaded and Captain Scott is right to be concerned," he said as severely as he could manage.

"Yes, sir," Doug said, and proceeded crisply to give the *Reliance* another weather report. The *Queen* had weather radar as well as the standard weather stations that were now dotted around the Mediterranean with every radio. It also had the computing power to coordinate all those data points into something approaching a real weather map. Outside the large windows of the *Queen*'s bridge, there was nothing but ocean in any direction. It was only the navigation computers that told him they were just over the horizon from Europe.

Lars' phone rang and it was Jane Carruthers on the line. "What's the problem, Jane?"

"It's not exactly a problem, Captain, but Menelaus wonders if he might join you for dinner?"

In spite of the fact that the *Queen of the Sea* was no longer exactly a cruise ship, dinner at the captain's table was still a matter of status. In a way, now more than it had been. Half the passengers on the ship were nobles or representatives of heads of state. Discussion at this captain's table had, on more than one occasion, changed the status of a nation.

"What does Her Nibs say?" Lars asked, referring to Roxane, the widow of Alexander the Great and quite possibly the highest-ranking noblewoman in the world at this time.

"It was her request."

"What's she playing at?"

"Trade concessions, Captain. Specifically, getting Ptolemy to take a caravan of fuel oil to Suez on the Red Sea."

"Well, in that case, certainly." There was no Suez Canal, of course, but Ptolemy was building a road from Pelusium to Suez. It was a straight road for the terrain, and was being built using wheeled wagons with roller bearings for the wheels and camels pulling the wagons, and being built from both ends. It was part road and part a series of way stations that should provide shelter in the event of sandstorms.

The important point from Lars' point of view was that with a fuel depot at Suez, or better yet, at the mouth of the Red Sea near the Gulf of Tadjoura, the range of the *Queen* would be greatly extended. It would be a major step to getting access to India and China.

Queen of the Sea, *passing through the Strait of Gibraltar*

The party was in full swing and the captain's table in the Royal Icon Restaurant was full. Roxane was there with Dag, and Menelaus was there with a Greek woman named Bethania; Marie was there as Lars' guest, and so was Staff Captain Anders Dahl. He was there stag. Anders had not gotten over the loss of his wife and family to The Event.

The tablecloth was white linen and had been made in a Trinidad factory from flax grown in Egypt. The wine was a Carthaginian red with overtones of strawberry. The waiter came over with a tray of Atlantic tuna steaks. Lars was served, but Marie had ordered super turkey lasagna.

Once the guests were served and the waiter left, Bethania "call me Beth" asked, "Why are you so anxious for a fuel depot in the Red Sea? From my reading, the *Queen of the Sea* couldn't even get there. The *Reliance* could, but it would use half its fuel doing it."

"We are better off than earlier cruise ships in the matter of fuel and range," Anders said. "Since we have flex-fuel engines, we have tankage based on fuels with lower energy densities. So using the semi-refined fuel oil from Trinidad, we have greater range than we might. We can go almost ten thousand nautical miles from full tanks."

"But around the Horn of Africa is almost eleven thousand of your nautical miles, is it not?"

"You're quite right, Beth," Lars agreed. "However, we are attempting to establish a string of fueling stations across the Atlantic, on islands that are unoccupied. We don't want to steal anyone's land."

"Are there such islands?"

"Yes. There are several we know about from our twenty-first-century references. The Ascension Islands, the Cape Verde Islands, São Tomé, and Príncipe, which are near the coast of Africa. St. Helena, where Napoleon died. We are working on determining which of those options to use."

"In any case," Dag added, "we are almost certainly going to end up needing a fueling station near the Horn of Africa. Cape Good Hope or Madagascar. Also, weather stations. The more of them we have, the better able we will be to predict the weather, and that's going to be important to everyone."

"Yet you still want my brother to ship hundreds of tons of fuel oil overland to fill a fuel depot on the Red Sea?" Menelaus asked. "What for?"

"India," said Roxane.

"You are still trying to use the *Queen* to attack the satraps of the eastern empire then?"

"Not at all," Roxane said just a little too quickly, with a glance at Lars and Marie. "The issue is the India trade. Cotton, tea, sugarcane, all sorts of things. And, for that matter, the China trade. Silk and spices. Pepper from India." Roxane stuck a fork in a pepper from Venezuela that was not quite a jalapeno and lifted it. "Black pepper is incredibly expensive once it winds its way through the southeastern empire." She was referring to those parts of Alexander's conquest that were east and south of Babylon. They were the overland trade route from India to the Mediterranean.

Marie gave Lars a look, then looked at Roxane and back. Lars got the signal. Whatever Roxane was saying to Menelaus, she did want at least the threat of the *Queen* bringing forces to attack the southeastern satraps and kingdoms from the rear.

The dinner went on and the discussion moved to the choice of islands in the Atlantic. St. Helena, according to Wikipedia, had a forest but no humans and no domesticated livestock. There was almost certainly animal life on the island, but the Wikipedia article didn't specify what sort of trees or animal life.

"Our best guess," Anders said as he set his wineglass on the table, "is that it has birds and reptiles, possibly land crabs of some sort. But mammals are unlikely."

"Why?" Beth asked.

"Because, while there are exceptions, mammals mostly get to islands by being carried there by men. Birds fly, even if they later become flightless, and reptiles and amphibians swim."

Menelaus agreed to talk to his brother about the oil transports.

Alexandria, Egypt
January 5, 319 BCE

Sitting in the open room in the satrap's palace in Alexandria, Ptolemy read the letter from his brother with interest. A warm breeze off the Mediterranean brought the smells of the sea to him, but they were far enough from the harbor that it wasn't overwhelming. He was almost sure that most of the letter had been composed by Bethania. Thaïs, who was sitting beside him, was completely sure.

"Do you think she's right about the islands?" Ptolemy asked his confidante.

"No," Thaïs said. "Oh, I am sure she has her facts straight, but she underestimates the difficulties."

Ptolemy lifted an eyebrow and Thaïs pointed at a map on the wall. "The Atlantic Ocean is a big place. A very big place. And in that big ocean, an island is a very small thing. We have compasses now, and decent clocks that will work on shipboard, but still, loading up a ship and founding a colony on St. Helena or even Cape Verde would be a risky undertaking, and what would we gain? Nothing but the annoyance of the ship people. If we occupy one, they will just choose another *and* resent our interference. No. Your original plan was best. Take the Red Sea from Suez to Tadjoura. If you can take the Gulf of Aden beyond it as well . . . perhaps Dioscorides . . ."

Ptolemy winced. "Have you ever been to Dioscorides?"

"No. I know Alexander established a colony there after taking Egypt, but I never had occasion to go there."

"I spent a horrible year there one week on the retreat from India. The place is all desert, with snakes and bugs and not much else."

"Sounds like a perfect place for a fuel depot. Take the oil by road to Suez, then by ship to Dioscorides."

"Except I'm not sure I want them to be able to skip Suez."

"That makes sense. Certainly, make them pay for it if they want a depot at Dioscorides. But the islands in the Atlantic . . . leave them to the ship people and New America. If nothing else, you don't want to get involved in the ship people argument over 'pristine natural environments' and the exploiting of them." Thaïs rolled her eyes.

Fort Plymouth, New America
January 6, 319 BCE

Anna Comfort pounded a hand on the table. She was the least comforting person that Al Wiley had ever met and as a politician he had met a lot of nut jobs before and after The Event. Somehow—Al didn't understand how—she had gotten herself elected as the representative for northern Trinidad. "The environments on those islands have evolved for millennia without the interference of man. Now you propose to repeat the environmental atrocities perpetrated by the Portuguese in our timeline before there is even any such nation."

"Yes," said Lacula, quite genially. He leaned back in his chair, and for a moment Al was afraid he was going to stick his feet on the large oblong elephant-ear wood table. "That's exactly what we propose." He waved at Al and the Congress.

Like so much of Fort Plymouth, even the constitution, the table came from many sources. The wood was provided by the Kalaki Nation from northern Venezuela. It was cut and cured right here in Fort Plymouth, using saws made by the *Queen of the Sea*'s modified and expanded machine shops, and finely carved and finished by native and Carthaginian craftsmen.

Even with the addition of the rest of Trinidad and several small territories on the coast of Venezuela and up the Orinoco, the Congress of New America was still not much bigger than a glorified city council. Part of that was because the first Congress had invoked citizenship and residency requirements which, while not as stringent as those back in the twenty-first century, still meant that seventy percent of the people living in New America were not yet eligible to vote. That would change over the next couple of years, but for right now the franchise was only held by ship people and three of the tribes on Trinidad.

"Unlike you ship people," Lacula continued, "we have lived our lives *in* the environment. We know it and its cruelty well. And I don't accept that a cougar has a greater right to live than my children."

"That is a completely false analogy. I am not proposing that dangerous predators be released into New Plymouth. I'm simply arguing that we have a moral obligation to protect those pristine environments that have not been encroached on by man."

Al let it wash over him. It was Fort Plymouth, but along with her other unattractive characteristics, was Anna Comfort's propensity for renaming things to suit her prejudices. Fort Plymouth was militaristic and therefore evil, and New Plymouth went with New America. The damned liberal nut job would run down eventually. She didn't have the votes to stop the island project.

"Actually, Anna does have a point," said Yolanda Davis, and Al stared at her in shock. Yolanda was part of the cleaning staff on the *Queen* before The Event and had married George Davis, a pipefitter who was on his annual vacation. She had strong support among the former crew and the Kaluga tribe, which occupied a good part of southwest Trinidad and were possibly the most Americanized of the locals. Still, Al was shocked to hear Yolanda mouthing liberal doctrine.

Then she added, "We may find things of value in those environments. Remember the nut potato. It had been lost over the centuries between now and

the founding of the first America. So had many of
our peppers and spices. Peppers and spices that are
bringing an excellent price in Europe. I recommend
that we send an environmental expert with the expedition, to see what can and should be saved of those
pristine environments. Don't do it willy-nilly like the
Portuguese did. Use the twenty-first-century knowledge of the ship people to see what can be profitably
exploited and to save and document the unique life
on the island."

"That's going to increase the cost of the project and
the project is already expensive," Lacula said.

"Not that much, Congressman Lacula," Yolanda said.
Yolanda always called Lacula by his full title. "We
are already planning a repeater station and a weather
station on Saint Helena, as well as the fuel depot."

"That's not the point and we don't have an environmental expert to spare. We only have Michael
Lockwood, who has a BS in environmental studies,
and we need him here," Anna interrupted. "An island
like Saint Helena is the sort of pristine environment
that needs to be studied carefully and only by experts."

"Kai Mumea has an interest in environmental studies. He's been working with Bob Jones on integrating
local plants into his farm," Yolanda said. "And he's
willing to go."

"That's exactly the wrong approach," Anna said, and
suddenly Al was having to work to suppress a smile.

He looked at Yolanda and for a moment considered
the possibility that he was looking at the next president
of New America. Not for years yet, but that was a
smooth move. Anna Comfort was never going to get
her way, but she had enough support to delay things

and possibly extort concessions to get her to shut up. But Yolanda had seen the problem coming, and by offering a compromise she'd cut the legs right out from under Anna. All Anna's support was going to switch to Yolanda's camp, and a fair chunk of Lacula's as well. Which meant that her friend Kai was going to get a post on the expedition to Saint Helena as soon as they could get the *Reliance* to make the trip. And that was going to garner Yolanda extra support, especially if Saint Helena, Ascension Island, and Tristan da Cunha became a state in New America. There was virtually no chance that so little an area of land would become multiple states, not if Al Wiley had anything to say about it.

And that's how the debate went. By the time it was over, the Congress had decided that the first mission would be to Saint Helena, and that they would take a sailing ship—a small sailing ship—on the *Reliance*. Most of the *Reliance*'s deck space would be taken up with disassembled fuel tanks. Basically large—very large—wooden barrels that would be placed on the island.

214–216 12th Street, Fort Plymouth, Trinidad
January 6, 319 BCE

Stella Matthews sat in a wicker chair in the upstairs living space, reading the paper aloud and eating breakfast. Carthalo was listening as he ate his super turkey egg and bacon breakfast sandwich. Carthalo, for all his skill and native intelligence, couldn't read. Not even his native Phoenician. He spoke some Greek and was picking up English at phenomenal speed, but his attempts at writing were first grade or maybe kindergarten.

"The radio station among the Kalaki reports that there is a cold front coming down from Mexico and we can expect cooler, drier weather tomorrow and probably the next day." She took a sip of her cocoamat and grimaced at the bitterness, then went back to reading. "The *Reliance* will be bringing precut wooden barrel parts from Egypt when it makes its return trip."

"Someone took—" Carthalo interrupted in his shattered English, "Egypt barrels shit."

"Crap," Stella corrected absently. "Egyptian barrels are crap. Anyway, it's expected to lower the price of barrels in Port Market."

She glanced at the second page. "They have busted glass for fifteen bucks a pound."

"Clear, colored?" Carthalo asked.

"Clear or colored," she again corrected absently. "The ad doesn't say. So probably colored."

"Clear *or* colored," Carthalo repeated. "Forget then. Need clear." He got up, tossed his yesterday's newspaper sandwich wrapper in the trash and headed for the stairs. "Must start melt."

The trash would be picked up and sorted for paper, food waste, and anything else of any possible use. Recycling was very in in Fort Plymouth. Not out of any environmental concerns, but because *everything* was too expensive to waste.

Stella spent another half hour on the paper, then went downstairs to the shop and got to work on the lens-polishing machine. She would get that bastard to work if it killed her. It wasn't like they could buy one of those from Egypt.

Reliance, *Mediterranean Sea,*
en route to Alexandria
January 7, 319 BCE

Captain Adrian Scott sat in his comfortable chair with his laptop computer on his lap and read the radio message on his screen. The laptop was hooked into the *Reliance*'s Local Area Network, which saved on paper and the much more important printer ink. The message was from Fort Plymouth. Adrian would have preferred to lay in his bunk and read it, but paper was expensive in the fourth century BCE, and ink was very expensive, even though the *Reliance*'s laser printer was now in Fort Plymouth and had been replaced with a dot matrix printer that used an inked cloth tape. So Adrian sat in his chair and read through Al Wiley's plan to set up a combination fueling station and small colony on Saint Helena Island in the Mid-Atlantic, thousands of miles from anywhere.

On balance, he rather liked the proposal.

In theory.

In practice, the *Reliance* was already working harder than a one-armed paper hanger taking fuel and cargo back and forth between New America and Europe. Once he had read through the darn thing, he got on the horn to Dan Neely. "You want to come down to my quarters and have a look at this?"

☆   ☆   ☆

Adrian laid on his bunk while Dan used the computer to read the message. Then Dan turned the chair around. "Can't do it, Skipper. Much as I'd like to, just two ships—us and the *Queen*—crossing the Atlantic is not enough. Take one of us out and the

whole economic house of cards that Eleanor Kinney
has built up could come tumbling down."

"Not going to happen, Dan. It's a gold- and silver-
backed system and the *Queen* has storerooms full
of refined gold and silver coins to back it. No, what
worries me is that almost every damn thing we ship
is vital. Even stuff like bales of cloth make a tremendous difference in the everyday lives of people from
Carthage to Babylon."

"We still need more ships crossing back and forth,
Skipper. Not less. Not because we took one of the two
ships that can make the trip out of action for weeks
while we set up fueling stations that won't be used
for who knows how long."

Poseidon's Beard, *Strait of Gibraltar*
January 7, 319 BCE

Captain Yabac gripped the rail firmly as *Poseidon's
Beard* heeled over onto a new tack. The name of the
ship was a reference to the white-foam wake the sharp
bow produced. A common expletive was "by Poseidon's
foamy beard." Carthage was a maritime power and
adopted gods from all around the Mediterranean.
Often they had several gods or versions of gods active
in the same area and getting in each other's way. That
was the case here. Melqart was often preferred as
the sea god by Carthaginians, but the Carthaginian
version of Melqart didn't have a beard, so the ship
was named for Poseidon.

Yabac looked up at the sails and they looked wrong.
For one thing, the *Poseidon's Beard* sported *sails*,
not a single square sail amidships. There were now

two masts and a bowsprit. She was also fore-and-aft rigged, rather than the traditional square rig. All of which made the *Beard* heel over much more than she did when she was square-rigged with two rows of rowers. Yabac didn't like it. He was often in danger of seasickness and the deck's angle was often greater than he liked.

Tubanic slid over to Yabac, grinning like an idiot and showing a broken tooth. "We're doing at least ten knots by my eye, Skipper, and not an oar in the water. Isn't it marvelous?"

Yabac tried to grin back but he doubted he did it very well. His hands were still white-knuckled on the railing and getting stiff from the force with which he was holding on. Tubanic was right. With sixty-four rowers to feed and water, the range of *Poseidon's Beard* was perhaps two weeks at sea if they were going to carry cargo of any worth. This rig required only a quarter the crew, so could sail four times as long. And rowers could only row so long at a stretch. They had been doing ten knots or better for the last three days since they left Carthage. An Atlantic crossing was possible now, as a practical matter.

"Stomach still bothering you, Skipper?"

"Never mind my stomach, Tubanic," Yabac growled. "How's the cargo? With this amount of heeling, I don't want those amphorae of wine shifting."

Carthage strawberry red wine was going for a *stater* a bottle in New America. At least that's what the radio said.

"It's fine, Skipper." Tubanic turned and waved at the hold but still held the railing with his left hand. Then he looked up at the sails. "Catao, you lazy ox.

You tighten that line, or I'll stripe your back, shoulder to arse!"

Yabac looked. The aft lugger was a bit loose, but not bad. "I think the wind is shifting a bit, Tubanic." Captain Yabac moved along the rail, hand over hand. It was demeaning for a captain to move so, but he'd rather look silly than go swimming. They ought to reach Fort Plymouth in three weeks, a month at the outside.

Argos, *Mediterranean Sea* *January 7, 319 BCE*

The *Argos*, out of Isola Grande on the Isle of Sicily, had never had rowers, but that didn't bother Captain Onasus at all. It did have a new sailing rig that had cost almost a hundred drachma and it was carrying wool and flax rather than wine. Onasus looked at the clock, a clock that had cost almost as much as the new rig. They made them in a factory on the *Queen of the Sea* and, for now at least, that was the only place in the world that *could* make them.

In fact, there were a whole raft load of things that only the *Queen of the Sea* could make and Onasus' backers had spent the cost of the *Argos* on clocks, sextants, compasses, and charts.

People were trying to make steam engines now and had been since the *Queen* had first showed them the designs shortly after they arrived in Alexandria. But the engines and, especially, the tube boilers that the *Queen of the Sea* made in their factories were still much, much better. Unfortunately, there were less than twenty of the things in the world, most of them in Fort Plymouth.

"The wind is falling off, Skipper," Pontius said. "I wish we had one of those new steam engines."

"If we have to, we can open the ports and row," Onasus shouted back. "That damn fantasy of yours would cost more than the rest of the ship." Pontius was in love with the idea of steam, and forgot that the charcoal to power would come out of their budget if they had one. And besides, the thought of fire on a ship made Onasus nervous. He looked at the sails then at the wake and shouted to the steersman, "Shift us a little to port, Cincinnatus."

As a ship from Sicily, the *Argos* had a mixed crew. Some Italian, some Greek, and a couple of Carthaginians. That was especially true now, when the *Argos* was making the first Atlantic crossing of any ship from Sicily, though there were rumors that Tyre and Carthage had sent ships. There was no reason Onasus could see to let the *Queen of the Sea* make all the profit from the Atlantic crossing.

Queen of the Sea, *Royal Sports Bar*
January 7, 319 BCE

The big-screen TVs were showing a rerun of the debate over the Olympic Games, but neither man was paying it much attention. For the first time in centuries, the religious games at the city of Olympia had been canceled last year. Partly due to the war and the new government, partly over religious issues and the differences between local Olympics and ship people Olympics.

"There are secrets," Gorloc told Mathis.

The commentators, one Greek and one ship person, continued to argue.

Mathis snorted and the Carthaginian shrugged back at him. "Don't believe me then. When Carthage has good steel while Rome is still struggling with carbon content, you'll regret your parsimonious ways."

☆   ☆   ☆

A table away, Calix listened and fumed. You just couldn't trust a ship person.

Queen of the Sea, *Carthage*
January 9, 319 BCE

Eric Bryant leaned against the rail and looked out at Carthage. The port of Carthage was still not deep enough for the *Queen* to dock, so instead they would be using one of the converted lifeboats—repurposed might be a better way of putting it. They had wood frame tie-downs on the roof, but mostly they were just lifeboats that were being used to ship passengers and goods from the *Queen* to her various ports of call. He looked over at his boss, Quitzko, the god king of the Suthic, a northern Venezuela native tribe from the interior.

The little cannibal wasn't actually a bad guy, once you got past how he was raised. But he needed a native guide, and not just to places like Carthage, but to the ship people. Even the ones in New America. Quitzko was a standard South Central American native. Black hair, black eyes, brown skin. He was five foot two, stocky, with a round face and scars on both cheeks from blood sacrifices that the royal houses of his tribe were expected to make to appease the gods and make the rains come on schedule. He had buckteeth, but not bad, and not overly crooked.

Eric shook his head again. To think that he would ever meet a real, honest-to-God cannibal! And, even weirder, get along with him. Eric wouldn't have believed it before The Event. But cannibalism as part of religious rights was almost common in Central America at this time. And besides, Quitzko insisted that he was happy to give up cannibalism and the god part of his rank.

"*Ssoche ta zi wi tek?*" Quitzko said, and Eric answered, "*Dask zi wi Socke.*"

The first was Quitzko asking if the Carthaginians had really built that harbor, and the second was Eric assuring him they had. Eric, it turned out, had a real knack for languages. Weirdly enough, especially the languages of eastern Venezuela three hundred years before the birth of Christ. Not something anyone back in Alabama would believe, even if they were here. But full immersion had a profound effect on Eric's ability to learn languages, and he was just back from six months living with the Suthic as the New America assistant ambassador.

"The Carthaginians are one of the groups in Europe with the highest tech base. Major traders. They pick up technology from just about everyone. Greeks, Romans, Egyptians. Everyone. In fact, word is they are headed for the Horn of Africa since the *Queen* arrived with stuff like sextants, clocks, and maps."

"What about steam engines?" Quitzko asked. The *Queen* made steam engines which were in use in New America, both to provide electricity and direct engine power for factories, and Quitzko wanted them for his tribe.

"Yes, probably. But I'm not entirely sure that I would trust them. I've heard they've had boiler explosions."

"You ship people . . ." Quitzko stopped, but Eric could fill in the "are soft" that Quitzko didn't say. It was true, at least by local standards. But, by ship people standards, the locals on both sides of the Atlantic were suffering from PTSD. Not just individuals. Whole nations. All the symptomology, paranoia, hypervigilance, flashbacks, and uncontrolled violence were not just present, but were so common as to be considered normal. They were trying, at least some of them. People like Quitzko were trying *very* fucking hard to civilize themselves, and Eric wanted to do all he could to encourage that. There were way too many locals and way too few ship people to depend on tech to make up the difference.

"Come on, boss," Eric said. "The radio says we have a meeting with House Hamil and the ship people radio crew in the city."

Quitzko nodded. He was wearing a leather shirt and a patterned llama wool dress, and locally made imitation tennis shoes. They were rubber soled. The Suthic had a small latex processing operation. Old women with wooden paddles stirred plant juice, ipomoea alba, into heated latex from rubber trees. They had been doing the same thing for centuries before the ship arrived. In fact, the name "Olmecs" meant rubber people, or latex people. The Suthic were descendants of the people that archeologists would call Olmecs, who had moved south after what was probably a series of natural disasters. They had a lot of legends of volcanoes and droughts and other natural disasters, proving that the gods were displeased by their failure to provide adequate sacrifices. It wasn't until the ship people showed up that they began to question those legends. And not all of them did yet.

Quitzko was a leading liberal light in the royal family

of the Suthic royal house and also the closest thing the locals had to an environmental nut job. He believed that the end of the Olmecs was caused by over-farming and a lack of environmental awareness. Which made him a supporter of Anna Comfort, and made him want to have other sources of food and trade, in case that sort of thing happened again.

One of the big legends that his family had was that the ancestor kings were sacrificed to the last babe in an attempt to appease the angry gods, which was how his family got their rank.

Carthage, compound of House Hamil
Three hours later

"Hey there," Eric said, holding out his hand. Oddly enough, in spite of the new languages he now spoke, he still had an Alabama accent, complete with a nasal twang that made banjos envious. "I'm Eric Bryant, from Gadsden, Alabama, and this is Quitzko, who hails from a bit further south."

"Hey there," responded Tina Johnson, and Eric found himself feeling more at home than he had since The Event. "We"—she waved at two older ship people, her parents, Eric knew from reports—"hail from Hokes Bluff, not too far from Gadsden, and this is Borka Hamil, the owner of the steam-engine shop you're interested in." Borka was a middle-aged Carthaginian woman in a sheer linen gown dyed a purple red, and held in at the waist by a belt of small gold face masks fixed together with small links.

They got down to it. The Hamil wanted rubber. Wanted it very badly. Mostly for seals, but for other things as well. And they were willing to sell them steam engines, slaves, strawberries, grapes, wine, wool, cattle, and—apparently—their children, to get it.

As they talked, Eric and Tina translating, he kept looking at Tina and finding her looking back at him. He was uncomfortable about the mention of slaves and he could tell Tina was even more unhappy, but they translated it honestly. That was part of the deal.

Quitzko apparently saw their expressions. He looked at them, then at Borka. Then he said, "Please translate this as accurately as you can manage. Our ship people friends have sensitive digestions. The very notion of slaves makes them quiver in the belly. So, for their sake, I suggest that we work out a deal. Have you ever heard of a contract of indenture?"

Eric translated just as accurately as he could, and was happy to do so. Because this was a compromise he and Quitzko had worked out. The Suthic weren't part of New America, in part because they refused to give up slavery. They, under threat of the *Reliance*, had officially given up human sacrifice, but that was as far as they were willing to go. They did lose slaves escaping to Trinidad on a regular basis, but the *Reliance* was still out there, so they didn't make an issue of the runaways.

Indentured servitude was still slavery, but it was limited, and at least nominally legal on Trinidad. At least the version that he and Quitzko had agreed to was. The Suthic had five forms of slavery, each with its own name: war slaves, debt slaves, crime slaves, land slaves, and sacrifice slaves. Debt slaves were slaves until the debt was paid off, war slaves were slaves for life, crime slaves had a specific time of slavery, depending on the crime and the judge. Land slaves were close to serfs. They had more rights than other slaves, but their condition was permanent. They were tied to a particular farm or grove. Sacrifice slaves were taken from war slaves or crime slaves, and sometimes from debt slaves, and given over to the church. They were then treated well for several months and then given to the gods, and eaten by the priesthood. That was the practice that was officially stopped, but which Eric suspected still happened, on a smaller scale, in private.

However, the ship people were having an effect. The fact that there was a place to run was causing some of the tribes to treat their slaves better. Others, of course, treated them worse. The Suthic were one of the tribes, or tribal groups, that were treating their slaves better. They were also more advanced than expected from the archaeological record, because it turned out that buildings, even wooden pyramids, that are built on wood stilts in river floodplains don't leave a lot in the way of archeological records.

"Anyway," Eric continued, "the slaves the Carthaginians sell to Quitzko will become debt slaves, indentured servants, with a set term of service and legal protections in the Suthic lands. And after their term is finished, they will be accepted as members of the Suthic people. Not exactly citizens—more like peasants, but free to get up and move if they want to. The Suthic aren't any sort of democracy."

Negotiations continued, and after another couple of hours it was decided that Quitzko would stay in Carthage for a few days and catch the *Queen* on its way back. Eric, of course, was staying with him. Which Eric thought was just fine. He couldn't get his mind off of Tina Johnson.

CHAPTER 5

MURDER ON THE *QUEEN*

Queen of the Sea, *Alexandria Harbor*
January 10, 319 BCE

Olympias looked at the screen on the computer in the Princess Computer Center on Deck 9 of the *Queen of the Sea*. Use of the computers was an expensive luxury even on the *Queen*, and there was always someone watching you. No food or drink was allowed in the room, and the staff enforced the prohibition vigorously.

That didn't bother Olympias. What bothered her was that the *Queen of the Sea* had computers at all. Of all the magic that the *Queen of the Sea* practiced routinely, the computers impressed and demeaned her the most. All her life Olympias had based her personal power on secret knowledge. Knowledge of plants and their properties, knowledge of tools and devices, knowledge of spirits, demons, and gods. Knowledge that only she and a very few others had.

Now she sat in front of a screen and looked at the properties of a plant that she had never heard of. A plant that grew in northeast Africa and produced a concentrated form of caffeine. Caffeine, a drug that could keep you awake. And a drug that she had never heard of. It was insulting that they should know so much and share it so freely with anyone who had the money to access their computer library. Such knowledge should be kept to royalty and the priesthood. Else how could they maintain their power? And without that power, the world would sink into barbarism.

Olympias had known that since she was a little girl. And it was still true, in spite of the insanity of the ship people. It had to be.

But the computer screen would not argue with her. It just sat there, displaying a coffee plant and describing the effects of caffeine on the human body and mind.

☆　　☆　　☆

Dag pulled up a chair at the table in the break room, and Travis Siegel looked up and scratched his beard. Travis was sixty and was a passenger before The Event. Now he was the foreman of the crucible-refining shop on the *Queen*. It used induction to heat metal in the crucibles, which allowed them to get very fine control over the chemical mix, making high-quality steel. They couldn't make a lot, not in comparison to a Bessemer, or even some of the crucible rigs they had back in the twenty-first century, but given the raw materials they could make really good steel.

"How they hanging, Dag?" Travis asked.

"Same as always," Dag said. He handed a bottle to Travis. "It's not coffee, but it's bitter as an old girlfriend's heart."

"What would you know about that, kid?" Travis complained with gusto, and got up to go to the cabinet.

He got two mugs and poured the dark green mixture of cocoa and yerba maté that was the most potent coffee substitute available. He stuck both mugs in the microwave and set the timer for one minute. For the next minute, Travis leaned against the counter and discussed the latest load of steel to come out of the crucibles. It was to be used in springs for wind-up clocks.

The microwave pinged and Travis pulled the mugs out. He passed one to Dag, who filled the mug the rest of the way with cream. Dag didn't take cream in his coffee, but this stuff was a different matter. It was in severe need of softening and sweetening, so after the cream he added two spoonfuls of granulated honey. He then sipped cautiously.

Travis emptied his mug with three chugs in quick succession. "That's the stuff," he said as Dag shuddered.

They talked for another few minutes while Dag sipped and Travis had another mug. Dag was starting to feel strange. His stomach was upset and his vision was getting blurry, with halos around the lights.

Travis rubbed his head and muttered about caffeine withdrawal headaches. Then he poured another cup and drank it cold. Then, he grabbed his chest and Dag knew something was wrong. Travis having a heart attack was bad enough, but him having a heart attack while Dag was seeing halos around the light fixtures was too much of a coincidence. Dag was an environmental officer before The Event and his first thought was that some sort of industrial pollutant had gotten into the air. He was still thinking that as he pulled his phone from the case on his belt and called 9-1-1. It was the same number on the *Queen* as it had been back in the twenty-first century before The Event.

"Poison," Dag got out. "Travis is down and I'm gonna be soon." Then he lost consciousness.

☆   ☆   ☆

"We were lucky not to lose Dag," Doctor Laura Miles said. "Dag said poison, but he didn't specify airborne, which turned out to be a blessing because it wasn't airborne. It was in that damn caffeine drink, cocoamat."

"Cocoamat is poisonous?" Lars Floden asked, looking at the mug on the table with sudden suspicion.

"It is if you flavor it with digitalis," Laura said. "The lab identified it. There was enough in that carafe to kill a dozen people. It did kill Travis Siegel."

"Olympias?"

"That's what I think," Daniel Lang said, "but there is no proof. If she did it, I don't know how. She didn't have access to the carafe that I can find. And that's a problem, sir, because we can't lock her up on suspicion. It's against the law and we absolutely have to be seen as obeying our laws. Half our status as neutral ground would go away if we violate our own laws."

"Plus, it would be wrong," said Marie Easley.

"Plus, it would be wrong," Daniel acknowledged with a nod. Daniel was looking about ten years older than he had when The Event happened.

Lars looked at Laura to catch her eye, then he shot a quick glance at Daniel Lang. She gave him back a slight shake of her head. "Later" that head shake said, clear as words.

Surprisingly, considering her medical condition, Laura was looking good. She had a heart murmur that required blood thinner and just after The Event they had thought she was on the soon-to-die list. But, using a combination of twenty-first-century chemistry and fourth century

BCE knowledge of medicinal plants, she and her medical staff came up with a drug produced from a local plant that thinned her blood enough to prevent the clotting. At least they hoped it did. Her staff was now twenty, two ship people doctors and eighteen local doctors from Athens, Macedonia, Egypt, Carthage, and New America.

They would have expanded the medical staff more, but there were only so many beds on the *Queen* and only so much room. The University of the Seas was probably the most exclusive and expensive school on the planet, in spite of all they could do. There were a hundred or a thousand qualified applicants for every slot and the number of slots was also limited by the other functions of the *Queen*: factory, United Nations, residence of at least one of the queens of the Alexandrian Empire and its toddler king.

All those functions took up space, and while the *Queen of the Sea* was a massive cruise ship—had been one of the biggest on Earth even back in the twenty-first century—it wasn't infinite.

☆   ☆   ☆

After Daniel Lang left to set more watchers on Olympias, Lars looked to Laura. "How's he doing?"

"There is nothing physically wrong with him. No, that's not quite accurate. It's the stress levels involved. Dan isn't really suited to a high-stress job because he stresses himself enough anyway. Have you ever seen pictures of American presidents before and after their presidencies? It's the constant stress. Stress has real effects on the human body. Usually, we have time between periods of stress to recover. There hasn't been much downtime since The Event. Besides which, Dan hasn't gotten over leaving his wife and kids back in the twenty-first century."

"What do you recommend?"

"A long-ass vacation and to get laid," Laura said. "Not that I think either of those is going to happen."

"How long a vacation?"

"A month at least. Preferably two or three months. But who would take his place? And how are you going to put him on vacation without it looking like you're firing him, or at least have lost confidence in him?"

"I don't know," Lars said, "but I would rather replace him for a few months than have to bury him and replace him permanently."

Roxane's suite
January 11, 319 BCE

Roxane wanted to be with Dag, but she couldn't stand to see him like that, with the plastic tube down his throat, needles in his arms and unable to move. So she was back here, plotting her revenge on Olympias. She didn't know how she could manage it, but she was going to . . .

There was a knock and her maid stuck her head in. "Ah, Olympias is at the door to the suite, asking to see you."

"She can take her demands—"

The maid shook her head. "Not demanding. Requesting. She was very clear about that."

And that right there stopped Roxane, because Olympias didn't request. She demanded. Even with Philip and Alexander, she had demanded. Which was why Alexander had preferred to love his mother from a considerable distance. Olympias making a request rather than a demand was the sphinx answering a question rather than asking one.

It took Roxane a few moments to process that, then she went to the bedside table, opened the drawer and took out the automatic pistol that Dag kept there. She checked it to make sure that there was a round in the chamber and the safety was off, then she went to the breakfast nook, sat at the table, and placed the pistol on the table about an inch from her hand. "Very well. Send her in."

Olympias came in. Her gaze moved quickly around the room, finding no guards, then back to Roxane at the table. Then she froze. Not for long, just for a moment. Long enough for Roxane to realize that she knew what the semiautomatic pistol was.

Olympias nodded then, a deep nod. Almost—but not quite—a bow. "You will not need that, mother of my grandson."

Roxane placed her hand on the pistol and lifted a sculpted eyebrow in question.

"I did not poison Dag Jakobsen. I swear this on the life of my grandson."

Roxane didn't let her mouth twist, but it wanted to. *On the life of her grandson.* Olympias' grandson was Roxane's son. Not a debt that Roxane would call due.

"I know, Roxane, but there is no oath I could hold more sacred. And if I lie, it will not be you but the gods that call the debt due."

Roxane knew that was true, but she didn't know that Olympias wasn't lying anyway. She didn't trust her former mother-in-law not to put her grandson at risk if the gain was great enough. "If not you, who?"

"I don't know," Olympias said.

And for the first time, Roxane heard real emotion in that voice. Frustration. She still wasn't sure, but she was starting to wonder. She waved Olympias to a seat. Not the chair across from her. She still didn't want Olympias that close. But a couch halfway across the room.

Olympias took the seat and they began to speak in earnest. Eventually, Roxane came to believe that Olympias was innocent. For one thing, the cocoamat was not one of Dag's preferred drinks. He drank it because they didn't have access to coffee, but he wasn't fond of it and always added cream and honey. It was a lousy place to put poison if your target was Dag. It made more sense, a lot more sense, if Travis was the target.

"You almost convince me, but it will not convince Daniel Lang. Nor, I think, most people. What do you want of me?" Roxane asked.

"I want you to help me clear my name."

"Why?"

"Because it failed to kill your Dag. If I had done it, he would be dead. I don't want my reputation sullied by a failed poisoning."

And that, at least, Roxane could well believe.

☆ ☆ ☆

After the meeting with Olympias, Roxane went to the daycare center, where her son was making a hash out of drawing the English alphabet, using a green crayon. Little Dorothy Miller was sitting beside him, telling him all about doing it wrong, near as Roxane could tell. In a cradle a few feet away, Eumenes' infant son was being gently rocked by his nanny.

Stateroom 536, Queen of the Sea

Calix watched the television as it reported on the poisoning and wondered. He was one of three aides to Arrhidaeus, Antigonus One-eye's representative to the USSE. *Why haven't they arrested Olympias? She is the obvious suspect.*

Then his phone rang and it was Cleon, his direct superior. "Did you see the news?"

"I am watching it now, Lord Cleon."

"Well, why haven't they arrested Olympias? Everyone knows she's a witch."

"Her rank is all I can think of, Lord."

"Ha! Even Philip would have arrested her over something like this. Dag Jakobsen ranks high among the ship people."

"Not that high, and much of that is because of his relationship with Roxane."

"Well, I want you to go see what's going on with the ship people guards. Offer to help or something, but go find out."

Calix didn't let a grimace appear on his face or in his tone. "Yes, sir. I will go right away." He had no desire to join the investigation and even less to be brought in contact with Olympias. Olympias knew him of old. Better if the world simply assume that Olympias was the poisoner and imprison her, or put her off the ship. He wanted her out of the way.

Lydia, east of the Bosphorus Straits
January 12, 319 BCE

Erica Mirzadeh didn't burst into the tent, but only because there were guards at the entrance. "You let me in!" she shouted. "That bitch Olympias has poisoned Dag Jakobsen."

"Let her in," Eurydice said, suddenly concerned, and the guard did. As Erica came in, Eurydice asked, "What happened?"

"She poisoned Dag Jakobsen."

"You said that already. What else?"

"Ah, well, that's pretty much all."

"What precisely does the message say?" asked Eumenes from the camp stool he was seated on. They were going over the plans for the pontoon bridge. They had a regular factory making pontoons. Eight-foot-wide and four-foot-deep frameworks, wrapped in tarred cloth and painted with more tar.

Erica Mirzadeh read the message, and it said even less than she had. There was nothing about Olympias in the message at all. Just that Dag Jakobsen and another man, Travis, had been poisoned and Travis had died.

"Did you know Travis Siegel?" Eumenes asked.

"No. I never met him. It's a big ship and we never ran into each other. Honestly, I never met Dag either, though of course I saw him on shipwide TV several times. He's usually with Roxane. It's not personal, not exactly. It's that that bitch poisoned one of ours."

Eumenes laughed and Eurydice wanted to. Philip pointed at Erica and shook his head in rebuke, all without looking right at her.

Erica blushed. "Sorry. We really do mean it when we talk about equality, but not that many of us came back in The Event and it's a bond between us."

"As it should be," Eurydice said. She looked at Philip. "Just because she is concerned about Dag doesn't mean that she thinks ship people are better than us."

"Ship people *are* better than us," Philip said. "They are healthier and better educated. But they should not act like it. It's against the ship people rules. People should obey the rules."

Erica Mirzadeh grimaced a little, but nodded. The truth, Eurydice knew, was that Erica was no more comfortable with Philip than most people were. It was getting better over time because Philip was acting as the primary computer for the bridge project and Erica was deeply involved. That threw them together and people got used to Philip's ways.

"That doesn't actually sound like Olympias," Eumenes said.

Eurydice turned to him in shock, and he looked back, consideration plain on his face.

"She scares me," Eumenes said, not sounding all that scared. "Always has. But a good part of the reason for that is that she has her insanity under control. This doesn't seem to me to fit her style."

"She takes credit for things she didn't do," Philip said, sounding aggrieved. "She took credit for my spectrum disorder."

"Which is probably a good thing, when all is said and done," Eumenes said. "If it were thought that the gods did it, things might have been much worse."

"Not why she did it," Philip said.

"No, you're quite right, love," Eurydice said. "She just wanted credit for having powerful and subtle magic. That's half the trouble with her. You can never know what's real and what's illusion."

"And that's what bothers me about this," Eumenes said. "It just seems too sloppy for her."

"Well, I think she just didn't understand what our labs could discover," Erica pointed out.

"Possible. But in her way Olympias is as careful a person as I have ever met," Eumenes said.

"And as evil," Eurydice said. "She had Philip murdered and forced me to commit suicide."

Eumenes looked at Eurydice, and she felt her face

heat. The truth was that while she despised Olympias personally—she was a vicious old harridan—she wasn't all that much worse than any of the rest of them. Perhaps even herself.

"She *would* have had Philip murdered. In a different universe," Eumenes said. "In any case, there is nothing we can do about this now. What about the tar?"

Erica Mirzadeh grimaced and came to the table. "It's being used up faster than we expected. And the shipment from Egypt is delayed again. I think Ptolemy may be being sneaky."

"You think he's—" Eumenes started to say, then stopped. "No. Ptolemy doesn't exactly hate Cassander, but the little coward isn't one of his favorite people. I don't see him actually conniving with Cassander, unless Cassander had more to offer him than he does. What concerns me is that whatever its cause, the delay could throw our timing off." King Seuthes had gone back to Thrace to prepare his forces. The plan was to have the Thracians make a display to threaten Lysimachus and draw some of his forces away from the Bosphorus when they had the parts of the bridge ready to be put together. There was no way that Lysimachus would pull all his forces out, but crossing the Bosphorus against two thousand would be a lot easier than crossing it against ten thousand.

They had signals to let Seuthes know when to act, but his preparations were going to be hard to keep secret. And if Lysimachus were to deal with him before they were ready to cross the Bosphorus and hit Lysimachus in the rear, things could get very bad for Seuthes.

Pella, radio shack
January 12, 319 BCE

Malcolm Tanada checked the final connection and sent the handshake. The handshake was the radio code in the computer that would tell the *Queen*'s radio that the message that followed was from Malcolm and tell his computer that the *Queen* was who they were talking to. It was a series of codes and responses loaded into his computer and the computers in the *Queen*'s radio room.

He looked at his computer screen and it took a minute before he was in. Well, not a real minute. A minute was a long time for a computer handshake, but it did take a full ten seconds, which meant there was a weak signal and a lot of interference. The bandwidth was going to be low, and it was going to take more time to send his files. He used the mouse ball and moved the cursor over the file and dragged it into the queue.

Then he waited, looking out his window at the city of Pella. Well, small town of Pella. Maybe ten thousand people lived here, which was a lot by fourth century BCE standards, but still a small town by Malcolm's. It was also a city of slaves. He could see them out his window, carrying water and food from place to place and working at trades in the open air.

He shook his head and turned back to the computer. The file contained about two thousand words of text, but also twenty or so pictures. It was the report that he put together as they were setting up the radio and included things like the fact that Thessalonike was now living in Pella and Cassander had a group of Macedonian nobles calling him king. Also the fact that very few of those nobles had anything good to say about Alexander the Great, and even fewer had anything good to say about Eumenes, Philip, Eurydice, Roxane or her son.

Royal Compound, Pella, Macedonia
January 12, 319 BCE

"Well?" Cassander said to Malcolm Tanada, then looked over at Thessalonike, who was watching from the sidelines. She hadn't agreed to marry him, not yet, but she had agreed to come to Pella. She was watching the ship person with the same sort of interest she might have shown if he was a great ape or an elephant.

Malcolm was the lead radio operator for Macedonia. And like most of the radio teams, he had a radio made by the ship people after they had arrived and a computer system that they had brought with them.

"The derrick is finished, sir," Malcolm said. "We're back in contact with the *Queen*. We can also reach Rome, Athens, and Alexandria."

The derrick, as Malcolm called it, was a wooden framework that was placed on top of one of the tallest buildings in Pella. It extended up another forty feet and from what Cassander was told, allowed the range of the radio to be greatly enhanced. He also knew that a link to any station was effectively a link to all of them because, like signal fires, they formed a network. So he didn't ask about Carthage or, for that matter, Trinidad on the other side of the world. "What about Babylon?"

"Nothing from that team yet, sir," Malcolm said.

Cassander grimaced because Malcolm insisted on calling him by the ship people appellation "sir," rather than majesty or my lord. According to the ship people it was a sign of respect, but carried no precise designation of rank. Sir could be said to a merchant you were dealing with or the greatest king in the world without giving offense.

At least, that's what the ship people said.

Cassander didn't agree. He found their failure to give him his proper title—king of Macedonia—to be a calculated insult. And if it were anyone but a ship person who used "Sir," he would have them killed for it. But the radio was vital, and even if he took it, it would do no good, because it needed another radio to be of any use and the other radio was far away and not under his control. The ship people would refuse to acknowledge any message he sent, even if he managed to make his radio work. It was an amazingly effective protection for the radio operators.

Cassander looked at Thessalonike and saw a little half smile on her face. He suspected that it was because of the lèse-majesté the ship person was showing him. Cassander really wanted to execute Malcolm then. The fact that he couldn't was probably amusing her greatly.

"I didn't really expect anything yet. First, they have to cross the frigging desert and travel down the Euphrates to Babylon. Then they will have to negotiate with Antigonus for access and a place to stay," Malcolm said.

Cassander knew all that, but it was taking a long time.

Syrian desert
January 12, 319 BCE

Susan Godlewski reached up and wiped her forehead
with a damp rag. It was raining in the Syrian desert.
Again. *Whoda thunk it*, she thought. Susan was from
Arizona. She was used to desert, which is why she'd
agreed to take this position. Well, that and the very,
very good money offered by Arrhidaeus and Eumenes.
They hadn't mentioned—*the dumb bastards*—that she
was liable to drown on the way. The desert sands were
now grainy mud, the wagon wheels were four inches
deep. and the wagons wouldn't go anywhere till the
rain stopped and the sand dried so that they could
dig out the wheels. The camels, on the other hand,
seemed to be enjoying the rain, holding up their heads
and licking their muzzles. Or maybe they were just
happy they didn't have to pull the wagons.

"Come in out of the rain, Susan!" shouted Karrel
Agot, a belowdecks crewman who took the job for
the same reasons that Susan had. He was about five
nine, swarthy complexion, with a Vandyke beard. He
was a Muslim still, in spite of The Event. He did his
daily prayers facing Mecca, even though Muhammad
wasn't born yet, anymore than Christ was. Susan shook
her head, but she couldn't feel that superior. She still
said grace, after all.

She went into the tent she and Karrel shared with
the twenty Persian mercenaries who had been hired
to protect them from bandits. "How's the rig?"

"Still in the boxes." The *Queen of the Sea* could
manufacture radios, even tuneable, fairly powerful
radios. The problem was output. Even with many of

the parts manufactured in parallel and in groups, the total output of the radio factory on the *Queen* averaged out to one mid-range radio a day. They could produce three short-range radios in the same time frame, but a long-range radio station like the one for Babylon took a month or so to complete. It wasn't just the radio, though making a transmitter that would reach from Babylon to Tyre was no mean feat. No, the problem was that a radio of that power needed a generator and a bank of batteries, circuitry-testing equipment, a steam engine to turn the generator and, most importantly of all, they needed to have electrical and general physical protection of the computer that ran it all, because the computer was completely irreplaceable.

To protect this highly valuable installation and the two ship people who were accompanying it, the *Queen of the Sea* had hired twenty mercenaries and equipped them with ship-made crossbows. They had wanted to do rifles, but rifles take long barrels and long barrels were much harder for the equipment on the *Queen* to produce. They also sent a couple of crates of grenades.

Palmyra was still a couple of days' travel and Babylon another couple of weeks after that. Susan wondered what she would find when they finally got to Babylon.

Antigonus' palace, east half of Babylon
January 12, 319 BCE

Antigonus One-eye, seated in a chair that made a good attempt at being a throne, gritted his teeth and waved at the Greek soldier. The soldier was one of Attalus' men and Antigonus didn't recognize him.

He was young, though, probably in his twenties. And from his clothing, probably a son of a noble house. He came under a flag of truce.

The man stood up from his bow and asked, "Have you gotten any word on the radio?"

Antigonus shrugged. "They were crossing the desert last I heard." Even for dispatch riders it took a week to reach the radio at Tyre and the signal fires were disrupted by the constant skirmishes between his and Attalus' forces. Dispatch riders could avoid the skirmishers, even if it did mean that they couldn't change their horses.

It had not been a good few months for Antigonus One-eye. After his initial not quite victory over Attalus, he was plagued with desertion and disease. Attalus gained troops in the first weeks after the attack and maintained his hold on the west side of Babylon. In fact, much of the infantry that Antigonus captured deserted back to Attalus.

Word from the *Queen of the Sea* that a constitution had been written and that Eumenes was made *strategos* for the empire had hurt him badly in status and authority, and with only the Euphrates between them, defection proved easy for the troops. Instead of moving west to take on Eumenes, he was stuck here holding Babylon against Attalus. He didn't even control the surrounding territory, not completely. Attalus had gotten a lot of his cavalry out of the city, slipping them out in the weeks after his attack, so there was regular skirmishing between Antigonus' cavalry and Attalus'.

"I don't see that it matters that much. I don't accept Eumenes' authority any more than I accept Attalus'," Antigonus told the envoy.

"And the queens?"

"I am loyal to the babe, but Philip is an idiot and now that Alexander's son is born, he has no right to the throne. That eliminates Eurydice. And as for Roxane, she is a woman and not Macedonian. Such cannot rule Alexander's empire."

His statement was nothing new. Attalus had been making his claims in the name of Roxane and that treacherous little bitch Eurydice since the day he arrived, and Antigonus had maintained his answer for just as long. He'd also sent envoys to the satraps of the eastern empire, asking their support and making promises. He'd sent envoys to Ptolemy too, though as yet all he had gotten from Ptolemy were delays and promises to consider. Ptolemy, the coward, was sitting in Alexandria and hoping that the winner of the war would be so weakened that he could take it all, or at least keep Egypt.

"And the wounded?" asked the envoy.

"We will take care of our own," Antigonus said. "As for the prisoners, they are traitors and get what a traitor deserves."

Attalus' palace, west half of Babylon
January 12, 319 BCE

Attalus paced back and forth, glancing at the table that was filled with maps. Maps of Babylon, maps of the surrounding territory. The stalemate continued, and Attalus was increasingly frustrated. Right after the battle, every day his forces had gotten stronger as Antigonus' got weaker. But then the defections had gradually trickled off. He'd gotten enough of his cavalry out of Babylon to relieve him of the need to find provender for their horses. But to do that, he was forced to slip them out a few at a time, and not all of them had joined his cavalry command. Some had gone to join Eumenes, and all too many had simply gone home. He had less than half the cavalry he'd started with, and only a third of the infantry.

He looked over at Menander. Menander had surrendered as soon as it was clear that Attalus was going to hold the west side of the city, and a month later had switched sides, joining Attalus' staff. Attalus figured the major reason Menander switched was because he didn't want to face Antigonus One-eye after losing the half of Babylon he was responsible for. "Dareios is back and Antigonus hasn't budged a finger width."

"Did you think he would?" Attalus asked.

"No, but I'm worried about what's going to happen when the ship people get here." Attalus had seen the *Queen of the Sea*, but Menander never had. The thing that impressed Menander about the ship people wasn't the great ship. What impressed him was the fortified wine that they had washed his wounds with after the battle. It was having his wounds sewn up and not having them fester or rot. Attalus could sympathize with Menander's point of view. He was even more injured at the battle of Sardis.

"I don't know. I know I don't want to be responsible for anything happening to one of the ship people," Attalus said. "From what I was told, Gorgias managed to kill two and they destroyed his fleet. And I know that Metello killed only one, and they hung him and killed half his army." That was an exaggeration, but still... pissing off the ship people wasn't something he wanted to do, even if they were hundreds of miles from any ocean.

"Well, when is Eumenes going to relieve us here?" Menander asked.

"He's up at the Bosphorus."

"Yes, just sitting there. While Antigonus has us trapped in this hole."

Attalus closed his eyes and thought. Eumenes' messages about his attack on Babylon hadn't been complimentary. Angry as Attalus was at the generals for the murder of his wife after Peithon lost at the Nile, he still resented the fact that Eumenes and not himself was made *strategos* of the empire. Eumenes was not Macedonian and it was just wrong to put him above a true Macedonian.

But the world was what it was, and Menander harping on it wasn't making him feel any better about it. Maybe when the radio got here Eumenes would send him better instructions. Or he could talk it out with the queens and get them to reconsider.

CHAPTER 6

PREPARATIONS

Royal Lounge, Queen of the Sea, Alexandria Harbor
January 15, 319 BCE

Ptolemy took his usual seat in the Royal Lounge. "Are you sure that this is worthwhile?" he asked the room at large.

Marie followed his gaze as he looked around the room. There was Roxane and Dag, who'd recovered from the poisoning. Digitalis washed out of the system in only a few days if it didn't kill you, which, with proper medical intervention, it usually didn't. But Travis Siegel had a heart condition and he had apparently ingested at least three times as much of the digitalis-laced cocoamat as Dag had.

Next to Dag were Eleanor Kinney and Amanda Miller, who by now was Al Wiley's ambassador at large. She and her daughter traveled with the *Queen of the Sea* and by agreement enjoyed diplomatic immunity from Carthage to Alexandria and north to the remnants of the Etruscan League.

Marie looked over at Lars, who looked at Eleanor Kinney. Eleanor was the ship's purser who was now the main architect of the monetary and banking system on the *Queen of the Sea* and in New America. She hadn't done it alone. She'd had the help of Amanda Miller, and a few other passengers with banking and money-management experience.

"I'm surprised," Eleanor said. "Eumenes seemed quite anxious to have us circle the Horn of Africa."

"Eumenes is acting as *strategos* for the empire," said Ptolemy. "His goal is to use the *Queen* as a threat against Antigonus' rear so that Antigonus can't bring the armies of his allies to the war that is going to be fought along the Euphrates. My concerns are more pragmatic. There is more trade between Egypt and New America than the *Queen of the Sea* can truly support. If you go exploring around the Horn of Africa, that will take the *Queen* out of service for months. And to stockpile the fuel you will need will require taking the *Reliance* out of the trade lanes as well. The market for super turkeys and llama, not to mention jade and gold decorative art, are helping our economy."

Marie looked at Ptolemy in surprise, but she got over the surprise quickly. Thaïs, his mistress—for lack of a better word—traveled on the *Queen of the Sea* for months and she was a very smart woman who studied intently. And apparently shared her thoughts with Ptolemy. She looked around the table and saw Dag's expression. Roxane, seated beside Dag, was showing nothing but polite interest, but Dag's face was easier to read. There was a cynical twist to his lips; not a very severe one, but it was enough. Marie looked back at Ptolemy and realized that the satrap of Egypt wasn't in any great hurry to see Eumenes defeat Cassander and Antigonus. As long as Eumenes was busy in Macedonia or Babylon, Ptolemy would be able to strengthen Egypt and the other territories he had gobbled up since Alexander's death.

With good planning—and just a little luck on Ptolemy's part—Egypt would be too powerful for the United Satrapies and States of the Empire to fight by the time they got around to trying to reimpose imperial control and make him give back Syria, the Palatine, the kingdoms of Nabataean and Judea.

"Surely," Marie said, "the goods that might be found in southern Africa or shipped by the *Queen* from India to the Port of Suez will add more to the empire's economy."

"Perhaps, but the—" Ptolemy held up a hand. "What is that expression that my daughter picked up from you ship people . . . ? Something about birds and hands?"

"A bird in the hand is worth two in the bush." Marie lifted an eyebrow.

"Yes, that's it. The transatlantic trade and the Mediterranean trade are birds in the hand. This trip to the south of the great desert is very much birds in the bush."

"That's not the only factor," said Eleanor Kinney. "There are going to be new trade ships. In fact, we hear that there are sailing, or at least primarily sailing, ships that are attempting the transatlantic crossing already. From Rome and Carthage, even from here. Exploration and establishing trade routes and weather stations will help the whole world."

"And," added Amanda Miller, "the sooner those

trade routes are established, the sooner ships from
New America and the Mediterranean powers can
follow in relative safety. Don't forget, Satrap, that
the weather predictions that our computer models
can provide are very dependent on the number and
spread of our weather stations. The weather stations
dotted around the Mediterranean help, but a storm
front from the Atlantic might send a hurricane to
Trinidad with almost no warning. Storms and rain,
high winds, all these things could destroy your crops
in the field if you are not warned."

Marie watched Ptolemy's expression as Mrs. Miller
went through this list of advantages. He didn't seem
convinced, but Dag was smiling and so was Lars.

Royal Palace, Alexandria
January 15, 319 BCE

"Did you get them to delay?" Thaïs asked.

"Not for a day, and I couldn't use the oil depot at
Suez, because they know we're building it anyway. I'd
like to know how they learned that."

Thaïs laughed. "Come, now! You know that the
radio team is here as much to spy as to provide
communications. Bruce Lofdahl is a nice man and
TinTin Wai is charming, if her accent is sometimes
hard to follow. But they are collecting information
on Alexandria and the rest of Egypt and reporting it
back to the *Queen of the Sea.*"

Ptolemy did indeed know that. He was just blowing off steam, another one of the ship people sayings.
This one hadn't made much sense to Ptolemy until he
had seen one of the new steam engines in operation.

"I know, but Menelaus says that the ship people are cooperating with Roxane. Even if they don't do anything so overt as dropping troops or shelling coastal cities, just sailing along the coast in sight of land will scare the crap out of Tlepolemus." That, at least, wasn't one of the ship people's catchy phrases.

"What's the word from Eumenes?"

"He's still at the Bosphorus and, according to Claudius, building pontoons."

"They should be getting close, shouldn't they?"

"Yes, but the Bosphorus is wide even at its narrowest point. It's going to take them a while."

"How long?"

"Figure fifteen feet between two pontoons, including the width of one of the pontoons. That's a hundred and fifty pontoons or close to it. There are the bridge sections that fit over the pontoons. But there will be different groups working on pontoons and bridge sections." He snorted. "From what Claudius said, they are even using a group to make railings for the sides of the bridge, but that won't take any more time. Just more hands working on it. It will take several days for each pontoon, but again they will be making several pontoons at the same time. A month and a half, maybe two months from when they started. Add two weeks for the time it took them to build the factory and arrange to have the wood and fabric brought in. Not today or tomorrow, but I would be surprised if it takes Eumenes more than another month.

"Then they have to tie them together. That's a week right there, and they will be doing it under the arrows of Lysimachus."

"Will they?"

"What do you mean?"

"They have the ship people rockets."

Ptolemy stood suddenly and strode across the room, then back. "I've seen the steam cannon, but not their rockets." Frustration was clear in his voice. "I don't have any idea how effective they will be. They might do very little, or they might wipe Lysimachus' army from the western shore of the Bosphorus as though they were a mighty broom."

"I saw a couple of examples while we were in New America, but it was only a few rockets, fired one at a time." Thaïs reached up and tugged on a curl of her dark brown hair. "They have the range to reach across the Bosphorus, I'm almost certain. But how accurate they will be at that range, I'm not sure. What I do know is that they often explode either just before or just after they hit the ground. It is like a grenade, but larger."

Now Ptolemy sat back down. Egypt had grenades. Gunpowder was one of the first bits of ship people knowledge the locals gained. Dinocrates started using black powder in construction months ago, and Ptolemy had a unit of grenadiers training with the small, throw-able bombs. They were fused, not contact, explosives, and there had been two very demonstrative accidents, where a grenade was lit, then dropped.

A total of seven dead, five the first time and two the second. Against a phalanx, grenades would be pure murder.

"Accuracy wouldn't have to be that great if the grenades in the rockets are large enough. Then there is the shock value. I've had to pull quite a few of my soldiers out of the grenadiers. Veterans who I would have called fearless are sometimes terrified of the things. It's the indiscriminate nature of the weapons. Not even that, exactly. With a flight of arrows, you can hold up your shield and if you hold it right, you have a good chance. With grenades, there is nothing you can do. You die, or don't. In the second accident, a man standing not five feet from the grenade was barely scratched, but a man almost fifteen feet away had a piece of shrapnel go right through his breastplate."

"The ship people's way of war," Thaïs said, "lacks in honor, I think." Thaïs followed Alexander the Great's army from Macedonia to India and back. She'd seen many battles and had been forced to wield a sword in defense of the baggage train in two of them. She respected war as a contest of skill, strength and courage. But the way the ship people did it.... She shook her head. It wasn't the better man who won when ship people fought. It was the man with the better tools.

And that meant that Eumenes was almost certain to cross the Bosphorus successfully. What would happen after that was less certain, because Eumenes only had so many of the critical venturi for the rockets.

Community center, Fort Plymouth
January 16, 319 BCE

Carthalo took his seat with a beer in one hand and a super turkey and bacon corn-flour wrap with lettuce, tomato, and green pepper in the other.

It was the 3:00 to 3:30 news report, the one that was in Phoenician. And most of the people sitting on the chairs in front of the television were from Carthage. About three quarters were former slaves, indentured or not. The rest were freemen who came looking for opportunity. And Captain Boka, who gave all his slaves their freedom, was seated next to his wife, who was a former slave. Carthalo wasn't sure whether to admire the captain or just acknowledge that he was a crazy man.

The news came on and Carthalo watched as he drank his beer. They talked about the rubber groves up north and the work on the copper-wire-pulling shop on 5th Street, then about where the two big ships were at the moment—which Carthalo didn't care about at all—then ended up with a report on the war in the Alexandrian Empire, which he cared about even less. He took a bite out of his wrap as the screen showed a map of the Bosphorus with a little red dot where Eumenes' army was supposed to be.

Then the report was over and so was Carthalo's lunch. He went back to the shop on 12th Street.

Lydia, east of the Bosphorus Straits
January 16, 319 BCE

The blacksmith took the cone in his hand and placed its tip against the round oblong of wrought iron. Then he struck the conical wedge with his hammer. He looked at the still-yellow oblong and hit it again to try and get his wedge a bit deeper. Then he lifted the whole thing and knocked it against his anvil to loosen the still very much unfinished venturi. Pharnabazus gave him one of the venturi that the ship people made as a model, but he built the tools to make the thing himself, working it out from the shape of the bells, one on each end and the hole between them.

He put the venturi back in the fire and selected a smaller punch. Even with the tools he had and starting from a blank provided by other smiths in Lydia, making a venturi was a lot of work.

On the other hand, *Strategos* Eumenes had promised to buy all he produced.

Eumenes' headquarters
Lydia, east of the Bosphorus Straits

"Not enough," Pharnabazus said. "Not to affect this battle anyway. And probably not to affect any battles that we will fight in the next three or four months."

"And the cost," Eurydice complained, "of one of those damned venturi is almost as much as a short sword. Worse, we can only use the venturi once."

"That is true, Majesty," Eumenes agreed. "Everything either of you have said is completely true. But even more expensive in the long run would be trying to cross the Bosphorus with only swords and arrows. We could do it, yes. But it would cost us a thousand men and more. If we can get a force on the far side of the strait with minimal casualties, they can hold it while the rest of our army crosses and our army is bigger than Lysimachus', especially if Seuthes is tying down half of Lysimachus' army with his attacks."

"How long, then?" Eurydice asked, even though by now they all knew the schedule by heart. She was just nervous.

"Another week," Eumenes said.

CHAPTER 7

CROSSING THE BOSPHORUS

Lydia, east of the Bosphorus
January 23, 319 BCE

Erica Mirzadeh watched from the radio wagon as the army formed up on the shore. She had a pair of binoculars that were made at New America Glassworks in Fort Plymouth. They were not very good binoculars, only 4-power and the right lens had a rough patch that was irritating. In fact, using them too much tended to give her a headache, but she was going to use them now. She had her phone in her box, but with earbuds and a small mic made back in the world before The Event, she was going to record the battle to the best of her ability and send back a report.

She swung her binoculars to the docks, where they were starting the bridge.

☆   ☆   ☆

Nikon shouted and the squad of war-captive slaves pushed the pontoon along the pier. The pontoon was in a little cart, really just a framework of leather and wood with wheels, but the wheels rolled and the cart meant he only needed six men to push the sixteen-foot-long, eight-foot-wide, four-foot-deep pontoons along the pier. They pushed, then pushed some more, then they reached the end of the pier and kept right on pushing. The pontoon went over into the water and the framework cart sank beneath it.

"Pull, you bastards, pull!" Nikon shouted, and the slaves pulled on the ropes that attached to the cart. Meanwhile, the Bosphorus wasn't waiting. Its current pulled the pontoon out of alignment, and the rope on the pontoon swung it in, so that it wedged the cart in place at the end of the pier. Nikon started cursing then, and he cursed for most of the rest of the day as the slaves used poles to push the pontoon far enough out so that they could pull up the water-logged cart, then, by muscle, pull the pontoon back into place so that the platform could be laid onto it and tied in place.

By the time the first pontoon had been placed and tied down, the sun was going down. Nikon looked at the upstream tie-down and noted the stress on it. They were going to need some way of holding the pontoons in place or the current was going to take them all the way to the Marmara Sea.

☆   ☆   ☆

Erica Mirzadeh didn't have a clue how to fix it. "It" being the whole series of interacting problems with the construction of the pontoon bridge.

"We need to redesign the cart," said Thales of Miletus, a soldier in Eumenes' army and, as he often pointed out, a relative of the philosopher of the same name.

"How do you mean?" asked Heraclitus, also of Miletus, with such an air of long-suffering patience that it came through clearly, even though Erica was still struggling with Greek unless she used the translation app.

Thales made a gesture that Erica had no trouble at all interpreting, then said, "We need to dump the pontoons without dumping the cart."

"Won't work," Heraclitus insisted, with what sounded like satisfaction in his voice. "You're ignoring the current. You can't drop pontoons in the same Bosphorus twice."

Thales rolled his eyes and Erica checked the translating app while she tried to figure out what Heraclitus was talking about.

Heraclitus pointed at the end of the pier, now extended by a sixteen-foot-square wooden platform supported at the far end by a pontoon. The pontoon was sixteen feet long, eight feet wide, and four feet deep. It had a raised section two feet wide going lengthwise from end to end. The wooden platform was tied to the shoreward side of the raised section of the pontoon. The idea behind the raised section was flexibility. If the waves on the Bosphorus lifted a pontoon, or a weight on the bridge pushed a pontoon down, this design would put less strain on the rest of the bridge. On the other hand, it had the unwanted side effect of having the pontoon stick out past the end of the bridge. Not good when you're going to be dropping the next pontoon off the end of the bridge.

"You dump the pontoon off the end there," Heraclitus said, "and the cart's in the way. The flow of the Bosphorus drags the pontoon, the pontoon pulls the ropes, the ropes pull the cart and the whole thing becomes a tangled-up mess. Not only does the cart get dunked, anyone caught in the wrong place gets dunked as well. And that's if they're lucky. If they aren't lucky, the ropes will cut them in half."

Nikon looked at the bridge, then he looked at Heraclitus and Thales, then he looked at Erica and said, "Dump the pontoon off the side of the bridge." With a sidelong glance at Heraclitus, he continued. "The upstream side. That way the Bosphorus will push the pontoon up against the bridge. Then we attach the next bridge section and use it to push the pontoon along to the end of the bridge, tie it off and do the next."

Erica Mirzadeh didn't know why he was looking at her. She knew radios, not building. Well, she knew computers before The Event and she was learning radios. But bridge-building wasn't her thing. Sure, she had helped with surveying of the Bosphorus, and even with the design of the pontoons. But mostly that was just getting on the radio and telling the engineering types on the *Queen* and in New America what they needed, then using the dot matrix printer to print out crappy images of what they sent back. "That sounds like a plan," she said. And it did. She didn't have any real idea whether it was a good plan.

Heraclitus looked at the single bridge section that had been added to the pier, then at the Bosphorus, then across the Bosphorus. "The current is strong enough here. When we get out near the middle..." He shook his head, real concern showing now.

"We'll have to run lines to pontoons to keep the river from ripping the bridge up."

And so it went. There were more problems on

the second day, but by the fourth they mostly had it down to a routine. Eight sections a day. By the ninth of February, they were getting close to the far side. Close enough that Lysimachus brought up oxybeles.

February 9, 319 BCE

Erica Mirzadeh looked across the Bosphorus at the oxybeles being pulled into place. Oxybeles were bows on a frame that were cranked back before firing. What surprised Erica was that they weren't all that much bigger than the crossbows that the Silver Shields on the *Queen* carried. She watched as they were positioned with care, then as they were cranked up, then as the commander of the oxybeles shouted and brought his sword down. Fifty or so of them went off as close to simultaneously as made no difference. It wasn't a huge barrage, but it made it all the way across the gap from the far shore to the end of the pontoon bridge.

Of the fifty bolts that were sent, four fifths missed cleanly. And half the bolts that fell among the engineers and pontoons didn't hurt anyone. Several of them did hit the pontoon that was almost ready to be put into the Bosphorus. Of the last five, three struck shields or armor, minimizing the damage they did, and two, by mischance, struck the same man. He was dead before he hit the ground.

Erica Mirzadeh looked over at Eumenes and Eurydice and waited for them to give the order to fire the rockets.

No such order was forthcoming. More men moved out onto the bridge, pushing more carts carrying pontoons and bridge sections ... and that was all.

For over three hours, while two more sections

were placed and tied down, while another anchor was dragged upriver by a small rowboat, dropped and cranked tight, while men died in increasing numbers... Eumenes and Eurydice did nothing at all.

Then, finally, Eumenes gave orders. But not orders to fire the rockets. No. He ordered a wooden shield put over the end of the bridge and the men back out of range of the oxybeles. Then he ordered five more pontoons to be put over the side of the bridge. Two on the upstream side and three on the downstream side, tied off with ropes. And that was all... until the sun set.

☆   ☆   ☆

"Pull!" Krakos shouted.

Makis pulled. He couldn't see what his pulling was doing because it was blacker than Olympias' heart out here, in spite of the torches. Another flight of bolts came and Makis ducked. Too late to do any good, but he ducked anyway.

"I saw that, you coward!" shouted Krakos. "Stop your cowering and pull, you gutless wonder!"

Makis pulled. The rope burned his hands in spite of the leather rags wrapped around them, and the air smelled of tar and dead fish. The pontoon moved. He could feel it through the ropes and hear the scraping. Then another flight of bolts came in. Part of it hit the shield on the end of the bridge, but several of the bolts came over the shield at a sharp angle and plunged into the planking of the bridge section. Hades, arrows fell all around them.

Makis heard a scream and the rope jerked as one of the gang fell away and the rest of them had to take up the slack. Makis was pulled forward a step, then another, and stepped on a soft black form in the night. The rope was attached to the pontoon by way of a pulley that was supposed to keep them safe by letting them pull from behind the shield.

Fucking idiots. Makis didn't know if he meant the idiots who designed the system or the idiots pulling the rope for a ship people silver talent. You couldn't spend it if you were dead.

All through the night, volunteers pulled those pontoons forward and tied them together with almost no light. Volunteers, who each received a ship people silver talent—or their heirs did. And at least a third of them died in the doing.

February 10, 319 BCE

The next morning, the end of the bridge was less than fifty yards from the shore, and now it wasn't the oxybeles they were facing. It was a thousand archers, who massed along the shore.

A thousand archers, backed by two thousand infantry carrying *sarissa*, the twenty-foot-long spears that turned a Greek phalanx into a fort.

For the first hour, Eumenes waited while Lysimachus deployed his troops in a packed mass on the far shore of the Bosphorus.

Eumenes pulled the binoculars from his eyes and passed them to Eurydice. "There should be more."

Eurydice looked, and grunted in frustration. "Do you think he's hidden them?"

"Where?" The far shore of the Bosphorus had trees and rocks aplenty, but they were back from the shore, at least here.

"Do it then!" Eurydice said.

Eumenes turned then and waved at a courier who rode down to a group of men who were set up in a protected spot near the shore. A few moments later, the first rocket fired. Then the first fifty.

Eumenes watched as the projectiles shot into the sky, trailing smoke and fire. Shot up and up, then arched over and started down. He followed their trajectory all the way across the Bosphorus. They were short. Not very short, but they struck the shore, half of them falling in the water.

☆   ☆   ☆

"No, no, no!" Philip of Macedon shouted before the rockets were more than halfway to the far shore. Then he shouted to the mortar men who were manning the tubes to adjust their azimuth. "Two turns." It was a shift in arc of less than half a degree, but it shifted the impact point almost thirty yards inland. The next salvo of rockets landed right in the middle of the archers.

And the next did the same, because a phalanx cannot move, not that fast. It can either stand or shatter.

This one shattered.

Not from a lack of courage.

From a lack of understanding, a lack of experience.

The men in that phalanx, at least many of them, had followed Alexander across the world, beating every foe they faced, all the way to India.

But fire falling out of the sky to rip them into small pieces when they couldn't fight back, when all they could do was run or die, was not exactly too much. It was too terrifyingly strange.

☆   ☆   ☆

Lysimachus was not in the right place to be hit by that salvo of hell, but he saw it and heard it. And if he wasn't the most honest of men, he was neither a coward nor slow of wit. Even before the second salvo of rockets landed among his archers, he realized that stopping Eumenes at the Bosphorus was no longer an option. He didn't know yet what options would work, but letting his army stand out there and get slaughtered was stupid, whatever happened next.

Lysimachus didn't order a retreat. He ordered a rout. "Have them run for the trees!" he shouted. "Don't try to keep formation. Throw away the *sarissa*, but get into the trees! Get away from that, that—" A short pause. "Whatever it is. Ship people magic."

Even so, it took time. Time while more rockets fell. Time while men ran without orders. Time while what had been an army turned into a terrified mob. Time that would be reflected in still more time trying to reconstitute his army.

☆   ☆   ☆

The rockets flew and the rocketeers watched. Then an order from Eumenes came. "Stop shooting."

Philip, hearing that, shouted, "Cease fire!" That was the proper command, not "stop shooting." He looked around, wondering why the order to cease fire had been given.

A sergeant looked at him and said, "Look there. They're running. Have run. The cowards are halfway to the trees. They won't be shooting at our bridge crews, not anymore."

Philip looked. Then nodded. Four hundred forty rockets fired, thirteen misfires, and only forty-five left. They needed more rockets.

February 11, 319 BCE

Nikon, bandage on his arm, ordered the last ramp into place and walked down it to the shore of the Bosphorus. At that, he was one of the very few injured in the battle for the Bosphorus. He was on the bridge during the night, dragging the pontoons forward under the bolts of the enemy.

☆   ☆   ☆

Erica Mirzadeh typed, then saved the file describing the battle. She sent the message open to the *Queen* for general dispersal. It would go to Athens, Alexandria, and even to Babylon, now that Susan Godlewski had arrived there, which was only three days ago.

Once the file was sent, she stood. "Okay, Tacaran Bayot. Let's get the gear packed up."

☆   ☆   ☆

Erica Mirzadeh wrapped the antenna wire around the spool as Tacaran Bayot packed up the body of the radio into a padded wooden crate. The radio was replaceable, but it was a thing of tubes and was more fragile than the integrated circuits and gorilla glass of a phone or the plastic case of a laptop.

Erica Mirzadeh swallowed bile. She had seen through her binoculars what it looks like when a mass of people comes under a barrage of rockets with black powder and shrapnel warheads. And now, even as she worked, the images of bodies being torn apart came to her and tore at her soul. She knew that if the battle had gone ...

No, that wasn't a battle any more than a man tied to a post and shot by a firing squad is a battle. But still, she knew they had no choice. They hadn't yesterday, and they wouldn't tomorrow. Not if the remnants of Alexander's empire were to turn into something worthwhile.

Tacaran was muttering prayers as he packed up the radio, and he wasn't the only one. Eumenes' army too was in a kind of shock as they took the eastern shore of the Bosphorus. The battle had been a cakewalk for them, but these were the cultural heirs of Achilles, for whom battle was a personal thing. No longer single combat perhaps, but still sword against sword, spear against spear, man against man.

Rockets launched across the Bosphorus by men sitting in protected comfort turning little knobs to adjust their aim? All while their victims were decimated and more?

It was just wrong.

How the army responded to it depended on the individual. The most cynical concluded that dead was dead and the job of the army was to make the bastards on the other side dead. But while that attitude was often expressed, it was a thin veneer. Something older, something left over from much younger men who had flocked to the banners of Philip II and Alexander the Great, to prove to the world, and to themselves most of all, that they *were* men.

Where, they asked often in the privacy of their soul, *was the glory in this?*

☆   ☆   ☆

Thales of Miletus sat his horse and looked at the hole in the ground. There was an arm sticking out of the hole. No body. Just the arm. And he thought about going home and giving up being a soldier. He was not yet thirty and had served in Alexander's army only for the last eight years. Even so, much of his work was fortifications, for Thales was a well-educated man of the upper classes. Alexander—or rather, Alexander's generals—had put his education to work. Especially Eumenes.

He was still sitting there looking into the hole when Heraclitus rode up, looked into the hole and said, "Everything changes. It's the nature of the world."

"Oh, shut up," Thales said. "I'm not in the mood."

"Neither am I," Heraclitus admitted. "It's true nonetheless. I believe it more now than I ever have. With the ship people, everything has changed."

"Well, if everything has changed, what in Hades are we doing here?"

"I think we need to find a new reason to stay, or go home," Heraclitus said.

Thales sat his horse, looked at the arm in the mud, and thought. After a few moments, he looked at his old friend. "I'm going to go see the ship people."

"Why?"

"To find out why they are out here fighting with Eumenes. Why they fight at all."

☆　　☆　　☆

Tacaran spoke Spanish, French, and English, with the addition of Greek since The Event. His Greek was still new, but he was less dependent on the translation app than Erica was, so he did most of the talking to the Greek soldiery, even though Erica had a college education and was in charge of the mission.

When the two well-dressed Greek cavalrymen came riding up, Tacaran held up a hand. "Sorry, guys," he said in badly accented Greek. "We've already packed up the radio and we won't unpack it till we get somewhere reasonably secure."

"That's not what we want," said the taller of the two men.

"What then?"

The cavalrymen dismounted and turned to face him. Then they hesitated, as though not sure what to say. The shorter man finally burst out with, "What are you doing here?"

Tacaran felt in his pocket for the pistol that had cost him a small fortune. He didn't have that much ammunition for it, but it was his "final friend" if everything went to crap.

"That's not what he means," said the other one.

"What does he mean?" Tacaran asked, still nervous.

"He wants to know why you work for Eumenes." Then, clearly searching for words, "Why you took the job."

"Took the job" wasn't the only way that phrase could be translated, but it was one of them, and Tacaran thought in this case it might be the right one. "How do you mean?" he asked. Then, not waiting for an answer, he said, "For the money, but that's not what you want to know. Is it?"

"No, it's not," said the shorter one. Then, wrapping his horse reins in his fist, he added, "I'm Heraclitus of Miletus and that's Thales. He was named after a philosopher, and he thinks it makes him have profound thoughts."

"And Heraclitus here was named after Heraclitus the Obscure, and that just makes him a pain in the arse."

Tacaran grinned at the two men. "Okay, my philosophical friends. That helps. Are you asking for the philosophical answer? Like 'what are we fighting for'?"

"Something like that, yes."

"Well, let me ask you then. Why did you join Eumenes?"

They talked about it for a few minutes, as they were taken down odd roads by the differences in language, and what they came up with was that Thales and Heraclitus had both become soldiers to prove themselves. And difficulties of translation aside, they were pretty open about it. Not at all ashamed, which Tacaran found odd. To Thales and Heraclitus, the notion that the toughest son of a bitch in the valley deserved to be honored and get everything he wanted simply because he was the toughest son of a bitch in the valley seemed perfectly okay.

It wasn't okay to Tacaran, but it happened. It happened in the twenty-first century all the time, but it wasn't supposed to happen. You were supposed to honor people for the good they did. For their devotion to God, or to the country, or . . . well, any number of things. But the only time you were supposed to honor them for being tough was when that toughness was put to a good cause. Well, maybe a boxer or a martial artist was an exception. But, in general, it was the content of their character and being a tough son of a bitch wasn't necessarily even a good thing. And that sent Tacaran back to their question to him as they walked along, them leading their horses, him walking beside the wagon that contained the radio and their gear.

Tacaran looked up at the wagoneer, who was following their conversation with interest. Then he looked at Erica Mirzadeh, who had gotten her phone out to try and follow along. "What do you think, Erica?"

Erica shrugged uncertainly, then said, "'We hold

these truths to be self-evident, that all men are cre-
ated equal. That they are endowed by their Creator
with certain unalienable rights. That among these are
life, liberty, and the pursuit of happiness.'"

Tacaran wasn't an American. For that matter, before
The Event he hadn't been all that fond of America, at
least not its government's policies. But he knew that
quote. Almost everyone on Earth knew that quote
in the twenty-first century. And basically, he agreed
with it, at least in principle. He knew perfectly well
that some people were smarter, some were stronger,
some were—he looked over at Thales and Heraclitus—
tougher. Even that some had hideaway pistols and
others didn't. But that wasn't the point. The point
was that the government shouldn't make distinctions
based on those things, either to take from those with
ability or to lock out those with less. "It's not like
the United Satrapies and States of the Empire has
abolished slavery, Erica."

"One step at a time, Tacaran. One step at a time."
Then she spoke to Thales and Heraclitus in broken—
well, shattered—Greek. "Eumenes and Eurydice, the
empire, they are trying to put a system in place where
people will be able to live out their lives in peace and
prosperity. That's worth doing. At least, I think it is."

Tacaran thought it was too. And the *Queen of the
Sea* was spreading the seeds of that dream all over
the world. At least, it was trying to.

CHAPTER 8

Setbacks and Stratagems

Queen of the Sea, *Trinidad, New America*
February 11, 319 BCE

Olympias sat at the table, clearly trying not to glare at
Marie Easley. She wasn't doing a good job of it, but
she was trying. Over the last month Marie had come
to realize that when she laughed at Olympias' spell
casting, she hadn't just embarrassed the woman. She
had done the equivalent of spitting on the Koran or
stomping on the cross. Olympias didn't just use magic
to influence others. She believed in it as much as any
Bible-thumping pastor or monk in a monastery.

The horror of it for Olympias was that most of
the cornerstones and rites of her faith had been lost
entirely as other faiths superseded hers. That her god
would not survive into the twenty-first century spat
on the notion of permanence that was so much a part
of almost all faiths.

Marie knew all that, but that didn't make the other
woman's simmering fury much easier to put up with.

Roxane looked between them and said, "The investigation has hit a standstill. Daniel Lang dusted the carafe for prints and took the prints of anyone that would have had a legitimate reason to touch it. There was one partial that didn't match up to Aida Pondong, who made the cocoamat, Dag, or Travis."

"And that partial didn't match any of my fingerprints," Olympias said. "I know. You told me days after the poisoning, when you made me put ink on my fingers and press the cards. Is Lang still insisting that I simply hired someone to put the poison in the carafe?"

"It's one theory that he continues to investigate," Marie said. "But I think even he has mostly given up on it. That leaves just four thousand or so other suspects."

"And he won't take everyone's fingerprints because it would be a violation of their civil rights. Yes, so you've said."

"Diplomatic immunity is even more of an issue," Roxane said. "Daniel insists that he needs probable cause."

"So you have said. Meanwhile, the whole ship continues to look upon me as an incompetent poisoner."

Then Dag Jakobsen came in from the other room with the three-year-old Alexander IV on his shoulder. "Not me. I'm quite sure that you're an effective poisoner. Snow White would have been dead as a doornail if it had been you."

Olympias looked at him for a moment then said, with apparent sincerity, "Thank you, Dag."

Marie looked at Dag, then back to Olympias. In spite of the mutual distaste, she felt a little sympathy for Olympias. She, personally, was convinced that Olympias was innocent, and being condemned in the general perception couldn't be comfortable. Unfortunately, it didn't seem likely to change anytime soon. The investigation was stalled and there was simply too much else to do to focus that many resources on it.

Queen of the Sea, *Fort Plymouth,* *Trinidad, New America* *February 12, 319 BCE*

"Can't the *Reliance* do that?" Lars asked. "Understand, Mr. President, I approve of the fueling station on Saint Helena, but can't Adrian deliver the necessary start-up equipment?"

"The *Reliance* is already on the way, as you well know," President Wiley said, frustration quite clear in his voice.

"I meant on the next trip, Mr. President." Honestly, Lars didn't like Al Wiley, even if he had grown to respect him. He was a competent politician and showed occasional statesmanlike behavior. He was also a good administrator, something that Lars would not have believed from Al Wiley's first reaction to The Event. But the man had a tendency to think of the *Queen of the Sea* as his navy and of Lars as under his command. But she wasn't, damn it. The *Queen of the Sea* was her own... well, not quite nation, but getting close to it. She wasn't under the authority of Al Wiley any more than she was under Ptolemy's.

"That will screw up the *Reliance*'s schedule, and more than that, several of the materials and components that we wish you to deliver to Saint Helena are most readily produced on the *Queen*." Then Wiley narrowed his eyes and asked, "What will it take, Captain?"

And the negotiation was on. Eleanor Kinney, his

chief purser and in these circumstances his chief negotiator supported by Marie Easley, took over and fought Amanda Miller, Congressman Lacula, and Al Wiley. There were complaints that to fulfill their desires would cause the raising of taxes on the still very young nation. That it would cause inflation as the unreasonable demands drove up the price of latex.

But three days later, the *Queen* sailed for Saint Helena and her holds held an abundance of preprocessed and purified latex, the natural precursor to rubber. Rubber products like seals, water bottles, and—most especially—condoms, were bringing a fortune in Alexandria and Athens.

Queen of the Sea, *Saint Helena*
February 23, 319 BCE

The *Reliance* was already there when the *Queen of the Sea* arrived. And a crew of workers were already building a tank farm.

"What are you finding, Captain Dahl?" asked Doug Warren over the radio.

"I don't have a clue, Doug. There are trees, I can tell you that, and birds out the kazoo. But I know very little beyond that, besides the fact that Yolanda Davis' pet environmentalist, Kai Mumea, is pretty keen on it all. I haven't seen him since we landed. He's been wandering the island, taking notes. I do think that this place can produce some good income. Mike Kimball says that the forests are old growth, with some potentially valuable woods. But the big prize is Madagascar."

Mike was a car salesman who, with his wife and

teenage daughter, was vacationing on the *Queen* when The Event happened. A political adherent of Al Wiley, he was appointed to the post of governor of St. Helena until such time as the colony grew to the point that elections were practicable. He was also the manager of the weather station and his wife was in charge of the shortwave radio station that would connect the island to New America and the *Queen of the Sea*. In total there were fifteen families and just over a hundred people in the colony, along with twenty-five people who were to stay on St. Helena only until it was determined where the refueling station on the east side of Africa was to be placed. As a matter of policy, New America was trying wherever possible to expand into territory where no one yet lived.

"If Madagascar isn't inhabited," Doug pointed out. The great and holy Wiki said that the first evidence of foraging was around 2000 BCE, but there was argument about when colonization started. Anywhere from *already there* to *not for five hundred years.* "Anyway I don't think you're going to get the skipper to go around the horn to Madagascar this trip."

"Why not? The *Reliance* is going to be stuck here for at least another couple of weeks, helping to get the station set up, and you could spend that time giving Madagascar a look-see."

"Why not? Because Eumenes has crossed the Bosphorus into Thrace and Roxane wants to get back to the Med as soon as she can."

"Hey, Doug. I grant that Roxane is hot, but she's not Helen of Troy to be launching fleets."

Doug Warren looked up then to see Captain Floden looking at him. "I'll give you the captain, Captain

Dahl." He handed the phone to the skipper, and went back to his job.

Thrace
February 23, 319 BCE

The arrows were coming in sheets as Lysimachus' archers fired and fired again, while Seuthes wondered how he had gotten so much of his army here so fast. He had to have abandoned the Bosphorus, and made a forced march up the coast of the Black Sea. The land was rolling hills and Seuthes was on a hill with his men formed up in the Macedonian style. They had the long *sarissa*, but Lysimachus was hitting him with arrows and Seuthes' men lacked the experience of Lysimachus' army.

An arrow thunked into the shield his shield bearer was holding up, but Seuthes barely noticed, he was so focused on trying to find a way out of the trap. This battle never should have happened. He looked east to where his cavalry was engaged with the larger cavalry of Lysimachus and cursed himself for a fool. He should have stayed in Chernomorets, forted up. More arrows and Lysimachus' infantry was moving up. That was the good news. Lysimachus didn't have that much infantry. Alexander's Anvil was smaller than usual. That might...yes, that might be a way.

He turned to his flautist and gave orders. Then the flutes screamed.

He watched as he sat his horse. His infantry, under the command of Cotys, his son, turned and, *sarissa* upraised, marched directly toward the archers. There was a screen of infantry between him and the archers and if his cavalry broke, the hammer of the enemy cavalry would pound him to pieces against Lysimachus' infantry. But it was better than standing here while his army drowned in a rain of arrows.

Telos waved his sword in a circle, pointed at the enemy, and his Thracian cavalry charged. He swung and missed, ducked under the Macedonian's counterthrust and was by, on to the next. He swung again, and hit. But most of the blow was deflected by the armor. The counter was way off, but the horses collided and his bay lost its footing. He leapt as it rolled and landed in the mud that the horse hooves had turned the field into. He struggled to rise and made it to his knees, then had to fling himself aside as one of his own men almost crushed him. A hand reached down and he grasped it.

Back on his feet, Telos looked around and could see little of the battle, just the fighting that surrounded him. He tried to get out of the melee so that he could see what was going on, but it took time. Time the rest of the army didn't have.

Cotys rode at the front of the infantry and reined his prancing horse to keep pace with the slow pace of the army. Arrows fell among his men and several came close to hitting him, but he paid them little attention. His attention was focused on the enemy infantry. The Macedonians were a mix of veterans and stay-at-homes, as were his men. Large numbers of Thracians had gone with Alexander to Asia and many had come home to Thrace and given service to his family. Cotys strove to be worthy of that service. There. The enemy were bringing their *sarissa* into position. He looked at Oineus, a veteran of twenty years with Alexander, and Oineus nodded. He lowered his sword and shouted, "Ready the *sarissa*."

The *sarissa* came down, and the armies kept moving.

An arrow came down out of the sky and struck between the breast and back plate of Cotys' armor, in the gap that was only covered by leather straps. The razor-sharp arrowhead sliced through the toughened leather like it was butter. Sliced through the muscles of his shoulder and into his shoulder blade where it quivered and shook and caused his shoulder to scream in agony with every move. Tears sprang to his eyes, but he sat his horse and stayed with his troops as the army marched forward and the *sarissa* crossed and interpenetrated. Men started to die on both sides, and he held his place shouting encouragement as the blood flowed.

☆   ☆   ☆

Telos reached the edge of the field and looked around. His cavalry was caught in a melee with a good part, the better part, of Lysimachus' cavalry, but a contingent of the enemy cavalry had broken away. It was even now riding down on the rear of their infantry.

☆   ☆   ☆

Seuthes saw the cavalry bearing down on his infantry and his son. But he had no force to send. Only himself and some of his household.

He charged.

☆   ☆   ☆

Through the pain, Cotys heard a flute signal. His head swung around and he saw the enemy cavalry coming. A cavalry charge is not an instant thing. He had a minute, maybe two. "Oineus!" he shouted. "Keep them going!" Then he rode for the rear.

He reached the rear of his sixteen-rank-deep phalanx, and shouted orders, the arrow still sticking out of his shoulder like a standard. "Rear rank, lift *sarissas!*" Time, while the men looked at him. Time, while the men, by main strength, lifted the twenty-foot poles to the vertical.

Cotys tried to lift his arm but it wouldn't come up. He did manage to shout, "Rear rank, face about!" Time, while they turned in place and saw the oncoming cavalry. Time, while he bled.

He tried to shout for them to lower their *sarissas*, but blood came out his mouth, not sound.

It didn't matter. The men in that rank could see the enemy cavalry just as well as he could. They lowered their *sarissas* without orders.

Almost in time.

Almost.

The cavalry hit the rear rank of his infantry and hammered it. But some of the *sarissas* had come down in time and the cavalry charge was blunted, if not stopped. Slowed as it rode over the half-prepared rear rank. Slowed long enough for the rest of their force to break Lysimachus' infantry.

Once the infantry broke, the archers ran.

Then the king and his bodyguard hit Lysimachus' cavalry from the rear.

The battle was a stalemate. Seuthes' forces held the field, if barely. But Lysimachus' men retreated, in good order for the most part.

☆   ☆   ☆

Seuthes looked down at the body of his son, Cotys. He cursed himself for a fool. He never should have left Chernomorets. He never should have allied with

Eumenes and Eurydice. For he knew that in that other history his son had ruled after him. A diminished Thrace, perhaps, but Cotys lived and fathered sons of his own. Seuthes' wife was dead these last ten years, and Cotys' sister Nike was barely fourteen years old.

Thrace
February 25, 319 BCE

Eumenes read the message, then passed it over to Eurydice, who passed it over to Philip.

"It's good that he's retreated to Chernomorets," Eumenes said.

"No, it's not," Eurydice said. "As long as he was out there pulling Lysimachus' forces out of position, we were in a better position to hit Lysimachus. Or, if he refused us battle, to bypass him and go after Cassander."

"It doesn't matter. With the rockets, Lysimachus can't face us in a stand-up battle."

"But we don't *have* the rockets. At least, we don't have enough of them. We need at least two thousand to break Lysimachus' army, you said. And even with the load we got yesterday from Lydia, we only have three hundred."

"But Lysimachus doesn't know that," Eumenes said. "That's why we have the wagon loads of the mockups in the baggage train." Eumenes looked over at Philip. The co-king of Alexander's empire was improving. He could stand to be touched and he spent time in his hug box every day. But he still had no real comprehension of deception and his approach to war was as an equation that had specific answers.

But war was an art, a thing of perceptions and

impressions. Bravery, the rightness of a cause, or at least its perceived rightness, all affected the outcome, not just of wars, but of battles. Right now, today, if Lysimachus' army was forced into combat, they would probably break with the first salvo of rockets.

Probably.

It wasn't a chance that Eumenes was willing to take, and conniving bastard that he was, Lysimachus wasn't stupid. Eumenes doubted the man had spent more than a waking hour without thinking about how to defeat an army equipped with rockets. Eumenes had done the same exercise. But it was unlikely that they had come to exactly the same answers.

For Eumenes, the answer was basically the same as the answer for bow or catapult. Get in amongst the bowmen or the catapulters and kill them. Wreck the catapults. He was also familiar with the notion of artillery duels from the ship people books, and from his own experience. But Eumenes' experience suggested that they were less decisive than the ship people seemed to think they were. Eumenes suspected that that was because artillery itself was less effective. He wished that he had been able to talk the ship people out of some cannons. Absent the powerful but tiny industrial base of the *Queen of the Sea*, this was a handcrafted world and handcrafting took a very long time compared to the ship people's magical machines.

So, for now, the rockets represented almost as much of a vulnerability as they did an advantage. A cavalry raid that got in amongst them and started fires would destroy his advantage, and at the same time be a crushing blow to his army's morale.

Cassander had to know that.

Pella, Macedonia
February 25, 319 BCE

Cassander did know that. He'd spent the months since he got home not just building his alliances, but thinking about how he would fight the new tools of the *Queen of the Sea* and the ship people. For the most part, Cassander thought the changes that the ship people wrought would help him more than hurt him. It didn't take strong arms or strong hands to wield a pistol. He knew that because he had paid Malcolm Tanada a small fortune. Not for his pistol, but to be allowed to fire it.

It turned out that Cassander was not a bad shot for a novice. And he had a smithy working on a copy of the six-shot revolver caplock that had been made on the *Queen* after The Event. He would have bought one from the *Queen*, but they were not selling them. Only ship people got the pistols.

A servant came in and Cassander waved him over. "Have the guests arrived?"

The servant ran through a list of nobles who had arrived and another group who hadn't. Cassander listened with care, taking note of who was early, who was late, and who wasn't coming at all.

He would remember.

If Lysimachus could keep Eumenes occupied long enough for Cassander to build his army, Cassander thought he could win. He had his father's alliances, and there was a strong core of Macedonian noble families who had hated Alexander the Great. That was the core of his army. And soldiers, some infantry but mostly cavalry, were joining his army in small contingents. Money was coming in now, hesitantly, but coming in. He would be able to hire infantry soon. But it all depended on local Macedonian politics and family alliances. Thessalonike would help with that.

Cassander, king of Macedonia, would today be married into the family of Philip II, and thereby bolster his claim.

"The queen?"

"She is in her rooms, preparing."

☆   ☆   ☆

Thessalonike paced in her rooms. There were beautiful rugs on the floor and wall hangings that kept the chill mostly out, but not entirely. The shutters were open for the light, but they also let in the moist, chill air. Thessalonike rubbed her hands together and adjusted her cloak, then paced back to the brazier. She was going to get married, and while not exactly thrilled with marrying Cassander, an old man to her thinking, and not a particularly fit or handsome one, that wasn't her major concern. Olympias, according to radio messages, was opposed to the marriage. And Thessalonike loved her foster mother, even if she was a bit terrified of her. She didn't want to be caught in the middle between Cassander and Olympias, but she could see no way out. If she refused to marry Cassander, this comfortable palace could become a very uncomfortable prison quickly.

A maid came in. Thessalonike spun and the maid made a hasty retreat. She took a deep breath. She was one of Olympias' favorites. She knew that. She had even been included in some of the rites of the Cabeiri. But politics were politics, and she was in Cassander's hands, not those of Olympias. She took another deep breath and used some of the techniques that she was taught among the cult of the Cabeiri for use when the holy drugs didn't work the way they were supposed to and the dreams became nightmares. She took another deep breath and visualized Axiocersus, god of death, of peace, and the quiet grave, and took into herself some of his quietude. She let Cadmilus and his excitable youth flow out with her exhalation.

Then she called in her slaves to dress her for the wedding. She would apologize to Olympias later.

CHAPTER 9

WHERE DO WE GO FROM HERE?

Queen of the Sea, *Saint Helena*
February 27, 319 BCE

"What do the passengers say? Jane?" Lars Floden asked as they sat at the conference table. It was the same conference table they sat at on the day of The Event, when Marie Easley came to tell them what was going on in this part of the world. And right now, today, that was what worried Lars most. They had Marie Easley to advise them about the Alexandrian Empire, the *diadochi*, and the culture of the fourth century BCE Mediterranean. They didn't have an equivalent for dealing with East Africa or India. They didn't even know for sure whether Madagascar was occupied.

"It's mixed, Captain," Jane Carruthers said. Jane was still in charge of the hotel function of the ship. The casino was under her authority, as were guest services, even if the guests were now the high nobility of the Mediterranean and some from South America. "The scholars, for the most part, want to make the trip around the Cape of Good Hope. The merchants and politicians want to go back to the Med. But it's not consistent. Roxane wants us to go around the cape, and so does Capot Barca from Carthage. His government wants to extend their trade around Africa and hope to get information about it and what they will face. There are several others of like mind, and some of the merchants are interested in possible new trade opportunities."

"Daniel?"

"I would love to make the trip, Skipper, just to get some real coffee." He lifted his cup of cocoamat and grimaced. "But, as for security, it really doesn't matter. I have my contingent of retrained Silver Shields and the augmented security staff. No one is going to take the *Queen* unless they have a lot more than we've been told. Not against steam cannon and caplock-armed Silver Shields."

The Silver Shields he was talking about no longer carried shields. They did have badges made of silver, polished and lacquered, in the shape of a shield. They wore them on the right breast of their new uniforms. Nor were they strictly the Silver Shields of Alexander. That was the core, and where the traditions came from, but now they included locals from New America as well as ship people, Carthaginians, Romans, and other Greeks. There were five hundred in all, and they were the *Queen of the Sea*'s marine force. They bunked six to a room and their families were in New America, because the *Queen* didn't have room for all of them.

The Queen, Lars thought, *doesn't have room for half the people it needs on board or half the industry or half the anything, really.*

"Eleanor?"

Chief Purser Eleanor Kinney said, "The bank is pretty full so we don't need the immediate income from the New America to empire trade, Skipper. And the long-term profits from sugarcane and the other stuff we will be able to pick up in exploring the world would be amazing. I say go."

"Marie?"

"It's a difficult decision, Captain. We need to be in two places at once. Plying the route between New America and the empire to tie them together and, at the same time, we are going to need the resources of India, China and the rest of the world." She shook her head, then looked back at Lars. "Madagascar, I would say. Find out if there is anyone there, and if there is, find out if they are people we can work with. If we can put a station there, we need it for the weather data anyway."

"Anders?"

"I'd like to go, Skipper," Staff Captain Anders Dahl said, "but Madagascar and back would nearly run our tanks dry. And if we go on up the East African coast to Suez, we won't have enough fuel to get back. We won't be dry, not quite, but we will be at Ptolemy's mercy and I don't trust Ptolemy."

"I don't think he's going to try anything like he did in Alexandria, sir," Dag said.

"Maybe not, Dag, but all he has to do is keep the fuel a few miles back from the shore and insist that he's having transport difficulties until our tanks are dry, and we'll have to make whatever concessions he wants or become a helpless island that can't even provide drinking water." The *Queen of the Sea* made drinking water from seawater with a system of reverse osmosis that required the engines to function. When they ran out of fuel, they ran out of everything.

"No, he can't," Lars said. "Oh, he can make things difficult for us, but the *Reliance* can make it to Suez with enough fuel to get us back here to Saint Helena. And once we got refueled, Ptolemy would not like what happened to Alexandria."

"Yes, sir. But does Ptolemy understand that? Or, more importantly, believe it?"

"I think he does," Dag said. "Or at least Thaïs does, and he listens to her."

Lars looked around the room. Then he nodded sharply. "Very well. Jane, inform the passengers that the *Queen* will proceed to Madagascar and in all probability from there to the port at Suez. I need to have a chat with Adrian. I don't want to make it too blatant, but I do want to be sure that the *Reliance* is not anywhere that Ptolemy can get his hands on it until we get refueled at Suez. And I want Ptolemy to know it."

"Well, Skipper," Anders said, "if he goes back to Trinidad for a full load of fuel, we'll have reached Suez, been refueled, and be on our way before he gets back here."

☆   ☆   ☆

Ten minutes later, in his day cabin, Lars picked up the phone and had the radio room connect him with Adrian on the *Reliance*. Adrian had changed. No, that wasn't right. But the *Reliance* was the property of New America, while the *Queen of the Sea* at this point was owned by its crew. "Well, Adrian, the consensus is we go. But I want something from you."

"Yes, sir?" Adrian asked cautiously.

"It's nothing too severe. I just want you to go back to New America and pick up another load of fuel. If everything goes well and Ptolemy has the fuel he says he has, we pick it up and everything is fine. But if he doesn't, if he tries to get clever, I want you out here with a full load of fuel and out of his hands."

"That won't be a problem, sir," Adrian said. "I just got word a Carthaginian ship arrived in Trinidad this morning. We are no longer the only link between New America and Europe."

"That's great, Adrian, and no, I hadn't heard. I've been in meetings all morning. Look, make sure that Ptolemy gets the word on what we're doing. Not blatantly, but make sure he knows that we are going to have access to fuel, no matter what he does."

"Not a problem, Skipper."

Alexandria, Egypt
March 1, 319 BCE

When Ptolemy walked into the private chamber he shared with Thaïs, she was lying on a couch on her side, reading a scroll. Her breasts were exposed and the breeze off the Med came in the window to caress her hair.

She looked up from the scroll and lifted an eyebrow in question.

Ptolemy handed Thaïs the sheet of paper he carried. Paper that was made in a factory right here in Egypt, printed in ink that was also made in Egypt, but printed on a dot matrix printer that was made from parts furnished by the ship people and New America.

Thaïs took the message and read. It was an apology. A personal apology from Captain Adrian Scott.

> *Sorry to tell you, but the New America Godiva chocolates you were expecting will be delayed. The Reliance will be making an additional trip to Saint Helena and probably on to Madagascar to put a fueling station there.*

She sat up and looked at Ptolemy. "You know this is not the message." It wasn't a question.

Ptolemy laughed. "Of course, I do. I'm not an idiot. It's a warning. No matter what we do, the *Queen* will have the fuel to do . . . whatever it should decide to do. What I'm asking is what you think I ought to do about it."

Thaïs leaned back on the couch and considered. Egypt had very little oil of its own, but it had been shipping it in from Trinidad whenever Ptolemy could get it. They had also informed Antigonus and the other eastern satraps that they were interested in acquiring it. That, along with the ship people knowledge, had by now resulted in two producing wells near the Persian Gulf. Whatever the ship people might have thought, not all of the oil wells in what the twenty-first century called the Middle East were deep wells. That meant that Ptolemy had access to more oil than expected, but at the same time he had more uses than expected too. Oil is a lubricant as well as a fuel, and the base for several products such as tar. Still, so far demand was mostly based on its use as fuel. An oil flame is more readily controllable than any other flame source. You can turn it up or down to control the heat of a steam-engine boiler or a pot of stew. The price of oil was increasing because, so far, demand was growing faster than supply.

She looked at a map on the north wall of the room. "In spite of the cost, I think you should send the fuel not just to Suez but on to Socotra."

"I'm still not sure it's worth it." Ptolemy followed her gaze. "We can't really charge them more in Socotra than we could at Suez, and the transport will cost rather a lot."

"I know, but the precedent is what's important." Thaïs stood and walked to the map. She drew an arch with her finger from the Port of Suez along the south coast of the Red Sea to Socotra. "It will strengthen our claim on the Red Sea and the Gulf of Aden. We already have envoys in Ethiopia looking for coffee."

"Not looking for. Have found," Ptolemy corrected, joining her at the map and pointing to a place on the northeast coast of Africa. "There is a tribe in a place the natives call Dassi where they are familiar with the tree. Some people chew the beans for energy, but it's not a particularly common practice because the beans are bitter. However, according to his letter, Amir is confident that he has found the right plant, and he has seeds. They bear in the dry season, which is just ending. He has three sacks full of the seeds. Even some seedlings that he brought back."

"Where is he?"

"Suez." They had named their port Suez after the ship people name for the same place.

"All the more reason for us to establish ownership or something like sovereignty over the Red Sea and the Gulf of Aden."

Ptolemy shook his head. "They won't accept that. We don't own the Red Sea. Not even much of its western shore. Much less the Gulf of Aden. It's not even part of Alexander's empire."

"That makes it better. We aren't rebelling against the central government or attempting to seize additional satrapies, just extending our territory and therefore the territory of the empire. Eurydice will probably support us, as long as we don't go after other satrapies. And Roxane might. Besides, it will give us major trade goods for sale to New America."

Sally's Bar and Party Palace, Fort Plymouth, Trinidad

Tubanic looked at the stage where the girls danced in synchronization and nothing much else. They were all natives from around here, none of them ship people, but the dance was supposed to be a ship person dance called the cancan. He looked over at Drakos, a crewman from the *Beard*, and grinned. The music was strange, with a pounding rhythm that reminded Tubanic more than anything of the beater on a trireme calling the rowing cadence. But it was complicated by other rhythms that flowed through and around the main beat, and the music came from a box that was called a speaker, not a group of musicians.

There were times on the trip from Carthage when he wondered if the trip was a good idea. Especially as they made their way south, island-hopping. The winds had kept them north of where they wanted to be, making the trip longer. He no longer felt that way. This was possibly the most successful trip he had ever been on.

After the dance ended, he called over one of the dancers and made arrangements in pidgin American. They proceeded upstairs.

A sailor with money in his pocket.

For now.

Capitol building, Fort Plymouth, Trinidad, New America

"I told you!" Anna Comfort insisted hotly. The woman, with her face framed in dark brown hair, straight and parted in the middle, waved toward the window where the sound of music was audible. "This city is turning into a den of iniquity."

Al agreed with her, as much as he hated agreeing with the loony-liberal congresswoman. He was uncomfortable with the blatant sexuality of the locals, even if he doubted that it was the women being exploited and the men doing the exploiting as Comfort insisted it must inherently be. "I don't disagree, Congresswoman. You know I supported the bill to outlaw prostitution, but we lost. The vote was overwhelming. So there is nothing we can do about it."

Poseidon's Beard wasn't the only ship in the port. The *Argos* arrived a day after the *Beard*, and the port bars were already packed with natives from all over the north coast of South America. There were ships from as far north as the Manguea states, where Mexico was in the twenty-first century. The trips up and down along the coast by the *Queen* and the *Reliance* let the people know what was here, and trade was picking up. However, the *Beard* and the *Argos* represented a major potential expansion because the radio system had already reported back to Carthage and Sicily that the ships had made the trip successfully. More would be coming. Many, many more. So Comfort was going to get worse.

If only there were a Boston to ship her off to. Someplace where she could complain, and he wouldn't have to listen.

Peninsula Port, Guayaguayare Bay,
Trinidad, New America
March 6, 319 BCE

The *Reliance* pulled up to the pier and ran out a hose to connect to the pipe. Most of the pier was wood, but they were importing concrete from Rome now. Not in large amounts, but someone was also working on producing portland cement. So that was going to change. The pumps weren't all that efficient either, so it was going to take two days to fill the *Reliance*'s holds.

Adrian Scott started the two-hour process of disconnecting the tug from the barge.

☆   ☆   ☆

The *Reliance* tug pulled away and turned for Fort Plymouth. "Get me a link to the *Queen*, Dan." The link went through the large station at Fort Plymouth, and was then bounced off the ionosphere using frequency-hopping to insure the bounce. It was an automated technique implemented since The Event, handled by the computers and mostly transparent to the user. But the *Queen* was now approaching halfway around the world from Trinidad so there was a noticeable delay. Adrian reported that they were refueling and would be

spending a couple of days here before heading back.
The *Queen of the Sea* gave their position, which was
on the west coast of Madagascar, where Morondava
was, back in the twenty-first century.

Morondava, Madagascar
March 10, 319 BCE

Dag looked around at the tropical wilderness. This was
a nice place to establish a fishing village, and they
had explored the area over the last few days. There
was no one here, nor any evidence of prior habitation.
That wasn't proof that there was no one on the island,
but it certainly supported the notion that any people
who might be here were not in large numbers.

The trees around here were mostly baobab trees.
They were old, too. The biggest in sight was sixty feet
tall and almost thirty feet wide by Dag's rough estimate.
There were a couple of hundred green fruit in the
high branches, again by Dag's rough guess. They were
green, furry, and about three quarters the size of a
coconut. According to Wikipedia, they were edible or
would be when they ripened in another few months,
by which time they would be the size of coconuts.

According to the *Queen*, it was raining on the far
side of the island, but the mountains in between had
removed much of the moisture from the air. The day
was hot and a bit humid, but not bad.

"Look over there," Makis said, pointing.

Dag followed his finger and saw the biggest bird
he'd ever seen. It was eleven feet tall, and it made an
ostrich look like a fashion model. It was an elephant
bird and not the first Dag had seen, but this was the

biggest yet. The elephant bird had become extinct sometime around the seventeenth century in the original timeline, but they were common here. They had dark brown feathers instead of the black feathers of an ostrich, but the big difference was the size. Elephant birds were thought to have weighed about a thousand pounds, but Dag suspected that that estimate was on the low side. The monster was blithely ignoring Dag and his escort of Silver Shields. They weren't the biggest animal on the island, but they were one of the biggest and much larger than any predator, so they didn't run away as ostriches in Africa did.

"That would be a lot of meat?" Makis asked hopefully.

Dag was tempted, but not because the *Queen* was low on food stuffs. It wasn't. But these birds had the potential to be a useful source of all sorts of things. "You want to carry that sucker back to the boat?"

Makis shrugged. "We could send for a wagon."

"You have a point." Dag pulled his phone from the specially added pocket in his shirt and opened the wooden protective case. He turned on the phone and called the ship. He discussed the possibilities with Eleanor Kinney, who promised to send a wagon and a butcher.

"Okay, Makis. You have a go."

Makis searched the area for a good place, walked over a little way and lay on the grassy ground. He took careful aim with the caplock rifle, and *BANG*.

The bullet, a fifty-caliber minié ball, cut the spine of the elephant bird like it was an ax.

The bird staggered around for a couple of seconds, then collapsed.

Dag and the rest went over and examined the bird. The musculature was impressive. Depending on how these animals responded to domestication, they might turn out to be a significant resource. Dag, as an environmental officer, knew quite a bit about environmental studies. And one thing he realized long since was that one of the best ways to survive as a species was to become a domesticated food and/or draft animal for humans. The surest route to extinction was to be a danger to man. With their modern knowledge, it was entirely possible that they could save the elephant bird from extinction by turning them into a food animal. Considering the culture of the world at this time, any other course as far as Dag could see led to extinction.

Dag turned to Sharon Thigpen, who was a manager of a jewelry store, and was now going to be the head of the Madagascar mission, the weather station, and the radio system. "Well, Sharon, it looks like meat is going to be available. Put someone on studying the life cycle of these creatures. If we can, I would like to ship some to other islands for domestication."

"Sure, Dag. We don't want all our eggs in one basket, even if it is almost the size of a continent."

There were twenty-three people, mostly locals, some from Europe, some from New America, who would be staying on in Madagascar. They would do some farming, but for now, at least, would mostly live off hunting and gathering. It was a dangerously small colony, and to get the volunteers Captain Floden was forced to promise that the *Queen* would come by at least once every six months and the government of New America was required to promise them massive personal land grants. Everyone in the colony owned at least a square mile of land. Including little Janel Thigpen, all of one year old, Sharon Thigpen, and her husband Tony's youngest child. Not to mention their older kids, Tegan and Nyssa.

The discussion turned to the station. Nine prefab buildings, none all that large, an oil derrick–style construct to support the antenna, and where all those things were to go. The station had a generator that ran off a low-pressure steam engine with a boiler made on the *Queen*. Compared to the folks at Jamestown in the original timeline, they were well supplied. But they were one hell of a small colony on one heck of a big island.

"When do you think we will hear from the locals?" Sharon asked, because Dag was the "expert" on locals.

"According to the last radio message from Ptolemy, he's sent a mission along with the oil ship. We'll meet it at Dioscorides. They have amphorae of that Egyptian beer you like and quite a lot of grain. Figure a month, maybe two. Long enough for your locals to do some hunting and for you to process the stuff into samples. Besides, we've left you enough freeze-dried food to last you six months, even without what you hunt and fish for here."

"Mostly it's the extra colonists I'm looking forward to, Dag. More than the food or the beer, you need people to make a colony."

CHAPTER 10

ROLLING SNAKE-EYES

Nenet's Dream, *Red Sea*
March 14, 319 BCE

Abial smiled up at the rigging of *Nenet's Dream*. Then he looked over at the *Cockle Shell* and frowned. Nadaka was a snooty bastard, and Abial would just as soon be nowhere near him. Besides which, *Cockle Shell* was carrying amphorae of beer, sacks of grain, and passengers, while he was loaded down with nothing but hundreds of amphorae of naphtha. Also, adding the supplies for the expedition had delayed them for a week, which was why he was still in the Red Sea.

"Do you think it's real, Skipper?" asked Hambid.

Abial knew what he meant. No one on the *Nenet's Dream* had ever seen the ship people ship, the *Queen of the Sea*. Ptolemy's governor in the new town of Suez said he had seen it, even been on it. But Abial was half convinced that the damned arrogant Greek was playing with the provincials. A ship the size of a mountain or the Great Pyramid—another thing that

Abial had never seen—that was just not believable. "We'll know in a few more days. The new way of rigging the sails works, so at least they weren't lying about everything."

That was true. The *Nenet's Dream* was doing eight knots in a light breeze off the port quarter. Even if she was heeled over more than he liked.

Nenet's Dream, *Gulf of Aden, near Dioscorides* March 20, 319 BCE

"Land ho!" shouted the lookout. Then... "Gods preserve us. Captain, it's real."

Abial's eyes followed the lookout's pointing finger, and on the horizon he could see a small bump rising out of the sea. But Abial was an experienced seaman. He could tell that the smallness was distance. "Two points to starboard. And adjust the sails."

☆   ☆   ☆

It was huge. "I have to go see the pyramids someday," Abial muttered. For the great white mass exceeded what he had believed possible. Maybe the pyramids did too.

Queen of the Sea, *Gulf of Aden* March 22, 319 BCE

Dag watched as the last of the amphorae was emptied into the pot and ordered the pumps to start again. It took them two solid days to transfer the oil from the amphorae on the *Nenet's Dream* to the *Queen's* tanks, through a combination of pumps and manual labor. Something that would have taken the *Reliance* about an hour.

And still their tanks weren't full. It wasn't anyone's fault, not really. It was just that the *Nenet's Dream* was tiny even compared to the *Reliance* and carrying fuel in amphorae wasn't the most efficient way to do it. Between being topped up at Saint Helena and the fuel they had here, the *Queen* had enough fuel to get back to Saint Helena and a little left over, but not a lot.

Dag picked up the phone and called the bridge. "All done, Skipper," he said once he got the captain on the line. "Give me twenty minutes to get the fuel lines retracted and we can be on our way."

"Maybe by the next time we get up this way, there will be a real fuel depot here," Captain Floden said, sounding tired.

"There should be, Skipper, now that the locals in this area have a better idea of what we need. And what we can pay for it."

Queen of the Sea, *Royal Lounge*

Captain Abial took another bite of elephant-bird steak. It was well done at the captain's request. Half-cooked food wasn't popular in a world where much of the meat carried parasites of one sort or another. On the other hand, Abial was entranced by the flavor, like the finest quality beef, but different. The wine was strawberry wine from Carthage and the vegetable was something called a nut potato from the other side of the world. All served on white ceramic plates and in glass goblets. It was the fanciest and quite probably the best meal he had ever eaten in his life.

"How do you like your steak, Captain?" asked Dorothy Faubion.

Dorothy was a dark-skinned woman like some of the tribesmen Abial had dealt with in his career, but she was clearly one of the ship people. She spoke the ship people tongue and used the small devices to translate for her. And that was a magic that still made Abial uncomfortable every time he saw it.

"The steak is excellent and the . . . everything is excellent. But I do wonder why you're going to such trouble over a minor ship's captain." It was a good question too. Three tables over, Cleopatra, a sister of Alexander the Great, sat dining with another ship person. Captains of cargo ships didn't dine in the same room with royalty, and they weren't asked by wizards how they liked their meal. Not outside of stories.

"Because we want you to make some changes in your ship," Dorothy said. Or rather, the device in her hand said. It spoke in Egyptian too, not Greek.

"What sort of changes?"

"We want to convince you to transform your ship into an oil tanker."

"What? I just brought a massive load of oil to you here. My ship *is* an oil carrier."

Dorothy picked up her phone and tapped the front of it several times. The phone spoke. "I'm sorry. We have a translation problem."

Another tap. "Please excuse me for a moment."

She got up, walked over to Cleopatra, and spoke for a few moments. Then Cleopatra stood and came toward the table where Abial was seated.

Abial stood quickly and tried to bow, though he was sure he made a mess of it. Abial wasn't used to bowing and scraping. He didn't deal with royalty. The minor nobility was bad enough.

Cleopatra waved away his bow, and said, "Do not trouble yourself. I am not here as a Macedonian princess, but merely as a translator. The ship people want you to convert your ship into a ship that is specifically designed to carry oil in large containers. Not amphorae, but containers so large that they cannot be lifted out of your holds. They will have to be built into your ship, and sealed with a special sealant they will provide."

"With all respect, Highness, that is insane. If the tank is built into my ship, how will we get the oil out?" Abial had a good idea how it would be done from his experience with the refueling of the *Queen of the Sea*. What was honestly of greater concern was how such tanks would affect his ship in regard to other cargo.

Cleopatra asked Dorothy something and Dorothy consulted her phone. Then the phone spoke in Greek and Cleopatra explained. "They will use pumps of the same sort that they used to empty the amphorae you carried."

"Yes, but I have no such pump."

"The ship people can sell you a pump."

"I don't think so," Abial said. "How would the conversion be done?"

They brought out drawings. And it was even worse than he had feared. They would divide his ship into six sections, using wooden frames, rods, and walls, which would in turn be painted inside and out with this tar they talked about. "After you have done that, my ship will be no good for anything but shipping oil. It won't even be able to ship wine, because the tar would affect the taste." That was a guess, but an educated guess. Resins of all sorts, and paint likewise, often affected the taste of food and wine. "Besides," he went on, "even if the coating didn't, you can never get all the oil out of an amphora and these large tanks would be the same."

Dorothy agreed with that, but said, "The idea is that the *Nenet's Dream* would become a dedicated oil tanker."

"And how often am I going to get an order like this last job?" Abial asked. "No. The risk is too great and the reward too small. And you want me to pay for it. Buy the pump, you said. Probably buy the tar too. I would be completely dependent on your schedule for my profit."

They bargained. They even got on the radio and called Alexandria to get an assurance from Ptolemy that there would be oil waiting at Suez. And that a large fuel depot was planned for Dioscorides. Finally, Abial agreed, but not before he got the *Queen of the Sea* to provide the pump, and the tar, and the designs, and let him pay them off out of oil transport fees, and never more than half the fee, so that he would always be paid.

The pump was steel, made in Alexandria, and weighed the better part of a ton. But someday, they said, there would be a steam engine available and it could be used with a propeller for speed as well as to use the pump. And that would be a good thing.

Someday.

☆   ☆   ☆

"We have a deal," Dorothy Faubion said as she entered Eleanor Kinney's office. "Captain Abial drove a pretty hard bargain and I had to get Cleopatra involved to help translate. But we got it. And we also have Ptolemy a bit more committed to the fueling station on Dioscorides, and I think once the Dioscorides station is full up we'll be able to get Abial to ship down to the station at Madagascar."

"Good. The captain wants us to get back to Europe as fast as we can. Eumenes has just been royally screwed by Lysimachus."

Pass north of Abdera, Thrace
March 21, 319 BCE

Eumenes looked up. The pass was between two mountains and the path was hemmed in by trees, but it was the only fast way to get to Abdera and the ships. Since crossing the Bosphorus, the fighting had been sporadic. The army moved north to take the pressure off Seuthes, and it worked. Lysimachus retreated, unwilling to risk being trapped between Seuthes in his stronghold and Eumenes' army. After that, things got worse as Lysimachus retreated, but sent his cavalry to harass Eumenes' army. What Erica described as pinprick raids that forced Eumenes to send his cavalry out as a screen, a wide screen with attrition on both sides. After the death of his son, Seuthes wasn't willing to go into the field against Lysimachus. "Let Macedonian fight Macedonian," he'd said.

Eumenes was winning, but he was having his army bled white as he did it. And after Lysimachus, he had Cassander to fight. So he and Eurydice had decided to retreat to Abdera and take ship to Amphipolis. They stole the march on Lysimachus, but to do it they had to move fast. Not an easy thing for an army to do and not something you could do at all while maintaining an adequate screen of scouts. The strategy was working, but Eumenes was feeling the hairs on the back of his neck standing up. Something was . . .

Twaaaaang!

The sound of hundreds of bows lofting hundreds of arrows interrupted Eumenes' thoughts and confirmed his worst fears. Somehow Lysimachus knew. Knew, and put a force in the mountains surrounding the pass.

The arrows fell and the infantry turned turtle, as they should, lifting their shields to protect them from the arrows. It helped, but there were a lot of arrows.

The cavalry was not nearly so well situated as the infantry. Their mobility was almost useless in the mountains, and there was no shield made that was big enough to protect a horse. The rain of arrows hurt the infantry, but decimated the cavalry.

Eumenes spun his horse and started shouting orders. The enemy had the height on them and if they stayed here they were going to die in a rain of arrows. Couriers rode ahead to tell the cavalry in front of the column to ride forward until they got out of range of the attack. Others rode to the cavalry in the rear to tell them to retreat back the way they'd come. More rode to tell the infantry to stay in formation. And, most important, they rode to get the rocketeers to send incendiary rockets up into the tree-covered mountainsides that hid the enemy archers.

But it all took time.

And while they were doing it, the rain of arrows continued.

☆   ☆   ☆

Eurydice rode forward along the path, looking at the flights of arrows, and realized that the attackers weren't Lysimachus' whole army. Couldn't be. There were not enough arrows and, more importantly, on the mountainside where the arrows were coming from, there wasn't enough room. She thought as she rode, and she was sure at first that this was just the first stage of the trap. That the rest of Lysimachus' army must be waiting up ahead to destroy the retreating cavalry.

But how?

They knew where Lysimachus was. They had scouting reports. She reached the cavalry contingent that was the army's advance guard, and was about to shout countermands to Eumenes' orders when she realized the truth in a flash. It wasn't an army. It was a raiding force. A few hundred men, no more. Sent ahead.

She joined the lead elements of the army as they rode forward out of the rain of arrows. Then, as they were turning to struggle up the mountainside, she saw that the rain of arrows had become a rain of fire. The enemy bowmen were now lofting flaming arrows and they were concentrating their fire on a small group of carts being pulled along in the center of the infantry. The rocket corps.

"Follow me!" she shouted, and rode up the hill with no regard for safety or survival. She had to get to those archers before they ignited the powder train. She barely noticed whether the leading cavalry was following her, but it was. At least, most of it was. More slowly, perhaps, but following. Some of them were racing up the mountainside as fast as she was.

She saw a horse pass her, then trip, and go tumbling down the mountainside. Another kept with her, and then another. They rode over rocks and around the trees that clawed their roots into the rocky ground on the mountainside.

And the army bled while they did it.

☆   ☆   ☆

"Rockets!" Sakis shouted as he grabbed the wooden rocket launcher out of the wagon and tried to set it up next to the wagon. That was against the rules, but fuck the rules. They were going to die if they didn't stop those archers.

"Here it comes!" Hristos shouted back. Sakis turned barely in time to grab the rocket before it hit him in the chest.

"Slow match!" he shouted as he prepared to drop the rocket into the tube.

Hristos pulled a flint and steel out to try and light the sulfur-drenched cord they used to light the rockets.

Then the flaming arrows arrived.

Most of them missed or were stopped by the roofs of the wagons. Almost all, in fact.

It would have been all, because the heavy wooden chests in the wagons would stop a flaming arrow cold. But they were trying to set up the rockets in the open and the chests were opened to get the rockets out. An arrow, one of several hundred shot, came down on a rocket.

The rocket, as it happened, that Sakis had in his hands. The bronze arrow tip, coated in olive oil and wool, slammed right through the thin wooden wall of the rocket, and the wood of the rocket body scraped away most of the burning olive oil and wool.

Most. But not quite all. The explosive-grade corned powder, the powder in the warhead of the incendiary rocket that Sakis hadn't had time to fire, ignited and exploded, sending burning shrapnel in all directions, killing Sakis, and igniting a barrel of corned powder. Which ignited another barrel. A wagon went up in a massive explosion.

That wagon ignited the wagons next to it, and a series of explosions like a giant string of firecrackers went off.

In less than five seconds, Eumenes and Eurydice lost every rocket they had.

And most of their rocketeers.

☆   ☆   ☆

Erica Mirzadeh held her hands over her ears and prayed. She was in the radio wagon, just behind the rocket carts. The explosions killed both her horses and deafened. A piece of burning shrapnel ignited the roof of her wagon.

Tacaran grabbed her arm and pointed. It was still a small fire, just a piece of fabric soaked in a mixture of naphtha and sulfur from one of the incendiary rockets. The force of the cart in front of them exploding had plastered it against the wall of their wagon.

Tacaran pointed at one of the barrels of water that their wagon carried. Erica blinked and nodded. Then Tacaran went for the other barrel of water and together they filled buckets and managed to douse the fire.

☆   ☆   ☆

Eurydice rode through the sounds of the explosions, and finally reached the archers. It was too late, but the Greek cavalry, equipped with ship people–designed stirrups, solid-treed saddles and the heavier lances that they allowed, rode over the archers.

☆   ☆   ☆

An hour later Eumenes, Eurydice, Philip, and Erica examined the carnage. They had been counting on the rockets to persuade the city of Abdera to open their gates. It wasn't that Abdera was on Lysimachus' side, at least not the populace. But Lysimachus had a contingent of his army stationed in the city. A garrison that would have surrendered if they'd still had the rockets, but now would likely resist.

Pass north of Abdera, Thrace
March 21, 319 BCE

It was dark by the time Erica Mirzadeh and Tacaran got the radio set up, and Erica's hearing had yet to return. The world still whispered through the echoes of explosions in her head. The stars were hidden by clouds, and the trees at the highest point they could reach near the pass made it even darker.

Tacaran set the last wire and Erica turned on the desktop computer that had come out of one of the *Queen of the Sea*'s computer rooms. The screen came up, lighting the inside of the wagon with an incongruous glow. Erica called up the program that controlled the tuning of the ham-style radio.

The computer ran the scan and reported five radios in range. Two of them, the one at Athens and the one at Alexandria, were active. The others had alarms set up. The radios were separate from the computers and made after The Event. They had set listening-frequency ranges, response ranges, and automated mechanical-response routines. The devices were a cross between Edison's telegraph repeater and the old Jacquard looms. But they worked. If it was an emergency, she could ring a bell in Rome, Pella, or Tyre. It wasn't necessary. The full system was up at Athens, so she used Athens as the repeater station. Athens' radio tower had been built on top of the Parthenon, after getting Athena's permission. Or at least the permission of her priesthood. It was appropriate enough, and the temple received a fee for every message that was transmitted through the station there.

"What has you up at this time, Walter?" Erica Mirzadeh typed. Walter Palmer was one of the passengers on the *Queen*. He was forty-three and was an air-conditioner repairman before The Event. He, his wife, and their fifteen-year-old son were the radio crew for the city of Athens. They had taken the job because Walter's wife Peggy Jane insisted that their daughter Caroline would benefit from spending a year or two in the Athens of Aristotle.

"Negotiations and trade agreements. Word that the local's ships are getting to New America has put the cat among the canaries and everyone is negotiating their deals. What about you, Erica?" appeared on her screen.

The connection was quite capable of sending voice or even imagery, but text used up much less bandwidth.

"We just got buggered by Lysimachus."

"Buggered? LOL."

"Not LOL, at all," Erica typed, thinking about the exploding ammo carts and flying body parts of the afternoon. "He had a small, I'm told, contingent of archers in the hills and..." Erica stopped typing and took a deep breath, then she started typing again. "Look, Walter, I need to talk to New America. People died today. They may be locals, but they are people, and people I have come to know."

"Sorry, Erica," appeared on her screen. "I sometimes type without thinking. I'll get you a link."

The Congressional Club, Fort Plymouth
March 21, 319 BCE

The Congressional Club was a small room in the community center, reserved for congress and guests. Well, reserved part of the time. It was set up sort of like the Royal Lounge on the *Queen*, but smaller and made of wood. Still, it had a waitstaff that mostly came from the crew of the *Queen*. Yolanda Davis followed the maître d' to the table and after shaking the hand of the head of the delegation from the Yaki tribe, took her seat. The Yaki lived in what on another world would someday be called Panama. He was looking around in wonder at the room. The tablecloths were white linen from Egypt. There were brass lamps with glass chimneys.

"Now, Kabkid, you will want to try the lamb stew. It will be a new experience and it's one of Chef Vincent Bashaw's signature dishes." The translator, one of Lacula's friends and an early immigrant to New America, spoke and she got the nod from Kabkid that she had wanted. Yolanda was on the committee for foreign trade in the congress of New America.

The food hadn't been served when a local dressed in a loincloth, latex sandals, and nothing else except a painted-on red, white, and blue New American signet came in the door, looked around, and headed directly for them. He was one of the congressional pages. She took the message. It was from the radio complex.

New America now had two radio stations, one for communications and one for broadcasting, but they were located in the same complex and shared a lot of equipment. It turned out that the same antennas could be used for multiple signals at multiple frequencies.

To: Congresswoman Yolanda Davis.
From: Erica Mirzadeh with Eumenes' army

Need to speak to you urgently.

Erica Mirzadeh

It took Yolanda a few minutes to extricate herself. Yolanda had been the steward for Erica's stateroom before The Event, and Erica was nice even back then. After The Event, in the pressure cooker that followed, they got very close for a while. Erica had introduced her to George Davis, the man she eventually married.

Radio computer room, Fort Plymouth

"What's happened?" Yolanda typed.

Then a whole report appeared on the screen. Apparently, Erica Mirzadeh had typed it out while she waited for Yolanda to get here. It described the battle and the effect on Eumenes' army. And it asked for help.

The *Queen of the Sea* was studiously neutral in the internal workings of the United Satrapies and States of the Empire. The government of New America had until now been officially neutral too. But its neutrality was like the neutrality of America before they entered the second world war, a neutrality that leaned heavily on the side of England. New America's neutrality leaned on the side of the queens and Eumenes.

As Yolanda read through the report, she decided that it was time for New America to lean a bit more. Lend-lease seemed like a pretty good idea right about now.

"I'll do what I can," she typed. "Hang in there."

Then she got up and left the radio computer room. She had to talk to President Wiley.

President's office
Two hours later

Yolanda looked at the president; the secretary of the navy, Richard VanHouten; and the commander of the army, Leo Holland, Jr.

President Wiley looked haggard. "I asked Richard and Leo here to see if we can determine whether the histories are wrong. Was Eumenes good or just lucky in our history?"

Leo Holland looked up and grimaced. "That's hard to say, Mr. President. The truth is that it's always hard to say, even with generals like Patton, Montgomery, Custer, and even Alexander the Great."

"Now I'm totally confused," Yolanda said.

"I understand how you feel, Congresswoman Davis. But do you want to know the true biggest difference between war and war games? It's the number of games you get to play. In chess, for instance, it's thousands. Or if you're a real aficionado, even more thousands. In war, for a given general, it can be one or two. And rarely breaks fifty. In war games, you can tell who's better because the same people play again and again. In war, skill or its lack, often get swamped by luck." He held up the description of the battle and the strategy that led to it. "Eumenes' strategy was risky, but not bad. A calculated risk, we like to call it. A roll of the dice. But the trouble with calculated risks is that sometimes you roll snake eyes and get screwed right through your pants. And that's what happened here."

CHAPTER 11

REACTIONS

Queen of the Sea, *off the Cape of Good Hope*
March 29, 319 BCE

The conference room was subtly changed by now, with paintings from Alexandria and South American face masks on some of the walls, but the big-screen TV that could show anything they wanted was still there. Though, at the moment, shut off.

Lars Floden carefully placed his hand flat on the table, not slamming it down as he clearly wanted to. "Al Wiley can do whatever he wants, but the *Queen of the Sea* is neutral." He was clearly angry, but to Marie Easley it was clear that he was angry at the situation, not the President of New America.

"That may be true," Anders Dahl said. "But if New America, and through them the *Reliance*, takes the side of the legitimate government, our neutrality is going to be pretty frayed in the eyes of the world whatever we say."

"Don't assume that the locals lack subtlety." Marie

Easley shook her head. "Murderers and slavers certainly, but they are also political operators as good as any lobbyist who ever bought a congresscritter back in the world."

"I agree, ma'am," Anders said, then gave a half chuckle. "But all that means is they will be better able to use it against us."

It was true, Marie knew, that the absolute neutrality of the *Queen of the Sea* was a powerful tool in their political arsenal. But they didn't just have to be neutral, they had to be *seen* as neutral. Up until now, that included all the ship people and New America. But from the series of messages over the last week, that was about to change. Roxane, as queen regent for Alexander, and Eurydice, gone to war with Eumenes and acting as queen regent for Philip, were about to sign an agreement with New America that, if not an alliance, was the next best thing to it.

It was a trade agreement that offered delivery of war materials to Eumenes' army. And that meant that if the *Queen of the Sea* didn't deliver the cargo, the *Reliance* would. The *Reliance* wasn't going to be an easy ship to take, especially now that it had steam cannons and black powder breech loaders. On the other hand, the *Reliance* only had about twenty feet of freeboard even unloaded. It was, as had already been demonstrated, much easier to take than the *Queen*. And without the *Reliance* and the fuel it carried, the *Queen* was going to have its options severely curtailed. On yet another hand, if the *Queen* did deliver the cargo, it would be seen as taking the royalist side in the current war within the empire. "I don't disagree, Anders. But I don't see much in the way of options either. The *Queen of the Sea* can't dictate policy to New America," Marie said.

"No, ma'am, but we own a share of the *Reliance*."

"That's right, Anders," Lars Floden said. "We own a share. Specifically, we own forty-two percent of the holding company that owns the *Reliance*. New America owns forty-six percent and as part of his agreement, Adrian Scott owns ten percent. The rest is owned by private investors, including, by the way, Roxane. Also, the *Reliance* is registered out of New America and Adrian is inclined to support Roxane and Eurydice in this. We don't have the votes to stop it."

"But Adrian is—" Anders started.

"The captain of the *Reliance*," Lars interrupted before Anders said something irretrievable. "It's his call. And, like it or not, it's not unreasonable from his position—or for that matter, Al Wiley's. An alliance with a stable Alexandrian Empire that owns a good part of the coast of the Med, and a land route to the Red Sea and the Persian Gulf, opens up trade with India even without the trip around the Cape of Good Hope. And the empire is a major trading partner in its own right, even without that. But broken up into warring factions, the Alexandrian Empire is almost useless as a trading partner. The whole technicalization program that New America's economic forecasts are based on becomes a lot harder. They are going to need nations to buy the steam engines and potatoes, and not broke third-world nations. Nations that have their own machines and tools, that have something to sell other than slaves and hand-spun thread."

"Skipper, I'm not saying they are wrong, not even that bas—not even President Wiley. But however good the reasoning, it still leaves the *Queen*'s neutrality in tatters."

All through the meeting, Dag Jakobsen had remained quiet, head down, looking at his slate computer and making notes on something. Now he looked up and said, "Are you sure that's a bad thing?"

Anders Dahl looked at Dag, opened his mouth, and closed it. Everyone in the room knew Dag's relationship with Roxane. It was only imperial politics that had kept them from getting married. Most of the Macedonians were willing to look the other way about Dag and Roxane, though Cassander, Antigonus, and some of the eastern satraps were using their relationship as a propaganda tool. But if Dag and Roxane were to get married, legitimizing any children Roxane might have and making potential competitors for the toddler Alexander IV, well, at least three satraps would go over to the other side, and it wouldn't do the army any good either.

All of which meant that Dag's opinion was suspect when it came to dealings with Roxane and the Alexandrian Empire. Which, Marie knew, was why he hadn't spoken up till now.

"No. I'm serious," Dag continued, staring at Anders. "And I am not speaking for Roxane here. I am thinking about the political situation of the *Queen of the Sea*.

"Neutrality can be taken too far. I'm not saying we should take sides, but we wouldn't be taking sides. Just delivering a contracted cargo. If Cassander can come up with the money and buy a cargo from New America, let him. Hell, if he can come up with the money and wants us to build him a stamp press, or ten tons of black powder, fine.

"But right now, New America has contracted for ten breechloading four-pounders. They are building the gun carriages in Fort Plymouth and the *Reliance* will pick them up and carry them to the Med. We have the induction furnaces to make the steel, and the boring machines to bore the barrels, and the other equipment needed to make the breech blocks which the government of New America is buying from us. And the government of New America is selling them to their trading partner at a profit.

"The fact is, we won't be breaching our neutrality. We just won't let that neutrality outlaw trade."

Pella, Macedonia
March 31, 319 BCE

Malcolm Tanada sat in a handcrafted chair with cushions on the back and seat and read the radio message. The comfortable accommodations in the plushly furnished radio room didn't help at all. It wasn't that he was fond of Cassander, but this was going to make his position less stable. Well, no time like the present, and he sure as hell didn't want Cassander getting this over the signal fires or by courier.

☆　　　☆　　　☆

The royal-audience chamber was much warmer now on a sunny day at the end of March than it had been in February. There was a cool breeze, but that just kept the day comfortable.

Cassander and Thessalonike were seated on two thrones, and there was a gaggle of courtiers wandering around in the large round room that had marble-covered pillars circling the hole in the roof.

The seneschal saw Malcolm, and waved him over.

Malcolm told him the basics. "New America has signed a trade agreement with Roxane and Eurydice."

"The *Queen*?"

"I don't know yet."

"Wait here."

The seneschal moved quickly to the throne and spoke to Cassander, who listened, then waved Malcolm over.

Malcolm bowed and Cassander grimaced. Normally, Malcolm made it a point to not bow, so this must be bad news. Malcolm handed over the sheet that he had printed out, and Cassander read. He didn't read quickly. Even a rich bibliophile in the fourth century BCE had limited access to books. You could spend only so much time on it before you had read everything there was to read. Even bookworms spent much of their time on other pursuits and got less practice than most ship people did.

Lips moving, Cassander finished the sheet and after a gentle cough from the other throne, he passed it over to Thessalonike.

"What else can you tell me?"

"Nothing, sir," Malcolm said. "I came here as soon as the first news came over the radio. I have my people watching for more, but I should get back."

Cassander waved him away, but Thessalonike said, "Wait a moment. Please send a message to Olympias for me, asking for any insights she has to offer."

Cassander nodded, but didn't look happy, and Malcolm made his escape as Cassander called over a string of courtiers.

Babylon, west side

Susan Godlewski sat on the inflated leather cushion on her chair and read the report with some relief. News of Eumenes' defeat at the hands of Lysimachus had hit morale on Attalus' side of the river fairly hard. Even though it was a raid and Eumenes was left in control of the battlefield, it was still seen as a defeat. Partly that was because the Macedonian nobility wanted Eumenes to be defeated, because it confirmed their prejudices even if it wasn't in their best interest. But partly because it *was* a defeat. Eumenes' rockets were gone, and those rockets had a morale effect even greater than their direct military effect. So did their loss.

But this would almost reverse that political damage. Roxane and Eurydice had an alliance with New America. That meant an alliance with the ship people. In theory, they were neutral here, but all of her people were on this side of the river. They only crossed the river to deliver messages, and then only after heavy negotiations.

She leaned back in the chair and waved at Karrel. "Take a look at this."

He walked over, leaned over her shoulder, and read the file off the screen. "That's not going to help relations with Antigonus."

It was true their neutrality, and the ship people neutrality in general, made them the natural negotiators for the siege. And it was a strange siege. Porous on both sides of the river. Both sides mostly free to come and go as they chose, but with Antigonus having at least loose control over the surrounding territory.

It was only their guard contingent that had allowed them to get into the west side of Babylon. And now that they were here, they couldn't leave. Not safely.

"I don't think it matters," Susan said. "Antigonus wasn't going to settle for anything short of surrender, anyway."

Karrel grimaced, but nodded agreement. The status quo was to Antigonus' advantage. He could come and go with relative impunity. In fact, he wasn't even here at the moment. He'd left a week before on a diplomatic mission to the Persian Gulf.

"So how goes the glass factory?" Susan asked.

Karrel stood up and went back to his seat where he was working on a set of plans. Using access to the few engineers that were on the *Queen of the Sea* when The Event happened, and Wikipedia, Karrel was designing a glass factory for Babylon. He had the land and agreements with the garrison and the citizenry.

"Pretty well. We have the building. It's just the crucibles and the kiln. We need refractory bricks. What about the hospital?"

"Alibaba is doing fine." Alibaba was Susan's nickname for the Persian doctor who was using them and the ship people knowledge to revolutionize medical care and drugs in Babylon. Alibaba made regular trips across the Euphrates from Attalus' west side to Antigonus' east side, and ran hospitals on both sides. After several successful surgeries, he was generally considered to be a miracle worker, as were his medical staff. He also charged a fortune. At least to those who could afford it. Hence the nickname.

This wasn't unusual. All the radio teams were doing similar things wherever they happened to be.

Carthage

Tina Johnson looked at her dad, feeling something more than surprise, but not quite shock. "Are they nuts, Daddy?" She'd just read the report from the *Queen* about New America's actions.

James Godfrey looked up from the report on strawberry production in the Carthage area and considered. "I don't think so. At least, Al Wiley isn't." He waved out the window at the brightly painted almost-adobe houses and buildings that made up the city of Carthage. "Look, Carthage may be an empire by local standards, but by the standards of back home it's a banana republic with a shortage of bananas. And way too many banana peels. They can make glass and now that we've taught them how, they can make clear glass. But not in anything like the quantity we need. They can't make rubber, they can't make power tools, and I wouldn't want to be standing near one of their steam engines. But the USSE is almost big enough to be a real country, if it's not chopped into chunks by the *diadochi*. Which is why Carthage, Rome, and what's left of the Etruscans are all scared of a United Satrapies and States of the Empire. They are justifiably afraid that they will be conquered."

"Do you think they will be, Dad?"

"Possibly. But, more likely, they will be absorbed relatively peacefully. The *Queen* is out there in the Atlantic, able to hit the coast anywhere in the Med, and now even to East Africa and India. And we are a civilizing influence."

Tina nodded. She and her family had made the ship people attitude toward human sacrifice perfectly clear, and they moved in the highest circles of Carthaginian society. Such sacrifices hadn't stopped, not entirely, but they had been fading out even before The Event and now . . . Well, there had been one since she and her family arrived. They refused to attend the ceremony and flatly refused to deal with the family that performed the sacrifice. With the things like latex and nut potatoes that were now coming out of New America and off the *Queen of the Sea*, that by itself had severely damaged the financial position of the family that performed the sacrifice. And the magic of the arrival of the *Queen* and the knowledge that the gods to whom the children were sacrificed didn't even exist two thousand years later had prevented a sequel. It wasn't illegal, but there hadn't been a repeat either.

She looked over at Eric Bryant and Quitzko. The Native American got incredibly sick with something a few days after the *Queen* left, and Eric spent several days haunting the radio station to get medical advice from the doctors on the *Queen* on how to take care of him. They couldn't tell Eric much more than "Just treat the symptoms," but it was enough. A week later Quitzko was back up and around.

But in the meantime, Eric became a friend. And something more. They had a lot in common. They were from the same chunk of Alabama. Tina even thought they had met once at an away game back in high school. But now everything was different. She found herself daydreaming about Eric. He wasn't anything like her husband who had died, but he was a little bit of home here in Carthage. And she had to wonder if he felt the same, because he was sure attentive.

"It is a good move," Quitzko said in careful English,

bringing the conversation back to the possibilities. "The Europes don't know how to make a nation any more than we do. It is all tribes. If the USSE collapses, New America will be all alone in the world. The only nation made up of..." He stopped and asked Eric a question in his own language.

Eric reached up and scratched his short beard while he thought, then said, "I think 'disparate people' is as close as I can come." Then he said something in Quitzko's language, and continued in English, "Basically, he means people from different tribes, but also from different cultures, speaking different languages."

"Disparate," Quitzko said like he was tasting the word, then he shrugged. "But you do it and we not do it."

"It's not easy," James Godfrey said.

CHAPTER 12

AT SEA

Fort Plymouth, New America
April 2, 319 BCE

The *Reliance* tug pulled up to the dock. The barge was back at the oil depot, being filled with oil. Once they were docked and tied down, Adrian left and caught a bike cab into the city proper. The bike cabs had unprocessed latex over the wooden rims. There was a small factory that processed latex from South and Central America rubber trees into everything from tires to water bottles. But it was constantly running out of sulfur, and calling it a factory was a gross exaggeration. Or would have been, back in the world. There, it would qualify as someone's small garage business. In the here and now, it was a factory. Fifteen employees, three ship people and twelve locals, six Indian, two Greeks, and four Romans. It had started in Fort Plymouth, but complaints over the smell had forced it to move. But the processed rubber was still too expensive to go on the tricycle

214

cab tires. They used the soft, unrefined latex to act as a shock absorber. Wheels were spoked wood, and the chain was a thick knotted cord. Along with the tarmac streets, a pedal trike pulling a rickshaw-style cab was barely within the tech of the new colony, at least for the town of Fort Plymouth itself. Outside town, there were no roads for them to use. There were ten of the cabs at last count.

The cab took him to the capitol building and he walked through the wood-paneled halls to the office of the President.

☆   ☆   ☆

"Have a seat, Commodore Scott," said President Al Wiley.

"Commodore?" Adrian didn't take the offered chair. He was too shocked by the title.

"Yes. The newly named *Ronald Reagan* has just finished its modifications." Al Wiley stood up and came around his desk, holding out a hand to shake.

Adrian shook the hand, saying, "Congratulations, sir, but..." Adrian trailed off because he wasn't at all sure what to say next.

The *Ronald Reagan* was a converted mega-lifeboat from the *Queen of the Sea*. It now had a second deck on top of the fiberglass roof with rotating rocket launchers, basically wooden tubes on a stand behind four-foot-tall wooden walls. They gave the ship the ability to launch salvos of black powder rockets. It also now had a set of small sails to augment the diesel engine, increasing its range a bit. The modifications were designed by Richard VanHouten, a retired electrical engineer and aficionado of shipbuilding history. Adrian, Captain Floden, Dag Jakobsen, Bernt Carlson and the *Queen's* boson, James Warner, had all gone over the designs and made suggestions. She was intended to provide coastal defense for Trinidad while the *Queen* and the *Reliance* were elsewhere.

"Ah..." Adrian paused, then went on. "But what does that have to do with me? And, more importantly, what does it have to do with the *Reliance*?"

"The *Queen* and the *Reliance* have both acted unofficially as the navy of New America since our founding. But Captain Floden is justifiably concerned that the *Queen*'s neutrality is called into question by our recent treaty with the United Satrapies and States of the Empire."

Adrian hid a smile as he noted that, as always, Wiley used the full name of the USSE, or called it the Alexandrian Empire, or just the Empire. Al Wiley found USSE to be altogether too close to USSR for his comfort.

"I understand, sir, but..."

"I'm getting to it," President Wiley interrupted. "It's a bit complicated. The *Queen of the Sea* is owned by the Queen of the Sea Corporation, which is registered in New America and owned by the crew and a few of the passengers who, for whatever reason, kept their share. The *Reliance* is owned in part by the Queen of the Sea Corporation and in part by the government of New America, along with the part ownership by you and some of your crew." Wiley held up his hand before Adrian could again ask what this was all about. "We want to change that. We, that is, the government of New America, want to buy the *Queen of the Sea*'s share of the *Reliance* and commission her as the New American Navy ship *Reliance*. Making her officially a ship of New America."

Adrian was shaking his head.

Al Wiley again held up a hand. "Hear me out. I admit I don't like the idea of this much mixing of government and private enterprise, but we are in a special circumstance. For now and for years to come, the government of New America is going to have to help in the kickstarting of the industrial revolution. It is our intent to divest ourselves of all these businesses just as soon as we can, except maybe the post office. But, for now, we need the *Reliance* as both a commercial presence and a New American military presence that is able to reach Europe. We have to do that to maintain the distinction between New America and the *Queen of the Sea*."

Adrian nodded. It made sense in the weird and twisted way that things had made sense since The Event. He agreed that having government mixing in business was a bad thing. He'd been a Tory before The Event. But he'd also run the *Reliance* up the Orinoco River to burn out the towns and villages that had been involved in the attack on Fort Plymouth. The military function of the *Reliance* was a reality, in spite of any desires to the contrary.

"We want to persuade you to buy a commission as commodore in the New America Navy with your share of the *Reliance*."

Adrian looked around and went to the chair he had been offered. His knees were suddenly weak.

As Adrian sat, Al Wiley leaned his hip against his desk. "It's actually quite a good deal for you, Commodore Scott. As a commodore and commander of the *Reliance*, you will still be entitled to most of what your share would have been with the *Reliance* in private hands. Your share of the oil and cargo transport money will be only slightly diminished with the *Reliance* as the flagship of New America."

There was something in Wiley's voice that made Adrian look at his face and what he saw there made it very clear that Wiley was unhappy about the whole notion of an officer of a New American warship having a share of the profits that ship might make.

"Why?" Adrian asked. "Why ask me to buy my commission and why give me a share?"

"Because it's going to be hard enough to buy the *Queen*'s share of the *Reliance*. New America isn't going to have a balanced budget this year and the Bank of New America is in truth only a branch of the *Queen of the Sea* bank. We need to get your shares for political reasons. The *Reliance* has to be wholly owned by New America, but we can't pay you what the shares are worth. And, to be honest, if you fought us over the issue, you would almost certainly win."

New America had a Supreme Court. It had three justices and all of them were American lawyers from the passengers. They were also a fairly conservative bunch, with strong views on the issue of private property.

"So what do I get to keep me from suing and what do I give up?"

"You get the status of a commodore in the New American Navy. That puts you on a par with a Satrap of the Empire. You get a regular salary and it's a pretty big one. And you and your crew get a share of the profits that the *Reliance* generates by carrying oil and cargo."

"And I lose?"

"A certain amount of freedom of action," Wiley

admitted. "You will be a man under orders. And you will be operating under the UCMJ as soon as we get it written."

Adrian felt a grin fighting through the receding shock. The Congress of New America had been haggling over the Uniform Code of Military Justice almost from day one. The locals, both Greek and Injun, had their own views of the rights and obligations of soldiers. Those rights, by local standards, almost always included things like sacks and gleaning. The ship people, on the other hand, figured that a soldier or sailor was paid by the government. And besides, murder, rape, theft, and arson caused political problems. That was no doubt another reason for Wiley's displeasure. Giving the crew of the *Reliance* a share in any profit the ship made was a precedent he clearly didn't want to set. "How is that going to affect the crew of the *Ronald Reagan*?"

Wiley grimaced. "As it stands now, the UCMJ makes a clear distinction between acts of war and other functions. So the *Reagan*, as primarily a warship, won't be generating the sort of income the *Reliance* will. On the other hand, and you should know this because if you take the deal, you're going to be the very first member of New America's admiralty, we are probably going to have admiralty courts. And if the admiralty court condemns a seized vessel as a pirate or a ship of a belligerent power, the crew will get a share of any proceeds. I don't like it, but we are stuck in a world where the distinction between a navy ship and a pirate is very slight."

Then President Alan Wiley stood up from his lean against his desk and said, formally, "Mr. Scott, will you accept the post of commodore in the Navy of New America and all the privileges and obligations of that post?"

Adrian stood up and saluted as best he could. Adrian had come up as a merchant seaman and never before served in the military. "I will, sir."

Navy Office, Fort Plymouth, New America
April 3, 319 BCE

The Navy Office was just that. An office in the capitol building. And not a very big one. The room was ten feet by thirteen feet, had two small desks—one for the Secretary of the Navy and one for his secretary—and one file cabinet that was about half empty. It was next door to the Army Office. The offices opened into a larger room that had half a dozen desks for clerks, most of them ship people and most of them on the high side of fifty. They were the rest of the government bureaucracy. The capitol building was a grandiose name for what was actually not very different from a block of the townhouses that made up the rest of Fort Plymouth. It was two stories, wattle and daub, on a platform held four feet off the ground by wooden stilts.

The Secretary of the Navy was Richard VanHouten, the electrical engineer and naval history buff who designed the refit of the *Ronald Reagan*. He was a balding man with horn-rimmed glasses and a slight stoop to his shoulders. And when he wasn't being Secretary of the Navy, he ran a ship design firm that was going to build cargo sailing ships for the coastal trade. He reached out and shook Adrian's hand and smiled, showing a chipped denture. The making of plastic dentures was a long way off, so dentures were irreplaceable. Or at least in regard to the quality they were used to before The Event.

"Congratulations, Commodore. Have you met Captain Boka, late of the Carthaginian navy?"

Captain Boka had a black beard that was both curled and perfumed, and long, curly hair. He wore a captain's hat and a white coat with four narrow gold stripes. He saluted in the Carthaginian manner, right hand facing outward, arm bent at the elbow and raised to the shoulder. Then he gave a bow, but a shallow one.

Adrian gave him a British navy salute, and no bow, thinking, *We are going to have to come up with some form of common protocol for naval personnel.* "It's nice to meet you, Captain. The *Reagan* seems a fine ship and I'd like to visit her sometime."

"At the commodore's pleasure," Captain Boka said in a clearly rehearsed phrase.

They talked some more and Adrian learned that Boka was a fairly proficient English speaker, though he had a strong Phoenician accent. He was also familiar with the political situation along the east coast of the Americas. And, surprisingly, an ardent abolitionist.

"I spent three years as a galley slave to Sicilian pirates, Captain. I have hated the institution ever since. It was just that there was no other option until you people arrived."

"Captain Boka freed his slaves, every last one of them, three days after the arrival of the *Queen* on its first visit to Carthage. It effectively ruined him, and his family paid his passage on the *Queen* to New America just to get him out of sight," VanHouten said.

☆　　☆　　☆

The ceremony was a bit pompous, but moving in a way. Adrian swore the oath that was very close to the oath taken by everyone serving in the USA military.

> *"I, Adrian Scott, having been appointed an officer in the Navy of New America, in the rank of commodore, do solemnly swear that I will support and defend the Constitution of New America against all enemies, foreign or domestic; that I will bear true faith and allegiance to the same; that I take this obligation freely, without any mental reservations or purpose of evasion; and that I will well and faithfully discharge the duties of the office upon which I am about to enter."*

And that was where Chief Justice Setsuichi Watanabe stopped.

"So help me God," Adrian finished on his own. He knew the reason that Watanabe stopped. Even back in the world in the US, that "so help me God" had been tradition, not law. Here in New America it was not even that, because many of the locals swore to other gods. They had people from Athens who swore to Athena. They had Indians who swore to Quatal, a feathered dragon god that was probably an ancestor of the Aztec Quetzalcoatl. At least, it was the god of knowledge and farming. But there wasn't a single god that was commonly worshiped in New America. Christianity—Catholic, most major Protestant varieties, Mormon—Islam and Judaism. All of them were expanding, but they were still in the minority even put together.

Justice Watanabe reached out and shook Adrian's

hand. "Congratulations, Commodore. You can buy a good uniform at the Agape shop on Baker Street. They do good work."

That wasn't a surprise either, having the chief justice touting a tailor. This was a different world. Smaller, more local. Fort Plymouth, the biggest and really the only city in New America—stretching the term "city" to the breaking point—had a population of less than five thousand. What made it seem like something of a city was more the degree of crowding into a small area than the actual size of the population. In the United States most of the ship people had come from, a typical town of five thousand people would spread out quite a bit. Here, for the sake of protection within Fort Plymouth's palisade and because a large number of the population weren't up to walking very far, that same five thousand people were crammed together pretty tightly. Being honest about it, much of Fort Plymouth bore a more than passing resemblance to a tenement slum.

The new Jacquard-style loom, a device of wood and string with only a few small metal parts, lowered the cost of weaving. The spinning wheels lowered the cost of thread, and so did the small hand-powered carding machines, but sewing was still very expensive and mostly done by hand. So the uniform was going to be a month's wages for a commodore and the sort of thing that left a lieutenant moderately deep in debt.

"I'll look into it, sir," Adrian said.

The New America Navy was not going to be very picky about uniform regulation as long as Adrian was the senior officer. On the other hand, as a commodore he had a greater obligation to lead by example. Which was probably at least part of Justice Watanabe's point. At the moment, Adrian was dressed in his ship's dress uniform, white with short sleeves. And, by now, it was getting quite frayed around the edges.

☆   ☆   ☆

For the next several days, Adrian found himself stuck in Fort Plymouth, taking care of the parts of his new job that had to be done here in the capitol. Then he boarded the *Reliance* for the trip to the Med.

Queen of the Sea, *Alexandria*
April 7, 319 BCE

Captain Lars Floden took the sheet from the steward and read the message.

> *Reliance on route to Thrace.*

Then he went back to the dinner conversation with Cleopatra, Sean Newton, Roxane, Dag and Epicurus. This was still the *Queen of the Sea*, and this was still the captain's table: white linen, fine china, silver flatware, the best food and wine, and people dressed in their best. "So, Sean, what do you think about the new agreement between the empire and New America?"

"I think it's a good thing overall, Captain Floden," said the large, beefy man who was going a bit bald. "It will facilitate trade and increase the market for New American goods." Sean had stayed on the *Queen*, but—using funds from his girlfriend Cleopatra, sister of Alexander—he had invested in several manufactories in New America and was rapidly turning into a tycoon. Cleopatra was thrilled with the situation, Lars knew. It meant that she was much less dependent on the income from her lands, which were tied to the political position she occupied and less than completely dependable. "As to the tactical and strategic situation, I don't have a clue. Cleo says it will help Eumenes, especially coming after that mousetrapping he got in Thrace."

Dag Jakobsen smiled. "Don't be too disappointed in Eumenes, Sean. From my read, it's the sort of thing that can happen to anyone. And Eumenes didn't let it stop him. Slow him a bit, maybe, but not stop him. He is besieging Abdera, and if Lysimachus is blocking him on the land route, he isn't in a position to attack him. And Eumenes has a good supply situation. Apparently he's been listening to Erica on the issues of food storage, canning, drying, and pickling."

"We already knew about pickling and drying, and even canning is only new by degree," Cleopatra said.

"Yes, dear, I know," Sean said with such a long-suffering tone that Lars had to suppress a laugh.

Cleopatra gave him a look, then she did laugh. "I know, I know. The improvements are significant in reducing spoilage. And in making storage and transport easier. But it's not like we were still figuring out how to make fire."

"How is he getting supplies?" Epicurus asked. "I mean, with Abdera in enemy hands and Lysimachus controlling most of the land between them and the Bosphorus."

"Mostly they aren't." Roxane waved a wineglass. "That's why food preservation has become such an issue. Eumenes was already quite a good quartermaster by local standards. Almost certainly the best in Alexander's army. Alexander used to talk about it quite a lot. As long as Eumenes was handling it, he never had to worry about supplies. Except for that trek back from India, and that wasn't Eumenes' fault. It was Alexander's. Anyway, after he met you ship people, he set up a bunch of local kitchen canneries in his territory, and he has wagon loads and wagon loads of preserved meats and beans, as well as other stuff. It allows him to keep his army fed with much fewer depredations on the Thracians. Meanwhile, Lysimachus is raping the land and Eumenes' army grows every day because of it."

"It grows." Dag frowned. "But it doesn't grow stronger. Just bigger. Most of the new recruits aren't veterans. They are farm boys who are escaping from burned out villages. And they are bringing their wives and mothers with them. That's why the alliance is such a boon. If the *Reliance* ever leaves Fort Plymouth, that is."

"You will be pleased to know, then, that the *Reliance* has left Fort Plymouth and should raise Abdera in eighteen or nineteen days."

"Does Eurydice know that?" Roxane asked.

"If not, she will soon," Lars said.

CHAPTER 13

OVER MY DEAD BODY

Abdera, Thrace
April 8, 319 BCE

Claudius Kokaliáris—in spite of the moniker Kokaliáris, which meant skinny—was in his middle forties, a stocky man. He had the famous Greek nose and a thick, luxurious beard that was going gray in spite of the fact that his hair was still black. He sat on a couch and read the message again. He looked around the room at his officers lounging here and there, working or drinking. More drinking than working.

The siege of Abdera was two weeks old, just long enough for it to be clear that Eumenes wasn't going to waste his army in an attempt to storm the walls. Now this. The message was sent by a herald, from Philip and Eumenes as his *strategos*, but Claudius knew what that meant. It was actually from Eumenes and Eurydice. And all it said was: *Reliance has left New America. Will arrive at Abdera Harbor April 27.*

He knew what that meant too, at least to him as commander of the city.

Claudius was one of Lysimachus' lieutenants. He was appointed to this post because of his proven loyalty to Lysimachus and because he was quite unpopular in Thrace, having spent much of the last three years as one of Lysimachus' top tax collectors. But Claudius was also, at his core, a very practical man. He knew for a fact that he couldn't hold the city if the *Reliance* got here. Even if it never fired a cannon or shot a rocket, just its presence would cause the city to rise up.

Claudius stood up and went to a table. Then he called over Silas, a slave. Silas was an Athenian and a student of Aristotle before falling on hard times. "Write what I tell you," Claudius said quietly. He could read, though not very well, and he wrote even more poorly.

"Eumenes, I will turn the city over to you, but not for free. I will need to leave Thrace and I will need money to live. What I can do for you is to open the north gate and stand down the troops just before dawn on a day to be agreed. But you must guarantee my safety and provide me transport to New America. And I want an account in the bank of the *Queen of the Sea* in the amount of fifty talents."

Silas looked at Claudius, eyes wide, and started to open his mouth.

"Quietly, Silas. Quietly, or I will have the skin of your back off."

Silas' mouth snapped shut. And Claudius considered. Silas was silent now, but he would need to stay silent or Claudius would find himself deposed before he could act. He wasn't Lysimachus' only man in Abdera and Nikomedes was stupid enough to think he could hold Abdera in spite of the *Reliance*. Sighing with real regret, he spoke again. "Also, my slave Silas, who I manumit the moment we are both on the *Reliance*."

Silas looked at him, eyes even wider, then they tightened in calculation. And, slowly, Silas gave Claudius a slight nod.

It wasn't nearly as deferential as Claudius would have liked, but they both knew how the world worked.

Negotiations proceeded for a few more days, but the outcome was a foregone conclusion. Claudius got forty talents, not fifty, but he would have been satisfied with thirty.

Eumenes' men slipped in the north gate of Abdera an hour before dawn on the fourteenth of April. There was very little fighting.

Abdera docks
April 14, 319 BCE

The captain of the single-masted merchant ship *Hericlease* was named Simon. He was dressed in a rag tied around his waist with a rope and a cloak that was, if anything, in worse repair. He had a short, graying beard and hadn't bathed recently. He smelled of salt air and Simon. Rather more Simon than salt air. Erica Mirzadeh considered investing in yet another soap factory. There was one in Lydia that she had gone halves on with Eurydice, and it made pretty good soap through the good offices of a local apothecary and some modern Wikipedia articles on the making of soap that Erica translated. Unfortunately, its product was still quite expensive by the fourth-world standards of pre-Christian Greece.

Erica Mirzadeh held her tongue and tried to breathe shallowly while Eumenes, apparently completely unaffected by the aroma, discussed shipping goods from Lydia to here. Almost from the moment that Erica had accompanied Eumenes, Eurydice, and Philip off the *Queen*, they had been starting businesses based on ship people knowledge. The vast majority of them were located in Lydia. They made everything from horseshoes to thread, from soap to dried soup mix.

"But what of pirates?" Simon was complaining.

"Come now, Captain. The straight-line distance between here and Canakkale is only eighty miles. Well, eighty of the ship people nautical miles. And I grant that you can't go entirely straight, but we are still only talking a day or two and—" Eumenes stopped as though struck by a new idea. "I know, Captain. For your safety, I will assign a platoon of crossbowmen to you for the trip."

Simon didn't look especially pleased by that, not to Erica's eye. He looked trapped. And that, in Erica's opinion, was all that was needed.

From Eumenes' expression, he was just as satisfied with the situation. He waved Erica over, and she pulled out the magnetic compass. It was the product of one of the new industries. The needles were heated, then exposed to an electromagnet. They made the needles in batches on the *Queen* and assembled the cases in a shop in Lydia. She also had a sextant and a set of instructions for both compass and sextant.

"This is the compass," she explained, holding it out

and letting him take it. She pointed at the needle and had him rotate the compass around so that he could see that the needle continued to point north. She showed him the markings on the little paper sheet and how to read them to tell which way the ship was traveling.

Then she introduced Ophion, one of Eumenes' most trusted cavalry officers. After learning how to use both compass and sextant over the months Erica had been with the army, Ophion was actually more skilled at their use than she was. "Ophion here will command the crossbow platoon, and he will also teach you the use of the navigational devices."

The *Queen* was making clocks now, mechanical clocks that worked quite well. But the army only had three, and none of them were going to be turned over to Captain Simon and his tub, which was almost as much in need of a good scrubbing as he was.

☆   ☆   ☆

Once they were off the ship, Eumenes gave her a look. "You ship people are the most fastidious people I have ever seen."

"Tell me that fat slob didn't stink."

"Oh, he stank. But I only noticed it because Tacaran, and now Eurydice, are constantly pointing it out."

Eumenes had bathed the day before, with soap. It was becoming the custom in his army. But a lot of that was the medical texts that were still being translated into Greek and sent to them whenever they were stopped and had the bandwidth.

They went on to the next ship and repeated the process with variations. Captain Iakchos, as it turned out, bathed every time he hit port and had his own stock of soap. Soap he bought in Lydia. He also had a compass that he bought in Lydia, but not a sextant, which had proved too pricey for his purse. He was happy with the sextant and the offer of ship's credit for the trip.

Eumenes reached into his breast pocket—an affectation at least in part, as to add a pocket to a tunic required hand-sewing the pocket onto the tunic, and in spite of the very low cost of labor, it was still not something poor people could afford. It was a way of demonstrating wealth without exactly flaunting it. From his pocket, he pulled a booklet. The booklet was a checkbook. It had a picture of the *Queen of the Sea* in the upper right corner on every check, something that would be very difficult to forge. Using a barrel as a table, he wrote out "Iakchos" on the PAY TO line and the amount, then signed it.

"When we get back to the station," Erica said, "I can radio the *Queen*, set you up an account, and send them the information that is recorded there, so the *Queen* will have it. You do need to be aware, though, that only you can cash the check. You can't sell it to someone else."

That was, by now, a standard spiel. Checks and *Queen of the Sea* bank money were sometimes accepted, and sometimes not. The wealthier and more educated the person was, the more likely they were to accept the *Queen's* bank money. On the other hand, the *Queen's* coinage was absolutely the best money anyone had ever seen. The coins were stamped consistently and the edges were reeded. That is, they had little grooves all around the edges to prevent clipping. The coins were also of a constant purity, and that purity was marked on the reverse of each coin. The front had a stamped image of the *Queen of the Sea* herself.

That was proving to be one of the biggest advantages of the royalists in the civil war. The money that Roxane and Eurydice spent through their agents was better and more trusted than the money of Antigonus, Cassander, or the other rebellious satraps. It was even better than Ptolemy's money, though Ptolemy was now in negotiations to have the *Queen of the Sea* mint Egyptian coinage for the bank of Egypt.

Alexandria, Egypt
April 14, 319 BCE

TinTin Wai adjusted her glasses, then looked through the microscope. It was impressive in its way, even if its magnification was only a little over a hundred power. It had taken the efforts of three glassmakers, a jeweler, two carpenters, and a brass smith three months to make. TinTin was in new territory. She was using the microscope to try and identify the bacteriological infection that was making Abaka sick. Abaka was the twelve-year-old daughter of a family of wealthy Egyptian merchants. She had the symptoms of tuberculosis, but TinTin wanted to be sure because the sulfa drugs that she, along with the help of the local apothecaries and the *Queen of the Sea*'s database—

There! There is one of the tubular little suckers. She was pleased at the confirmation that the microscope was working and useful in identifying the disease. Happy that it worked. Still, the prognosis wasn't good. There were surgeries that could be tried to relieve the symptomatology, and the sulfa drugs would at least impede the disease. But those drugs were poison. They would destroy the liver with regular use.

She sat up and stretched, then waved Kadmos over. Kadmos was a doctor in the mold of Hippocrates, both an experimenter and good with patients. He was, in fact, second chair of medicine in the newly formed University of Alexandria. TinTin gave him her stool and he looked. It took a minute. Then he said, "Yes, yes. I see it. It is much like the image I saw on the computer, but different as well. Harder to see." He spoke in English with a Greek accent that TinTin thought was even worse than her Cantonese accent. Whatever Bruce said.

The door opened without a knock. "Sorry to interrupt, Doc," Bruce said, "but I need TinTin."

"What? Oh, fine," Kadmos said in Greek with a pronounced Spartan accent. The difference between Athenian Greek and Spartan Greek was about as great as the difference between Southern and Bronx, with the Macedonians off somewhere in Cockney Land.

"What do you need?" TinTin asked.

"Word just came in. Eumenes took Abdera yesterday."

"And?"

"And Ptolemy has a message to send to Antigonus."

TinTin lifted an eyebrow as she moved to the door.

Bruce shrugged. "It's in code," he said as he stepped back out of the room.

TinTin waited until the door was closed to ask, "What code?"

"A variant on the military code that they were using with the signal fires."

"Cracked?" TinTin asked. She was careful even here in their offices.

The ship people enclave was a large four-story building near the Temple of Serapis. The temple was new, built since Ptolemy had become Satrap of Egypt. In it there stood a newly made statue of the god Serapis. Fifteen feet tall, made of painted terracotta, and dressed in robes. Serapis had aspects of Osiris, but also a Greek look about him. The temple, reminiscent of the Acropolis in Athens if smaller, was made of marble columns. TinTin could see it every time she looked out the window of her suite in the four-story apartment building that was now the ship people enclave.

On top of the ship people enclave was the radio tower, and the radio room was on the top floor, but protected from weather and accident. On the bottom floor was a ten-room hospital for the wealthy. On the second floor, where they were now, were the labs and shops, mostly occupied by Greek and Egyptian scholars and master craftsmen loaned to them by the University of Alexandria. On the third floor were rooms that they rented to visiting ship people, of which there were several at any given time. Either from the ship directly or from Judea, where there was a small colony. And on the fourth floor, along with the radio room, were the apartments of Bruce Lofdahl and TinTin Wai. Bruce was leading her to the stairs. An elevator was being added as a demonstration project, but it wasn't finished yet and TinTin had no intention of using the thing even after it was finished.

"Did you carbon copy Her Nibs?" TinTin asked. The ship people enclave had more locals than ship people by an order of magnitude, at least. And some of them were spies. So TinTin and Bruce had taken to speaking obscurely, if not exactly in code.

"Yep. And I would bet Strom Borman has cracked their code, even if it is a book code." Bruce was grinning like he knew a secret.

"Maybe." TinTin conceded the probability, though she was less confident. A book code was, by its nature, the hardest of all codes to crack. Even with the software and computing power of the *Queen*, you had to have something for the formula to work on. And that meant you had to have the book the sender used. Or you had to make your own by making guesses. Besides, TinTin had never met Strom Borman and didn't know much about him, except that he was supposed to be some sort of mathematical genius.

"I'd say it's a pretty safe bet, TinTin," Bruce said. "Not so much because of Doctor Borman, but because I would bet that Eumenes or Roxane had a copy of the main book. Or at least can make a good guess about which book it might be."

By now they were on the third-floor landing and Bruce motioned her to his rooms. Again, TinTin lifted an eyebrow, but she went with him. As soon as they went through the door, TinTin faced Ahura, whose smile at seeing Bruce disappeared as soon as she saw TinTin.

"It's just business, sweetie," Bruce said.

Ahura was eighteen or nineteen. They weren't sure which. She was an orphan and a slave whom the enclave bought and manumitted. She started as part of the cleaning staff and set her cap at Bruce the moment she first saw him.

TinTin didn't see it, at least not physically. Bruce was on the wrong side of fifty and chunky, with horn-rimmed glasses and a hairline that was in full rout.

But he was a nice guy who hadn't tried to use his position to importune any of the staff, so Ahura had gone after him. And got him. Which was fine with TinTin, whose tastes went to the Arnold Schwarzenegger type.

Ahura tried to smile at TinTin but didn't make a great job of it. Bruce led TinTin into the office. Then, waving her to a chair, he went to the locally made wheeled office chair. "Ptolemy is trying to buy oil from Antigonus."

"How do you know?"

Bruce pointed at a bookshelf. TinTin went to look. It was a bound book, *Government* by Aristotle. It was clearly not one of the scrolls that the locals used as books. She pulled it out and looked. It was a printout that used their dot matrix printer and it had the text in Greek and English.

"There is a copy on my keyring flash drive. Plug it in, and *ta da*."

"So you knew all along," TinTin said.

Bruce grinned even wider. "Best way to keep a secret, don't tell anyone."

TinTin shook her head in disgust. "So tell me about the oil?"

"Ptolemy is building steamships at Suez."

"Why?"

"Because the *Queen* can't be everywhere, and she is neutral besides. And while the *Queen* isn't there, a steam gunboat will control the Red Sea, and a few of them could control the Arabian Sea and the Persian Gulf as well. I think that Ptolemy is getting ready to make a try for most of eastern North Africa and maybe India."

TinTin considered. She was rather cynical. Not paranoid, just mostly convinced that a lot of people had a large helping of self interest and rather smaller helpings of loyalty and honor. Especially among the locals. "I don't know, Bruce. How is he going to control the captains of those ships once he builds them?"

"I don't know, but Ptolemy is pretty good at this sort of thing."

"No. He's pretty good at controlling an army on land. A ship at sea is a whole different kettle of fish. The idea of loyalty to the state or government, even loyalty to kings . . . it's not really there yet."

"Alexander."

"Which is why they called him 'the great.' Remember that Persian guy whose soldiers killed him and brought Alexander his head? For them to get in trouble for doing that, they had to do it. Can you imagine someone chopping off the queen of England's head, or even the President's, and giving it to the enemy just because their side lost?"

"TinTin, you're a cynic."

"I'm a realist. I know you're fond of the locals. Hell, I'm fond of them. But don't you start believing that they are civilized. Anyway, what's the word on the *Reliance*?"

"I think we are going to have to wait till they get to Abdera before we find out."

Abdera, Thrace
April 27, 319 BCE

Commodore Adrian Scott looked around the airy room with the parquet floor, and the incredibly expensive wall hangings. It was a very nice place and they were digging out the paths for sewage pipes to install toilets. He'd seen them as he came in, proudly pointed out by one of Eumenes' aides. "I'll forward your request, *Strategos* Eumenes," Adrian said. "But I honestly doubt it will be granted." The request was to have the *Reliance* ship a load of troops from here in Abdera to Amphipolis. Not a long trip or a dangerous one, at least not for the moment. But it would drag the *Reliance* right into the middle of the war.

"Is there nothing you can do, Commodore Scott?" Queen Regent Eurydice asked. "Can't you persuade your President Wiley?"

"I suspect that President Wiley would like to help you, Your Majesty, but he doesn't operate in a vacuum. We have a constitution and an elected government. And the government must be respected even if it doesn't do the wisest thing." Adrian was fudging here more than a bit. As much as the notion of agreeing with anything Anna Comfort said galled him, in this case he thought she might be right. The *Reliance* had once been boarded and taken by locals, and acting in support of Eumenes was just asking for it to happen again. Keeping New America out of "foreign entanglements" made a lot of sense.

It wasn't like the USA back in the world. New America was still a very small nation with a very small population, and technology would only take you so far against numbers.

Meanwhile, Eumenes was looking at Adrian like he didn't quite buy it. Not surprisingly. Adrian was a ship's captain, not a frigging politician.

"Let us set that issue aside for now," Eumenes said. "At least until you get word back from your President.

In the meantime, what can you tell me about the situation in the rest of the world?"

Adrian looked at him. "That I can do. Cassander is using the time to try and consolidate his control over Macedonia and using printing presses to print proclamations and broadsheets describing Eurydice here as a usurper. And you as a peasant clerk with delusions of grandeur. He is making much of how you got mousetrapped in the pass."

"What does mousetrapped mean?" Eumenes asked. "I can make a guess. But I don't want to misunderstand."

For the next few minutes Adrian found himself describing mousetraps and how they worked. And as he talked, he realized that the introduction of mousetraps might save a million people from death due to malnutrition or disease in the next decade or so. Mousetraps, for the Lord's sake. It happened now and then. The simplest thing, the most seemingly inconsequential, unimportant thing, and it was the difference between life and death for people he would never know. "I'll get designs for them, *Strategos*, and give them to you." Then it was back to the political discussion and the situation in Babylon and Alexandria. Babylon was still a stalemate and Ptolemy was building steamships in Suez.

"He's going to be trouble," Eurydice said hotly.

"Perhaps, Majesty, but Ptolemy is a careful commander. He is not a McClellan, but neither is he Lee or Grant."

Adrian blinked. He wasn't entirely sure who McClellan was, though he recognized Lee and Grant from movies about the American Civil War.

Eumenes looked at Adrian and started to laugh.

"He reads all the time," Eurydice said. "Erica Mirzadeh is charging us enough money for a company of infantry, just in paper and ink for printouts for Eumenes here." She looked at Eumenes and added, "Captain Scott is English, not American."

Eumenes thought. "World War II, then. He is not Patton or Montgomery. More Bradley. He does not lack courage, nor is he frozen by overestimation of the enemy's power, but neither is he a bull to be enraged by a slap on the nose. He won't seek revolution, but will attempt to get as much as he can at the negotiating table and be satisfied with that."

"Unless he becomes convinced we are weak," Eurydice disagreed. "I don't read as much as Eumenes or my husband, but I know the world."

"It's a big world," said Philip. "In five dimensions."

Philip was always near Eurydice, but usually silent, drawing his mathematics on sheets of parchment.

"Five?" Adrian found himself asking. "I would have thought four. Or maybe eleven."

"Maybe eleven," Philip said. "But at least five. Two timelines, which requires at least two temporal dimensions."

Adrian was now totally out of his mathematical depth and dropped the matter. "If you say so." Turning back to Eumenes, he said, "I think I agree with your assessment of Ptolemy, especially with Thaïs to advise him."

"What about the murder attempt on Dag?" Eurydice asked.

"It seems to be stalled for now. I did talk to Dag the last time that we were both in port together and he seems convinced that Olympias is innocent."

"That's what Roxane says, but I don't believe it. Why is there no evidence?"

"With all respect, I didn't say there was no evidence. I said the investigation was stalled. There is evidence. They have a fingerprint off the carafe of cocoamat, but that fingerprint didn't match Olympias or anyone on her staff. It's possible that she bribed someone on the serving staff, but even there we know that it wasn't anyone who was supposed to be there. They volunteered their fingerprints to a man and all have been eliminated from suspicion. Which only leaves about four thousand possible suspects."

"Four thousand?" Eumenes asked.

Adrian smiled and shook his head. "It's a little complicated. Before The Event, the *Queen* had room for five thousand in relative luxury, or at least relative luxury for the passengers. But since The Event, almost half the passenger rooms have been converted into factories to make use of the *Queen's* power plants. That knocked the *Queen's* capacity down to around three thousand passengers. Maybe a few less. But also since The Event, several of the staterooms that would have held a single passenger have been converted into bunk rooms that hold six, and sometimes eight. But that only brings them back up to approximately five thousand people on board. Of those, we already had fingerprints for at least some of the passengers and many of the crew. Since the incident on the *Queen*, it's been required that all the Silver Shields be fingerprinted as part of their induction, just like anyone who joined the military was back in the world before The Event. Together that eliminates about a thousand people for whom they have fingerprints on file. None of them match the prints on the carafe, leaving around four thousand people that were on the *Queen* who haven't been eliminated."

"Very well." Eumenes agreed. "Four thousand. How will you trim that number to something more reasonable?"

"That's why the investigation is stalled, *Strategos*. We have rules in place to protect the rights—"

Eumenes held up his hand. "Yes. The Bill of Rights of the empire is based in large part on the Bill of Rights of your United States."

"Not *my* United States. I'm a Brit," Adrian said, smiling again. "But we had the same basic rights, even if they were ordered a bit differently. The point is that those rights are respected on the *Queen* and in New America. They aren't things to be put aside when they become inconvenient. That is one thing that Al Wiley and Captain Floden agree on. So do I, for that matter."

Eumenes leaned back in his chair, unconvinced. But it wasn't Eumenes who had the last word, not this time.

Philip III of Macedon, for the very first time Adrian had ever seen, looked someone in the eye. Dead in the eye. "You will violate the rights laid out in the empire's Bill of Rights over my dead body."

Eumenes stood then, and bowed profoundly to one of the kings of the Alexandrian Empire.

CHAPTER 14

POISONER?

Reliance, *Abdera, Thrace*
May 3, 319 BCE

The *Reliance* turned sharply to port as it left the Bay of Abdera. It was empty of oil and the decks were piled high with wool, soap, and anything else that the locals could come up with. Al Wiley, under pressure from the isolationists in the New American government, declined to use the *Reliance* to transport troops. In compensation—and very quietly—the government of New America did cosign a note to the Queen of the Sea Bank that would almost double Eumenes' drawing account. Commodore Adrian Scott left the bridge and headed to his flag cabin, his mind running over the situation.

Roxane and Eurydice's government would have to pay the money back, but not until after the war. And by then they ought to be able to do so quite handily out of the profits of the various industries that Erica Mirzadeh, Tacaran, Eurydice, Eumenes, and—through Erica—Cleopatra had started. A very conservative estimate was that the production of cloth and most metal goods would double over the next two years. But that was the least of it. Even now trade and production were both up from one end of the Mediterranean to the other.

It wasn't one thing. No magic bullet named "Tech." It was tech, but tech wasn't one thing. It was a thousand thousand things, some mechanical like the shape of a hammer, the function of copper wire in carrying electrical current, the interaction of lye and fat. Some social, legal, political, or economic, like representative democracy or fractional reserve banking. And, most of all, it was the interaction.

The introduction of carding machines and spinning wheels, making the production of thread easier and less expensive, and the new automated Jacquard-style looms lowering the cost of making cloth even more, while at the same time fractional reserve banking increasing the money supply drastically. So more people had the money to buy cloth. Most of all, the knowledge that an economy could expand was still just starting to sink in around the Mediterranean. The common perception in the fourth century BCE before The Event was that the world was a diminishing place, with each generation the same as the last or maybe a little worse off. The common perception in the twenty-first century was that the world had gotten better and was going to continue to do so.

Now, slowly and doubtfully, the fourth century BCE was starting to accept at least the possibility of improvement. That there were other ways of getting rich than stealing it from your neighbors. It wasn't the first time that Adrian Scott had thought about that, but now, as he walked slowly across the tug and climbed the stairs to the deck of the barge portion of the *Reliance*, he took the thought a step further. That was the difference between Eumenes and Cassander, Antigonus, or the rest. Eumenes wanted the world to be the way the ship people saw it. Cassander, Antigonus and the rest of Alexander's successors didn't. They had spent too many years wading through too much blood in Alexander's wake to accept that there might be a world where their actions were not justified by grim necessity. What must it be like to wade for a decade through the blood of your victims to carve out an empire, then learn that there was another way?

Adrian reached his flag cabin, a building built onto the deck of the barge portion of the *Reliance*. The New American Marine sergeant at his door saluted, right fist to left chest, and Adrian reminded himself that he needed to regularize salutes and drill and ceremony in general for the Navy and Marines.

**Queen of the Sea, *Mid-Atlantic,*
en route to Alexandria
May 5, 319 BCE**

Calix sat in the Royal Buffet, drinking Carthaginian strawberry wine, and watched Olympias across the room. He wasn't sure whether he was relieved or deeply offended that Olympias had simply failed to recognize him. He was not involved in the investigation into the attempt on Dag Jakobsen's life. He offered, but his offer was declined. It didn't appear he was even a suspect, though, and most people looked at Olympias with deep suspicion.

Then First Officer Navigation Elise Beaulieu came in with her two guards. They were a belowdecks crewman of the ship people and an Indian from Venezuela. And they were all armed. Elise with her famous pistol and the other two with post-Event-made cap-and-ball revolvers. There was a swagger about them. A swagger that Calix noted Beaulieu didn't share. She talked with them casually and waved hello to people in the dining hall as she made her way to the line and selected her meal. It was only a few minutes past dawn and, in spite of his best efforts, Calix's eyes followed her as she collected scrambled eggs, bacon and rolls. Calix noted that while she got her tray and one of her guards did the same, the other waited until they had both reached a table before he went back to the line to get his own tray.

Then Cleopatra came in with the ship person Sean Newton, and Calix hid a grimace. The cult of Cabeiri was not pleased with Olympias, but it was even less pleased with the ship people. They denied the gods. If they were to be believed, didn't even *remember* the gods. There were political reasons to disrupt relations between Roxane and the ship people, but for Calix that was almost beside the point. To have the royal house of Macedonia marry into the ship people was a betrayal of the cult and Cabeiri. And Cabeiri would punish Macedonia and the royal house.

Then things got worse. Cleopatra, with Sean Newton, walked over and sat down with her mother. Olympias spoke cordially to Sean Newton, who responded with apparent cordiality.

☆   ☆   ☆

Sean suppressed a frown. He believed Cleo when she insisted that her mother hadn't tried to murder

Dag. But the things Cleo admitted Olympias had done were enough to make her a war criminal back in the world. They were not going to get back to the world, however. It wasn't going to happen no matter how much he might wish otherwise.

"What is bothering you?" Olympias asked, then gave him a careful look. "You miss that other world, do you not? The world you came from."

Sean felt his mouth fall open and snapped it shut. *How could she know?* He looked at Cleo, and she was looking smug. Her mom might be a mass murderer, but she was not slow-witted. Sean looked back at Olympias. "Got it in one."

The old woman smiled with red-lipsticked lips, and Sean suppressed a shudder. "What did you want to see me about?" he asked.

"I understand that you are advising my daughter in matters financial."

"I guess you could say that," Sean acknowledged.

"I have access to certain funds."

She did too. Over the next fifteen minutes or so, they went over the process to invest Olympias' ill-gotten gains in new businesses. Then Sean and Cleo got up, shook hands, and left. On their way out, they said hello to Elise, and then—for just the briefest moment—Cleo froze.

☆   ☆   ☆

Cleopatra had just turned away from Elise when she saw him. He was looking at her with a sour expression and she wondered. She knew him. She wasn't sure from where, but the Greek man at a corner table was someone she had met before. And he had been looking at her the same way, with disapproval sprinkled with lust. The fragment of memory froze her for a moment, then it was gone.

☆   ☆   ☆

Cleo was moving again and Sean moved with her. But even as he did, he scanned the room, trying to think what might have upset her. The Royal Buffet was around three-quarters empty at this time of the morning, and Sean tried to figure out who had been in Cleo's line of sight when she froze. There were four possibilities, and while trying not to look like it, he took note of them all.

☆   ☆   ☆

Calix noticed Sean Newton looking at him, then noticed the same careful examination of the other people in the room. But he was distracted as one of Elise Beaulieu's guards got up and the small, dark-haired ship person woman said something in English.

☆   ☆   ☆

Sean leaned over and spoke into Cleo's ear as they left the Royal Buffet. "What was it?"

"I'm not sure. It was the Greek with the sideburns and the oiled hair," Cleo said as they walked along the Lido Deck by the swimming pools.

"I saw him. What about him?"

"I'm not sure. He seemed familiar."

"More than familiar, I think. From your reaction."

"What do you mean by that?" Cleo was starting to sound irritated.

"If he had just seemed familiar, you would have gone over and greeted him. Instead, you froze for a moment. It wasn't much," he hastened to reassure her. "Just an instant. I wouldn't have noticed if I hadn't had a hand on your arm. But you froze and covered.

So somewhere in the back of your mind, you saw him as a threat."

"You sound just like my mother," Cleo said, and Sean wasn't at all sure how to take that.

He thought for a moment and asked, "Is it someone associated with your mother?"

"I don't know." Cleo sounded frustrated, which didn't bode well for his prospects of a pleasant day. A happy, relaxed Cleo was a lot of fun. A frustrated Cleo wasn't at all.

So Sean started looking around for a distraction, then suddenly he stopped dead in his tracks. He didn't cover it nearly so well as Cleo had. It took him at least a second or two to recover.

"What?"

"Poison," Sean said, watching her face. Then he said. "Cabeiri?"

"That's it!" Cleo said. "Something to do with the Cabeiri."

Carefully, Sean asked, "Cleo, could he be working with your mom?"

He waited, watching her face, while Cleo thought it through, then said, "No, I don't think so. If she was involved, he'd be dead by now. First, because he failed. And second, because she wouldn't want the loose end out where it might be found."

"I understand, but that's a pretty hard sell to a jury, love. 'My mom didn't do it because she's such a frigging sociopath that if she had, and she had used him for it, she would have already killed him.'"

"I know, but it's true, anyway."

"I think we should talk to Marie Easley."

"Why Marie?"

"Because Daniel Lang will pull him in and start questioning him. Then what happens?"

"They take his fingerprints and compare them."

"Not without arresting him. And he can't arrest him without probable cause. And you vaguely remembering that he was with the Cabeiri at some point in the past is not evidence." Sean considered. "In fact it's almost worse than no evidence because of separation of church and state."

"Okay. But why Marie Easley?"

"Because I want to know who this guy is before we do anything else. If he's a merchant or a student that's one thing. But what if he's someone important?"

"If he were someone important, I would know him," Cleo said. And Sean knew it was true.

"Yes. But I'd still like to talk it over with Marie Easley."

Cleo looked at him and for just a second Sean was sure that she was going to tear into him. But she didn't. Instead her expression went from angry to considering, then she nodded. "All right, Sean. I'll trust your judgment."

Queen of the Sea, *Deck 9, computer room*

Marie repeated the Etruscan word, then turned to Thana, the young Etruscan woman she was working with.

Thana nodded and pointed to the papyrus scroll and made an *oo* sound as in school but just a little bit different. Thana spoke Etruscan, Latin, and Greek. She also read Etruscan and had brought a small library of the history of the Italian peninsula from the Etruscan point of view. A view that described Romulus and Remus as a pair of bandit chiefs who had been raised by a she-wolf only in the sense that their mother was a real bitch.

They were working together to develop an Etruscan lexicon for the translation app. One that would be able to understand spoken or typed Etruscan and translate it into Greek or English.

There was a polite tap and Marie looked up to see Sean Newton and Cleopatra.

"Do you have a moment, Dr. Easley?" Cleopatra asked.

Thana stood up and bowed, then exited quickly. Not quite running. Thana was from a minor noble house located in a small Etruscan city. She was not the sister of Alexander the Great and was acutely aware of the difference in rank.

"Apparently I do now," Marie said, not entirely pleased with the interruption.

"Sorry, Marie," said Sean, "but it is fairly important, though I'm not sure how urgent it is after this long."

Marie turned her chair a bit more so it faced Sean and Cleopatra more directly. "What's this all about?"

They took seats at Marie's table and explained about Cleopatra's almost recognition and Sean's hunch. After she heard it, Marie wasn't at all sure that there was anything there. In fact, she thought it more likely than not that, whoever it was, it was just someone who had a passing resemblance to someone that Cleopatra had met. And even if it was someone she'd met, and someone who had been, or even still was, a member of the cult of Cabeiri, that didn't mean he was the poisoner of Dag Jakobsen and Travis Siegel.

"What do you want me to do about it?"

More vague explanation followed, and Marie was forced to agree that Daniel Lang wasn't the best person for this. Daniel was a cop at his core. A good cop, but mostly a beat cop and administrator, not a detective. But even more importantly, he was a cop and restrained by the rules that cops worked under. If he got evidence, he was going to have to act on it. Whereas, if this was anything more than smoke, they needed to know a lot more before they acted.

"If this is real," Marie said cautiously, "we need to know a great deal more than that he was the one who did it. We need to know *why* he did it." She leaned back in her swivel chair and tapped her finger on the formica table that held the computer. "Sean, are you sure that the person you saw was the person Cleopatra recognized?"

"I think so, yes. There was only one guy with sideburns among the people I could see in the direction Cleo was looking. And we've discussed the rest of how he looked, the oiled, curled hair and so on. Her description matches the guy I saw."

"Fine. Tomorrow you're getting up early and having breakfast in the Royal Buffet. Don't be obvious about it. Don't look for him, but just notice if he shows up."

"And if he does?"

"If he does, wait a few minutes, have some cereal or something, then go to a phone and give me a call."

"And if he doesn't?" Cleopatra asked.

"If he doesn't, Sean is going to become a regular in the Royal Buffet for breakfast until he does show up. Was he with anyone?"

"No. He was alone at the table," Cleopatra said.

"It was the way he was looking at me that caught my attention."

"Do you have a slate or a phone, Sean?" Marie asked.

"Nope. I sold my phone to the ship before we hit Trinidad the first time."

That was disappointing, but not surprising. The *Queen of the Sea* offered three thousand dollars in ship credit for phones in the first months after The Event. By now, the going rate for a cell phone was fifteen thousand dollars ship money.

"Cleopatra?"

Cleopatra shook her head. "I considered one, and on a couple of occasions I have rented one from ship's stores. But with the amount of investing we've been doing, it just never seemed necessary. The ship's wired phones work well enough, and they come with the suite."

"Fine. Go to one of the phones and call me, but make sure it's out of sight of Sideburns. Tell me where he's sitting and I'll come take a look and see if I can get a picture."

Queen of the Sea, *Royal Buffet*
May 8, 319 BCE

Sean Newton rubbed his eyes and yawned. He and Cleo didn't normally get up this early. He looked down at his eggs and toast and wished he had some coffee. He took a swallow of milk and looked up to see Sideburns staring at him. He stared back, and Sideburns looked away. Sean went back to his breakfast and tried not to sneak peeks at Sideburns as he got his meal and passed out of Sean's view. He had another bite of toast, and then stood up and headed for the hall off the Royal Buffet where there was a courtesy phone. On his way he gave a quick glance and saw Sideburns seated at a table behind his.

He dialed Marie's number, which was not her room number anymore. Firstly, because six months ago she'd moved into the captain's suite, and secondly, because the numbers had been reorganized so that unlisted numbers were possible.

The phone rang and a grumpy male voice said, "Yes?"

"Sorry, Captain. I'm trying to reach Doctor Easley."

The phone was passed and an even more grumpy woman's voice said, "Marie Easley."

"He's here, Doctor Easley." Somehow calling her Marie didn't seem appropriate right now. "When you come in through the middle corridor, he'll be at a table three to the left and two behind the one I'm sitting at."

"Give me fifteen minutes."

"I'll give you all the time you want, Doctor. But I can't speak for Sideburns."

Marie grunted and hung up the phone.

Sean set the phone back in its cradle and went back to breakfast. He was not the least bit sleepy anymore. On his way back to his table, he stopped and picked up a serving of sausages and hash browns.

Sean didn't care for hash-browned nut potatoes, but he wanted a reason to have gotten up.

He left the hash browns on the table and finished his eggs, toast, sausage, and milk. He was polishing off his toast when Marie Easley came in and went to the egg station. She ordered eggs over easy and looked around while she waited. She didn't seem to notice

Sideburns, but nodded to Sean. After she got her eggs she came over, sat across from Sean, and asked him about the glass factory near Mount Ida in Lydia.

They talked about the factory that was located where Akçay would be located in the twenty-first century. It was making glass panes now, though one side of them was still rough so they weren't any good for looking through. They worked fine for letting light in, though, so there was an excellent market for them. About halfway through Marie's breakfast, Sean noticed Sideburns walk past. He winked at Marie and she nodded slightly.

Once Sideburns was gone, Sean said, quietly, "Do you recognize him?"

"There is no need to whisper, Sean," Marie said in a normal voice. "And no, I don't recognize him, but he does look familiar. I think he is with one of the delegations."

So it proved. Over the next few days, Marie did a search of the passenger list. Every passenger on the *Queen* had been digitally photographed and a picture ID printed for them. They were dot matrix black and white pictures, printed on locally made rag paper, but having a *Queen of the Sea* ID card was a matter of significant status anywhere on the Mediterranean coast.

Marie Easley was going through the digital photographs, as they had color and were better quality. One thing that hadn't made it back was facial recognition software. The cruise line had it, but it was on the docks back in the world, where people's passports were checked. Marie did a sort by gender, eliminating all the women. That helped, but in the fourth century BCE, most cultures were still very male dominated, so most of the passengers from around the Mediterranean were male, and that was even more true among the Greeks. She also, for the first pass, eliminated all the locals from New America and those from Carthage to Rome, guessing that he was probably Greek. That got the list down to about eight hundred names. The states and satrapies of the Alexandrian Empire were disproportionately represented in the students at the university, as well as in the political delegations and among the merchants.

She had been going through the remaining photos for the last hour, when she saw him. He almost slipped past. In the picture, he had the sideburns but the hair was lank, not oiled and curled. So Marie clicked, glanced, clicked again, then stopped, went back, and examined the picture. Even if the printout would be black and white and pretty grainy, the image on her screen was clear and brightly colored.

Calix, a member of Arrhidaeus' delegation from Antigonus. Arrhidaeus was Antigonus' representative to the *Queen of the Sea*, not to the government, because Arrhidaeus had refused to sign the constitution. That left his diplomatic immunity a bit frayed about the edges, but still there, as a necessary part of the neutrality of the *Queen of the Sea*.

Marie leaned back in her chair and thought, *Well, what do we do now?* If Calix was arrested, or even questioned, things were going to get official very fast. And Arrhidaeus was going to start complaining that it was all a smear against Antigonus and the *Queen's* neutrality was a sham.

214–216 12th Street, Fort Plymouth, Trinidad
May 8, 319 BCE

Carthalo lifted the pen and dipped it into the small bottle of ink. It was a glass bottle that he made, with considerably greater ease than he was having forming letters on the paper sheets. Blowing glass was a new skill, but not hard to learn if you had spent your life working with the stuff. Touching the metal tip to the side of the ink pot, he drained off the excess ink and carefully drew what he thought was a lower case b.

"No, that's a d. The b has the line on the other side of the circle," Stella said. "B is for butt, and the line is behind the b."

He looked and she was right. Learning to read and write was hard enough. Learning to do it in English was much worse. But he was convinced that he needed the skill in this new world. Wikipedia was in English, so was the daily paper.

He needed to learn how to make better lenses for glasses and for telescopes, microscopes, and other devices. He needed to be able to discuss copper, bronze and steel wire with the craftsmen who made them and shaped them so that he could buy glass frames. And just so he could talk to people. People from Rome, Etrusca, Athens, Macedonia, and Thrace, as well as the tribes and nations along the coasts and rivers of Venezuela. Here in Fort Plymouth, it seemed that everyone was learning ship people English.

By now there was a largeish contingent from Carthage here in Fort Plymouth. Iron makers, cloth makers, spinners, all sorts of people.

There was a slap on the front door and Stella got

up to see who it was. She came back a few moments later with the morning paper. She read him the headlines as he carefully drew the c, then the d, the e, and the f.

"The Carthaginians have elected a new pair of *shophetim* for the year. What's a *shophetim*?"

"They...they're sort of like judges and presidents rolled into one, but there are two of them elected each year. And if they can't agree, it goes...Never mind. It's a stupid system and I never got a vote anyway, being a slave."

"Gotcha." She read on. "The election of the new *shophetim* was delayed by almost six months as the wrangling over the new developments in Alexander's empire and Formentera Island seriously disrupted Carthage's political balance."

Carthalo snorted. Then cursed as his pen slipped and ruined his e.

Stella kept reading. "The investigation into the death of Travis Siegel is ongoing, but there are no new developments of note, and Congresswoman Comfort is asking why."

CHAPTER 15

MELEES

**Queen of the Sea, *Cleopatra's* suite
May 9, 319 BCE**

Marie Easley was brought in by Makis, one of Cleopatra's personal guards. Even on the *Queen*, people of Cleopatra's rank had to have guards as a matter of status. Makis was, in fact, Cleopatra's personal assistant and was one of her top advisers when she had been the queen regent of Epirus. He saw that Marie was seated in the lounge and went to fetch Cleopatra.

Marie had checked out a slate from stores. It was easy for her because she was both the captain's paramour and because of her status as expert on local custom.

Cleopatra came in. "Sean is in the drafting office." The drafting office of the *Queen of the Sea* was a room near the front of Deck 5 inboard. It had been three staterooms. Now it was converted into a drafting shop that had five old-fashioned drafting tables and a plotter hooked up to the computer system, all built onboard ship since The Event, and all busy twenty-four hours a day, seven days a week, with a long waiting list for their use.

"That's fine. We don't need him for this." Marie held up the slate as Cleopatra came over.

Cleopatra looked at the picture and read the name. "I remember now. He was an acolyte among the Cabeiri. He was a bit younger than me, and I was only seventeen at the time. He didn't have the side-burns, just little wisps of beard, but he looked at me with that same mix of lust and resentment that struck me when I saw him the other day. He...what's the phrase...'gave me the billys' even then."

Marie grinned. "You mean 'the willies'?"

Cleopatra shrugged. "Whatever. But now I under-stand why my mother didn't recognize him. She was high priestess and he was a minor acolyte from a middling family, barely a member of the nobility. She would have seen him as little more than a slave. Not seen him as a person at all."

"Another thing for him to resent," Marie offered.

"No," Cleopatra disagreed, taking a seat at the table. "At least not then. The way Olympias treated him was the way she was supposed to treat him. He only resented me because he wanted me and couldn't have me, not because of anything I did or didn't do."

Marie shook her head, not in negation, just to try and clear it. She knew that Cleopatra was right, intellectually. But emotionally accepting it was a com-pletely different matter. The mindset that accepted being treated as a thing was just too different from anything she had ever dealt with before The Event. "Do you think he could be our murderer?"

"If he stayed with the Cabeiri, he would certainly have the ability," Cleopatra said, rubbing her temple with her right hand. "But why would he?"

"That's the question, isn't it? But that assumes that he actually did it. I think we need to try to confirm that part."

"Yes, surely. In the meantime, though, just for my own peace of mind—" Cleopatra turned and called, in a clear but not overly loud voice, "Makis, would you come in, please."

Cleopatra had been taking lessons from Sean in ship people etiquette, Marie noted, and was doing quite well at it.

Once Makis came in, Cleopatra showed him the slate and read him the entry. "Find out what you can about him. Without letting him know anyone is asking."

"Of course, Your Highness." The word he used was Greek and fell somewhere between highness and majesty. It was the appropriate title for the queen regent of Epirus.

Once he left, Cleopatra turned back to Marie and asked, "How do we prove whether he did it or not?"

"Fingerprints," Marie said. "Leave that to me. Assuming that he's the person we're looking for, though, what does that mean? Do you think Arrhidaeus is giving him his orders, or is he doing it on his own?"

"I don't know. It could be Arrhidaeus, but he would be after Eurydice more than Roxane. After all, it was Eurydice who stole his army from him, not Roxane. For that matter, even for Antigonus, Eurydice is more of a threat than Roxane. She was the queen Antigonus had giving out those proclamations, and she is the one who ran away from him to the *Queen*, then revoked just about every proclamation she made while he had her."

"Not necessarily. If Roxane is killed, Eurydice becomes the only queen. And Antigonus has a much better chance of getting his hands on Eurydice than he does of getting them on Roxane."

Cleopatra nodded. "True, but the cocoamat wasn't for Roxane, and it certainly wasn't for my nephew. Dag drank some, but it was primarily for Travis. Why would Calix want Travis dead?"

"The steelworks?" Marie asked. The steelworks started with surprisingly good iron bought mostly from Carthage, where they had been making iron for centuries, using additives that were lost until the invention of the Bessemer process.

"You would know more than I would."

"I'm not sure. Travis was an architect before The Event, but he had taken classes in structural engineering and metallurgy in his training. He remembered the basic percentages and he knew how to judge and test. He was the best person for his job, but not the only person. Jennifer Stables took over for him and has been doing a fine job. I don't think we lost more than a load or two, if that."

"Could it have been personal?"

Could Jennifer Stables have ordered the hit? Jennifer was a potter before The Event. She had less knowledge of the formula of metals, but more of heating stuff. And she had been picking stuff up from Travis until the day he died. They hadn't gotten along very well. Travis was an "old-school Neanderthal," and Jennifer was an "artsy-fartsy liberal."

"No," Marie finally said. "Not Jennifer Stables. She

doesn't have the temperament for something like that."
And it was true. Marie could see Jennifer following
Gandhi or Martin Luther King, Jr., but shooting
someone or having them poisoned didn't fit.

"Perhaps someone else who disliked Travis or saw
some advantage in his death?"

"Not from what Daniel Lang has said. Travis could
be irritable and irritating, but he didn't have any serious enemies that Daniel could find."

"That seems to bring us back to Dag, but again I
don't understand the advantage," said Cleopatra.

"That's the problem," Marie said. "And the reason
I don't want to go through Daniel Lang for this. For
one thing, it's entirely possible that your mother is
the target."

"My mother?"

"Yes. She has a reputation that has lasted for a couple
of eons. If someone is poisoned, Olympias is the logical
suspect in the mind of everyone from Babylon to New
America. Assume for a moment that we operated the
way, say, your father operated. A woman with Olympias'
reputation comes into Philip's capital and suddenly
someone is poisoned. What would Philip do?"

"Have her killed, probably. Unless she was politi-
cally powerful. Even then, he would have her exiled."
Cleopatra nodded. "I see what you mean. But what
would what's his name... Calix gain?"

"I don't know. What's your mother's relationship
with the Cabeiri these days? For that matter, what
is Calix's? Who would we contact to get information
from the Cabeiri?"

"Thessalonike?"

"That doesn't sound like a good idea," Marie said.

"Why not?"

"She's married to Cassander!"

"So what? Thessalonike was raised by my mother, protected by my mother. She's not in love with Cassander. It's a practical, pragmatic relationship. And she's clever, even if she is a sociopath."

Marie lifted an eyebrow.

"I've heard my mother called that. And Alexander. And my father. Everyone in the family but my brother Philip. So I looked it up."

Marie nodded. "Can we trust her?"

"Of course not. But we can use her."

Marie looked at Cleopatra and noted the complete lack of anything resembling conscience in that last statement. Cleopatra didn't regret that she couldn't trust Thessalonike. She didn't feel guilty about using a young woman who was, in effect, her adoptive sister. Marie noted—for far from the first time—that Cleopatra was as cold and calculating as any of the rest of them. *It's a crying shame.*

Pella, radio station
May 9, 319 BCE

Malcolm Tanada yawned, took a sip of the watered retsina, and grimaced. He looked around the radio room. There was a hand-carved wooden desk specially built to protect the laptop computer with a built-in run for the charging cable. New, actual glass, windows let in light without letting in rain.

He shifted his shoulders and went back to the Wiki article on water purification to see if he had missed something. They couldn't produce the membranes that were used to filter water in the twenty-first century, nor the clear glass and UV lights to disinfect water that way, but chlorine was poison, and in too large a dose it could kill you just as dead as the diseases that it stopped. The computer pinged an incoming packet.

He called it up. It was a private message from Cleopatra to Thessalonike. He used the touchpad to drag the file to the printer without looking at it.

When the message printed, he folded it up and looked at the clock on the computer screen. It was synced with the clock on the *Queen* and it read 10:15 P.M. local time.

In an age before electric lights, that was well after just about everyone's bedtime. The letter would wait for tomorrow.

May 10, 319 BCE

Thessalonike took the letter from her servant, opened it, and began to read. Then she took the letter to a small lamp and held it over the flame as she thought. Once it was lit, she dropped it on a brass tray and let it burn. She did have connections with the Cabeiri, but the organization wasn't strong here. Not since her father Philip II's death. Alexander hadn't been a member and hadn't wanted to be. She went to her table and started writing her own letter in code. The Mysteries were not for everyone. Certainly not for Cassander. She would ask about Calix and Olympias, but she would not decide what to do with the information until she got it. And that was going to take some weeks. Her courier would have to find the mistress, the high priestess of the Cabeiri cult in Macedonia.

Having done that, she put on the new gown made of white linen and went to see Aella, the wife of Ennis, who commanded over two hundred cavalry.

☆   ☆   ☆

Aella bowed, but not like she really meant it, Thessalonike noted. Thessalonike didn't make an issue of it. She needed Aella, and Cassander needed Ennis' horses. Instead, she waved Aella to a chair and had servants bring the new distilled drink called ouzo. It was a product of a distillery that Malcolm Tanada had introduced.

"The ship people have such wonders," Thessalonike conceded as the slave poured. "But they have such strange ideas. Ideas that threaten the very fabric of our world. Worse even than Alexander's putting upstarts like Eumenes in command of Macedonian nobles."

Aella nodded and her eyes shifted to the slave girl who was pouring the wine. By now it was common knowledge that the ship people opposed slavery, but still Aella didn't appear to want to speak of it in front of the slave, in case she was the only slave in Pella who didn't already know. Or, as if Aella felt that if she didn't say it in front of a slave, it wouldn't be real.

Thessalonike waved the girl away, and said, "Yes, their views on slavery are a horror, but those views are really just the point of a long and heavy sword that if not blocked will rip society asunder. They are even more fanatical democrats than the mob at Athens."

"They want to make us all into peasants," Aella said, almost hissing. "They think I am the same as that two-footed animal."

The word she used was one of several that the ship people translated into slave, and Thessalonike felt herself in agreement with Aella's outrage and, at the same time, with the ship people's imagined judgment of Aella. But none of that showed on her face as she nodded in sympathy with the older woman. That, after all, was the essence of politics. "That is why we must defeat Eumenes. Having him, Alexander's half-blooded son, or the idiot Philip on the throne would be bad enough. But following behind Eumenes comes the ship people, their constitution, and letting the mob dictate laws to the nobility of Macedonia."

"What is the military situation?"

"Eumenes is held up in Abdera, but our spies tell us he is buying ships, bringing them to Abdera, and having their sails refitted and rerigged. He is creating a massive flotilla and he has the walls of Abdera positively festooned with the ship people weapons. The ones they call cannons."

Abdera, Eumenes' headquarters
May 12, 319 BCE

The walls were not festooned with cannon. As Eumenes looked out, he could see only six real cannons. There were a dozen more that looked like cannons but were made of wood. They, like the six real ones, had come off the *Reliance*, along with the gun powder, the new cloth, and plate armor, the canned fruits, and the beans. Abdera was well supplied for now and it was likely to remain so. Eumenes controlled the Bosphorus and he had effective control of the Sea of Marmara. No one controlled the Aegean Sea, but it would be exceedingly difficult for Cassander to move an army across it to hit Lydia.

Morale was surprisingly good, in spite of the lack of action. Eumenes looked over to the parade ground where Eurydice and Philip were inspecting the troops. Increasingly, Philip was out and about where the army could see him. He still didn't look at people, but he examined a soldier's appearance out of the corner of his eye and missed very little. From frayed cloak to worn sandals, he noticed. Then he would murmur to Eurydice, and Eurydice would see to getting the problem fixed. It showed the troops that Eurydice and Philip cared. There was a knock, and as Eumenes turned to look, a guard brought in Tacaran.

"Yes?"

Tacaran didn't bow. The two ship people—and, increasingly, their local aides—didn't bow. One local assistant had assumed that if he didn't have to bow to people of higher rank, commoners had to bow to him. He no longer worked for the ship people, and the lesson hadn't been lost on their other local assistants. It hadn't been lost on Eumenes or Eurydice either, because Philip had pointed out its implications with pedantic insistence. Eumenes felt his lips twitch in an almost smile at that memory.

"*Strategos*, I got an email from a friend of mine on Malcolm Tanada's staff," Tacaran said, without waiting to be asked. "Seems he's friendly with a slave in Thessalonike's quarters. And..." Tacaran looked at the guard, then sent Eumenes a questioning look.

"Saburo is," Eumenes paused, then said in Ship People, "okay."

Tacaran shrugged and continued. "Anyway, Rico Gica is a friend from before The Event and one of those guys who couldn't get laid without endowing a whorehouse. But the change in our circumstances has produced at least a limited change in his attractiveness. One of Thessalonike's slaves made a pretty big play for him and he went for it."

Eumenes gestured for Tacaran to get on with it.

"It matters, *Strategos*. At least I think it may matter. We all figured that she had been ordered to seduce him, and Rico thought we were probably right, but didn't care. He talked to his girl all the time, learning Greek in the process and teaching her English and...Never mind. The thing is, Thessalonike got a letter from Cleopatra—"

"Cleopatra is Thessalonike's half sister."

"I know, and she gets letters from Cleopatra every week or so. Mostly instructions on how to do ship people stuff. The thing is, she keeps those messages, all of them, in a special chest. This message she read and burned immediately.

"Rico's girlfriend saw her do it."

Eumenes had been standing by the window while Tacaran spoke. Now he walked over to his desk. It was a new desk, built right here in Abdera to ship people designs. It had drawers and cabinets and a chair on little wooden wheels. Eumenes sat in the chair and waved Tacaran to another. "What do you think it means?"

"It could mean that Rico's slave girl is switching to his side, but I think it means that Thessalonike wanted you to know about the message and the fact that she burned it."

"Either way, it means the message is important," Eumenes said. "Thank you, Tacaran. I will send a message to Cleopatra and find out what I can."

"I'd consider it a personal favor if you tried to keep Rico and his girlfriend out of it. He's not actually a bad guy. Just sort of clumsy in the way he deals with women."

"I'll do what I can."

After Tacaran had left, Eumenes sent Cleopatra a carefully worded message and went back to work. The latest reports from Babylon were in his inbox and he started to read.

Sixty miles north of Babylon
May 12, 319 BCE

Pharnabazus drank from the plastic cup. It was a gift from Eumenes and Eurydice. Then he looked at it. It had small animals drawn on it in bright colors and an unrealistic style, and it had a lid that you could take off to clean it, but you could drink through. It was, according to Eurydice, a sippy cup, because you sipped from the little hole on one end of the top. In Pharnabazus' opinion, it was the perfect thing for drinking beer while on horseback. Having had his drink, he tucked his sippy cup back in his saddlebag and rode on. They were two miles from the Euphrates and his scouts had just spotted the dust raised by a cavalry troop.

They rode on, and five minutes later he could see the dust, just as he was sure the other cavalry contingent could see his. A scout rode up. "They are Antigonus' men, General. Two companies, from what I saw. Perhaps a hundred sixty riders. No camp followers and no infantry."

"In other words, another scouting party just like ours," Pharnabazus said. Then he considered. He only had about a hundred men, and not-quite-two-to-one odds weren't good odds. Half his men were lancers with the new saddles and heavier lances held under one arm. The other half were bowmen who would fight from the chariots by pulling up their horse, then firing from the chariots. On the other hand, the new solid-treed saddles, and the heavier lances that they made possible, should mean that his charge would be more effective. His bowmen would be firing from the light chariots, so had longer bows. Which, again, should make them more effective. "How were the enemy equipped?"

"I wasn't close enough to tell, but they didn't have the long lances. And I didn't see any chariots."

That was something then. Pharnabazus looked back at the two-wheeled carts that most of his horsemen pulled behind their mounts. "How far?"

"Two miles, General."

Pharnabazus raised a hand and turned to the column. "Lancers, mount up. Get out of those chariots, you lazy bastards! You're cavalry again. And armor the horses."

The men got out of the chariots and moved forward to the horses, then removed the long reins that the chariots required and flung the hardened leather armor over their horses' necks, tied it in place, and then mounted, using their stirrups, and helped each other with their lances. It took a few minutes, but if the horses complained about the extra weight on their backs, they were still basically fresh. Well fed and watered, and they hadn't been carrying the grain, water, and armor for the morning's ride.

"Move out." The column continued, still pulling the chariots.

The chariots were a mix of ancient Egyptian and ship people devices. They used ship people knowledge to improve a chariot design that the Egyptians and Babylonians already had, and converted it to carry supplies rather than as a battle platform.

They rode on toward the enemy. Five minutes later, topping a hill, Pharnabazus saw the enemy. The scout's estimate was a little off. Pharnabazus didn't think there were more than a hundred fifty fighting men in the enemy column. The difference was pack horses.

Pharnabazus smiled. This was working out better than he'd expected. "Form lines!" he shouted.

The riders fanned out in an orderly manner, as they had been trained to do. Less than a minute later, they were no longer a column of twos, fifty horses long. They were a double line, fifty horses wide, with the lancers in front and the bowmen behind, sitting on the crest of the hill.

"Lancers, drop chariots."

Fifty men pulled the lanyards that held the chariots to the saddle rigs that the horses wore. The traces dropped to the ground as the pins holding them in place were removed and there was a general neighing and stamping of hooves. The horses knew the routine by now.

"At the walk," Pharnabazus shouted, and the lines started down the hill, the bowmen maneuvering their chariots around the dropped chariots of the lancers. Looking down the hill, Pharnabazus smiled.

☆　　☆　　☆

Udom the Lucky, commander of one twenty-eight and the son of a prominent noble in Philip II's court, watched the events on the top of the hill in consternation that had almost the flavor of panic. That was impossible. All those men, the next best thing to a merchant caravan, pulling their little carts along behind them.

Then, in an instant, half the carts were left behind and the wagoneers became cavalry. An arrant thought jibbered in Udom's mind. *This had to be Eumenes, the carter's son. Who else would think of turning carters into cavalry?*

He sat his horse, watching the carters riding down on his column with those long, heavy lances that Rafal told him about. He should have believed Rafal, and not called him a sniveling little coward.

Vaguely, through the shock, he heard his sergeant shouting at him. "Sir, we need to form the men!"

Suddenly the shock was gone, and Udom the Lucky started shouting orders. "Form ranks! Bowmen to the rear and prepare to fire!"

He was supposed to have sixty-four bowmen and sixty-four lancers. In fact, he had fifty-three bowmen and sixty-two lancers. His men had the ship people–style stirrups and solid-treed saddles, but they still used the standard *xyston*, a long cavalry spear with a spear point on each end. *Xyston* were held in the middle and were not the heavy wooden poles, almost as long as a *sarissa*, he saw across the field. The enemy were riding down the hill and one of them rode a little ahead, riding back and forth, yelling at them to dress their ranks as though Udom and his men didn't matter at all. Then Udom recognized him. "That's Pharnabazus!" Udom shouted, pointing with his spear.

☆　　　☆　　　☆

Pharnabazus glanced over when he heard his name. He looked across the field. It was perhaps a hundred yards. Then, caught by an impulse, he turned his mount and dipped his lance. "That's right! I'm Pharnabazus!" He looked at the Greek officer in bronze breastplate embossed with nipples and abdominal muscles. He shouted, "Who are you? Your family will want to know how you died."

The overdressed Macedonian didn't answer. Instead, he shouted for his archers to shoot.

There was a flight of arrows. Not a rain of arrows. Barely a drizzle. Shields came up and were struck. The leather armor on the horses stopped, or at least slowed more, but a few got through to wound horse or man. Three hit Pharnabazus and one his horse, but they were all stopped by the armor and shield.

Pharnabazus was faced with a dilemma. He really should get back with the troops. Being out here all by himself was an invitation to concentrated attack. A fact amply demonstrated by the fact that three arrows hit him and a half dozen more hit around him while he had more men than the enemy had bows. On the other side of the scale, it wouldn't do his commander's dignity any good at all to go scurrying back to his lines like a frightened doe.

He compromised by turning and riding back in a sedate manner. The next flight of arrows proved that his decision wasn't the best of all possible decisions. It seemed every bowman the enemy had was targeting him. Most of those arrows arrived where he'd been when they were launched, a few yards behind him. But one hit Thunderbolt, his horse, in the flank. It was a glancing blow, cutting down the side and leaving a gash, and Thunderbolt made his displeasure plain by rearing and trying to bolt. So much for his commander's dignity. He did get the horse under control, but it meant he missed the final seconds of the charge and was clear of the melee.

Pharnabazus had just gotten Thunderbolt back under control when his men hit the enemy's front rank. In a way, the fact that so many of the arrows were aimed at him helped his men. Not a single one of his lancers fell to enemy arrows. They hit the enemy lancers in formation, lances extended, and for the most part ran right over them. Four of his men went down when their lances went wide and they were unable to avoid or shield from the enemy's counterblow, but it had to be twenty of the enemy lancers who went down in that first charge. At least twenty, and that left the enemy drastically outnumbered in the melee.

It was then that Pharnabazus, observing from a little up the hill, saw the drawback to the heavy ship people-designed lances. They were great for the initial charge, then effectively useless. "Drop your lances, you morons!" Pharnabazus shouted. "Use sword and ax."

Some did and some didn't. Some were already dropping their lances before Pharnabazus told them to. Some never had the chance. Then Pharnabazus saw the overdressed Macedonian again.

Pharnabazus still had his lance, and room to use it. He charged.

☆   ☆   ☆

Udom the Lucky wasn't all that lucky. He almost never won at dice or cards. But he was experienced and was very good at keeping track of what was going on around him, even in battle. He heard the horse charging from an unexpected direction, and his brain picked out the sound through the sounds of melee all around him. He turned his head in time to see Pharnabazus charging down on him. He kicked his horse, who lunged forward, trying to get out of the path of that lance. The lance followed, and Udom twisted in his saddle in a desperate attempt to interpose his shield. By now he knew that his *xyston* was useless against that monster.

He made it too. Got twisted around, got his shield up... and got knocked right off his horse anyway.

Udom hit the ground hard about fifteen feet from where he had left the saddle of his horse, after bouncing off one of his men and almost knocking him over. He was not aware of any of it clearly. The world had become a blurry mass of confusion and pain. He shook his head and saw stars. But even through that, his awareness reached out to try and warn him. He heard the hooves hitting the ground, coming right for him. He managed to turn his head and saw the horse.

But he couldn't move. Not even when the big black horse with Pharnabazus on its back rode over him and crushed his expensive bronze breastplate into his chest, breaking his sternum and driving shards of rib into his heart and lungs. Then Udom was aware of nothing at all.

☆   ☆   ☆

Pharnabazus saw the Macedonian kick his horse and shifted his aim. He was shocked when the Macedonian managed to get his shield around in time. He felt the jolt of impact in his bones. His lance shattered even as it threw the Macedonian off his horse. Pharnabazus dropped the remnants of his lance, spun Thunderbolt, and drew his sword.

There was one of his men in a melee with two

of the enemy and still trying to hold onto his lance. Pharnabazus shouted, "Drop your lance, Conon!"

He rode for them, not even aware of the Macedonian noble that Thunderbolt trampled in passing. Then he swung his sword and hit one of the enemies while Conon blocked the other's ax strike with his shield.

"Drop your lance, I say!" Pharnabazus repeated. "Draw your sword, you idiot!"

"How am I supposed to do that when people are whacking at me?" Conon complained. But he did finally drop the lance. At which point, another enemy attacked and Conon was busy with his shield again, even as he tried unsuccessfully to get his sword out of his scabbard.

Pharnabazus looked around. They were winning. The initial attack more than evened the odds and most of the melee had been two or more of Pharnabazus' men on one enemy. At that point, the enemy had very little chance. Even as he looked around, Antigonus' force broke and the remnants rode away. When the lancers broke, the archers turned and rode away with them while Pharnabazus' chariot-based archers rained arrows on them.

Two hours later

The sun was lowering in the afternoon sky and the dead were laid out in rows. Out of a hundred men, Pharnabazus had lost three, with five more wounded in the melee. The enemy had lost twenty-three, eighteen lancers and five horse archers. It was about as one-sided a battle as Pharnabazus had ever seen in a lifetime as a soldier. It was more one-sided than Alexander's victory over Darius III at Gaugamela, though much smaller, of course.

"We need a fast way of switching weapons after the initial charge, General," said Conon. "It wasn't that I didn't think about dropping the cursed lance. It was just that there was no time to switch weapons and the lance was better than nothing."

"No, Conon. You're wrong. Not about needing a quick way to change weapons. I agree about that. But once you were in the fight proper, the lance was worse than nothing. Certainly worse than a few moments of nothing while you switched weapons."

Other members of the scouting party came forward to discuss what had gone right or wrong with the battle. Much more had gone right than wrong, but half the purpose of this patrol was to discover the effectiveness of the chariots and the new saddles and lances. The chariots especially, because they were the invention of one of Attalus' cavalrymen in conjunction with Karrel Agot, who had come up with the cotter pins for detaching the chariots, and the wire-spoked wheels. Pharnabazus would have to thank Karrel Agot the next time he saw him.

The bronze strip-twist wire was made by hand by a group of craftsmen in Babylon. Craftsmen who had been making wire for decades. The only thing new was using it in wheels.

CHAPTER 16

CONSUMMATION

Babylon, west side
May 15, 319 BCE

Karrel Agot wiped his forehead with both hands and closed his eyes for a moment. There was very little breeze even though all the windows in the third-floor room were open. The oil lamps were barely enough light to work by. He leaned back over the table, positioned the ruler, and used the pressed-charcoal stick to draw a line. The west side of Babylon now had windmills on the roofs of several buildings along the Euphrates River. Those windmills lifted water from the Euphrates up to water tanks atop the buildings and then used the height of those tanks to provide water pressure all over the west side.

Well, not *all* over the west side. Here and there around the west side, where the people could afford it.

But the process was making the whole hanging gardens thing much easier to manage, and even allowed the occasional flush toilet. Of course, those toilets emptied right back into the Euphrates. Which made the situation no different than it had been before they got here. But Susan had a bee in her bonnet about it.

It wasn't that Karrel disagreed. He just had way too much to do. It wasn't fair to call Susan a woolly-headed intellectual, but it was certainly true that she had a great deal less experience with mechanics and hydraulics than he had. She also didn't know much about fortifications. And the most recent word Karrel had from his sources in East Babylon was that Antigonus was bringing up more forces. The time Karrel spent designing the sewer system that Susan insisted upon was time he couldn't be spending on improving the fortifications on this side of the river. It was all very well to protect them from disease, but if Antigonus' troops took the west side, they were going to die anyway.

Babylon, east side

The courier gave Antigonus the message from Atropates, the satrap of Media. It was flowery and full of praise, but offered no armies. His excuse was rebellion in his satrapy, fomented by the knowledge the ship people brought. Antigonus knew the real reason. That reason was Babylon. He was pinned here by that idiot Attalus and unable to attack Eumenes. That made him look weak to the eastern satraps.

Antigonus crushed the letter in his hand. He was angry, but not truly surprised. Nicanor of Parthia was sending an army of two thousand. A pittance, but better than nothing. Asander retreated from his satrapy of Caria with his personal retinue, but no great force. Tlepolemus of Carmania was trying to stay out of it, like Atropates—praise, but no aid. Sibyrtius, satrap of Arachosia, was sending troops, but the distance was great. Stasanor of Sogdiana was sending an army, but again, the distance was great.

Stasanor had read the ship people records of what he had gotten in Triparadisus and was angry with Eumenes that he hadn't gotten the promotion in this history. That was unfair to Eumenes, who had nothing to do with the decision.

Antigenes, the commander of the Silver Shields, was nominally the satrap of Susiana, but he hadn't been there since the mess at Triparadisus. Antigonus himself was effectively the satrap of Susiana, but Susiana was not going to provide troops either. Antigonus' control there was not strong and the satrapy was a drain on his manpower because of the garrisons he had to keep there.

Leonnatus came in. "The windmill is up on the Bactor Tower."

The Bactor Tower was a three-story building next to the Euphrates and the windmill placed atop the stone building was another five stories tall. It had five long fan blades and would lift a great deal of water up to a water tank. It wasn't only Attalus who was improving the city of Babylon. By agreement, Antigonus had access to the radio in West Babylon and the Wiki, which to Antigonus seemed like an oracle, if more pragmatic in the information it provided. That access was part of the ship people attempt to seem neutral in the war between him and Eumenes. So, like Attalus, he got information from the ship people on subjects like sanitation and windmills. That information was making Babylon over, even as the city remained divided.

The windmill and water tank on the Bactor Tower

performed two functions. One was as a water supply, but the other was as power storage. What the ship people called potential energy. The windmill pumped the water up to the tank, where it stayed till needed. Then a pipe took the water down to a generator that was almost entirely made right here in Babylon. The copper wire was made here, the coils were wound here, and the brushes were made here as well. They weren't the graphite brushes that the Wiki article talked about, but the earlier brushes that were actual wire brushes made of many short copper wires bound together.

Antigonus was not willing to have his access to the ship people and the Wiki flow through West Babylon. He would have a radio of his own.

"What about the tubes for my radio?" Antigonus asked.

"The *Queen* reports that they have been dropped off in Alexandria and any delays at this point are Ptolemy's doing, not the ship people's," Leonnatus said with some bitterness.

"What does Ptolemy say?"

"That they are in a warehouse in Alexandria and he will arrange for their transport in exchange for oil."

Antigonus nodded. "Give him his cursed oil. We have the wells working near the Gulf. At least some."

Leonnatus was not a great commander, but he had proven quite adept at understanding the ship people devices and techniques. That made keeping him around worthwhile, because the ship people's way of doing things was changing the world, and doing it much faster than Antigonus would prefer. "What about the powder mill?" Antigonus asked.

The formula and techniques for making what the

ship people called black powder was all over the
empire by now. And after what Eumenes had done
with rockets at the Bosphorus, Antigonus no longer
doubted their effect on war.

"I still say we should move it out of the city. One
spark and we could lose a city block," Leonnatus said.

"Then make sure there are no sparks," Antigonus
said. "You know that if we put it outside the city,
Attalus will send a raiding party to destroy the works."

"So put it farther east, in Media or Susiana."

"Stick to your toys, Leonnatus," Antigonus said.
"Leave strategy to those of us who understand it."

"Yes, Satrap," Leonnatus said sullenly.

☆　　☆　　☆

For the next two months, Leonnatus played with
his toys while news flashed around the world on radio
waves. While the *Queen of the Sea* made two trips
to the Mediterranean and another trip to Saint Helena, Madagascar and the east coast of Africa up to
Dioscorides, and Eumenes and Eurydice and Philip
arranged for a small fleet of sailing ships.

Abdera docks
July 18, 319 BCE

Philip III of Macedon, co-king with his nephew
Alexander IV of the United Satrapies and States of the
Empire, stood on the deck of the *Argos* and thought.
He paid no attention to the waves slapping gently
against the sides of the ship or the smell of the sea.

He had duties. And now he was almost able to
perform them. He could stand to be touched, at
least some, and he was functional. In a way, it was

less of a trauma for Philip than it would have been for a ship person. Victorian morality wasn't existent at all in this century. It was simply that until the ship people had come, he was unable to be touched without going into hysterics. That was different now, with the use of the squeeze box and the marijuana water pipe that he smoked to decrease the tension. The marijuana made the world vague, and he didn't like that part. But it held the panic at bay, as well.

He looked down the dock and watched the sailors and soldiers loading the ships. They would be leaving soon, to go to Amphipolis, or perhaps all the way to Therma, only a short distance from Pella. Eurydice was pushing for the Therma option because Eurydice was addicted to risk. She was brave in everything, and sometimes too brave. Convinced that she would win, no matter what the odds. It made people want to follow her. Alexander had had the same thing, and more of it. Eumenes didn't have that, but in Philip's judgment, he was the more intelligent planner. And that implied that Amphipolis was the better plan.

But Philip couldn't see how it was a better plan. Philip was very good with numbers and he remembered what he read. Everything he read. But the interactions of people didn't make sense to him and he knew that. It seemed to him that going to Amphipolis would put their army between Cassander to the west and Lysimachus to the east. He was sure that Eumenes saw that, but Eumenes wanted to do it that way anyway. And Philip couldn't understand why.

☆　　☆　　☆

Eumenes laid the letter from Paul Howard on his desk. Paul was a ship person living in Trinidad. The letter was a discussion of *The Tactics of Mistake*, a book by an author named Dickson. The book itself hadn't made the trip through time, but Mr. Howard was a science fiction fan and a true bibliophile with a phenomenal memory. The basic idea of the book had come to this time in the brain of Paul Howard and a single Wiki article. It was something that Alexander had done almost by instinct, and Eumenes had done sometimes with intent, and sometimes by accident. What you did was give the enemy a tempting target, make it look like you had slipped up, so they would rush in to take advantage. Then, when they left themselves exposed by their attack, you counterattack.

He looked at the map on the wall. It covered the northern Aegean Sea and surrounding territories from the Bosphorus in the east to the edge of the Adriatic Sea in the west. It was from the ship people charts and colored in by hand, and it took up most of the wall. It was backed by cork and had little steel pins with painted wood tops stuck into it, to indicate troop concentrations and the locations of important people. Alexander would have traded his horse for it, Eumenes was almost sure.

The specific mistake he was trying to engineer by his insistence on Amphipolis as their target was to pull Lysimachus out of Thrace so that Seuthes III could retake his state. Tactically, that wouldn't help them that much. They would still have—as Paul put it—"Cassander to the left of them and Lysimachus to the right." They would be just as boxed in in Amphipolis as they were in Abdera.

But that wasn't why he was doing it. They had to be seen as the legitimate government, and they had to be seen as keeping their promises. That meant that having promised Seuthes Thrace, they had to give him Thrace. Get Lysimachus out of Thrace. And Eumenes didn't have a big enough army to force Lysimachus out of Thrace by main force, not without destroying Thrace in the process.

Partly that was because Eumenes was fighting a war on two fronts, here and around Babylon. But in large part it was a function of what might be considered a third front. The resources that were being poured into industrial development, roads, mines, pumps, steam engines, and so on, would pay massive returns in a few years. But right now they were as much a drain on his resources as fielding another army would be. It was only made worse with the knowledge that the ship people disapproved of slavery. The Event—he wouldn't call it a miracle though many did—that brought the ship people to this time, gave the ship people and their views a holy aura in the minds of many. The ships themselves, the *Queen of the Sea* and the *Reliance*, added to that effect. So far, there had been three slave revolts in the empire. And putting them down pulled armies out of the civil war. On the other hand, the same thing had happened in Macedonia, pulling away part of Cassander's army.

Another thing that Paul Howard wrote him about was a doctrine called tactical defense and strategic offense. Eumenes got up and went to the map. Using a measured string, he measured out the distances again. It was almost a ritual by now. How many days would it take Cassander's army to reach Amphipolis? How many to reach Therma?

The door opened and Eurydice came in. "Measuring again? It will take Cassander at least four days and probably six to reach Amphipolis. Therma, he can reach in one if he is lucky, but more probably two.

"I still say two days is enough to fortify Therma well enough to stop Cassander if you insist on waiting for him to attack." She held up a hand as Eumenes looked at her. "Never mind. You are *strategos* and Roxane agrees with you on this. Or at least Dag does, and Roxane listens to Dag."

Eumenes lifted his open hands. "Thanks to Athena. You're going to stop insisting..."

"Not until we are at sea and the captains open their sealed orders, which will bear Philip's seal and all our signatures. If we are going to be tricky, we should be as tricky as possible. Cassander can't move from Pella until he knows where we are going. So, best if he doesn't know until we get there."

Flagship *Argos*, off Amphipolis
July 19, 319 BCE

Eurydice looked at the long shadows that the wall of Amphipolis cast in the evening sun. The sea was shading to a darker blue as well, as the captain of the *Argos* shifted sail and adjusted his rudder. She looked through the binoculars and saw the garrison of Amphipolis. Forming ranks, but they didn't know where to go. The standard method would be to beach the ships near the town and disembark. And it was clear as she watched that the garrison had assumed her fleet would do just that.

By now they realized that wasn't what was happening. They just didn't know why.

☆   ☆   ☆

"We'll slaughter them," Gordias crowed.

Cepheus wasn't so sure. Neither of them had served with Alexander, but Cepheus liked to read. As a boy he'd read the reports on the war in Persia with obsessive interest and he knew that Alexander trusted Eumenes, and Eumenes was usually successful, even if he was a Thracian wagoneer's son. The books the ship people brought back suggested that Eumenes was even smarter than the reports from Persia indicated. That didn't fit with him doing something this stupid. Neither did it fit Cepheus' concept of Eumenes' character. The man was a clerk. He'd been a clerk when he served Philip II and when he served Alexander, and he was still a clerk, all his little numbers lining up. Eumenes would never scale the walls, leaving his bodyguard behind. It wasn't in the man, and neither was storming along a narrow dock against prepared squares of infantry and archers.

"Get to your men, Cepheus. I want those *sarissa* steady when the arrows fly."

Cepheus left. It was Gordias' command.

☆   ☆   ☆

Eurydice no longer needed the binoculars. There were solid blocks of *sarissa*-armed infantry at the end of each of the seven piers. They were small blocks, thirty-two-man squares, four rows deep and eight columns wide. There were similar-sized blocks of archers behind them.

The docks were long, almost three hundred feet from the shore to the ends. Ships were supposed to tie up along their sides. Seven docks gave room for fourteen large ships to dock.

"Drop sail!" shouted the captain, and the winch

was released. The sails came down quickly and the ship slowed, coasting on momentum toward the end of the dock. Then there was a shout from the docks and a flight of arrows was shot at the ship. The infantry put up their shields, and the crew, working under the watchful eyes of armed soldiers, tossed lines to the dock posts and started pulling the ship in. All while under a steady rain of arrows. The bow of the *Argos* reached the end of the dock, then a few feet more, and a gangplank was dropped onto the dock. A picked unit ran down the gangplank and formed a shield wall. Behind them came the rocketmen, carrying their rocket stands and rockets.

Men died, struck by arrows, and their place was taken by the next in line. All in minutes, very few minutes, though to Eurydice watching, it seemed to take hours.

☆   ☆   ☆

Cepheus watched as the soldiers disembarked and formed a shield wall, but a shield wall with no *sarissa*, as though they had no interest at all in advancing. He saw the other troops coming down the gangplanks and doing something behind the shield wall, and was tempted to advance. A shield wall without *sarissa* could never stand against a troop armed with the long spears.

☆   ☆   ☆

Then Dexios, the commander of the rocketeers, waved a small red flag at Eumenes. Eumenes looked around, held up his hand in a signal to wait as he looked across the quays at the other ships that had docked and were unloading rocketeers.

Eurydice looked around. The other commanders of

rocketeers were waving their flags one at a time as
their units got ready. Eumenes waited until the last
of them was ready, then he brought his hand down
like he was chopping a neck.

Nothing was happening. Cepheus looked around
and there, on the next dock over, on the prow of a
ship, stood Eumenes with his arm raised, and two
bodyguards holding shields before him. He wouldn't
even be visible to the archers directly in front of him.
He stood there for what seemed a long time, then he
dropped his arm. Cepheus looked back at the docks
and saw that shield wall open. Not much, just enough
for something to pass through.

The rockets fired.
They didn't fire at the bowmen. They fired directly
at the pikemen blocking the docks. The rockets barely
arched at all, making smoky lines of fire from one
end of the dock to the other, then striking the pike
formations, and a moment later exploding as their
fuses reached the explosive charges.

Cepheus heard the sound. He even saw a rocket
fly by him, only a foot to his left. Then there was a
loud noise. And nothing more.

Then, and only then, did Silver Shields disembark,
check their ranks, and march down the docks to the
shore.

Gordias saw the rockets rip his pikemen to shreds,
and saw the shredded pike squares crumble under

Zeus' own lightning bolts. He stood there in shock as the pikemen, seeing the Silver Shields forming up, turned and ran. It wasn't until one of the pikemen ran by him that he realized that the battle was lost.

He thought about surrendering, but he couldn't surrender to Eumenes. He just couldn't. He thought about charging and dying gallantly on his enemy's *sarissa*, but he couldn't bring himself to do that either.

So he, too, turned and ran.

When Gordias ran, the defenses collapsed. It wasn't a large garrison, or a particularly good one, after all. Amphipolis was a burned-out husk, destroyed by fire and sword in October of 320 BCE. It had half a year to recover, and most of the wreckage was gone, but new building was barely begun.

Inn in Amphipolis, new headquarters of Eumenes' army Three hours later

In an inn near the center of the city, Eumenes looked up at the shadows cast by the setting sun. The fleet had docked, letting off their army. On the morning tide it would sail back to Abdera and pick up more men. Patrols were out and Eumenes had finished a cursory inspection of the walls and fortifications.

He looked over at Philip and Eurydice where they were seated across the room talking. Philip reached out and took Eurydice's hand and her face turned bright red. Eumenes didn't know what that was about, but didn't think it was his business.

He turned back to the table and using a pen made in New America and a bottle of ink, he set out to write

an explanation of his actions to Seuthes. The time for
secrecy was past in regard to Seuthes. Seuthes had to
know, to have time to act on the knowledge before
everyone else realized why they took Amphipolis.
But he still didn't want Cassander and Lysimachus
to realize what he was doing.

☆   ☆   ☆

"I think I can," Philip told Eurydice, not wanting to
promise too much. It was still hard for him to touch
people and even harder to be touched. But he was
getting used to it, and it wasn't fair to Eurydice to
prevent her from having this thing that most people
wanted so much.

Philip wanted it too. Just as he wanted to be hugged
and held, but couldn't stand it when he was. But now
he could stand it. He would spend fifteen minutes in
his hug box and smoke a doobie. Then he would try.

"Thank you, Philip. I know it's not easy for you,"
Eurydice said, squeezing his hand hard. She had
learned that gentle touches were harder for him to
deal with than firm touches.

"I want it too, Eurydice. I just never thought I
could have sex before."

☆   ☆   ☆

Philip woke up and he was next to Eurydice. He
almost panicked. Her arms were around him and she
was holding him, but it was a soft touch that slid
across his skin like a silken trap.

It took a real effort not to jerk away, but he managed
it. Last night had been clumsy, but functional. Slowly,
he pulled away and Eurydice squeezed him, trying to
hold him. That made it a little easier. His body knew
how to deal with being held tight. It relaxed him.

The door opened, and a servant came in, looked at them, and went out. That was a good thing, Philip decided. The servant would spread the word and it would enhance Eurydice's reputation. And his, he guessed, but he didn't care about that part.

Or perhaps he did. He had always been a freak. Philip's damaged son. Alexander's damaged brother. But never a person. Always a thing. This might change that, at least a little. The word would spread.

CHAPTER 17

PLANS AND PROGRESS

Queen of the Sea, *Arabian Sea*
July 20, 319 BCE

Joshua Varner, sitting in the radio room on the *Queen of the Sea*, didn't jerk this time. He was ready for it. Everyone was expecting a report from Erica Mirzadeh. What got him was the lead.

> *Eurydice and Philip have had sex. Don't blame me. Eurydice insisted that I report that. Apparently, it's even more important than the fact that Eumenes took Amphipolis yesterday. Locals are weird.*

In fact, Joshua was pretty sure that Eurydice was entirely correct about the relative importance of the two events. The improvement in Philip III was the talk of the Mediterranean and went a long way toward cementing the ship people's reputation as magi of the highest order. Plus, as Philip got better, it improved the legitimacy claims of the USSE, suggesting that the gods favored it.

That was something that still freaked Joshua out. He had never given it any thought before The Event, but somewhere down in the depths of his soul he'd assumed that before the advent of Christianity, people hadn't been religious. That no one had really believed in Zeus and Apollo, Athena, Bacchus, and the rest. They were just superstitions, cults, not real religions. Like believing in astrology or fortune-tellers, the province of crystal-worshiping nut jobs, not decent, ordinary people. But it wasn't that way. Most of the people on the *Queen*, responsible people, diplomats and scholars, merchants and as close as this century had to scientists, believed in the pantheons. And they believed in them just as firmly and with just as steady a faith as any good Christian from Georgia back before The Event. And since Joshua was a good Christian, that real faith called his into question. Somehow, Christianity was supposed to be different. Better, more real. And it wasn't, not to Gaius Pontius of Rome or Capot of Carthage.

As Joshua thought about that for the hundredth time, he was making copies of Erica's report for Roxane, the captain, and Dr. Easley.

Queen of the Sea, *captain's conference room* July 23, 319 BCE

Lars Floden looked around the conference room. Jane Carruthers nodded, then gave a sidelong glance at Roxane. Marie Easley smiled at Jane's look, but the smile died quickly. Dag and Roxane were both smiling as they took their seats, and so was Anders. Eleanor Kinney sat next to Jane and started whispering in her ear. Lars took his seat at the head of the oval table and looked over at Roxane.

"Well, Roxane, how do you feel about the news?" Lars asked. He was really curious too. Roxane had claimed from the beginning to be in favor of Philip and Eurydice's role in the government. But this meant that there was at least the potential of a child to compete with Alexander IV for the crown. A whole line of alternate monarchs.

Roxane's smile wasn't half, or twisted, or sardonic. It was closer to beaming than anything else. "I am thrilled and I'll be even more thrilled if Eurydice has a child."

"What about your dynasty?" asked Staff Captain Anders Dahl.

"I think I would like my dynasty to be doctors and engineers. Maybe ship's captains or wealthy playboys. People who don't get their heads chopped off because of a family squabble."

Dag was grinning. "Alexander IV, on the other hand, disapproves of the idea because he's the emperor of his daddy's empire and Dorothy Miller is threatening to throw him over for Philip's son. Of course, they're only children, so that might change over time."

"I am more concerned with the strategic position that Eumenes seems to have left himself in," said Marie Easley. "I don't see what advantage he's gained from taking Amphipolis. Aside from the psychological effects, that is."

"Good," said Roxane. "If you don't see it, maybe Cassander and Lysimachus won't either."

"Don't count on that," Marie said. "I'm a historian, not a general. But what is the advantage?"

"I'm curious too," Lars said.

"Excuse me, Captain, but this is one of those situations where the *Queen of the Sea*'s neutrality means you lack a need to know. It would be a bit like the Allies telling Switzerland where the D-Day invasion was taking place," Dag said.

"I see." Lars leaned back in his swivel chair and considered. Dag was learning to be a diplomat, and getting pretty good at it too. He was offering to let Lars in on the secret, but implying a price. "The *Queen* is, of course, officially neutral. But we all know that our neutrality occasionally favors the USSE in practice. What are you looking for, Dag?"

It was Roxane who answered. "I would like to visit the Persian Gulf, Captain. This is our third trip around the Cape. There is plenty of oil on Dioscorides."

"It's still two thousand miles, Your Majesty. What is there in the Persian Gulf that is worth the cost involved either to the *Queen* or to the overwhelming majority of our passengers? A trip to Sri Lanka would use less fuel and probably offer more in the way of business opportunities."

"Oil, Captain Floden. Oil. There are functional wells at the mouth of the Euphrates. What I want to do is encourage their expansion so that there will be an adequate source of fuel on this side of the Atlantic. That will increase the *Queen*'s effective range and make trips farther east easier for the *Queen*, for the *Reliance*, and for the steamships that are being built both in New America and in the empire."

"What does President Wiley say?"

"Oil is, of course, the major export of New America. In fact, the oil sold to the *Queen*, and to the empire and Ptolemy, represented almost thirty percent of New America's income last year. And thirty percent is a major part of the income of the government of New America—more than taxes, if not as much as the tariffs on trade goods. Naturally, President Wiley is concerned about the introduction of major competition..."

"In other words, Big Al is opposed to the idea," Staff Captain Dahl said. "That's a point in its favor right there, Skipper."

"President Wiley has done an excellent job, Staff Captain," Lars Floden said repressively. "Anders, I wasn't a fan of his politics before The Event either, but given what he had to start with, I don't think Gustavus Adolphus could have done as well. Not Washington or Lincoln either. New America has no slavery. It has free elections and a growing population. It is the industrial center of the world..."

Roxane coughed.

Marie Easley laughed.

Anders Dahl snorted.

What the captain had just said was both true and not true. New America at this point had more ship people than the *Queen of the Sea*. On a per capita basis, it produced more than any place on Earth, except for the *Queen of the Sea*. However, that was on a per capita basis. The USSE had a lot more capita than New America, and was industrializing just as fast as it could. That was also true of Carthage, and Carthage was starting out ahead of the USSE in terms of tech base. And on that per capita basis, even including the diplomats, merchants, students, and rich, indolent passengers, the *Queen of the Sea*, with its massive electrical generators and built-in infrastructure, produced more per capita than any place on the Earth.

Lars looked around the table and the comments stopped. "All right. You all know what I meant. But back to the point. President Wiley doesn't want it. What about the passengers?" He looked at Jane.

"Believe it or not, Arrhidaeus is in favor of it," Jane Carruthers said. Then, at Lars' expression, continued. "Officially, he is opposed and will claim to be opposed in his messages to Antigonus. But remember, Arrhidaeus was a general in his own right under Alexander, and had enough rank so that he got command of the army after Perdiccas was killed. He knows half the satraps of the eastern empire, and he wants access to them other than through Antigonus."

"Also," said Eleanor Kinney, "he is working on a deal with Capot Barca on advancing the India trade."

"There is no India trade," Marie said.

"Not yet, Professor. But many of the merchants are confident that there will be. Without the income from Phrygia, the stipend that Antigonus is providing his diplomatic mission is barely enough to pay Arrhidaeus' fare on the *Queen*. So he is trying to work his way into a deal. Any deal. He isn't stupid. He's looking to his retirement."

"I'm not sure how that does us any good, Eleanor. Antigonus is still opposed to the trip up the Persian Gulf, and Arrhidaeus will be screaming just as loudly that we are violating our neutrality."

"I don't think that's going to matter. We will have enough plausible reasons to make the trip that we can argue it was justified on purely financial grounds," Eleanor said.

"And Arrhidaeus assures us that we will have at least one official request from a satrap that both sides have endorsed," Jane said. "Probably Tlepolemus, satrap of Carmania. And that will give us all the political cover we need."

"You're in favor?" Lars asked.

"Yes, for two reasons," Jane said. "Well, more than two, but two really major reasons and they are both named oil. The main oil producer is New America. The main oil transporter is the *Reliance*, now owned by New America. The only other oil transporter is Ptolemy's Egypt." She glanced over at Roxane. "Sorry, but the degree of control you have over Ptolemy's actions is very slight." She looked back to Lars. "Ptolemy's Egypt, which gets most of its oil from New America, but some from the Persian Gulf. Between them, they represent the fourth century BCE version of the Standard Oil Trust. Without any desire to impugn anyone's motives, we need to develop and maintain alternative sources of oil."

"She's right, Skipper," Anders said. "And I don't mind impugning their motives. The only reason Wiley isn't on the comm daily, threatening our fuel supply, is because he doesn't have to say it out loud. We already know it. Ptolemy is worse. We have to buy our fuel from New America, and we have to get it from fueling stations that are owned by New America and Ptolemy." He turned, not to Jane, but to Roxane. "Do you really think that you can get us an oil supply in the Persian Gulf?"

"I think so, yes," Roxane said. "Especially with Arrhidaeus' help."

Lars looked around the table, collecting nods from Marie, Jane, Eleanor, Anders, Dag and Roxane.

"Very well then. Jane, announce the proposed schedule change to the ship's passengers and ask for comment. The *Queen* isn't a democracy, but we do want to keep our passengers reasonably happy."

"Who knows, Captain. We might pick up some more passengers," Jane said.

Lars leaned back in his chair again. "Okay, Dag, you got the trip to the Persian Gulf for your girlfriend. Now give. Just what does Eumenes have up his sleeve?"

"It's all about Thrace," Dag said.

"Thrace?" Anders asked in surprise.

"Anders, let him explain. Dag, explain."

"There is a group of military historians and science fiction buffs in Fort Plymouth. It's not a big group, half a dozen of them, including a guy named Paul Howard. Eumenes has been consulting with them, looking for ideas and knowledge about how wars will be fought in the future. Anyway, Paul Howard told him about a strategic doctrine in a science fiction book. It's called..." Dag went on to describe *The Tactics of Mistake* and how Eumenes was planning to use it.

Kazanlak, Thrace
July 23, 319 BCE

Seuthes III listened to the report in surprise bordering on shock. Why would he do it? Eumenes was smart, that much was obvious from a single meeting. And he was a Thracian, even if he was the son of a wagoneer. Making a mistake like this seemed very much out of character.

"Eumenes is an idiot, Sire," said Seluca, "but I see a possibility here. Lysimachus will rush east to attack Eumenes in coordination with Cassander. He will want to be in on the kill to cement his reputation..."

Seuthes listened with only half an ear after that. He had met Eumenes and Eumenes most certainly was not an idiot. Overly careful, perhaps, but never an idiot. *There had to be a reason, a good reason, for Eumenes to take Amphipolis. But what?*

Seluca's "possibility" penetrated his thoughts.

Could it be? Would Eumenes make such a move to give me an opportunity?

Seuthes felt a pang of guilt. After Cotys fell, Seuthes had retreated to his stronghold and sulked. Blamed Eumenes and Eurydice for the death of his son. He contributed nothing to freeing Thrace after that. Eumenes had every reason to be angry with him. Every reason to abandon him as he'd abandoned them.

"With Lysimachus pulling everything out of Thrace to concentrate on Amphipolis, we can sally. Move down the Black Sea coast to the Bosphorus, link up with the troops that Eumenes left there, and then move east. If Eumenes holds out long enough, we might even be able to hit Lysimachus from the rear," Seluca was saying.

It had to be, Seuthes thought. *Eumenes did it on purpose to give me an opportunity, like a swordsman shifting his position in a battle so his mate could get a shot at the enemy's back. It might not be the stuff of legends, but it won wars.* Seuthes felt his lips twitch in a smile. "You've convinced me, Seluca. But what makes you..." Seuthes stopped. Eumenes hadn't said that was what he was doing. No courier had arrived.

Why not? Perhaps it was best not to voice his guesses. "Why do you think that Cassander and Lysimachus will be able to crush him?"

"They will have better than two-to-one odds, Sire."

"And Eumenes will have walls, and rockets to defend his walls." Seuthes waved a hand. "Never mind. Time will tell. Prepare the army. I want to be moving as soon as we can."

En route to Amphipolis from Pella
July 26, 319 BCE

Cassander pulled up his horse, stood in his stirrups and rubbed his butt. *Four days on the march, and we are still less than halfway there. With the Companion Cavalry spending more time arguing precedence than riding.* He hated this. The new saddles were a great improvement and he was using one, if half his cavalry refused them. Carefully, he lowered back into the saddle and winced. As good as the new saddles were, he needed more padding. *Maybe a sheep skin?* he wondered. But no. The Companion Cavalry followed him, but they laughed behind their hands at his use of the new design for a saddle.

His mind wandered back to the real question. Why had Eumenes fucked the goat again? First the loss of his whole supply of rockets because he didn't take the time to put out scouts. Now this? It made no sense to take Amphipolis. Amphipolis was the wrong place.

He turned, wincing a little as his bum rubbed on the saddle, and looked at his army. It was a strung-out mess with little cohesion even within the units. The infantry was better than the cavalry, but not much. The rocketeers were a bunch of scholars he had collected, and half of them were slaves. They walked along beside their carts. And the rest of the army had taken to calling them "the Eumenes brigade" or "the carter's brigade."

☆   ☆   ☆

Paulus was from southern Italy. He'd gone to Athens to study and been drafted into a levy sent to fight Antipater, where he was captured and sold. He could read and write in Greek and Latin. That had gotten him sold to Cassander for use in the rocket company, and he really didn't want to be here. Paulus remembered what happened when the black powder in the warhead ignited early, and didn't want to be anywhere near a rocket.

One of the Greeks rode by and spat on him. Paulus didn't do anything or say anything. He was afraid. He looked down at the ground and tried not to breathe any more than he had to. The air was full of dust raised by hooves, wagons, and marching feet. He wondered what they would see when they finally got to Amphipolis.

Amphipolis
July 26, 319 BCE

Everywhere Philip looked, people smiled at him. The men and a lot of the women made gestures and laughed. He sort of liked it, even if he didn't know how to respond. He just nodded and went on. He climbed up onto the wall and looked along it. In his mind's eye he saw its shape and how the shape fit with the shape of the earth around it. It was a curtain wall, or it had been six days ago. Now wheelbarrows full of earth were being dumped along its outer surface to give it some depth, in case Cassander had cannon.

Rockets weren't that much threat to the walls, but even a small cannon would take down the sort of thin curtain walls that Amphipolis had.

Cassander could have cannon. The bellmaker's art already existed, and the same process used to make a bell could make a cannon. The issue was the expense. At least, that was what Eurydice and Eumenes said. It didn't make sense to Philip. He still wasn't good at guessing what things were worth. He looked over at the gate and saw a weakness. He turned to the stairs that led down the wall and went quickly down, then made his way to Dymnos, Eumenes' chief engineer.

Dymnos didn't smile at him. He rolled his eyes. Which Philip saw out of the corner of his eye as he looked at the wall. "There is a weakness..." Philip went on to explain why the posts of a join would likely fail if a rocket hit that spot and how the earthen ramp made it even more likely.

"You're right, but only if the rocket or cannon ball hits just the right place. We don't have time to fix everything. Cassander will be here any day now, and Lysimachus will be here almost as soon."

"No. Lysimachus is still concentrating his forces. He hasn't even started the march yet."

Dymnos moved around so he was in front of Philip's eyes. Philip looked away. He couldn't help it.

"How do you know?" Dymnos asked.

"Ships left Abdera yesterday and arrived this morning," Philip said to the wall. "Briarus says that Lysimachus had fifteen thousand men and is waiting for another five thousand."

Dymnos whistled. "How many men does Briarus have?"

"Seven thousand, mostly militia, but he has a good store of rockets and he has three cannons."

"Why does Abdera get cannon?" Dymnos complained.

"Because they only have seven thousand men. If Lysimachus decides to attack, he has to be broken before he reaches the walls. This is where we are concentrating the enemy."

"Why? That's what I don't understand," Dymnos said. "Why here, where we are going to have to face both Cassander and Lysimachus?"

Philip looked at the wall, then he looked at the joist in the ramp that went up to the top of the wall, then he looked at the paving stones. He didn't say anything because he didn't know, and not knowing made Philip intensely uncomfortable.

Amphipolis, Royal Residence

"I hate not telling him," Eurydice said.

Eumenes looked up at the sad expression on the young woman's face. Usually the eighteen-year-old wore an expression that wandered between certain and belligerent. Now it was pensive. "You know that Philip doesn't understand about secrets."

"I know, but he hates not knowing things."

It was true. Certainly, Philip knew a very great deal, but his understanding was often lacking, especially in matters of human interaction. Philip knew quite well that there were almost certainly spies for Cassander in their ranks. But he would fail to make the connection between spy and "don't talk to them about secrets."

Still, that look on Eurydice's face worried him. Eurydice had always cared for Philip. Even come to love him in a way, like you might love a horse or a dog. But with the change in their relationship, she had changed the way she thought of Philip. "Philip has made a great deal of progress, Eurydice. But he still has a long way to go before he can be trusted with state secrets. Now come over here and look at these plot lines. I want to be sure the rockets are properly placed."

"I don't know why you're fussing," Eurydice complained. "Philip approved them and the fire plan has been vetted by experts in Fort Plymouth."

Fort Plymouth, New America
July 26, 319 BCE

Paul Howard sipped the cocoamat and read the sheet. He couldn't bring food or drink into the computer room of the Fort Plymouth Library and Bookstore. No one could, and there were armed guards at the door who checked people to make sure they didn't have anything to eat, drink, or smoke when they went in. So Paul sat out here in the dining/reading room where you could eat, drink, smoke, and read through the printouts and make notes. Never in his life had Paul imagined he would find himself as a military adviser to generals in two nations.

Paul set the cocoamat down and scratched his beard. What he was looking at was the design for a fort that would be the main defensive center of Caracas. They were using the modern name. The local tribe had joined New America only a few months ago and not everyone had agreed.

In general, the tensions between not so much the ship people and the locals, but between the locals supporting the ship people and the locals opposing the ship people, were getting more intense as the legal sovereignty shifted from this or that tribe to New America. And those disagreements were getting more and more belligerent as the locals learned about smelting iron and steel and making gunpowder. The "ship people magic" was becoming less magical, and some of the locals were intent on regaining their god-given right to cut each other's hearts out. Hence Fort Caracas, with earthwork defenses and rocket carts, an underground powder magazine, and a two-hundred-man militia.

Paul wasn't the designer. He was a consultant, using his memory of forts and cities real and imagined to help inform the choices. He didn't have the final say about how the fort would be built, but he was making a decent living making notes and suggestions that would be acted on higher up the political food chain.

Fort Plymouth, Capitol Building Plaza

General Leo Holland, Jr. stood on the steps of the capitol building and watched as the sergeants ordered the men through their paces. Leo was a Marine master sergeant fallen on hard times. After twenty years in the Corps, he was reduced to being an army puke and—worse—an officer.

He wasn't the only one from the military who had been on the cruise. There were officers, even, and quite a few army pukes. But in the organization of New America's military after The Event, he'd ended up with the job, mostly because the real officers had all—as a unit—taken one step back.

"Attention!"

The men snapped to attention, their rifles on their shoulders. The rifles were new and of a new design. Leo thought of them as rifled slug-throwing shotguns. They broke open to load like a shotgun but they had a narrower bore, forty-five caliber. They fired a copper-coated lead slug using black powder in a waxed-paper cartridge with a brass cap. Basically a shotgun shell, because paper shells were way easier to make than brass, and cost a lot less. Brass was expensive in the here and now.

"Ground arms!" A hundred and twenty steel butt-plates hit the flagstone plaza.

Leo started down the steps as the sergeant, a Silver Shield who had done twenty years with Alexander the Great, shouted, "Parade rest!"

His army had many of the structures of the USMC, but it was also influenced by such diverse services as Greek Silver Shields and Native American warriors. It was Leo's job to integrate those traditions to form the core of the military tradition of New America. Drill and ceremony was an important part of the new tradition.

The shotguns were long barreled, about as long as a Kentucky longrifle, and they had three-foot bayonets on the ends. In part because a Silver Shield felt naked without a long stick with a point on the end.

Leo reached the bottom step and started his inspection. His men wore boots, like it or not, and a lot of them didn't. They wore long pants in camouflage colors whether the brass liked it or not, and a lot of them didn't. Tie-dyed green and brown was expensive. They were an elite professional service. One that had started out with rank inflation.

"Well, Kepko," Leo said to the Native American third in line, "I see you got your stripe back." Kepko had a strong preference for whisky and a tendency to become belligerent on drinking it.

"Sir, yes, sir," Kepko said, keeping his face straight and his eyes straight ahead. The left one was a little swollen, but it was still steady. Kepko was a corporal, not a lance corporal. In normal circumstances he would act as a private, but in an emergency, when the citizen soldiers swelled the army's ranks, he became a squad leader. It could be hard on a man to be bounced up and down in effective rank depending on circumstance. But President Wiley was intent that the army be both a professional service and an army of citizen soldiers, "so that the citizens would know what was on the line in war." Personally, Leo thought it was really because the idea of a citizen soldier was part of the American tradition. Well, it was part of Leo's tradition too. So the New America Army was both an army and a cadre for a much larger army that could be called up quickly.

Next came an exception. A ship person, Nathan Corbier's family had served in the US military for every generation since the first buffalo soldier right after the Civil War. He'd turned eighteen since The Event and if he couldn't be in the US Army, he would be in the New American Army. Out of over four thousand passengers and crew on the *Queen of the Sea* there were less than one hundred in the military, and a total of seven who were not officers or senior NCOs. Not because they were lacking in courage or patriotism to the new nation they were building here, but because there were too many more important jobs that they could be doing. The same was true of Nathan Corbier. He had a 3.2 GPA at Roosevelt High back in the world. What he ought to be doing was reading Wiki articles in the computer center of the library and helping to design machines or chemical processes. Not grunting on the confidence course or standing in formation.

And that was what the kid was going to be doing, like it or not. As soon as he finished Advanced Infantry Training, he was going to be transferred to the weapons development board. It might be a very good thing to have a man who'd been trained with locals adding his input to the geegaws those old fogies were coming up with.

☆   ☆   ☆

John Little, the leader of those old fogies, was at that very moment cursing the input from locals. John was a practical man and an experienced businessman. Back in the world, he had run a restaurant in Philly, a bar in San Antonio, a shoe store in Atlanta, and a clothing factory in Yonkers. In New America, he had a factory that made gardening and farming supplies. He knew how to run a business and a production line. So did the damn Greeks, or at least they thought they did. Unfortunately, their notion of how to increase production had a lot to do with more hands and almost nothing to do with better equipment. Better equipment, which they insisted would cost a lot of money, take time to build, and more time to train the operators. Better equipment that they insisted they didn't have either the time or the money for.

"All I want is an electric boring machine," he muttered to himself as he went over the notes on yet another proposal to hire more people and use the hand-powered boring tool and guide that were well-established innovations that worked. The most irritating thing about it was that they weren't entirely wrong. A power borer was an expensive piece of equipment that would take months to build and could be easily broken by misuse. As any number of mid-twentieth-century devices they had built already had been. It had lots of power and trying to drive the boring tool in too quickly could burn out the handmade electrical motor before an inexperienced operator knew there was a problem. But using hand tools was a dead end. It meant that a rifle would take at least a hundred hours to bore. And just using more workers would, in the long run, be more expensive even if the new minimum wage law didn't pass over Al Wiley's veto, which it very well might.

Fort Plymouth, President's Office

"Damn it, Yolanda. I thought I would have your support on this," Al Wiley said.

"I'm sorry, Mr. President, but the deals some of these companies are getting people to sign amount to slavery." Yolanda held up a hand to stop the President from interrupting. "I know it's only a band-aid, and I know that minimum wage laws are an invitation to cooking the books. I honestly don't like them much more than you do. But there is a bleeding wound in our economy and if a band-aid is all I've got, I'm going to use it."

"All you're going to accomplish is to start an inflationary cycle," Al said, but he didn't say it with much heat. That argument had raged back and forth for decades in the universe they'd come from, and while he'd always faithfully expounded the Republican Party line, he'd privately had his doubts. After all, the minimum wage had been raised plenty of times and he'd never seen where any great disaster had ensued.

The real issue in the here and now was slavery. Not slavery in New America—not even the indentured servitude they had been forced to accept to get the needed workers from Europe. The threat was the slavery in Greece, Carthage, Rome, and the rest of the Med. Also slavery from Mexico to Brazil among the native tribes. Slavery that produced goods that competed with the goods produced by paid workers in New America. And, in New America, even the indentured servants got some salary.

So far the advantage of New America in industrialization had kept the balance of productive capability tilted on the New America side, but the Carthaginians were copying the advanced tools and machines, then using slaves to operate them. Al was worried this new minimum wage law was going to make it easier for places like Carthage to undersell them. Especially in Europe, where they had lower transport costs.

He'd like to believe the arguments advanced by the proponents of establishing a minimum wage, that it would boost productivity rapidly enough to keep offsetting the cost advantage of using slave labor. They pointed to the experience in the old USA where the northern states had kept industrially outpacing the southern ones—in large part because the higher wages in the north kept drawing immigrants. But...

If they were wrong, things were going to get problematic.

Sometimes Al wondered why he had ever taken this job, but the truth was that he didn't know anyone else who could do it half as well as he could. And Al Wiley had a very strong sense of duty.

214–216 12th Street, Fort Plymouth, Trinidad

Stella Matthews listened to Marigene Morgan bitch about the new minimum wage bill that was probably going to pass over Al Wiley's veto. "The damn locals don't stay on the job long enough to learn the job anyway. If we have to pay them four dollars an hour, they'll be quitting at the end of the first day. And don't you look at me that way, Stella Matthews," she added. "Carthalo is an indentured. He can't quit and run off to hunt super turkeys or go fishing."

"Why would I want to?" Carthalo asked. "I can get a super turkey sandwich at the community center for a buck and a half anytime I want one. And I have an account in the bank."

"See? That's what I mean," Marigene said. "I have Stone Age hunter-gatherers who spend just enough time sewing hems to buy a knife or a file, and then run off into the jungle. I can't afford to pay trainees four bucks an hour. You have a craftsman from a civilized nation. Of course you can afford to pay him more. And you take half his salary back to pay off his indenture anyway."

That was true. At least sort of. Carthalo was salaried, not hourly. But there were rules about how many hours you could work an indentured in a day or a week, or you had to give them comp time or overtime. And figuring it that way, Carthalo made about six bucks an hour and kept three. Well, two fifty an hour, after taxes. But Stella had very little sympathy for Marigene, especially not after Stella had to pay Marigene two hundred and eighty bucks for a pair of hemp overalls for Carthalo. Which Marigene justified by repeating "hand-sewn" ad nauseam. True or not, it was ridiculous how much clothing cost in the here and now compared to back in the world.

Stella decided to change the subject before the temptation to smack Marigene overcame her. "So, what's all the excitement about Philip III and Eurydice about? They're married. Why so much noise about them having sex? And why did it take them so long?"

Two minutes later she knew she had made a mistake. Marigene was as enamored of the USSE royal house as any Princess Di worshipper back in the world. Stella got chapter and verse on Philip's spectrum disorder, while Carthalo, his break over, escaped back to the kiln, where this batch of glass was about ready.

CHAPTER 18

EXIT, LYSIMACHUS

Reliance, *off Abdera*
July 30, 319 BCE

Commodore Adrian Scott stood on the bridge of the *Reliance* looking at the army surrounding Abdera and worried. New America had a treaty with the USSE, but that treaty was barely more than a trade agreement and it specifically didn't include taking any active part in the suppression of internal rebellion. And this was looking like one heck of an internal rebellion.

Lysimachus now had twenty thousand men investing Abdera and there was a trireme heading for the *Reliance*, flying the USSE signet. By now some of the ships used flags, but not this one. It had a pole with a sculpture of a griffin on the top.

Briarus was standing in the prow of the trireme next to the staff, and Adrian just knew that he was out here to try and get New America to shoot at Lysimachus.

The situation was complicated by the fact that

Google Maps was wrong about the shape of the local coastline. Say rather, it was out of date. By about twenty-three hundred years. The coastline had moved in that time. Abdera in the fourth century BCE was on the coast, not near the coast. The coastline in the here and now circled around the city so that to the east there was a breakwater: a semi-artificial peninsula that stretched out into the Aegean Sea almost a mile. That breakwater kept the harbor quiet, but it was outside the city walls. That put the breakwater in the hands of Lysimachus. It wasn't all that close to the docks, but still...

☆　　　☆　　　☆

General Briarus stepped onto the deck of the *Reliance* and lifted an arm in a Greek salute. "Good afternoon, Commodore."

"Good afternoon. What brings you here? Considering the army outside your gates, I would think the royal governor of Abdera would have better things to do than pay a courtesy call on a trading partner of the empire."

Briarus waved a hand negligently back at the city before he walked over and reached out for the forearm grip that was the equivalent of shaking hands in the here and now. "I'm not worried about Lysimachus. He would break his teeth in the taking of Abdera and he knows it. Besides, the latest word we have is that Seuthes has come out and is moving down the Black Sea coast to link up with us at the Bosphorus. What's going to happen to Lysimachus if he loses half his army taking my town?"

Adrian didn't buy it, not quite. Briarus was just a little too bluff and casual.

"No, Commodore," Briarus continued, "I'm mostly here to borrow your radio. Also to order a radio and radio team for Abdera. Oh, and to inform you that we have a full cargo for you and we'd like you to pull into the docks to facilitate cargo transfer."

"What sort of cargo can a besieged city have?" Adrian asked as he turned and led the Greek bearing cargo to the radio room. His lips twitched and he added, "I warn you, General, we already have all the wooden horses we are prepared to ship."

Briarus looked at Adrian in confusion for a moment, then his eyes widened. He started to laugh.

☆   ☆   ☆

Adrian sat in the radio room at Briarus' invitation and listened.

"Yes, *Strategos*, the *Reliance*'s arrival is quite convenient. We have rather a lot of cargo that we would like to ship, first to you at Amphipolis, and to Mount Ida and Sardis. I have Commodore Scott here with me and I hope you can prevail upon him to bring the *Reliance* to dock to facilitate the cargo transfers both ways. Meanwhile, here is the military situation . . ."

He gave a full, if rather glowing, report to Eumenes and Eurydice.

Eumenes endorsed Briarus' request.

"I am concerned about two things, *Strategos*," Adrian said into the mic. "First, that our docking will be seen as endorsing one side in your civil war, and second, that we will get caught in the cross fire if Lysimachus decides to attack while we are docked."

"As to the first, Commodore," said Eurydice over the radio, "you're not on the *Queen of the Sea*. You're a commodore in the New America Navy and New

America has a treaty of trade with the legitimate government of our empire. Far from docking being an act beyond your scope, failing to dock could be seen as a breach of the treaty your government has with us."

"As to the military threat," Eumenes added, "I think it is very slight and made even less by your presence. Lysimachus will not want to commit an act of war against New America when, whatever its official policy, it's known that the *Queen of the Sea* will act to punish anyone attacking the *Reliance*."

"Let me contact the government in Fort Plymouth," Adrian said. "I know I'm a commodore, but I'm new to the rank. And besides, we have a radio. Might as well use it."

Everyone agreed to that, and Adrian made his call. Then everyone waited for most of a day while Al Wiley, Richard VanHouten and General Leo Holland talked it over. Eventually, word came back that the *Reliance* was to go ahead and dock at Abdera.

Abdera docks
July 31, 319 BCE

The electric crane on the *Reliance* lifted the pallet of preserved fruit from the deck and carefully lowered it to the wagon sitting on the dock to carry it away. It was a jerry-rigged system, but better than the human-powered cranes that were available in places like this.

Even so, this was going to take at least three days. Especially since Abdera really did have a cargo. Several hundred tons of smoked fish, a fair chunk of the annual output from the northeast coast of the Aegean Sea.

Lysimachus' camp
August 2, 319 BCE

It is still there, Lysimachus gloated, as he stood by his tent in the camp. It stank, as all such camps stank and always had. He ignored the stench from long experience and because of the glowing beacon of wealth before his eyes.

The *Reliance* still sat at the Abdera docks after three days. Three days while Lysimachus readied his army, terrified that the prize would escape before he was ready. Abdera was unimportant. With Eumenes and Philip gone, there was nothing in the town worth taking. It was no more than a convenient place to gather his troops while keeping some of Eumenes' forces tied down. But the *Reliance* . . . that was an empire's ransom.

Lysimachus had heard the stories and he even believed them. The *Reliance* was a ship made of steel, that was clear. But it had been taken once, and if it was lost again, when the *Queen of the Sea* came to the rescue . . . well, the *Queen of the Sea* was on the other side of Africa. It was also neutral, which Lysimachus' gut told him meant that the *Queen of the Sea* lacked the courage to act unless forced to it, and it had an excuse not to act now. The *Reliance* was owned by New America, not the *Queen*.

Lysimachus knew how the world worked. He knew there were those, like Alexander and Lysimachus himself, who took what they wanted. And there were others who were afraid. He knew that those who were afraid could be forced to fight by backing them into a corner or challenging their pride. He'd seen Alexander do it often enough. He knew that was what happened when the *Queen* retook the *Reliance*. And he knew how to arrange things so that Lars Floden wasn't forced to act. He had it all worked out.

He called over his lieutenant, Dexios. "Do it. At dawn, or as close to it as you can, so the sun will be in their eyes when you launch the boats. We'll make a general attack on Abdera's walls, but I doubt it will succeed. And I will pull the men back once we have their attention. It won't matter. Once we have the *Reliance*, Abdera is ours for the taking, anyway."

Abdera breakwater
August 3, 319 BCE

The boats were small, what a later age would call jolly boats or dinghies. These had no sails, but places for six to eight oarsmen, and rope ladders rolled up in the bow. They were a mismatched conglomeration of whatever Lysimachus' army could find in the surrounding fishing villages. And they moved out moderately quietly just as the sun lipped over the hills to the east.

☆   ☆   ☆

Pedro Baca was born in a village about two hundred miles south of Panama, or what would be Panama in a couple of thousand years. And his name wasn't Pedro when he was born. Pedro was the name of the *Queen of the Sea*'s passenger who had hired him when he got to Trinidad six months before. Now he was a deckhand on the *Reliance*. Enjoying a pipe of tobacco on the morning watch, he glanced in the direction of the sunrise. But the light was blinding, and he shaded his eyes with the hand holding the pipe. He saw shadows on the water but didn't recognize them. But he was conscientious and curious, so he looked again. Those were boats. And the ones in the lead were halfway from the breakwater.

"Captain!" he shouted, then he turned and ran for the tug. The Articulated Tug Barge that was the *Reliance* had a large oil tanker barge which had a slot in its stern into which fitted the tug portion, which had the engines and most of the crew quarters. By now, two years after The Event, the barge portion of the ATB *Reliance* had a small town built of wood on its deck. And it was in that town where Pedro Baca lived. It took him almost three minutes to get around the containers and workspaces to the barge, but he was shouting the whole way.

☆   ☆   ☆

Commodore Adrian Scott heard the commotion. In fact, he was awakened by the commotion and more than a bit irritated at the idiot yelling nonsense outside his door. Adrian came out of his door in his undershorts and a ragged robe from before The Event to see Pedro shouting and pointing. Pedro was a good worker and working his way to a seaman first rank. Which, for a moment, Adrian thought was about to retreat to seaman third.

Then his eyes followed the hand holding the pipe and saw the bright morning sun and dark shapes on the water. He looked harder, even as the heavily accented "boats!" Pedro was shouting finally penetrated his sleep-fogged brain.

As it turned out, Adrian's lack of early morning sharpness didn't matter at all. He wasn't the only one on the *Reliance*, and Commander Heiron, late of Athens, had the watch and was already giving orders.

Lines were being cast off, and the engine was started. Adrian, still in his robe and undershorts, went down the ladder, feet in slippers. On the deck of the tug, he ran for the command deck and his mind started to catch up with events. As they did, he remembered the last time the *Reliance* had been captured, and he remembered that the reason they were captured was because they were running away from a night attack and ran right into pirates. Adrian hadn't been on the *Reliance* when that happened. The captain of the *Reliance* at the time had died at the hands of the pirates. The situation wasn't parallel, not even close, but that wasn't the only factor.

There was also the reputation of New America to consider. Adrian wasn't a fan of gunboat diplomacy. At least, he hadn't been back in the world. In the here and now, he knew that the *Reliance* couldn't run. Not more than a few hundred yards to get some sea room. Adrian wasn't American. He was English, and if he didn't have Nimitz or John Paul Jones as his spiritual ancestors, he did have Horatio Nelson. Suddenly "Rule, Britannia!" was playing in the back of his mind, complete with bagpipes. Adrian hated bagpipes.

He reached the command deck and looked around. By now, and from this angle, it was easier to see the boats. They were tiny little things, but there were a lot of them. Fifty or so, each packed with half a dozen soldiers in Greek armor. Not the fancy bronze breast-plates that the rich guys wore, but the cloth-and-plate stuff that the ordinary soldiers wore.

The *Reliance* was backing away from the docks, doing perhaps five knots. The jolly boats were struggling to keep up, much less catch them. He tapped a switch and looked at the open sea behind him. Then, almost to his own surprise, he quite calmly said, "Stop all engines. Prepare the guns." He paused just a moment, then added, "Oh, yes. Battle stations."

The claxon started blaring in the battle station sequence. They had drilled it. And drilled it more since the *Reliance* had been acquired by New America, but they honestly weren't up to the standard of the movie navies. Well, maybe comedies, but not serious movies.

By the time the crew were reporting ready, the flotilla of jolly boats were getting close and Adrian gave the order to fire.

☆　　　☆　　　☆

The jolly boat didn't have a name. And the seven men aboard it, six soldiers rowing and one in the stern with a steering oar, might as well not have had names either. The black powder cannon filled with grapeshot didn't care at all. And the men pointing it at them didn't care much either.

All the men on the jolly boat saw was a metal tube pointing in their direction. The bore of that tube didn't look big to them, not at all. They had never seen anyone killed by a gun of any sort, and there were no cultural references to psychologically adjust the size. It was just a tube pointing at them.

A tube . . . then a lightning bolt and thunder all at once, and the six rowers were so much tenderized meat.

The commander of the boat, at the stern, was still alive for the moment. His legs were gone and he was bleeding out, but he was still aware and saw the puff of smoke from that little hole in the metal stick that was still pointing at what was left of the boat.

What was left of him.

Not much of either, as it turned out.

He lived long enough to see the stick shift, turn
to point at another boat.

But he was underwater, sinking and drowning, by
the time it was reloaded.

In the boat that the cannon turned to—a boat full of
men who had seen the effect of that first shot—panic
reigned. But only for a moment. The commander of
the boat was a quick-thinking man. Not a good man
by even the standards of the time, but a brave one
who kept his head in a crisis. He started shouting
orders so soon after the first blast that he couldn't
hear himself because his ears were still ringing. What
he shouted, again and again, was, "Back oars! Back
oars! Back oars! Row, you bastards, row!"

And it worked. By the third repetition, the men
were rowing away from that hell ship just as fast as
their backs could manage.

The gun captain noted that their first shot was a bit
low, and he also took note of the fact that the next boat
was backing away just as fast as it could go. Perhaps
if he were thinking a bit more clearly, he might have
decided to let it go. It was no danger to them now that
it was running, and there were other targets. But this
was combat, and his brain was focused on just one thing.

Killing the enemy before they could kill him.

He shifted the aim, then waited a moment, and
shouted, "Fire!"

The lanyard was pulled and the cap went off.

The cannon sprayed death again, and another boat
was turned into raw meat and driftwood.

Adrian Scott looked around. The enemy was in retreat. Two of the boats had gotten up to the hull and tossed up ladders. At which point, crewmen tossed down grenades.

And that was that.

Adrian had been on the bridge back in 321 when the *Queen* ran over Gorgias' fleet, but he hadn't been in command. Somehow that made things different. Adrian was both colder and hotter. In fact, he was personally furious, more furious than he ever remembered being in his entire life. "Take us out, Commander Heiron. I want you to put us on the other side of the breakwater."

It took a few minutes. The *Reliance* was a fuel ship, not a battleship. She backed away from the piers, turned using a combination of rudders and electric motors in the bow of the barge, and went around the breakwater in about fifteen minutes.

That fifteen minutes was plenty long for Adrian to see the attack that Lysimachus had launched and to place the enemy in his mind. Long enough for him to realize that if they could get far enough in, they would place themselves on the enemy's flank in a position to fire all the way down the enemy's line. Adrian knew there was a term for that sort of fire—a French word. *Enfilade*, if he remembered right.

"Commodore," said Captain Andrew Ramage, "we're coming into shallows." He pointed at the depth gauge.

The ATB *Reliance* had a sonar depth finder in the tug and another in the bow of the barge. It was standard safety equipment and Royal Cruise Lines had been picky about that sort of thing. For which Adrian was exceedingly grateful. Now the computer screen showed the seabed shoaling up. The *Reliance* had a draft that varied by as much as three meters, depending on load. And while the tanks were mostly empty, the cargo stacked on the deck had them low in the water.

The seabed was coming up on four meters and that was close to the keel. Adrian considered. They were at ebb tide, or close to it. He tapped keys himself. Even if they grounded, the high tide should lift them off the shore. He checked another datapoint for the sonar. The seabed was a bit rocky, but mostly silt. Then he looked at the battle along the walls of Abdera. The angle was still wrong, but it was getting closer.

"Keep going, Captain. I'll risk the grounding. These sons of bitches need a lesson."

Thirty seconds later, still not quite in position, the hull of the barge grounded on silt. There were some rocks down there too. Adrian could hear them scraping the hull. The *Reliance* was probably going to need a new paint job below the waterline, not a trivial endeavor.

"All portside guns, open fire."

Outside Abdera

Lysimachus would have liked to be in the assault of the *Reliance*, but he simply had too much to do. Moving an army to attack a walled city isn't all that complicated, but it's not easy.

You have to be able to get your men to charge up to a wall where they know they are going to be stopped while they place scaling ladders. When they know that even after the scaling ladders are in place, they are going to be going very slowly because only one man can start up a ladder at a time, and climbing a ladder with armor on and carrying a sword is not easy. All the while, the bastards on top of the wall are going to be dropping everything from flaming arrows to buckets of boiling pitch down on their heads.

It takes a powerful combination of threats and promises. And if your army is made up, in large part, of the sort of men who didn't follow Alexander's standard, it's even harder. More threats, more promises, and, very important, the commander needs to be right there with them, sharing the risk.

So Lysimachus was right there with the men, riding his horse, wearing his bronze armor, and giving orders as the army approached the walls of Abdera. And he was busy. So busy that he didn't notice the *Reliance* moving up on the far side of the breakwater until he heard the thunder.

He looked around and in a flash of insight knew that he had tried to have intimate relations with a crocodile. And the crocodile wasn't pleased. He wanted to run then, but he didn't.

Whatever else you could say about Lysimachus—and there was a lot you could say—he wasn't a coward. He held it together in the face of disaster and started giving orders to save as much of his army as he could.

The thunder came again and he saw the smoke from the guns on the *Reliance*. He also saw the sudden gaps through his army, as though a great sword wielded by Zeus himself had cut them. He kept giving orders.

They were, as it happened, the wrong orders, but that wasn't really Lysimachus' fault. He had seen engines of war before, trebuchets, catapults, and the like . . . but nothing like this. The best orders he could have given were probably just "run for your lives!" But there really wasn't any way for him to know that. Instead, he tried to hold his army together and make an orderly retreat.

All that did was keep the army in a nice tight mass, so the cannons had a nice big target that they couldn't miss.

Then Lysimachus' army got a stroke of very good luck. The black powder guns were firing balls now, since the range had gotten too great for canister. One of the four-pound balls hit a rock and bounced, spraying rock fragments around. One of the larger fragments struck the throat of Lysimachus' horse. The horse went down and landed on Lysimachus' right leg, pinning him to the ground. Meanwhile, another rock fragment hit the shoulder of the mount of one of Lysimachus' bodyguards. That horse reared and spun and its left front hoof came down on Lysimachus' chest.

It took Lysimachus almost five minutes to die, but he wasn't paying any attention as his army—suddenly without the glue of his presence—shattered into thousands of individual panicked men. Lysimachus didn't think of much of anything for the last five minutes of consciousness, except for the pain washing through him.

CHAPTER 19

GODS AND SCIENCE

Abdera walls
August 3, 319 BCE

Briarus stood on the wall of Abdera and looked out at the army. Well, no. He looked out at the fleeing mob that wasn't an army anymore. And though the individual men might be soldiers again someday, this army was gone. He didn't blame those men a bit. Not the least tiny dash. If those blasts of death had been aimed at him, he'd be running too.

He wanted to run right now. Briarus was an experienced commander. He'd fought for half his life and more. He'd seen swords spill out men's intestines and been splashed with the gore.

But he had never in his life been as frightened as he was right now, even though he wasn't in the least danger. He looked over at the ship sitting quietly on the far side of the breakwater and no longer firing its cannon, and remembered the not quite contempt, but certainly not respect, that he had felt for Adrian Scott . . . and his balls tried to climb into his gut.

He turned to an aide. "Hold the walls, but make no sally. I need to go talk to the"—he stopped and swallowed a lump in his throat—"them." He pointed at the *Reliance*.

☆   ☆   ☆

On the trip through the town and along the break-water to approach the *Reliance*, Briarus tried to decide what aspect of the *Reliance*'s actions had so frightened him. Part of it was clearly that it was new. He knew death and war, but this was a new sort of death and a new sort of war. But that wasn't all of it. It wasn't lack of discrimination. A flight of arrows or a boulder tossed by a catapult is indiscriminate too. But a man could understand a bow or a catapult just by looking at it.

He groped for a word that would describe what horrified him and couldn't find it. He couldn't find it, because the word didn't exist in any language he spoke.

The word was "mechanical," but in the twenty-first-century sense of the word with its connotations of uncaring power. Different from the "deus ex machina" he was familiar with. Just as powerful, but without the moral focus. As though the gods stepped in, but then stomped on the army without caring who got crushed. He didn't get it worked out by the time he reached a point where he could wave to call a boat. He still didn't have it worked out as he climbed out of the boat and up the rope ladder to the deck of the *Reliance*. But at least by then he had himself under control.

He saluted Commodore Scott with a firm fist to chest. And thanked him for his aid without any notice-able quaver in his voice.

Commodore Scott looked out at the battlefield, then looked back at Briarus. "I was angered by the attack on my ship, General. I'm afraid that caused me to be a bit less than fully circumspect in handling the *Reliance*. It shouldn't be much of a problem, though. When the tide comes in, we should be able to get off the shore well enough."

Briarus noted that the commodore didn't even mention the enemy army or the use of the cannons. As though such things were without any importance at all. He asked for permission to use the radio room, and that boon was granted. He neither asked Commodore Scott to stay or to leave, but the commodore left him in the room with the radio tech.

There was no delay. The radio tech was already making reports and Eumenes was in the radio room in Amphipolis. Once the radio man knew that he wouldn't touch anything, he too left so that Briarus could give his report in private.

He did. He told Eumenes all of it. What had happened. What he thought it meant. And he found himself telling Eumenes how he felt. "They are like gods, but gods in hiding. They go along, seeming like ordinary people, and then they sweep away an army like a child sweeping away straw."

"They are ordinary people, Briarus," said Eumenes' voice over the radio. The radio that had seemed only a useful toy yesterday, but now seemed somehow to be more. "It is simply that they have tools we don't understand. But we *will* understand them, and that understanding will come sooner than we might prefer. What matters for now is that Lysimachus' army is broken. Send messengers to Seuthes and coordinate with him. He is the king of Thrace and Abdera is part of his kingdom. You're a guest there."

They talked then about the rights of the federal government as they contrasted with those of the satrapies and the states. The federal government had the right to move troops through any state, but if they did any unreasonable damage, the federal government could be held liable by the courts. Briarus listened and asked questions, and it sounded silly and convoluted—the next best thing to idiotic. The sort of silliness that the ship people were prone to.

Briarus swallowed again. And he wondered if there might be a connection between the silliness of a court that was separate from the legislature and the executive and the cannons that could rip an army to shreds. And a commodore who could defeat an army with just a single ship.

In point of fact, there was such a connection although it was not direct. The sort of industrial society that could produce a ship like the *Reliance* also tended to produce democratic governments. Even the worst dictatorships it produced were much more egalitarian and merit-based than the hereditary autocracies that Briarus was familiar with. You didn't need to be of noble blood to rise high in Hitler's Germany or Stalin's Russia.

But the immediate cause of Lysimachus' army being routed was much simpler. It wasn't even the disparity in weapons so much as the disparity in experience with those weapons. A Napoleonic-era army would not have been routed by the sort of carnage produced by the *Reliance*. Those soldiers were accustomed to standing up to twelve-pounder field guns, not the piddly four-pounders being used by the *Reliance*. But they were

accustomed to cannon fire. To the men in Lysimachus'
army, the gunfire had been purely terrifying.

Amphipolis

The spy sat in the inn drinking sour wine and listening
to the soldiers less than an hour later. He was a wine
merchant, but he rounded out his income, and insured
his continued prosperity, by providing Cassander with
information. In this case, he would have to sneak out
once the sun went down.

He went to the tavern that was frequented by the
ship people radio operators and by their local support
staff, and listened. It wasn't hard.

Once the sun went down, he bribed a guard and
was let out a sally port, then made his way across the
field to Cassander's camp.

Cassander's camp, outside Amphipolis

Cassander sat on the camp stool and listened to the
spy carefully. The oil lamps, newly designed with glass
tubes on top, filled the tent with a ruddy golden light.

He tried to believe the man's report, but it wasn't
easy. He thought back to the demonstration that the
Queen of the Sea made when they dropped off the
radio crew. He tried to imagine what those steam
cannon would do to an army, and couldn't. He knew
it would not be good, but he honestly couldn't imagine
what it would actually feel like to have that rain of
death falling on him.

What was quite clear was that whatever it was like,
it was more than Lysimachus could handle. He found

that both surprising and disappointing. Cassander had never liked Lysimachus, but the man was brave. "You have done well to bring me this news. You have your king's thanks." He gave the man a purse and waved him away. His bodyguards and companions started talking as soon as the man was gone.

"It's a trick," his brother Philip Lípos didn't quite shout. "They bribed your spy or tricked him."

Others chimed in, agreeing with Philip Lípos, or disputing his statement. Cassander listened and considered. He was always careful with these men. They were either the most prominent nobles in Macedonia or their sons. He needed them and the retainers they could bring to battle. Personally, Cassander was confident that his spy wasn't betraying him, and rather less confident that he had not been fooled. The question that bothered him now was what to do about it.

He got up from the camp chair, another innovation of the ship people. It was a chair made of sticks with a cloth bottom and back. It was both lighter and more comfortable than the wooden camp stools he was used to. It also folded up for easy transport. He looked at that chair and realized he needed a way to sink the *Reliance*, not to take it. Two tries had proven that was impossible, but to sink it, to remove it from the game entirely . . . That might be done. A large enough charge of the black powder that even now powered the rockets that he sent over Amphipolis to burn its buildings. But until he could do that, he needed to be out of the range of *Reliance*'s guns. That meant ceding the coast to Eumenes and Eurydice.

Then he looked back at his staff and knew that he couldn't do that. They wouldn't stand for it. "Coward" was a word all too often used to describe Cassander, son of Antipater. It limited his options in a way that Alexander's had never been. And even, in a way, that Eumenes' options weren't. Eumenes might never have killed a boar, but he had killed men, even generals, in single combat. No one truly doubted his courage, even if they disapproved of his lineage.

That left Cassander with a very large problem. He needed to retreat from the siege of Amphipolis and he needed to do it without seeming to retreat. And as he framed the question, he had the answer. When is a retreat not a retreat? When you're just moving to attack elsewhere. He felt a smile twitch his lips at that thought. But only a twitch, because whatever mask he put in front of the matter, behind the mask he was facing a war that he'd been winning yesterday but was losing today.

He would need to send a message to Thessalonike and have her start working on a bomb big enough to sink the *Reliance*. The Cabeiri might help with that. They were skilled in magic and were rapidly learning the magic of the ship people as well. But they had no love for the ship people.

Pella, Royal Compound
August 6, 319 BCE

Thessalonike read the bundle of sheets, and as she read she began to wonder if she had bet on the wrong horse when she married Cassander. The USSE Constitution still didn't seem to her to be a workable system. But Eumenes kept winning and satrapies kept going over to the USSE. She would send messages to the Cabeiri, for such a bomb might well be of use anyway. But she would also send messages to Cleopatra and Olympias, begging their forgiveness, and asking their aid and opinion.

Her situation was complicated by the fact that she was three months pregnant. She felt her belly, even though there was nothing to feel yet. So far this had been an uncomplicated pregnancy. She suffered morning sickness, but as bad as it felt, her midwife insisted it was mild. She could abort the child. Her fellow initiates in the Cabeiri knew the drugs, but those drugs were not safe. They sometimes left the woman barren and, more rarely, killed her. More importantly, if Cassander discovered she had aborted his child, he might well have her killed himself. And the chance of Cassander finding out was much too great. Sometimes Thessalonike thought the ship people's insistence on using devices instead of slaves might be wisdom instead of softness.

She went to her desk and began to write letters in her own hand. Then she stopped. Her desk was a Greek table with modifications based on ship people ideas. It had a set of niches across the top where documents could be rolled into scrolls and placed. It was inlaid with mother of pearl and onyx. There, before her, three slots from the left, was the letter she received from the present high priestess of the Cabeiri on the subject of Calix.

She remembered what it said.

> *Calix is a despicable little toad, but he's skilled and he is not so insane as Olympias. The last word we have from him is that he was working for Antigonus. We would prefer that his employment*

not be passed on to Olympias. The Cabeiri are a religious order. We follow the teachings of the goddess and her consort, and we protect the privacy of our members, just as we expect our members, especially those of high station, to protect the order.

Thessalonike had gotten the hint. She was told because she was the queen of Macedonia. Olympias wasn't the queen of anything anymore. She'd respected that call for silence until now, not responding to Olympias' repeated requests and telling Cleopatra that the order was being reticent. But now... Now it seemed that the women on the *Queen of the Sea* might be her only hope. She wrote:

I have finally gotten word from one of my contacts in the Cabeiri. Calix is considered a skilled poisoner and spy. My contact says that he worked for Antigonus at one time, but my contact doesn't know who he is working for now, or even if he is still active as a poisoner and a spy.

Queen of the Sea, *Persian Gulf, Tiz*
August 8, 319 BCE

Lars Floden looked out at the small town on the northern shore of the gulf. They were about two hundred knots east of the narrows where the Persian Gulf turned into the Gulf of Oman, about where Chabahar was on Google Maps. In the here and now, Tiz was an important port, and while not the capital of Carmania, was its largest port.

It was no Alexandria and certainly no Miami, but it had docks that would accommodate the ship's boats. And it had access to oil. Not local, but Tlepolemus could get his hands on it, and was in the Royal Lounge right this minute, selling out Antigonus.

Lars grinned, stepped back from the rail, and went back inside. The *Queen* had spent the last week and a half right here, while Tlepolemus sent ships to agents in Persia and Susiana to get loads of oil. There were tours of the countryside—read desert—and, among other things, Tlepolemus was profoundly interested in desalination techniques.

And that was another matter. The membranes for the reverse osmosis water purification system had a working life expectancy of around five years, and that assumed adequate pre-filtration with activated charcoal. They were making activated charcoal now. They had all the processes and those processes could be replicated in the here and now. Also, the polymer-membrane canisters, when they did wear out, could be disassembled and the membrane washed, which would extend their working life at the cost of decreased efficiency. But how much it would extend their life was an open question. Sooner or later, they were going to be reduced to what they were about to sell Tlepolemus: evaporative desalination. Saltwater, heated right to boiling, then the steam collected. It worked, but had a very high energy cost. Which was why ships used saltwater for toilets and washing until the reverse osmosis process was developed.

But the problem with the power purification was reflected in other areas as well. The *Queen of the Sea* was an almost new cruiseliner, six months out of the builders' quays when The Event happened, just long enough to notice and catch any problems. But The Event was followed by a very tough two years. The *Queen* was gutted to install factories where they had the electricity, computers, and—almost as important— the waste disposal facilities. Even if sometimes that meant getting out in the middle of the ocean and dumping poisonous garbage, with the excuse that the *Queen* was just one ship and the oceans were very big. Anyway, the *Queen* was, in the first month after The Event, converted into a factory ship as well as a cruise ship, a cargo ship, a college, and a floating United Nations.

"Lars?" Marie asked as she walked up to him.

Lars turned and smiled at Marie's worried expression. "Just thinking about the *Queen* and the fact that she's become a floating United Nations."

"It's not, you know," Marie said. "A United Nations, that is. It's neutral ground, but there is no treaty that everyone has to sign. The *Queen* can't condemn the genocide in wherever, the way they were always doing back in the world. In a way, it's more like a floating Switzerland."

"Granted. But that wasn't the part I was thinking about. I was thinking about the future and how we are going to make a ship that has a life expectancy of thirty years when she had dry docks and a support infrastructure last without those things."

"Now who's being a worrywart?" Marie said severely. Well, trying to be severe, but the smile was there in the undertones. "The *Queen* is good for at least another five years before she needs an overhaul. We've talked about this. In fact, if I recall correctly, the first time we discussed it was two days after The Event, on our way to Alexandria for the first time. Food was the first issue, then fuel."

"Food and fuel have both been solved, at least for the most part. There is a refinery in Trinidad now that is making diesel. Not great diesel, but plenty good enough to run the ship's boats. And we have the resources to buy all the food we could ever need. Why else would Tlepolemus be so willing to bow to Roxane and little Alexander?"

"Loyalty to his father and to the dynasty, plus a desire for stability and good government."

Lars snorted a derisive laugh.

"No, it's true. Not all of the *diadochi* were monsters. It was the situation. I think most of them would have been willing to have either Philip or little Alexander on the throne if they could have been sure that the others wouldn't use the weakness of the child Alexander or the autistic Philip. Not all of them, I grant. The more I look at it and examine the data available in the here and now, the more I come to believe that Cassander, under the orders of his father, did indeed have a part in poisoning Alexander. Or at least a part in introducing the pathogen that killed him. Part of that is simply that I've been able to correlate the information, but part of it is what I've learned about how they do things here and now. That hoof that the histories talk about is a fourth century BCE petri dish. A way of carrying a certain class of poison that has been used for the last fifty years or so."

"Olympias?" Lars asked.

"About the hoof, yes. But she didn't realize that Cassander was involved. Didn't understand how Alexander's last illness could be intentional until we put our heads together. And by the way, Lars, if Cassander or any of Antipater's children should ever board the *Queen*, you want Olympias chained in her cabin for the duration of their stay."

"Noted," Lars said, then added, "How's it going in there?"

"Fairly well. Glass-topped troughs with black bottoms a bit inland from the ocean, seawater pumped in, then the sun allowed to evaporate the water. When the sun goes down, the water condenses on the glass and drains into a second channel in the trough so that you get clean water suitable for drinking and agriculture. It won't turn Carmania into a garden, but it should help them feed themselves. And the glass factory that Tlepolemus will have to build to make the glass for the lids is going to cost a fortune. Which will be paid for by a loan from the federal government. Which Roxane can do, because of the New America alliance."

Marie leaned on the railing, and since Marie was a short woman, that lifted her arms, and that did interesting things to her chest. Then she continued talking to the ocean, or maybe the port.

"That wasn't what I came out here to talk to you about. We have new information on the poisoning of Dag and Travis."

"What is it? And why haven't you told Daniel about it?"

"It's not actionable. At least not yet. And Commander Lang is a good cop, but not a particularly good investigator."

Lars wanted to argue, but couldn't. Daniel was a good man and a good officer. He was all sorts of good things. But he didn't read mystery stories as a hobby, and if he saw a bloody body and a bloody knife beside it, he didn't look much deeper. He was, Lars knew, still convinced that Olympias had somehow been involved in the poisoning, even though all the evidence said she couldn't have done it.

"All right. What do you have?"

"Cleopatra recognized someone in the . . ." She told it all. How Cleopatra had recognized the man, how she had found the picture to confirm it, then identified the man as part of Arrhidaeus' entourage. How they realized that he was part of the cult of Cabeiri, and how they'd sent off for information about him and learned that he once worked for Antigonus.

Lars listened to it all the way through, then said, "It doesn't track. Why go after Dag?"

"We aren't sure. We think it may be a shot at Olympias."

"Pretty stupid if it was," Lars said. "We eliminated her based on fingerprint evidence and lack of access early on."

"Not really, Lars," Marie said. "Remember that the locals' mindset very much includes magic." Marie paused, then said, "This is a bit difficult to express. We, you and I, grew up with Sherlock Holmes and all the other detectives. We watched TV with cops who used the motive-means-opportunity triangle. For us, if you're going to frame someone, the first thing you do is make sure they don't have an alibi and that they do have the weapon used, or one like it, and that they have a reason.

"But that's just not how people think here and now. They think in terms of motive, sure enough.

But Olympias has a motive to kill Dag, and to a lot of people's minds an excellent one. Dag is having sex with Alexander's wife. Widow, actually, but Alexander was Alexander, and Olympias' son. So most people will look at Olympias and assume she will ignore the fact he's dead and be pissed about the betrayal.

"Then, Olympias is a witch. A famously powerful sorceress and she's right on the same ship as the victim. That mostly counts as means and opportunity rolled into one. It didn't occur to them that we would be able to tell who touched the carafe, or that we could eliminate her from the list of suspects based on that and her known location at the precise time of the poisoning." She shrugged. "Basically, they're more general in the way they look at crime. Not so detail oriented. No, that's not right. It's more a different set of details they look at." Marie gave Lars a sardonic half-smile. "Some of the things they pay attention to make no sense at all to us. Among other things, Olympias is an accomplished astrologer and knows the way she knows the sun comes up in the east that she has personally talked to Zeus and Athena, as well as Axiocersus, and his son, Cadmilus."

Lars nodded. He knew by now that Axiocersus and Cadmilus were aspects of the four-part god of the Cabeiri cult. And he was not overly impressed by any of the cults of the here and now, not even the pre-rabbinic Judaism as practiced in the Second Temple.

"Lars...Never mind. Just remember that they believe it, and not just the 'suckers.' The high priestesses as well. What I was trying to get at was that it's not unreasonable for them to think that we would react the same way they would. So it is entirely possible that it was a shot at Olympias."

"All right, I'll accept that much. What do you want to do about it?"

"We have a plan to get his prints, but we need to be able to compare them to the print from the carafe."

CHAPTER 20

ESCAPE AND CONSEQUENCE

Queen of the Sea, *Persian Gulf, Tiz*
August 10, 319 BCE

Calix knew something was wrong. He was an initiate to the mysteries of the Cabeiri and he understood his feelings in a way no one not an initiate could. The hairs on the back of his neck were standing on end and he knew that was because Cadmila was warning him. Someone was watching him. Someone who was a threat. Calix was more comfortable with the female aspects, Cadmila and Axiocersa, rather than the male aspects, Axiocersus and Cadmilus.

He set his tray down at his favorite table in the Royal Buffet and went to get a mug of milk. As he moved, he watched.

The mugs were new, ceramic, made in Alexandria using a glaze developed in cooperation with the ship people. The tables were molded plastic, after only a couple of years not even badly marred. And by now Calix was used to the place. He got his mug of milk then went back to the table, feeling more nervous with each step. He looked out the large window to the promenade and beyond it to the coast and the city of Tiz. *Perhaps? No. Whatever the threat was, it didn't come from Tiz.*

He looked around the dining hall again, searching for the threat more with his mind and his feelings than his eyes. He couldn't place it. He knew it was here in the dining hall, but not what the threat was. There was Cleopatra's ship person, but he wasn't even glancing in Calix's direction. He was just eating French toast and drinking papaya juice. And yet it seemed almost as though he was avoiding looking in Calix's direction.

Maybe.

Calix couldn't be sure, but he trusted his instincts. There was danger here. Abruptly Calix rose and left the dining hall, leaving his tray on the table.

☆   ☆   ☆

Sean Newton didn't notice Calix leaving. He was too busy *not* looking at the man. So he finished his French toast and, grimacing, drank his papaya juice. He wished they had orange juice. There were lemon, lime, orange and even grapefruit trees growing in New America, because the cooks started saving seeds almost as soon as The Event happened. But the citrus trees would take at least four more years to produce fruit, and even then who knew how well it would work. The papaya juice was just blah. He finished it anyway, and got up, ostensibly to get another cup.

He managed to glance at Calix. No Calix.

The tray was there. The cup was there. No Calix. He was sure it was Calix's tray. Well, almost sure.

He went back to his table, picked up his tray, and put it where it belonged. Then he looked at Calix's table again. The tray was still there. He went over and, carefully avoiding the places on the sides where Calix would have carried it, picked it up by the catty-corners and took it with him back to Cleopatra's suite. No easy feat that. The trays weren't designed to be carried that way and he almost dumped the mug of milk twice on the trip.

Queen of the Sea, *Cleopatra's suite*
Two hours later

Cleopatra sat in her favorite chair, with Marie Easley on the couch and Sean at the bar fixing a pot of yerba maté.

Marie looked at the tray and said, "There will come a time when we have to bring Daniel in on this."

"Yes, but I'm not sure that it's now," Cleopatra said.

"What we need is a lawyer," Sean said. "We need to determine the legality of this."

Marie pulled her cellphone from the case at her waist and called Phyllis Fall, the *Queen of the Sea's* chief justice and the criminal court judge.

☆   ☆   ☆

Phyllis Fall had been an assistant DA for twenty years and was on her anniversary trip with her husband when The Event happened. Robert Fall, her husband, died three months after The Event, when the drugs that kept his COPD and asthma under control ran out. Now she lived on the *Queen* and ran the *Queen's* court system as well as presiding over the criminal cases that occurred on a ship at sea.

She looked at the tray and then at the three conspirators. "We have a problem and it's thanks to you folks." Then she paused. "Was Roxane involved in this?"

"Yes," Cleopatra said. "It was Roxane who called me in. Olympias went to her to protest her innocence."

"Then we have an out. Though I don't like the precedent it would set. Why the heck didn't you people just call in Daniel Lang?

"Never mind. There are two ways I could look at this," she muttered, then said, more loudly, "Okay. You, as private persons, have invaded the privacy of another private person, which leaves you liable to a civil action. You didn't, that I can see, commit any criminal act. Picking up an abandoned tray isn't a crime. Nor is dusting it for prints, which is what I imagine you're going to do next. It is an invasion of this fellow Calix's privacy."

"What's the other way you could look at it, Phyllis?" Marie asked.

"That you were acting as agents of Roxane, who is a head of state. That would make you police agents of the United Satrapies and States of the Empire. But I am not going to do that, because it would set all sorts of really bad precedents."

"What sort of bad precedents?" Cleopatra asked.

Justice Phyllis Fall looked at Cleopatra. "Precedents that might lead to a charge of mutiny on the high seas against Roxane."

Cleopatra shifted away from Phyllis visibly, and for a moment Phyllis thought she had succeeded in quashing the discussion. But Marie Easley was in the room.

"How on earth can you get there? Even if Roxane was involved, even assuming she was acting as regent of the Alexandrian Empire?"

Phyllis looked over at the small woman and, too late, remembered that never in her life had Marie Easley left a can of worms unopened. She sighed in defeat. "It has to do with police powers and the authority of governments. On the *Queen*, the captain is the seat of government. It is a ship at sea, which makes it the most dictatorial dictatorship in the history of the world. Captain Floden has delegated that authority to me, to Daniel Lang, to Jane Carruthers, to Eleanor Kinney and others, but he has not, in any sense, given it to Roxane for her to act as a police or government agent in regard to anyone on the *Queen*. It would be a usurpation of the captain's authority and that's mutiny. Because if it's not, then the *Queen* is under the authority of the United Satrapies and States of the Empire. And, Marie, before I set that precedent, I will watch Roxane hang from a yardarm if I have to build the yardarm myself."

Marie tilted her head slightly, as though looking at the situation from every angle. "Very well. We will consider that the actions Roxane took in this matter were as a private citizen, concerned over the welfare of her, ah, boyfriend."

"Good choice!" Phyllis said.

"Very well. We were and are acting as private individuals not endowed with any police powers," Marie said.

Phyllis nodded. "Nor acting in cooperation with the police until and unless you have credible evidence to present. Which"—she looked at the tray—"you don't. Not until you find prints on that tray."

Queen of the Sea, *Calix's room*

Calix paced back and forth in his room. It was a small room, so there wasn't far to pace in any direction. But this was wrong. He tried to think, but his guts were tied in knots. He could not escape the feeling of being watched...hunted...pursued. He decided to take *sabazios*, a potion made with certain mushrooms and used to commune with the gods, which was supposed to be restricted while on ship. Not forbidden, but restricted to specific places and ceremonies.

He didn't abide by those restrictions and using his contacts had managed to get the ingredients of the potion smuggled onto the ship. He locked the door to his room, and dug into the locked wooden box in the safe. It took him almost an hour to prepare the potion. Then he laid on his bed and turned the TV to one of the relaxation channels that played quiet music and displayed moving lights.

He drank the potion and watched the screen, letting himself float in the magic. He dreamed and in his dream he was talking with Cadmila. She stood and walked around the room, looking at the ship people magic. She touched the water glass on the desk. Where her finger touched, the glass was marked with her symbol in flame. "They know the secrets, child, at least some of them." She turned to face him, wearing a man's short skirt, one breast exposed, and held out her hand. On each finger glowed her symbol, her secret name. "They understand that everything we touch, we change, and it changes us. The connection remains. If you fail to obscure it, they will find it." She shook her head, clearly disappointed in him. "You should have been more careful, but you left yourself on the carafe." She reached behind her and lifted a carafe like the one he had put the foxglove juice into, and on it his name was written in Greek letters as clear as day.

☆　　☆　　☆

Slowly, he woke. Groggy, with head pounding, he went through the steps to remember the dream and to tie them to the working world. *Fingers leaving… Fingerprints.* He remembered now. One of the things about the investigation. Olympias' fingerprints were not on the carafe. They had mentioned it again and again when they were explaining why they failed to arrest her for the poisoning.

After that, for a while, Calix was careful not to leave anything with his fingerprints anywhere they might be found. But as time passed and nothing happened, he got sloppy.

He remembered suddenly. The tray. The tray in the dining hall. And clear as day, Cleopatra's lover… so careful to *not* watch him. That was what Cadmila was telling him. They would be coming. He had to get away, but he must follow Cadmila's instructions. He would erase the traces. But how…?

Ah, he thought. *A sacrifice using fire. Fire purifies. Fire gives to the gods. I will give my fingerprints to Cadmila.*

It took several hours to prepare. Spreading the alcohol and wax and oil, setting the candle in a corner so that nothing would light until it burned down. Lighting the candle with the Bic lighter. Then taking the Do Not Disturb sign and wiping it down with a cloth. And holding it with the cloth, placing it on the door, wiping down the door. Then he picked up his backpack, and left.

It was no trouble getting off the ship. He just showed his ship ID and got on one of the boats taking sightseers to Tiz.

Queen of the Sea, *Cleopatra's suite*

Gavin Piang gently tapped the mug with the horsehair barber brush dipped in fingerprint powder. He blew gently to expose the print and pulled his digital camera from the case. He photographed the print and went on to the next.

He took fifteen minutes dusting everything. The tray, the mug of milk, the plate, the flatware, even the toast. He didn't get a print from the toast, but he tried.

"Okay, folks. I have four complete and nine partials mostly from the cup and the bottom edge of the plate."

"What now?" Cleopatra asked.

"I upload them to the print database in the ship's computer and compare them to known prints," Gavin said, and he knew but didn't say that this was the part that was at least nominally illegal. Gavin was from the Bahamas. He was working on the cruise ship to get enough money to finish his degree in criminal investigation. Then The Event, and everything changed. He knew about chain of evidence and illegal use of ship's facilities. He found himself looking to Marie Easley for reassurance that what he was doing was all right. But he didn't find it. Not really. Still, he knew Travis. Not well, but he was a ship person and even if that wasn't supposed to make a difference, it did. Besides, no one was supposed to be murdered on the *Queen*.

He took the camera and his slate over to the ethernet connection and plugged them in. He called up the print database and transferred everything, then ran the prints through all the open cases.

He got a match. The partial on the middle finger of the left hand. Probably. The mug had the match, and from the fact that it also had an index finger again, probably, and their position on the cup, he figured the odds were eighty percent or better that it was the left middle on the carafe. It was also only an eight-point match, not a ten, but Gavin was convinced. "This is the guy all right. You got to tell Chief Lang."

"Yes, quite right," Doctor Easley said.

Queen of the Sea, *chief of security's office*

Daniel Lang hung up the phone, not sure how he felt. He was pissed that they went behind his back, but at the same time he was happy that there was a new lead. He called Judge Phyllis Fall and, on the basis of the match, asked for a warrant to arrest one Calix on suspicion of murder. "He's part of Arrhidaeus' diplomatic cadre from Antigonus. It says here that he's an assistant to the trade envoy, a guy named Cleon."

"And you say you have his fingerprints, and they match the print on the carafe that was used to poison Dag Jakobsen and Travis Siegel?"

"That's what my informant claims."

"All right. I will issue the warrant on that basis, but be ready for some flack from Arrhidaeus."

Queen of the Sea, *Calix's room*

The candle burned, inching closer to the oil-soaked rag tied around its base.

Queen of the Sea, *chief of security's office*

Daniel Lang, warrant in hand, gathered up two Silver Shields and headed for Deck 5. The elevator took them to the deck smoothly, and they exited crew country and entered passenger country. All the while, Daniel was thinking that this guy must not be very important to the delegation. Deck 5 was the lowest deck that had passenger rooms, and the rooms here didn't have balconies, just portholes. And the interior rooms didn't even have that, and now were mostly used as factories of one sort or another. They were the cheapest rooms that you could get on the *Queen*. The rooms used for slaves that were freed just so they could accompany their former masters on the *Queen*.

Just into passenger country, the fire alarm sounded. Daniel, through some instinct, knew without doubt what was going on, but they were near the bow of the ship and Calix's room was halfway to the stern. He started running, but people were coming out of the rooms in a panic, and the fire alarms blared. Half of them were carrying, or trying to put on, life vests.

"Coming through!" Daniel shouted. "Make a hole!"

Some tried. Some didn't seem to understand. But the overall effect was to keep him from getting to Calix's stateroom for forty-five vital seconds.

Queen of the Sea, *Calix's room*

The fire blazed up and the sprinkler came on, but it was an oil fire and it takes a lot of water to fight such a fire. By the time Daniel got to the already hot door handle and opened the door, all he did was feed the fire more oxygen. It was only a few seconds later that a Silver Shield went to work with a fire extinguisher. It put out the fire all right, but any prints that the fire had failed to destroy were destroyed by the white foam from the fire extinguisher.

On the docks at Tiz

Calix looked around as he stepped onto the dock. Tiz's dock was wood on stone pilings and the streets were cobblestones. The buildings were rock, brick, or adobe mixed together. There were five ships aside from the *Queen*'s ship's boats, but the largest of them was little larger than one of those.

Calix walked quickly, but he walked and didn't run. He slipped by the hawkers selling everything from fried fish to treasure maps and made his way into the town of Tiz. He needed to find a stable and a money changer, not necessarily in that order. He looked around.

The town proper was up a hill from the shore and as he climbed the hill the look and even the smell of the place changed. It took him a few minutes to find a stable.

Queen of the Sea, *Tiz*

Knowing it was too late, Daniel Lang called debarking and instructed security to detain Calix. As expected, he was informed that Calix was already off the ship. A moment later it was verified that he was off the ship's boat and somewhere in Tiz. Daniel started to curse the idiots and amateurs who, in the glee to "help," had managed to warn the murderer of Travis Siegel, giving the bastard time to escape.

Queen of the Sea, *Briefing Room*
Two hours later

They were all there. All the little helpers. Roxane, Marie Easley, Olympias, Cleopatra, Sean Newton, even Dag Jakobsen. As well as Captain Floden, Gavin Piang—who damn well should have known better—and Judge Phyllis Fall.

He listened to it as they explained what they did. But not why. So he asked.

There was a lot of looking back and forth, then Olympias laughed like the cawing of a crow. "Because you are a city guard, not an initiate of the mysteries. Not an initiate of Cabeiri, not an Illuminati, not what you people call a detective." She pointed at her hips hidden by the table, and continued, "You got your nose into my scent and couldn't smell anything else for it. They will not tell you because they are soft and you are their friend. But you are not the man to run a real police force that investigates things done in the real world."

Daniel looked at the psychobitch from hell and realized that she might well be at least a little right.

Then he looked around at the rest of the people in the room. Roxane was looking him in the eye with sympathy, but not support. Cleopatra...He could tell she agreed with her mother. And so did Marie Easley, though she didn't seem happy about it. He looked at Lars Floden, his captain and, he had thought, his friend. Lars was looking at him, but couldn't quite hold his eye. "Do you agree with them, Captain?"

"Not exactly, Dan," Lars said. "But you have been under a lot of stress lately, and..." He trailed off.

"Did you know about this?"

"Yes, I did. The concern was that you would approach Calix without enough for an arrest and, ah, spook him into making a run for it."

"You mean like causing him to light his stateroom on fire and jump ship?"

Olympias laughed again. "Yes, precisely like that." Then she sobered, and it was Olympias who looked him in the eye and said it. "And in spite of the way things turned out, they were right. Their error was that they thought *they* could do it. They should have given me his name. He wouldn't have run then. He would have died in agony."

"Maybe." Daniel looked her in the eye and finished, "But then we would be no better than you."

Olympias surprised Daniel at that point—and probably everyone else in the room—because she laughed again and Daniel could tell it was a real laugh and not derisive. Almost open...probably as open as Olympias ever was.

Daniel looked around the room and realized that right at this moment he liked Olympias more than anyone else at the table. She might be a psychopath, but at least she wasn't a hypocrite. He stood up slowly, very controlled because he was furious. "I am going to have to give this some thought," he said. But the truth was in the back of his thoughts. He had already made up his mind. He had to get out. Get away from these people.

He turned and walked out of the room.

☆   ☆   ☆

Daniel sat in his cabin on the *Queen of the Sea* and worked on the laptop computer that he was issued as the head of ship security, but he wasn't working on ship's business. He was writing out his résumé. He would send it out over the network to every government that had a radio. Maybe the locals would have a job for him. Someone had to have a use for a good cop.

Alexandria, Ptolemy's new capital
August 11, 319 BCE

Ptolemy read the message and passed it over to Thaïs with a lifted eyebrow.

She read it and said, "Make him an offer. Meanwhile, I will send a letter to Roxane asking what happened."

☆   ☆   ☆

For the next several days the news that Daniel Lang was looking for a job was the talk of the radio network. Roxane, Cleopatra, Olympias and many other on-ship locals were asked what happened and why.

And the offers poured in. From the edge of India to Trinidad, from Egypt to northern Gaul. Most of those offers had nothing to do with police work. They wanted him because he was a ship person. They wanted him to build steam engines, iceboxes, and radios. A few,

Ptolemy and—oddly enough—Cassander, offered him a job as a cop. Ptolemy's offer was for chief of police for the city of Suez. It was a good offer. He would have equal rank to what amounted to the mayor of Suez.

Daniel considered it. Seriously. He also considered Rome's offer and the offer from the Samnites, both of which offered him considerable rank and money. Three days later he was still considering his options.

Queen of the Sea, *Daniel Lang's stateroom*
August 14, 319 BCE

Daniel got up when the knock sounded and opened the door to see Olympias standing before him. He remembered her honesty in the meeting room and waved her into his stateroom.

"Thank you," Olympias said, which surprised him. "I have come to ask you a favor."

"Ask?" Daniel asked. "I thought you didn't ask even Alexander the Great or King Philip."

She laughed and if there was a certain amount of bitterness in it, there was a self-awareness that still came as something of a shock. "I am not a fool. You ship people have changed the world and, at least for now, you have changed the rules."

Daniel felt himself grinning. "So I shouldn't count on more requests? Instead, I should look forward to demands?"

Olympias shrugged.

Daniel waved her to a chair and asked, "What's the favor?"

"You have received a job offer from Cassander?" She lifted an eyebrow.

"I'm not going to assassinate him for you," Daniel said, and laughed.

"That's not the favor. You should listen before you speak," Olympias commanded.

Somehow, that made Daniel more comfortable. A polite Olympias was altogether too much like a vegetarian lion for him to find it believable. He gave her a little seated bow and, grinning, waved for her to continue.

"My protégé . . . that is the word, yes?"

"Depends. Who are you talking about?"

"Thessalonike."

"Yep. Protégé sounds right. What about her?"

"She is in danger!" Olympias said harshly, and Daniel, with years of interrogation room experience, and even more time talking to victims of crime, knew that the harshness hid real fear.

Gently, he said, "Tell me about it. All of it. Leave nothing out."

Then he listened as she gave her take on the political situation. Thessalonike's reasons for marrying Cassander and her assessment of Cassander's character. "I think he will kill her if it looks like she is considering escape. Possibly even if he's not sure. He knows that Thessalonike is my student and will realize that I want him dead very badly. That makes her a threat to him. That by itself might not be enough to make him kill her, but if it looks like she has reason to escape, he will kill her because her death will hurt his cause less than her escaping. Especially if she leaves poison in his cup on her way out the door." Olympias smiled as she finished, clearly liking that idea.

Daniel nodded. That sort of balancing of risks was pretty common in organized crime, whether it was a street gang selling drugs to soldiers or the real mob bosses having informers murdered. Cassander sounded like every thug boss he had ever investigated in twenty years as a military police officer.

"I want Thessalonike protected." It came out like a demand, but by now Daniel knew that it was a plea—and a rather desperate one at that.

"You want me to take Cassander's offer and once I get there you want me to make sure Thessalonike is safe?" He nodded. "What's in it for me? Understand, if I take Cassander's offer, I'll keep her safe. But why should I take Cassander's offer instead of Ptolemy's? Suez is going to turn into a huge port. It's going to have lots of crime and just the sort of crime I am trained to fight."

"What do you want?"

"I want the Cabeiri. Its leadership. Who's in it, what they do. Why whoever it is went after Travis Siegel and killed him on my watch."

"You think it was Travis, not Dag?"

"The same logic that you insist proves you didn't do it applies. If they were after Dag, why use the cocoamat?" Daniel grimaced. "You were right. I was too fixated on you to see it."

"I don't know why it was done. Probably Calix was paid to kill your Travis Siegel." She shrugged.

"But who paid him? And why?"

"How should I know? It could be one of your ship people, for all I know."

"No. We didn't know he was Cabeiri, so none of us would have known who to hire. That's part of the reason I want to know about the Cabeiri. I want to know who would have known that Calix was an assassin for hire."

"Antigonus might well know. There are others. The

Cabeiri have tendrils everywhere." Suddenly Olympias stiffened. She just sat there for several seconds while Daniel waited. "Yes, Daniel Lang." She hissed like a really angry cat. "I will help you bring down the Cabeiri. I will help you find them and grind their bones into dust."

"Ah . . . Why?"

"It was them! They gave Cassander the poison. They killed my son, Alexander the Great."

Daniel didn't know if Olympias was right or not and, honestly, he didn't much care. He had his way in now.

For the next several hours Daniel Lang and Olympias talked and plotted.

124–126 12th Street, Fort Plymouth, Trinidad August 15, 319 BCE

Carthalo used the tongs to open the door into the kiln and Stella Matthews shaded her eyes from the glare of the white-hot glass in the kiln.

Carthalo was dressed in wet overalls and a bronze faceplate with the eyes made of darkened glass. It was the equivalent of a shaded visor. He dipped the long spoon into the molten glass and lifted a spoonful while Stella waited with the knives at the worktable made of polished granite.

He turned away from the kiln, his overalls steaming, and popped the spoon up and down, flipping the glowing—and very dangerous—gelatinous mass into the air as he moved. He got to the table and dumped it in front of Stella.

Then, as she used the knives to spread the still-flexible mass into a sheet and cut it into sections, he went back and closed the door to the kiln.

When he got back to the table, he started working on his part, while Stella cut small two-inch squares and placed them in ceramic lens molds, then took the mold top and bottom, and placed glass and all into a vise. Closing the vise, she forced the glass into a basic lens shape. These weren't for their use. They were to go to the optometrist on 4th Street, who would grind them into prescription lenses.

"So," Carthalo asked as he used a stone rolling pin to flatten a glass square, "have you heard why Daniel Lang is looking for a job?"

"I only know what I read in the papers, Carthalo. Ship people don't have a secret information source that we hide from the rest of you."

"So you claim," Carthalo said darkly, then laughed at her.

She would have thrown something at him, but hot glass wasn't something to play with.

"I heard from Kasos that he wanted more money. But Marcus says it's because he let that Greek Calix get away."

"I heard he was a spy for Ptolemy," Stella said.

"From who? Your secret ship people club?"

"No. From Maresi. She has a job with Yolanda Davis. Apparently he was part of Ptolemy's delegation."

"I heard it was Antigonus' delegation, but Arrhidaeus is claiming that they had nothing at all to do with any crimes."

"Maybe." Stella looked at the little four-inch squares that Carthalo was making. They would be going into lead frameworks to make windows, like the windows that now adorned both floors of the double townhouse, partly for themselves, but mostly as an advertisement.

Once flattened and shaped, the squares would be reheated using a liquid-fueled blowtorch to remelt the surface to smooth them into clear, if slightly wavy glass. She grinned at Carthalo. The way he was doing it, they wouldn't need much smoothing.

She looked around. They were in back of the house in a half shack that held the kiln, and Carthalo now had an assistant, a native teen who was interested in glass because he loved glass. They made lenses, small windowpanes, glasses, bottles, and small decorative pieces for sale to the Native Americans and for export to Europe.

Stella had lost thirty pounds since The Event and it wasn't because she was starving. What was left was more muscle and less fat by a healthy margin. She wondered idly when they would be able to make a full-length mirror. Issues of high politics on the *Queen of the Sea* didn't really matter that much to her anymore.

CHAPTER 21

GAMES

Queen of the Sea, *Tiz*
August 15, 319 BCE

"Are you sure?" Captain Floden asked.

But Daniel noted that Lars didn't try to talk him out of it. And that made him a bit more sure. He nodded. "Yes, Captain." Then he waited as Lars Floden stood, walked around the desk, and offered him his hand. He took the hand and shook it, trying not to feel resentment.

Daniel would stay with the *Queen* for the next two months while he brought his replacement up to speed, and the *Queen* traded around Africa on its way back to the Med.

Alexandria, Egypt
August 15, 319 BCE

Ptolemy held up the polite refusal, looking at Thaïs. "Why?"

Thaïs was lounging on a couch while an electric fan blew a gentle breeze across her. She sipped her

367

drink with a little wrinkle of concentration in her forehead. "I don't know, and it worries me."

Ptolemy walked over to the large cushioned chair next to the lounging couch and sat down. "Tell me about Daniel Lang."

Thaïs lay back on the couch, closed her eyes, and began to speak. "He was perhaps the most 'ship people' of all the ship people. The least willing to accept that our way of seeing the world had any validity at all. All of us were barbarians to him and he made little distinction between you or me or a tribe of cannibals in South America."

"Then why...I get it." Ptolemy deliberately used the Greek translation of a ship people phrase. "If we're all cannibals, what's the difference?"

"No!" Thaïs' eyes popped open and she sat up. "He's not stupid. He would have tried for a bidding war for his services and gotten the best deal he could, if that were the reason. There must be something he wants. Something we don't have."

Ptolemy snorted. "Well, whatever it is, Eumenes will have it soon."

Eumenes' headquarters, Amphipolis
August 15, 319 BCE

Eumenes looked out his window and over the walls as Cassander's army moved away from the city in good formation, and smiled.

The victory against Lysimachus at Abdera was finally taking effect. According to his spies in Cassander's camp, Cassander was only now firmly enough in command of his army to make the move away from the coast, in spite of the *Reliance* delivering several tons of dried, salted fish over a week ago—and delivering it without so much as a peep out of Cassander's army.

Eumenes almost giggled. He didn't, of course. It would be wholly inappropriate for the *strategos* of the United Satrapies and States of Europe. Then the impulse to giggle died as his thoughts moved on in the standard route. He turned away from the window and went back to the map on the wall of the third-floor room that was his office and war room.

The map was large, made up of twenty-four of the ship people sheets. The paper was locally made, but printed at great expense by the printer on the *Reliance*. It showed this part of Alexander's empire. It was mounted on cork from the Iberian Peninsula and had pins stuck in it, showing where Cassander was going.

Abdera. And from Abdera up into Thrace, wherever Seuthes "ran."

But Seuthes wasn't going to be running. Eumenes turned to the table and picked up the two-day-old radio telegraph that described the king of Thrace's arrival in Abdera with his daughter Nike. The message made it clear that Seuthes was in Abdera to stay. Then there was the next message from Seuthes, the one that requested that Nike be made a lady-in-waiting to Eurydice. A series of messages, in fact, that arranged for Nike's transport by ship from Abdera to Amphipolis. She would be arriving in two days.

From some of those telegrams, Eumenes suspected that Nike's arrival had less to do with Eurydice than it did with himself. He suspected that Seuthes was setting him up with the girl, but she was just a girl. He might be wrong, though, because if you wanted your daughter to learn how to be a queen there probably wasn't a better teacher than Eurydice, unless it was Roxane.

The door opened and Eurydice came in, followed by Philip. As he usually did, Philip smelled lightly of marijuana smoke. He scanned the room, looking everywhere but at Eumenes, and walked over to the map on the wall.

"Is Cassander leaving a blocking force to maintain the siege?"

"He doesn't appear to be." Eumenes waved at the window. "But I don't intend to sally until he is well away and we have sent out scouts."

Eurydice nodded, but there was a dissatisfied twist to her lips. Eurydice wasn't happy about letting Cassander's army leave without an attack.

"We have no reason to attack. We have to wait for your new lady-in-waiting, after all." Eumenes looked down at the messages again.

"Why me?" Eurydice complained, sounding about twelve years old. "Roxane would be a better choice. Let the little princess learn to powder her nose from her."

"Seuthes wants her to learn to lead armies," Philip said, still looking at the map. "We should delay the move east."

"We've talked about that," Eurydice told her husband.

"You didn't listen," Philip said, then turned and faced Eurydice and repeated, "You didn't *listen!*" shouting the last word.

Eumenes' head came up, and he stared in shock at the usually quiet monarch. He looked at Eurydice, whom the ship people had nicknamed "the Philip whisperer."

She was looking shocked. Then she said, "I thought we listened?" Her tone was questioning.

"Food production!" Philip said, just as he had said before. Many times before.

"You said that before."

"You didn't listen." He didn't shout this time.

"I listened, but maybe I didn't understand. Explain it to me, please."

Then Philip started repeating figures. So many amphorae of grain, so many pigs, so many goats. It went on for fifteen minutes and seemed to Eumenes to be a fairly full description of the annual production of food and materials of all of Macedonia and Thrace. Then he said "food production" again, and began another set of numbers. This time each followed by the name of a town or city.

"What are those numbers?" Eumenes asked.

"Number of dead."

"Dead how?" Eurydice asked.

"Starvation, malnutrition, disease."

Fort Plymouth, New America
August 16, 319 BCE

Al Wiley held up the radio telegram and looked around the room. "Well, is his autistic majesty correct? Is there going to be a famine over there in Europe?" Al tried, but he wasn't comfortable around the mentally challenged, no matter what problems they suffered. He had sympathy for them, but he preferred to be sympathetic at a distance.

Everyone had read the telegram, or at least they should have. He looked over at George Sevier, the former mayor of Jackrabbit, Utah, a town of three thousand or so, surrounded by farm country. George and his wife were on the *Queen* for Al's daughter's wedding and was the natural choice for interior secretary because he studied land management before going into politics.

George shrugged. "If these numbers are right, he could well be. I don't care how much of a savant Philip is, the uncertainty comes from the accuracy of the source data. Frankly, if his numbers are anywhere near accurate, I would be surprised if you didn't lose more, even without a campaign during harvest season. For the Lord's sake, Al, any time you have armies marching across fields, you're going to lose crops. With folks living as close to the edge as they do in this time, one bad season is starvation, and two in a row is *mass* starvation."

"What my friend is saying," Yolanda Davis said, "is that Philip is right in principle, even if he isn't in the specifics."

"What do you think we ought to do?" Al asked the table in general. The table included his cabinet as well as representatives from congress.

"Well, they aren't asking our permission for any action they take. They simply want a read on whether Philip III's numbers add up," said General Leo Holland. "I say we give them our best guess on that, but I also think we should focus on food production for a while. Any we don't eat, we can export."

Docks, Amphipolis
August 17, 319 BCE

Eumenes, along with Eurydice and Philip, waited on the dock as the ship *Tiberius*, under the command of

Captain Iakchos, was tied up and the boarding ramp run down. Then a set of four armored soldiers, followed by a small, skinny girl, a middle-aged woman, and four more armored men-at-arms, came down the ramp.

Eurydice walked out in front and greeted Nike, the daughter of Seuthes and princess of Thrace. "Welcome to my service, Princess Nike. May Thrace benefit from your time here. This is my husband Philip, emperor of the United Satrapies and States of the Empire." She waved at Philip, who nodded to the ocean, nowhere near where Nike was located. He wasn't at his best among new people.

"And this is Eumenes, *strategos* of the USSE," she finished, and Nike bowed all around.

☆   ☆   ☆

Back in the office war room, Eurydice, following her mother's custom with daughters and ladies in waiting, included Nike in the conversation. "You need to know what's going on," she started, then spent fifteen minutes catching Nike up on Philip's issues with the ongoing war.

Nike, totally unsure of what she was supposed to do, simply nodded. Partly because she didn't understand why Philip should care. Mostly, the people who might die during a famine wouldn't even be his serfs and slaves. But she kept her mouth shut.

Then Eumenes started talking and she noticed how old the carter's son was. He must be forty. His hair was going gray, and he had lines around his mouth and eyes. But his eyes were steady and his voice was calm and reasoned. Boring. He droned on about the possibility that even if they stopped their attacks, Cassander wouldn't stop his. Cassander was off balance now, and if they pushed hard he would be dead and in the ground by the end of the year. Which seemed to Nike to be the best option.

But because he was so boring, her mind wandered to the Olympic games, the games her brother planned to attend, but were cancelled for the first time in centuries because of the arrival of the ship people and the changes they wrought, including these people winning rather than losing and her brother being dead.

"We need some way to convince Cassander and Antigonus to halt hostilities for a few months and give the empire time to recover, time to import food to keep the death toll down," Eumenes said.

"Why?" Nike blurted. "Who cares? Those who die will be serfs and slaves. No one who matters. Not like my brother, who should have been at the Olympic games last year, not getting ready to die in a battle that never would have been fought without you." Then, realizing what she'd said and who she said it to, Nike turned and fled the room.

☆   ☆   ☆

"And I suspect that Nike just summed up Cassander's attitude," Eumenes said. "Any ideas?"

"The truce of the Olympics?" Eurydice asked, but not like she thought there was much chance of it working.

"The truce never actually stopped the fighting. Besides, the Olympics were supposed to happen last year. And for the first time in centuries, they were canceled due to war."

"Use that," Eurydice said. "Let us make it up to the gods by making these games and their truce greater. Offer an expanded Olympic truce to Cassander, from now until the Olympics. Not just free passage to Olympia, but no battles until after the games. No raiding, no looting, nothing."

"You think Cassander would keep to that?"

"No, not entirely. But he would pretend to, and that would limit his depredations."

"Will it buy us enough time? Even if this was the wrong year, the games should have happened by now."

"We make them fall games." Eurydice waved that objection away. Once she got her teeth into an idea, she was loath to give it up. "And while we're at it, we propose that we expand the games to include women and non-Greeks. And that we hold off on fighting until it's settled."

Eumenes shrugged. "It's worth a try. I'll send the proposal to the satraps and kings, as well as the city-states. And an extra message to Ptolemy about shipping more grain from Egypt. Athens and the other city-states will probably sign on. They weren't happy when the games were canceled last year."

Queen of the Sea, *Indian Ocean,* *approaching Madagascar* *August 18, 319 BCE*

Roxane sipped the cup of real coffee, grimaced, and passed it over to Dag.

Dag smiled. There still wasn't much coffee to be had, so he was just as pleased for Roxane not to acquire the habit yet. He sipped the coffee and sighed in contentment. Then, at Roxane's "Humph," set the coffee aside and went back to the telegraph message. "What do you think?"

"I think we should pursue the war and feed Cassander's body to the crows," Roxane said. "I don't know what's gotten into Eurydice." Then she smirked. "Well, I do know what's gotten into her, but I can't imagine Philip's such a good lover as to have this sort of effect."

"Crude woman!" Dag said.

"Victoria and her insane notions are two thousand years away in a different universe, praise the gods. All the gods from all the pantheons. Even Jehovah is not so crazy."

Roxane was wearing a negligee that was purple, but so transparent as to leave very little to the imagination. And Dag did thank the gods, at least for her attitude about sex.

He brought himself back from thoughts of a bit of after-breakfast exercise. "I disagree," he said. "I understand how you feel and in a strictly military sense you're absolutely right. And there were a lot of people even in the twenty-first century who thought that military, or more broadly security, necessities should trump all other considerations. But by the time The Event happened, most people had realized that that was a road that only led to police states and slavery for the citizenry.

"You don't just have to win the war. You have to have a nation to rule after you've won it. Doing this—and doing it publicly so that everyone knows you are doing it for your people in spite of the military cost—will go a long way to insuring the loyalty of the common people. And they *do* matter."

Roxane sighed and leaned back in her chair, giving Dag a nice view. Then she said, "I know. I want to agree with you, but I am afraid. I don't want to give Cassander time to regroup. I don't want to give Antigonus time to persuade the eastern satraps that we are too weak to rule. I don't want my son to be murdered in his bed while his mommy is fed to dogs."

Dag got up, walked around the table, knelt, and kissed her. "I know, love. It's scary doing the right thing."

Roxane kissed him back. And the co-emperor of the USSE chose that moment to wander in and proclaim, "Eww, mush."

Totally killing the mood.

The ship people, Roxane thought, *are a bad influence.*

Cassander's camp, near Abdera
August 20, 319 BCE

Sitting in his tent with the walls pulled up to allow a breeze, Cassander read the radio telegram with poorly concealed glee. *Idiots*, he thought. He looked at the messenger in his bronze breastplate and ship people–style britches and boots. "This is real?"

"Yes." The messenger didn't sound pleased or the least bit respectful. Which irritated Cassander, but not much, considering how good the news was. "It's not my fault you chose to follow a carter's son and a mental defective," he said, sneeringly.

The messenger started to respond, but Cassander waved him silent. "Whatever the ship people choose to call him. Nor do I doubt his numbers. But that is the core of his defect, don't you see? He knows the numbers, but has no sense of which numbers count. And even less which people count. A carter's son is your *strategos*, Melanthios. Of course he wants to protect the lesser people. He's one of them. And Alexander's doxy Roxane is no better. She never had the guts for necessary action. The only one in the whole bunch with any worth at all is Eurydice, and now that she's getting fucked she's gone soft. They lack the stomach for war."

He looked at the man and could see the words behind his eyes. *"Where is your boar, Cassander?"* But the messenger didn't say them, so he let it pass. *My boar was Alexander the Great.* But that could never be said aloud and was dangerous even to think.

Once the messenger was gone, Cassander called together his commanders, and explained to them that this was a gift from the gods, that Eumenes' weakness gave them the time they needed to regroup. His commanders were less pleased than he expected.

☆   ☆   ☆

Walking out of the tent, Giorgos, a commander of cavalry, turned to his brother, Arsenios. "I don't like it. That clever carter's son has a plan. This is a trick of some sort."

"Maybe, but we have word from father. The war and the weather combined to cut this year's wheat crop in half. We are going to need that grain if we are to feed our people this winter."

"What? You think that Eumenes actually cares about *our* people?"

"Maybe. Or maybe Philip does."

"You're not saying we should be on Eumenes' side?"

"No, I guess not." But Arsenios sounded doubtful, and Giorgos realized the carter's plan. Eumenes was making himself and the queens look like they cared for the people of the empire—even the ones in rebellion. They were doing it to gain support. He didn't see a counter for it, though.

Alexandria, Egypt, Royal Palace
August 20, 319 BCE

"I will be happy to pay this year's taxes in grain," Ptolemy told his daughter Eirene. "And we will ship the grain to them in steam-powered ships."

"And what is that going to do to the price of grain in Egypt?" Thaïs asked.

Ptolemy stopped gloating, but it was still a good plan. For the next two months Ptolemy shipped grain to Amphipolis and Abdera, where it was divided into smaller loads and shipped to towns and estates throughout Macedonia and Thrace. Egypt didn't have enough on its own, so the massive farms on Sicily were also brought into play, which almost—but not quite—started the third Greco-Punic war.

Olympia, Greece
October 16, 319 BCE

Nike stood behind and to the left of Eurydice as they stood on the platform while athletes—not just from Greece, but from the rest of Alexander's empire and even Carthage and the Italian states—paraded before them. It was a marvelous spectacle and she didn't even mind that Cassander was on his own dais a few yards away with his wife, Thessalonike. These games would put all the others to shame. There were gymnastic competitions and pole vaulting, as well as the foot races, boxing, wrestling, and chariot races. The gymnastic competition had a women's section, as did the music and dance competitions.

Just offshore, the *Queen of the Sea* and the *Reliance* rode at anchor, and passengers from as far away as New America crowded the stands.

☆   ☆   ☆

For all of ten days, the expanded games were played. And politics were played as well. The imported food was making a difference, but it wasn't an unmixed blessing. The line between gratitude and resentment is both narrow and blurry. Philip got a lot of thank-yous, but not a lot of oaths of loyalty.

But the fact was that that wasn't why Philip did it. He did it because even with the advanced technology that the *Queen* brought, they would be a mostly handmade culture for decades to come. And that took hands. Hands connected to full bellies, for best results and greatest productivity.

214–216 12th Street, Fort Plymouth, Trinidad
October 18, 319 BCE

The big-screen TV in the community center started its life in a sports bar on the *Queen of the Sea*. Now it was, in a way, back to its old function. Though Stella didn't imagine that a chariot race taped by a bunch of cellphone cameras and edited with the *Queen of the Sea*'s video-editing suite was what ESPN had in mind back in the world.

It was moderately exciting, but she felt no need to jump up and down the way Carthalo and half the men in the audience were doing.

She shook her head, grabbed a slice of super turkey burger pizza and her beer, and waited for the race to end and them to get to the good stuff. The good stuff was the men's wrestling, done in the traditional Greek style, the wrestlers oiled up and naked.

The race ended with the favorite winning and the side of the screen showed the odds and the payout, and a number of the audience took their tickets to the window to collect on the bets. Carthalo tore his ticket into little bits and tossed it in the air like confetti. He wasn't the only one. The Carthaginian charioteer he'd bet on wasn't dead last, but that was only because the Etruscan charioteer took that "honor."

The commercials came on. There were commercials for beer, for brown potatoes, for corn fritters, for bottled "tabasco" sauce. Anything and everything. And not just from here. There was an ad from Carthage for cotton tunics, and one from Thrace for scented bath soap.

Then the wrestling came on and Stella found herself distracted for a while.

☆   ☆   ☆

"You want another beer?" Carthalo asked. Stella nodded vaguely and Carthalo grinned to himself. It was good to see Stella interested in something other than the books and how broke they were. He took the mug and went to the counter to get more of the corn beer that was on tap.

Besides, they weren't that broke, not anymore. They were producing glass at a good rate and selling it as fast as they could get it made. They'd just gotten a new contract yesterday, to provide the glass for windows on one of the ships they were building next to the harbor. They were going to have to hire more workers. He put that thought away. He used a printed bill to pay for the beer. Carthalo didn't have one of the ship people cards like Stella had. They couldn't make those in the here and now.

He took the beers back and set Stella's in front of her. He wasn't interested in the wrestling. He was neither Greek nor female. But Stella was, and that was something that Carthalo wanted to encourage. After all, they were on the other side of the world and he was right here.

CHAPTER 22

STUCK IN THE MUD

Katerini, Macedonia
October 28, 319 BCE

Daniel Lang escorted Thessalonike and Cassander off the *Reliance*. The *Queen* was officially neutral ground, but Cassander didn't trust that neutrality, not when it had, at the moment, both queens Roxane and Eurydice, and both emperors Philip and toddler Alexander IV, on board. Not to mention Eumenes and Olympias.

Daniel couldn't really blame him for that, but the truth was that the greatest danger—by far—was from Olympias. As to the *Reliance*, Katerini was as close as it was willing to get to Pella. The inlet that connected the sea to the city was too narrow and shallow for Commodore Adrian Scott to trust. Also, Daniel suspected that Adrian didn't trust Cassander's promise of free passage. For which Daniel didn't blame him a bit.

Once in town, they called for a steam barge. Steam engines and, more importantly, their boilers, were still very expensive and the best ones came from the

Queen of the Sea. But Cassander now had three of them, one for a factory in Pella, one for the royal barge that went from Pella to Katerini, and one that Cassander was being very tight-lipped about.

☆　　☆　　☆

The trip to Pella was quite comfortable, at least for Daniel. He wasn't the slave feeding coal into the boiler. He was seated on the deck, watching the birds and smelling the salt air, while he drank a cup of watered wine. Not great wine, but watered wine was the custom, in response to bad water. Nowadays, distillation was becoming available and the amount of alcohol put in water was much more controllable, so you could purify your water without the sour taste if you wanted to. Daniel sipped and grimaced. They didn't want to.

The cheese was good, though. And the scenery was nice, in a not quite tropical way. He slapped his arm as a mosquito decided it was time to dine, then went into the cabin and closed the screen door. The screen was cheesecloth, not wire, but it worked and let some air through.

The door opened and Cassander came in with Thessalonike and one of his younger brothers—this one named Phillip, but called Lípos. He was a beefy young man. Daniel guessed he was in his mid-twenties. He had crooked teeth, but big shoulders. He was wearing a fancy bronze breastplate over a short-sleeved linen shirt and ship people jeans. His were green, not quite olive drab.

Daniel stood and waited while Cassander and Thessalonike took seats and Lípos took station by the door.

Thessalonike waved Daniel to a chair, getting a

sharp look from Cassander, who, after a moment, said, "Sit, sit."

Daniel sat.

Cassander looked at Daniel and began to speak. "We are here to discuss your duties. We wish you to act not only as the...what is the phrase... 'boss of police'?"

Daniel nodded. It was close enough. The Greek word *Archigós* meant chief, and *Afentikó* meant boss, so it was an easy slip.

"We also wish you to set up a school to teach our police to use ship people law enforcement techniques." The word Cassander used was *Oi nkárntens*, which meant guardsman, but that was about as close as local Greek came to cop.

Daniel nodded again. This was expected. "What sort of authority am I going to have in regard to hiring and firing?"

They talked for about an hour and Daniel noticed early that when Cassander said "we" he was using the royal we, not including Thessalonike or Lípos in the discussion. Also that Thessalonike wasn't happy about that, but was not making an issue of it. Lípos, still standing by the door, didn't seem to care.

More to the point, Cassander made it clear that Daniel was pretty limited in his hiring and firing practices. Among other things, he was getting a title, but unlike most of the titled nobility in Macedonia, Thrace, and the other Greek states, his didn't come with family to avenge him.

"If you were to kill Metró Archelaus, his family would come to me to punish you. And if that didn't work, they might take action on their own. So it behooves you to be careful using that ship people gun of yours."

The gun in question, a six-shot black powder cap-and-ball revolver made on the *Queen of the Sea*, was even now openly displayed on his belt. Daniel had over a thousand caps and a mold for making lead bullets in his bags. He noticed that Lípos was grinning. "I will be careful, Your Majesty. However, if push comes to shove, you are going to lose some of your nobles."

"Good!" Cassander nodded. "They need to learn to respect you."

Lípos was still smiling.

Pella, Macedonia
November 1, 319 BCE

The police headquarters office was located in the same building that housed the radio. Partly, that was because Daniel didn't have his own computer and would be sharing theirs. Malcolm Tanada and Rico Gica were the only ship people here and he knew that Rico was the "chief of station," the ship people chief spy in Pella, which just meant he was the computer geek while Malcolm was the effective ambassador from the ship people to Cassander. Daniel would not need to set up his own spy network, which wasn't anything new for a cop. Police work was all about informants, whatever shows like *CSI* made it look like.

But that was upstairs. Here and now, Daniel was standing in a room roughly ten feet by fifteen, with no furniture and no door in the doorway or windows in the window frames. He would need to order glass from Carthage. Carthage had a glassmaking industry before the *Queen* arrived. Now it had a clear glass-making industry, and if the glass was only flat on one side, it still let in the light while keeping out the cold. He looked over at Zoilo, the Greek slave whom Cassander had assigned to him.

"So, it looks like we are starting from scratch," Daniel said in his Macedonian-accented Greek. He'd picked up his Greek from Silver Shields and from the computer translation programs that got most of its pronunciations from the Macedonians.

Zoilo nodded, but didn't speak. Not all that surprising. During the trip to Pella, Zoilo didn't use two words if he could get away with one. Daniel didn't know whether that was just with him or with everyone.

"We're going to need a door with a lock," Daniel said.

Zoilo pulled a waxed slate out and started writing.

Pella, Office of the Police
November 2, 319 BCE

Thessalonike walked into the office, looked around, and sniffed. Well, waddled into the office. She was six months pregnant and her movement was affected.

Daniel didn't blame her for the sniff. There was still no door, and not even shutters in the window frames. No furniture but a single couch that was doubling as Daniel's bed. Zoilo was sleeping on a pallet on the floor, and that was rolled up in the corner. She looked at Zoilo and he got up and left.

Then she walked over and sat on the couch. "Olympias says I can trust you."

"Within limits." Daniel stayed standing. "Olympias and I have an agreement concerning you." Daniel wished he still had his phone with its translation app, but it was owned by the *Queen* and he was watching his expenses.

They talked in fits and starts, and mistranslations and careful rephrasing about the political situation and what Daniel might be able to do to keep her safe if things went to hell.

"Philip Lípos is leaving to take command of the army tomorrow. The army will be heading into Thrace to defeat Seuthes."

Daniel nodded, trying to keep his expression bland.

"You doubt Lípos' ability?"

Daniel shook his head. Then looked at the young woman and decided that his best course was honesty. "I don't know enough about Lípos to have an opinion of his ability as a general. I do know that he will be going up against a general who history counts as only slightly less capable than Alexander the Great himself, and one—maybe the only one—who gets the twentieth-century military axiom 'amateurs study tactics, professionals study logistics.'" He shrugged. "That's not why I'm here. I'm here to make a professional police force and to make the streets of Pella as safe as the corridors of the *Queen of the Sea*."

"Can you really do that?"

"Not a chance. But I'll get as close to it as I can." He smiled, and she smiled back. She had dimples and a little gap between her two front teeth.

There was a cough from outside. Daniel looked at the door to see two young men, teenagers really, walk into the room. They were wearing the nippled bronze breastplates that were so popular with the Macedonian nobility.

They were laughing until they saw Thessalonike. Then they stopped, and gave her a bow. One of them said, "You should be in the palace. Not out among peasants without even your ladies."

Daniel looked at them, then at Thessalonike. He wasn't sure of the status here. She was the queen, but she was female, and women weren't supposed to act on their own. That was most of the reason that the Macedonian nobility was outraged by the queens regent. Especially Eurydice. And Daniel wasn't sure how the dynamic fit in this situation.

Thessalonike stood up, sniffed, and gave the boys a look that would freeze half a lake. "I am your queen. You will not speak to me in that fashion."

The boys stiffened, and one of them started to advance on her. That was enough for Daniel. His hand dropped to the pistol on his belt, and the second youngster grabbed the first's arm.

Suddenly Daniel had a thought. "Queen Thessalonike," he said, "the king said that if I killed any nobles I would have to deal with their families mostly on my own. What families am I going to have to deal with after I kill these fellows?"

It was partly his horrible accent, and partly the way he was using the Greek words that made both young men and Thessalonike look confused as they worked out what he was saying. But it was his hand resting on the butt of his pistol that made the point when they finally worked out the words.

After she parsed his sentence, she pointed. "That is Bastian of the house of Papados. The other is his cousin Demos."

The boys were looking at the pistol and it was

clear that they were familiar with them. Not really surprising. Malcolm had one just like it, and shot at a small pistol range he'd built next to the radio shack. "And what brings Bastian and Demos to police headquarters?" Daniel asked.

"I believe they are two of your police captains," Thessalonike said.

Daniel looked at her, then back at the boys. They had dark curly hair and—not following Alexander's example—they were letting their whiskers grow, but neither had much in the way of beards. "How old are you?"

"Fifteen," Bastian said.

"Sixteen," Demos added.

"Oh, my God," Daniel muttered. Then he took a breath. "Gentlemen, run up to the radio shack and ask Rico Gica for a copy of the Greek translation of the police manual. Then find a place to sit and read the first chapter while I discuss the organization of our police force with the queen."

The young men looked at him like he'd just killed their dog. It was Bastian who said, "We don't read Greek. At least, not well."

"I think there may be a Macedonian translation," Daniel offered. "Marie Easley has been studying Macedonian since we got here. Rico will probably have to download it from the *Queen* and print it, though."

"Ah..." Bastian said. "Almost *no one* reads Macedonian."

Daniel felt like whimpering. Even he, who was no great reader, knew the value of education.

Thessalonike looked at Daniel, then back at the boys. "Have your tutors read them to you." Then to

Daniel, "Their tutors will be Greek slaves, probably Athenians."

That didn't make Daniel Lang feel one bit better. Slavery was illegal on the *Queen* and in New America, but to the best of Daniel's knowledge, nowhere else on Earth, not in this day and age. So leaving the *Queen of the Sea* meant that he would have to deal with slavers and slaves. And, for that matter, Daniel was going to have to enforce the property rights of slave owners. He knew that, but he didn't like it.

☆   ☆   ☆

Once the boys were gone, Daniel and Thessalonike got down to cases. Lípos was in charge of the army because Cassander couldn't afford to be in command of the army if it lost to Eumenes, and when Cassander's army went after Seuthes, Eumenes would almost have to come to Seuthes' aid.

Once again, it was made clear that this war was as much about politics as battles. He wondered what was going on with Eumenes.

Amphipolis
November 3, 319 BCE

Philip III, co-emperor of the United Satrapies and States of the Empire, drew the symbol on the sheet as the discussion passed over him. They were talking tactics, and while the individual actions made sense, they didn't fit together for him. So he worked on determining how much time would be saved by a steam hammer versus the cost of making one, and how soon the steam hammer would pay for itself.

Eurydice came over and squeezed his arm hard.

Which didn't make him jerk the way he would have if she touched him gently.

She looked at the calculations and nodded. She could follow some of them now. Then she turned back to the discussion.

☆   ☆   ☆

"My father says you should prepare to attack Pella," Nike said. Seuthes now had a radio team in Abdera. "He says that he can hold out against Lípos for months."

Eurydice nodded agreement. In her opinion they should attack Pella whether Seuthes could hold out or not. Chop off Cassander's head and the whole rebellion would die. At least the rebellion in Macedonia and Thrace. All of the "Greek" states. She knew that Roxane and Eumenes disagreed. She even understood their reasoning. They had to be seen as defending the states and their legitimate kings.

"In that case," Eumenes said, "we need to get ships here to take our army to Pella. I want to go by sea because they can tell where we march, but they won't be sure where we're taking the army if we go by sea. For all they will know, we could be sailing for Tyre to reinforce Attalus at Babylon." He snorted a laugh—something Eurydice found irritating—and continued. "I almost wish we could do that. I don't like the reports we're getting from there. Antigonus One-eye is winning the cavalry war in the area around Babylon."

"Frankly, I'm shocked Attalus has lasted this long," Eurydice said. "He has kept Antigonus locked in Babylon for months. He can last a few more while we deal with Cassander."

West Babylon
November 3, 319 BCE

Karrel Agot helped the kid onto the bed. He was three, maybe four, with a distended belly from the malnutrition that was making the switch to out-and-out starvation. Rations were getting scarce in Babylon. Boats still got through, bringing food and other things from up- and downriver, but they had to make the trip at night and hug the bank once they got in sight of the walls, which gave Antigonus' patrols a shot at them.

The people of West Babylon weren't starving yet. Not most of them, anyway. But the poor were always the first to suffer as a siege closed in and food got scarce. Karrel dipped the cloth in the broth and put it next to the kid's mouth. It was goat broth thickened with wheat flour, not the milk that the kid really needed, but it would have to do.

☆   ☆   ☆

Susan Godlewski sat at the table with Attalus, Menander, and the rest of the general's staff. It was a decent but not overly fancy meal. There was bread, cheese and, of course, olives. A sour wine that was cut with water. Out the window, they could see the river wall. It was a short wall compared to the outer walls, because the river was expected to provide part of the defense and because the other side of the city across the Euphrates River was taller.

"But every day we hold out is another day for Eumenes to catch Cassander," Attalus said, just as though that had been his plan from the beginning. It hadn't, of course. By now Susan knew the history. Partly through anger and partly through arrogance,

Attalus attacked Babylon trying to prove that he was a better general than Eumenes, and at the same time trying to kill the murdering bastard who had his wife killed. Attalus got caught in a trap of his own making and only survived by luck. None of that changed the validity of the statement, however. As long as West Babylon held out, Antigonus was stuck in East Babylon. And every day Antigonus was stuck here, he got weaker and the empire got stronger.

"I don't disagree, Satrap, but the poor are starting to starve. If we don't do a better job of sharing out the rations, we are going to lose West Babylon to disease, if we don't lose it to betrayal first."

Attalus' face got hard and Susan was quick to add, "It's not disloyalty. It's hunger. If your wife was starving, what would you do to save her?"

"It's not just the sharing of rations," Menander said, "it's getting supplies in through the blockade. Antigonus' cavalry owns the east side of the Euphrates, and we don't own the west side, not really."

East Babylon

Boulos the slave sat on his pallet of bound reeds with a small knife and whittled. He had a pattern and two chunks of wood. The pattern was in bronze, two cups with a narrow tube between them, a tall cup on one side and a short, fat one on the other. And if Boulos didn't finish it to the overseer's satisfaction, he would be beaten. Though skilled, a childhood of chronic malnutrition had left him not overly bright, and a life lived in a world where questioning authority got you killed left him profoundly incurious.

So Boulos slid the short-bladed steel knife over the wood, taking off a paper-thin sliver at a time, and gave no thought at all to what he was making. That was up to the masters, not to him.

☆   ☆   ☆

One of those masters, Rahel of Rhodes, a cavalryman in Antigonus' army, was trying to fit a venturi onto the body of a rocket. Rahel was a reasonably well-educated man by the standards of Rhodes. He could read, write, do basic math, and had never missed a meal until he joined Alexander's army at sixteen, and not often since. He picked up the often read *Ship People Basic Physics* and reread the section about every action having an equal and opposite reaction, and still couldn't quite get his head around the idea that it meant they needed venturi. A hole in the back for the gas to escape should work. He shrugged, put the booklet down, and went back to the rocket.

It was all magic, anyway. It didn't really need to make sense. The venturi was just part of the spell.

He looked at the fins. Those made sense to him. They were like the feathers on an arrow. They would make the rocket spin and the spinning would keep it going straight. Then he got up from the bench and nodded to the overseer, a slave but higher ranking than the average. "How many? And how soon?"

"It's slow work, master. And new designs . . . we don't know which parts matter, so we can't scrimp anywhere. It will be months before we have the number of rockets that *Strategos* Antigonus demands."

Rahel nodded and looked over at the palace where the increasingly irritable *Strategos* Antigonus resided.

☆   ☆   ☆

Antigonus One-eye stood on the balcony of his palace and looked across the Euphrates River at the thorn in his side. *I'm winning.* He had to keep telling himself that, because it didn't feel like it was true. He looked at the antenna rising up from the tallest building in West Babylon, so tall that it could speak to Fort Plymouth on the other side of the world. That radio told him what was going on in Macedonia and Thrace. It let him send messages to all the satraps of the eastern empire, and without it the fragile alliance would have already collapsed. But, at the same time, it told everyone of every loss that Cassander's army suffered and, worse, it was portraying the rebels in West Babylon as courageous defenders of empire.

He turned and looked down at the shop. It was located in East Babylon, just a few blocks from the palace, and in it he was building the rockets and the boats that would open a way into West Babylon and end this farce.

CHAPTER 23

DANCING IN THRACE

Lípos' army, en route to Seuthopolis
November 7, 319 BCE

Lípos sat his horse and looked around. His army was heading inland, ignoring Abdera and the coastal cities entirely. They were going to Seuthopolis, the symbolic center of King Seuthes' power. If Seuthes stayed on the coast, he would be abandoning the temple of Hephaestus, Zeus, and Sabazios which was his primary duty and source of authority.

Lípos laughed. *Seuthes and Eumenes probably think that I'm headed for Abdera to put it under siege. Cassander may be a gutless conniver, but he's smart.* He took a wineskin from his belt and had a drink, then rode back to the head of his army.

Amphipolis, headquarters of Eumenes' First Army
November 9, 319 BCE

Eumenes looked at the soldier. He was a standard Greek infantryman with his *sarissa* broken into its two parts and pointed at the sky. He had one new feature, a patch sewn onto his tunic. It was red with a white sword and the legend "1st Army." The patches were delivered by the *Reliance* last time it came through, and were part of the transformation of Alexander's army into the Army of the Empire. The introduction of unit numbers and names was going to introduce a basis for unit pride that wasn't based on Alexander or any general, but on the unit and the army and government. He checked the man's *sarissa* for cleanliness and condition, then returned it and stepped to the next man.

A clerk came running up and Eumenes turned to look at the man. Then he reached out and the man put a sheet of paper in his hand.

It said: *The army of Philip Lípos is not where it is supposed to be.*

Eumenes folded the sheet and went back to his inspection.

☆   ☆   ☆

Back in the headquarters after the inspection, Eumenes looked at Eurydice, who was standing by the map, muttering, "So where is he if he's not on his way to Abdera?"

"We don't know. We've sent out more scouts, but it looks like he may have gone north."

Eumenes walked over to the map. Pella was almost due west of Amphipolis, and since Lípos' army didn't take ship, Eumenes had expected it to travel northeast to avoid Amphipolis on its way to Abdera. Perhaps along the far side of the Strymon River Valley, or perhaps even farther north. Eumenes looked at the pins in the map indicating where the earlier scouts had looked.

"Eumenes, I think we have to delay moving on

Pella, at least until we know where Lípos has gone," Eurydice said. "We can't afford to attack Pella and have Lípos fall on our rear."

"I'm more concerned with what he might be doing in Macedonia or Thrace while we are investing Pella, but I agree that we need more information before we move."

November 11, 319 BCE

The scout was muddy and his hair was plastered to his head by the rain. But he saluted Eumenes fist to chest, then bowed to Eurydice. "I saw them, Majesty," he said to Eurydice, and at her gesture he went to the map and put his finger on a spot almost fifty miles due north of Pella. "Wherever he was going, he wasn't heading for Abdera."

"Where can he be going? This makes no sense!" Eurydice said.

"It could be that he is simply going out of his way to avoid the coast," Eumenes said. "Remember, not all decisions are rational. And with our alliance with New America, he may wish to avoid coming anywhere near range of the *Reliance*'s cannon."

"You think Cassander is that frightened of the *Reliance*?"

"Not really, no." Eumenes scratched his chin. "Cassander is afraid of the *Reliance* certainly, but he is more afraid of looking like he's afraid of it. So rather than go along the coast just out of range of the *Reliance*'s guns, he makes some excuse to avoid the coast altogether."

"You sound like Philip," Eurydice said, smiling. "I think you're overthinking it."

Eumenes chuckled. "Perhaps, but it feels right." He turned to the scout. "Go find some hot food and a place to dry off. We need to think about this."

Once the man was gone, Eumenes said, "What about the ship people?"

Eurydice shook her head. "I don't think so. They have to be careful. Part of the deal that keeps them safe is the promise that they don't act as spies. Would you want Tacaran spying on us?"

Eumenes snorted at that.

"It's true they can pass on what others tell them, and they can certainly send messages for spies just like anyone else, but they can't gather information for us against Cassander, or for Cassander against us."

"I understand. But see what you can find out anyway."

Amphipolis, radio section

Tacaran Bayot sipped his coffee with the care of a connoisseur long denied the delicacy. It was shipped here from Egypt. Ptolemy had a source and was making friends and influencing people by shipping small amounts of the holy beans to the radio operators and ambassadors around the Med. He grimaced. More than two years without had left his taste buds unprepared for the bitter flavor. He went to the sideboard and got milk and sugar—well, granulated honey.

Erica Mirzadeh and the servants watched. Erica with unveiled amusement, and the servants slightly more careful of their expressions. But only slightly. Several of the servants were former slaves whom Erica and Tacaran bought and manumitted, then hired. But they were free people now, and if loyal to Erica and Tacaran, they were not particularly subservient.

There was a knock and then Eurydice was ushered into the room. Tacaran waved at her, then sipped his coffee and sighed in bliss. "Would you care for some coffee, Your Majesty?"

Eurydice sniffed the air. "That smells lovely."

"Don't be fooled," Erica said, holding up a glass of red wine that was actually made of glass. Most of them were ceramic, but the Carthaginians, who were producing glass beads and artworks before The Event, had used ship people knowledge to produce clear blown glass and were selling glassware at a premium around the Med. "Coffee smells glorious, but tastes as bitter as an ex-lover's heart."

"Yes, it does," Tacaran agreed, then sipped happily. "It's what is known as an acquired taste. Since you're just starting out, I suggest goat milk and honey to soften the flavor."

"I'll take it without." She paused a moment, thinking. "Ah . . . yes. I will take it straight."

Tacaran shrugged and fixed her a cup of black coffee. She tasted it, grimaced, but kept sipping. She took a seat and looked at Tacaran. "Have you heard anything from Rico Gica recently?"

Tacaran looked around, then said, "Salucas, Alala, that'll be all for now. We'll call you if we need anything."

The two servants left and Eurydice grimaced again. She knew that the ship people didn't think you should tell secrets in front of servants, even loyal servants. She even knew they were right. But she often forgot.

"No," Tacaran said. "Is there some reason I should have?"

"Lípos is going north."

"Okay?" Tacaran looked at Erica, who looked back and shrugged.

"We were expecting him to head east. Fairly close to due east. Passing just to the north of us and traveling along the coast to Abdera. That's why we're still here, hoping he would think we were going to hit him from behind. Instead, he is going north. Far enough north to add at least a week to his trip to Abdera."

"Are you sure he's going to Abdera?" Erica asked.

"Where else would he go?"

"I don't know. You're the general. Tacaran and I just run the radio."

Eurydice rolled her eyes.

"I can send him a message and ask what he knows, but don't expect too much. You know we aren't supposed to act as spies. And before you roll your eyes again, that thing with Rico Gica's girlfriend was gossip, not spying."

"Then ask him for some gossip." Eurydice stood. "Good coffee. I'll have to order some."

Pella, Radio Building

Rico Gica lay on the bed with one arm around Sara as he looked at the timber ceiling. Sara wasn't her actual name, but it was a name he could pronounce, and her real name started with an *s* sound. She giggled the first time he called her Sara, so he assumed that she was okay with it. Rico was from Port-au-Prince, a short black man with crooked teeth. He was self-educated and knew electronics from fixing busted radios back in the world. On the ship he had been a steward. But he could read a circuit diagram better than he could read English, or even his native French, so he got this gig as radio tech.

Sara snuggled closer and Rico tried to figure out a way of convincing Thessalonike to sell him Sara. So far he hadn't had any luck with that. His plan was to free her, but he hadn't told anyone that.

There was a knock at the door and he got up. "Yes?"

"You have a message in the radio room." It was one of Malcolm's servants, a manumitted slave whose name Rico couldn't pronounce. He had a lot of trouble with Greek names. He had a lot of trouble with Greek, period, but he understood it a lot better than he spoke it.

"What is it, Ricardo?" Sara asked. She called him Ricardo instead of Rico. He thought it was her response to his calling her Sara, but he liked it.

"Just a message. Go back to sleep." He put on his tunic and his pistol, then slipped on the sandals, and went upstairs to the radio room. "What have we got?"

"It is in your mailbox."

The computer mailbox, he meant. The computer was installed in a purpose-built desk. He sat at the desk and logged onto the computer. The room on the top floor of the building had a tube radio built on the *Queen of the Sea*. Attached to the radio was a surge-protected cable to the computer. There was also a surge-protected charging cable that went from the hundred-watt pedal-powered generator that was also a product of the *Queen*.

He checked his mail. It was from Tacaran, a roommate on the *Queen* before The Event.

*I hear that Cass's bro has gone north, not east.
Do you have any notion why that might be?*

*P.S. Keep this on the down-low, buddy. The little
queen wants to know.*

Tacaran Bayot

Rico read the message with some concern. This
was the first he'd heard about Lípos, and unless she
was told not to Sara would have told him. That left
only two possibilities . . . well, three. Sara was told not
to tell him, Thessalonike hadn't told Sara, or Thessalonike didn't know.

He thought about what he might do. He liked
Tacaran and there was a loyalty between the ship
people. But he loved Sara. He didn't know when that
had happened, but he loved her. And if he was ever
going to get her freedom, he had to be someone that
Thessalonike could trust.

All the way back to the room, he balanced loyalties,
but there was never any question.

He crawled back into bed, snuggled up to Sara,
and whispered in her ear. "Your mistress will want
to know that Eumenes' army knows that Lípos took
the army north."

"What?" Sara jerked upright, stared at him, looked
around, then lay back down and whispered in his ear.
"Lípos went north? Are you sure?"

"Tacaran Bayot is."

☆   ☆   ☆

Sophronike listened to Rico's explanation. She knew
that Thessalonike would have told her if she knew.

After all, she was more than Thessalonike's slave. She was also an apprentice to the Cabeiri in her own right, trusted with the lesser secrets and initiated into the rites. And she had proved her devotion when her mistress ordered her to seduce the ugly little ship person. She knew, or at least strongly suspected, that Rico wanted to free her. But she didn't want to be freed. She was a trusted confidante of her mistress and thereby in a position of importance in the governance of Macedonia and accepted of the Cabeiri. She had no desire to give that up for some odd ship person notion of freedom. No one was free in the way that ship people thought of the word.

But she listened to Rico with care, kissed him gently and thanked him for telling her. Then, after he went back to sleep, she slipped out of bed and went to inform her mistress.

Thessalonike's rooms, Pella
November 12, 319 BCE

Cassander was nowhere in sight, of course. Once Thessalonike started showing, he avoided her bedchamber. Sophronike knocked quietly on the door panel and was admitted by one of Thessalonike's guards, then allowed into the queen's bedchamber. The room was dark, shuttered against the November chill, with a small fire in a portable bronze firepit and a lamp in the corner. She moved carefully to the couch the queen was sleeping on. She whispered to Thessalonike, who was lying on her side, one leg over a reed pillow.

"What?" Thessalonike woke. "What are you doing here?"

"The army is going north!"

"What? How do you...? No. Of course, you got it from Rico. Where did he get it?"

"You knew?"

Thessalonike levered herself up in the bed. "No, and I don't believe it, not yet." She got up and moved to the chamber pot. Sophronike waited while Thessalonike finished.

When the queen returned to the sleeping couch and sat, Sophronike waited some more. She could tell that her mistress was thinking. Finally, Thessalonike spoke. "Go back to Rico. I need to study this matter."

☆   ☆   ☆

That morning after the sun came up, Thessalonike called on several of her agents. They were women and a few men who were connected with the army. People who could find out where the force under Lípos went and why. It took three days and a very drunk cavalryman talking to his young lover, who "wanted to learn strategy."

Thessalonike's rooms, Pella
November 15, 319 BCE

The lad was fifteen and well formed. He knelt on the small rug on the marble floor. That, after all, was what it was for. Then he bent forward and placed his forehead on the floor. This wasn't the respect to a queen, but the respect due the gods and their representatives. Thessalonike nodded her approval, then said, "Rise and speak."

He rose, but stayed on his knees. "The army moves to Seuthopolis. According to Pantheras, it will discredit

Seuthes when his holy city is captured and the temple to Dionysus is seized. They will burn the temple, proving that Seuthes can't defend even his temple. He will have to respond and will charge north, where he can be defeated well away from the support of the *Reliance* and its guns."

"And what of Eumenes?"

"I asked Pantheras about that. He said Eumenes is a Thracian wagoneer's son. If he tries to sally north in support of his king, his army will abandon him. Or, at best, he will be defeated once he is in the open field with no walls to hide behind." The boy looked up pleadingly. "He really said that."

"I don't doubt it," Thessalonike assured him. "Continue."

"That is all of it, Majesty." Then he blurted, "Do you think they will really desecrate the temple?"

"Unless . . ." Thessalonike stopped. "Don't worry about it." She waved the lad out.

Once the boy was gone, Thessalonike stood with some difficulty and walked to the north wall of her room. She pulled a bell pull. She could barely hear the chime on the other side of the wall, but quickly the door opened and her personal guard came in. "I need to see Sophronike."

☆   ☆   ☆

An hour later Sophronike arrived from the radio room, while Thessalonike was seated at her writing table with one of the new fountain pens. She didn't rise, but waved the girl over, saying loudly, "I have a message for Olympias. You will take it to your friend in the radio room. Make sure he gives it priority. I need more rubber hot-water bottles."

As she passed the sheet to Sophronike, she said quietly, "Tell Rico that Lípos is moving on Seuthopolis."

Army of Lípos, Thrace
November 15, 319 BCE

Lípos cursed his army. He did it quietly, under his breath, lest his prickly subordinates hear the complaint and spend an hour sitting in their saddles, insisting it was someone else's fault. Less than ten miles a day his army was making, and he wasn't traveling anything close to a straight line. Miles out of his way for every hill or grove, stopping by noon every day to rest their horses and forage for food. He looked around. They were riding single file down a path between trees and it was raining. The infantry behind them would stop complaining about the dust the horses kicked up, and complain instead about the muddy bog that two thousand horses left after they crossed the ground.

He kept riding. Around noon they reached the end of the trees and rode into an open area made up of grazing land for sheep. And a contingent of his cavalry rode off to steal some sheep for dinner. At least they were Thracian sheep now, not Macedonian.

He waited in the rain as slaves set up his tent, then climbed off his horse, tossed the reins to a groom, and went into his tent. A slave waited with a damp towel, and Lípos suppressed a biting comment. The rain wasn't the slave's fault.

Amphipolis
November 15, 319 BCE

Tacaran Bayot handed the message to Eumenes, not really sure what it meant. He looked at the map and saw Seuthopolis marked by a wine-red star. Appropriate enough for a temple to Dionysus, he supposed, but it was in the middle of nowhere. There was nothing there.

He was surprised when Eumenes started cursing in what, best Tacaran could tell, were the Macedonian, Persian, and Phoenician languages. And perhaps Egyptian. Then Eumenes stood, went to the map and, using strings and pins, measured out the route and, calculating out loud, figured the time it would take to get Briarus, Seuthes, and their combined army from Abdera to Seuthopolis.

"Maybe," Eumenes said to the map. "Or maybe not." Then he turned back to Tacaran. "I need you to get a message to Abdera. Seuthes is to move to Seuthopolis, taking only his fastest cavalry, and prepare the city for a siege. Briarus is to hold Abdera using only the infantry." He paused for a moment, staring at Tacaran, then asked, "How quickly can the radio operators at Abdera move their equipment?"

Tacaran considered. Charles Blevins was sixty-two, and before The Event was overweight, but otherwise in good health. Not forced-march good health, but good health. His wife Alice Blevins was forty-five and in decent shape. On the other hand, they wouldn't be marching. They and the radio gear would be on two-wheeled chariots pulled by two horses and surrounded by cavalry. "They ought to be able to keep up, depending on how long they have to do it for."

"I think three days. Two and a half if they are lucky. They will go slow to save the horses the first day. Then . . . Never mind." Eumenes waved it away. "Tell Seuthes to take the radio with him. If we can have it in Seuthopolis, we can coordinate."

☆ ☆ ☆

Once Tacaran was gone, Eumenes called in his staff and started preparations to get his army under way. There wasn't that much to do. They were ready to march on Pella until this happened.

On the other hand, Eurydice wasn't happy. "This is perfect. We go to Pella while Lípos is all the way up in central Thrace and take the city. We have rockets and the *Reliance* can get within range with its rockets. We will have Cassander, Thessalonike, and Macedonia before Lípos even gets to Seuthopolis."

"But if we do that we will be out of position to support Seuthes," Eumenes said.

Eurydice looked at Eumenes like he was crazy, then slowly shook her head. "I am sorry about that, Eumenes. I truly am. But the needs of the empire outweigh the needs of a single king within it. Seuthes will just have to hold out until we get to him."

Nike, daughter of Seuthes, was staring at Eurydice. "You would betray my father?"

Eurydice turned to her. "Not betray, no. But I must put the needs of the empire above the needs of any kingdom in it, no matter how well beloved." She turned to Eumenes. "We march on Pella."

"No, Majesty. I am *strategos*. Pella will still be there a month from now, or three months, if that is what it takes. We would not only damage our alliance with

Seuthes, but our reputation with all the states and satrapies within the empire would be compromised."

"That is a political decision, Eumenes, not a strategic one. It is a decision for the queen...ah, queens. Not the *strategos*."

"Then let us hear from the other queen."

They argued until they got to the radio room and called Roxane on the *Queen of the Sea*.

Queen of the Sea, *Atlantic Ocean* *November 15, 319 BCE*

Roxane picked up the phone and muttered, "Yes?"

"We have an urgent radio communication from Amphipolis."

"Put it through." Yawning, she lay back in the bed, head on her pillow, and used the hand not holding the phone to push her hair out of her face.

Eurydice spoke from the earpiece. "Eumenes is being difficult. You need to tell him to go to Pella."

Almost, Roxane agreed. She was still half asleep, after all. But she was just a little too familiar with Eurydice's tactics. "Is Eumenes there?" she asked, and yawned again.

"Yes, Majesty," came Eumenes' voice. "Lípos is attacking Seuthopolis."

"What?" Roxane asked, trying to... "What!" Suddenly, without consciously willing it, Roxane was sitting up in bed. Dag grunted at the motion. "Now?"

"No. He's days away. We got the information, indirectly from Thessalonike, about an hour ago. The plan is to discredit Seuthes as priest king of Thrace."

"What do you want to do about it?"

He told her. Over the next few minutes, she got the whole tale, not just Eumenes and Eurydice's version, but also Nike's concern.

"All right," she said at last. "You both have good points. Very good points. Nike, Eurydice isn't being uncaring. She is being a commander in the field. A hard job, and one your father understands. He will tell you the same. However, on balance, I have to support Eumenes in this. It isn't that Eurydice is wrong, but that we will be seen by many as betraying our vassals.

"I say go after Lípos and catch him between the walls of Seuthopolis and your army. Then deal with the snake in Pella."

CHAPTER 24

STAGE DRESSING

Abdera
November 15, 319 BCE

Alice Blevins was at the radio when the message came in. It was in Greek and she wasn't good at Greek yet, but she could recognize the recipient's name and that was all she needed at the moment. She loaded the printer with paper and printed out the message, then called one of the Thracian soldiers who were assigned to them as runners and bodyguards. She folded the letter and handed it to the guy. He was about twenty, with curly black hair and a mustache that he'd copied from Charles Blevins. "Urgent for Commander Briarus," she said, then enjoyed the view as he turned and ran out of the radio room.

☆　　☆　　☆

It was almost fifteen minutes later that the commander of their guard came in, shouting orders. Then argued with two of the other guards/assistants before turning to Alice and saying, in a broken smashup of

Greek and English, "Need to *gobbledygook* tear up *gobbledygook* radio to run to *gobbledygook* Thrace."

"Charles!" she yelled at the top of her lungs. "Get your fat ass in here."

It was Charles' break time, and he was taking a nap.

He came in and there was a quick confusing conversation in Charles' slightly better Greek.

Then everything went right to hell. Charles told her they had to go to Seuthopolis, and "right fucking now." Then, under the eyes of the Thracian guard, they disconnected the batteries, took down the antennas. There were three of them. Packed up the desktop computer and screen, packed everything in wool and wood, and loaded it onto two two-wheeled carts, then climbed onto another chariot and left before nightfall, and well ahead of the army.

☆   ☆   ☆

"They are away?" Seuthes asked.

"Yes," Briarus agreed. "I still think it's a risky move, sending them ahead with a guard of only twenty. There are still bandits running rampant through Thrace."

"I know. But we are going to need that radio in Seuthopolis, and we are going to need it there as soon as we can get it there. Now, about the rest of the army—" And they talked about who was going to go and who would stay here to defend the port.

Approaching Seuthopolis
November 18, 319 BCE

Around ten in the morning, an utterly exhausted Alice Blevins looked down into a valley and saw a hill near its center. On that hill was Seuthopolis, perhaps fifteen miles away. It was a small place, just a few large buildings surrounded by a stone curtain wall, maybe thirty feet high. There was a village outside the walls and a vineyard outside that.

Another two hours brought them to the gates. Large wooden things, wide enough to let in six horses abreast. All Alice wanted to do was sleep, but on the trip here it had finally sunk in that they weren't running like this to get out of the area to be attacked. They were here because this was where the attack was going to fall. She looked over at her husband and said, "And you said this was going to be a soft gig."

Charles shrugged. "It's easier than staying in Fort Plymouth and trying to start an industry with hand tools while we run out of money."

Alice looked at Charles. He was looking all of his sixty-two years after the trip and she was worried about him. Which only made her madder. That was the argument he used to get her to agree to come to work for Eumenes and Seuthes. "Tell me that after Cassander burns this whole place to the ground with us in it."

"Hey, the walls are brick, not easy to burn," he said, pointing as they rode through the gates.

Once they were through the gates, they were on a brick-paved street that looked to be around fifteen feet wide. They followed that street about two hundred feet to a large open square, an agora, or market square. At the far end of the square another street teed into it and beyond that there were a couple of short blocks and the palace compound. That was where they were headed. Where they could rest.

Palace of Seuthes, Seuthopolis
November 19, 319 BCE

Somebody banged on the small brass gong mounted next to their door. The sound of it was a bit deeper than a doorbell, but served the same function. The sun was just coming up.

It was still last night, as far as Alice was concerned. She pulled a pillow over her head.

The next thing Alice realized was that a group of men were standing around the bed she and Charles were sharing. "What the flaming hell!" she shouted, grabbing for the blanket. "What are you people doing in my bedroom?"

"Lípos has been sighted. He will be here by the end of the day," Hristos, their Silver Shield and translator, said. "The holy brother here says that you must get the antenna up as soon as possible. It must be seen by the Macedonians that we have ship people radio and ship people here."

☆   ☆   ☆

Charles sat up. Unlike Alice, he went from asleep to awake in nothing flat. One of the men standing around their bed was Mucapor, the high priest of Sabazios. "Come on, Hristos. You know that we won't be able to whistle up cannons, even if we get the radio up and running. And just getting the radio tower set up won't get the radio working." Their radio was a tube job, built on the *Queen of the Sea* post-Event, with some of its innards cannibalized from pre-Event components. To make it work better, they strung a set of long wires as high as they could get them, which was standard practice and known all over the Med these days. The wooden towers to hold them were locally made.

"Don't matter. As long as the wires are up on the tower, it will work."

"What will work?" Alice asked, beating Charles to the punch by half a breath.

"It will frighten Lípos. The auguries have shown it."

From the sound of it, Charles wasn't sure whether Hristos believed that or not. But he was pretty sure that Mucapor did believe it, and he was in no mood to start a religious war when only he and Alice were Christian, and he wasn't *all* that sure of Alice.

"Fine. Let us get dressed."

Some talking in what was probably Thracian. Then, Hristos said, "Hurry up."

They were left alone. Charles got up and started getting dressed, talking all the while to let Alice know that today wasn't going to be a sleep-in day no matter how much she wanted it to be.

By the time he was dressed, Alice was sitting up, looking flamethrowers at him. He tossed her some clothes from their pack and made a hasty retreat.

☆   ☆   ☆

The roof of Seuthes' palace was flat and a triangle of logs was being put up under Charles' direction by the time Alice climbed the ladder to the trapdoor leading to the roof. "You need me for any of that, Charles?"

"No. Set up the computer and do a systems check."

The lead-acid batteries, except for one, were with Seuthes' army, which was supposed to be behind them, and so was the pedal-powered low-voltage generator used to charge them. What they had with them was the computer, the radio, and the antenna wire and one battery. The system would run for about two hours without the other batteries and the generator.

Alice was turning to go back down into the palace when Charles said, "Before you go, have a look." He pointed west. There was a column of men in armor carrying the long spears of the Silver Shields, and beside it were two columns of cavalry. *There must be five thousand men*, Alice thought. Not that she knew crap about estimating military strength.

☆   ☆   ☆

On the walls of Seuthopolis, Mucapor watched the army, hoping desperately that he was reading the auguries correctly. Priest King Seuthes had sent him instructions, and he knew the stories about the ship people, but Mucapor was not the priest king. He was just a senior priest, and King Seuthes' seneschal, and the ship people were throwing all the world into chaos and uncertainty. He turned away from the approaching army and looked at the palace. Already the wooden tower was rising. It would be visible from outside the walls before Lípos' army had the city surrounded. All he had to do was hold Lípos here for a few days, until Seuthes brought the army to their rescue.

Lípos' army, outside Seuthopolis
November 19, 319 BCE

Lípos looked at Seuthopolis with relief. Finally!

Then one of his officers rode up beside him and pointed. At first he couldn't make out what it was, then he remembered the tower in Pella. *A radio. How did they get a radio here?*

Radios meant ship people. And Lípos knew what would happen if any harm came to those ship people. It was made perfectly clear in the agreements. Besides, Dag Jakobsen had killed a dozen men by himself, with just a small ball of ship people magic, when he made his escape from Tyre. Everyone knew what a radio meant.

But there couldn't be one here. Couldn't be.

He called his bodyguards and rode ahead to within shouting distance of the walls.

☆   ☆   ☆

Hristos watched the party of riders approach the wall. He thought that was Lípos. He pointed and asked Mucapor if he recognized the rider.

"I don't know. He could be Philip Lípos. I know he's not Cassander."

"Cassander stayed in Pella. At least according to the radio message we got," Hristos said. Then he shouted, "Where's your brother, Lípos?"

There was no answer, and Hristos wondered if he were wrong about who was out there.

☆   ☆   ☆

Lípos was wondering too. Not about where Cassander was, but about how they could fail to know if they really had a radio. He started to think that the tower might be a ruse. A ploy. The product of a messenger rider and a pouch of instructions.

"You tell me!" he shouted back. "Get on your radio and call him."

"He's in Pella, too afraid to come himself," came the snarling reply.

"You're guessing. You don't have a radio. There are no ship people here."

"Come and see for yourself. Or are you the same kind of coward as your brother?"

"I'm not the sort of fool to trust a Thracian dog," Lípos shouted.

"Wait there, then," came another voice with a strong Thracian accent.

☆   ☆   ☆

A few minutes later a single man on a black stallion rode out the northwest gate and straight toward him. The horse was black as night, with a white flash over its left eye and white socks. It was also overfed and groomed. It had to be one of the holy herd, as the sanctuary of Sabazios maintained. Sabazios was, after all, often depicted as a rider on horseback. Besides, the rider was wearing the robes of a senior priest of Sabazios.

He rode all the way to Lípos, then said, "In the name of Sabazios, I guarantee your safety. Come and see the radio and the ship people who operate it."

Lípos considered. He had grown up in politics and knew that the priests of the various gods lied as often as anyone else, but that they were careful about lying in the name of their gods. He also knew that his brother Cassander was afraid of the ship people. He looked the priest in the eye and couldn't tell. "I will discuss it with my officers," he said as haughtily as he could manage.

He jerked his horse's head around and kicked it in the side. It tried to rear and he had to rein it hard to keep it under control. Then he rode back to his lines, followed by his bodyguards.

He couldn't attack if the ship people had an operational radio. If they had an operational radio they probably had rockets. And who knew, maybe even the cannons that struck like lightning.

☆   ☆   ☆

Mucapor, with effort, kept his face bland until he was halfway back to the walls. Then he couldn't help it. He started laughing. He stayed on his horse, laughing hysterically all the way back into Seuthopolis.

"It went well then?" Dryas, captain of the city guard, asked from the gate house on the wall.

Getting himself under some control, Mucapor shouted back, "He's going to consult with his staff! That buys us an hour at the least." Mucapor looked at the sun in the southwest. "They won't attack today."

"That much is good," Dryas said, not nearly as pleased as Mucapor.

Mucapor's smile weakened in the face of Dryas' obvious concern. "Surely Seuthes will be here by tomorrow."

"Don't depend on that, Eminence," Dryas said. "The ship people and their guards made good time and a small group can always travel faster than a large one. I doubt King Seuthes' army will make more than twenty-five miles a day, and they will average less."

"That's still only two more days."

Dryas looked down at him and shook his head. Mucapor knew what Dryas meant. They had discussed it in private, and it needed no airing in public. They had less than five hundred men at arms. And if Seuthopolis was crowded with refugees from the surrounding villages and vineyards, they were good for growing grapes, not for fighting wars.

He went to see the ship people.

☆   ☆   ☆

422 *Eric Flint, Gorg Huff & Paula Goodlett*

Charles and Alice Blevins listened as Mucapor told Hristos what was coming. Then, as Histros, in a combination of broken English and Greek, told them what he'd said.

"It's not that Cassander's army will target you," Histros finished. "But when an army takes a town, the troops are likely to get out of hand. Much better for all of us if they don't attack. Is there anything you can suggest?"

Alice curled her straight graying hair around one finger as she thought. She wished she had her guitar. She always thought better with it in hand, but it was at home in Arizona, twenty-four hundred years away. She looked over at Charles.

"The only thing I can think of is the trick some rebel general pulled on McClellan in the Civil War," said her husband. "He marched his troops around in a circle, hidden part of the time, so that it looked like he had a much larger army. McClellan believed it, and refused to attack. I don't remember for sure, but I think that was when Lincoln fired off the telegraph message saying that if McClellan wasn't going to use the army, he would like to borrow it."

Alice laughed while Histros looked confused.

Then Charles got a funny look in his eyes as he looked at Alice. "The other thing I remember was the rebel officer was into amateur theatrics. Sounds right up your alley, Alice." Then, as Histros was looking even more confused, he said, "When we met, Alice was the guitarist and lead singer for The Dulcets." At the blank looks he added, "A band." Then, "A group of musicians who play together." Finally getting nods of understanding, he continued. "And every year she gets at least one part in some play or another at the community theater, when she's not doing set dressing." Then he had to explain that.

While he was explaining, Alice tried to think, but she drew a blank. It was Mucapor who gave them the idea.

"Can't you make the rockets we have heard about?"

Now Alice had it, and so did Charles from the grin on his face. It took them an hour to explain and some of the papyrus that the temple had to make the drawings that the craftsmen would use to make and paint the wooden mockups of launchers and rockets.

Then, for much of the night, they helped as wood was cut on wood lathes and painted with charcoal and grapeseed-oil paint to make them look like iron. The question of how accurate they had to be came up. And the answer was, they weren't sure. Who knew if there might be veterans in Lípos' army who had seen Eumenes' rockets and rocket launchers?

Even so, at the end of a night's labor, they had a total of ten "rocket launchers" and fifteen "rockets." Not enough for one salvo, even if they were real. Then it was the time for the McClellan trick. As each rocket was carried up to the roof of a building, it would be lowered back down to the street out of sight of Lípos and his men, then carried around the corner into view to be hauled up again.

Lípos' army, outside the walls of Seuthopolis
November 20, 319 BCE

The sun was well up when Lípos mounted his horse, looked around at his companions, and led them to the gate in the northwest wall. They rode slowly, careful of their dignity, up the hill, through recently abandoned houses to the opening gate. They were met by the same priest, who was called Mucapor. Looking down the street, Lípos saw men with ropes lifting some sort of contraption onto the roof of a building. It looked a little like the frame for a ballista without the ballista, but that was all Lípos could tell. He pointed it out to his companions, and Mucapor rushed them on.

They rode all the way to the palace and were led to a room on the second floor where a table was set up with a strange device and a woman in front of it, and a man leaning over her, looking at the same part of the device. The device glowed with an image. They were introduced and an old man introduced himself as Hristos and claimed to be the translator for the ship people. They were dressed oddly enough, if richly. The woman wore blue pants that fit her body so tightly that for a moment Lípos thought she was painted like some northern barbarian. She was also wearing a shirt of many colors in a complex pattern and a brown leather vest and beads. She was wearing a silver crown with polished blue *kálaïs* and rings on several of her fingers. The style of it all was strange, but strangest of all were the large clear lenses she wore on her face.

The man was older, pudgy, with pants of the same sort as the woman but looser. His shirt was much the same as hers, but he wore pointed-toed riding boots and clearly he was of lesser rank. He wore no crown, but a felt hat of a strange shape.

Lípos couldn't tell anything from their names. Alice and Charles might mean anything. He asked about sending a message to Cassander.

Hristos spoke to the ship people and they talked together, then spoke to Hristos again.

"Certainly," Hristos said to Lípos. "If you will write it out or tell it to me, I can write it for you. They will send it to Pella. He is at Pella, isn't he?"

Lípos cursed himself for a fool. He had a codebook back at camp, but he hadn't brought it with him. Nor did he have a pre-written message ready. "I will send one to you by messenger." Lípos looked back at the device and the image on it. The image was familiar somehow, but he couldn't quite place it. He pointed. "What is that?"

All of a sudden there was discussion back and forth in that strange language of theirs. What appeared to be arguing. Then the woman said something final. The man shrugged. So did Hristos. Hristos turned back to him and said, "That is a tube for launching rockets."

Now Lípos had it. The framework being lifted onto the roof that looked sort of like a stand for a ballista, but different. It was that. They had rockets.

He had to get out of here.

Lípos watched the side streets as they approached the gate. It was hard to tell from this angle but he was pretty sure that the rockets were in place on several roofs. They would still be well hidden by the northwest wall. Seuthopolis was on a hill with the Tonzor and Golyama Varovite rivers protecting three sides, with only the northwest wall without a river protecting it. He would be leading his army up that hill when he attacked. He wouldn't even be able to see the launchers that killed his men. They were still lifting the rockets to the roofs as he rode out the gate. They must have been doing it all the time he was at the palace. They must have thousands of the cursed things.

Radio room, Royal Palace, Seuthopolis
Two hours later

Charles Blevins tightened the screw that connected the radio to the battery then flipped the switch to turn it on. It was already hooked up to the laptop. He waited as the tubes warmed up and the readouts reached their targets, then signaled Alice. She clicked the icon and hooked up the computer to the radio by way of the ethernet cable, then called up the radio program. She clicked an icon telling all the stations in range that they were online. They got back a link from Pella that was clear and had no need of any enhancements. They also got replies from around the Med, including the *Reliance*, which was just the other side of the Pillars of Hercules, but for those they needed a fair amount of bit checking and retransmittal of garbled code. It was handled by the computer and mostly transparent to the user. *Thank God*, Alice thought.

Alice pulled up the mail queue and sent off the messages to Cassander and Eumenes. Eumenes wouldn't get his until Tacaran Bayot and Erica Mirzadeh set up their radio when the army made camp for the night.

CHAPTER 25

SPY VS. SPY

Royal Palace, Pella
November 20, 319 BCE

Malcolm Tanada handed the radio message to Cassander, who read the message, then looked at Malcolm with a furious expression on his face. *"How did you find out?"* he demanded.

"Find out *what*?" Malcolm asked, shocked at Cassander's tone.

"How did you find out that Lípos was going to Seuthopolis?"

"Lípos is in Seuthopolis?" Malcolm asked. "Then how did he send you a message?"

"The Abdera radio has been moved to Seuthopolis." Cassander sat forward in his throne, his hands gripping the armrests like claws. "How did it get there?"

"Got me. It's been offline the last few days. Technical stuff, not my area." As soon as he said that, Malcolm realized that Rico must have known what was up or he would have been a lot more worried than he seemed to be.

Rico knew, and didn't tell him. Rico's girlfriend... Malcolm looked at Thessalonike, who sat in the throne near Cassander's. Not on purpose, but as he put what was happening together, he realized that she must know what was going on and he sure as hell didn't.

Cassander followed his glance, then looked at Thessalonike, who was trying to look as shocked as Malcolm actually was. She almost carried it off. Malcolm was sure that Rico would be fooled, but he wasn't. And he was pretty sure that Cassander wasn't either. For a frozen eternity of perhaps three seconds, everyone was staring at Thessalonike. Then Cassander turned back to Malcolm. "My apologies, Mr. Tanada. Would you please try to find out when the radio team left Abdera for Seuthopolis?"

"I can ask, Your Majesty, but I can't make them answer unless they choose to."

"I understand, and thank you. But do please ask," Cassander said in a tone of voice so oily you could lube your car with it.

Cassander waved his hand, and Malcolm happily made his escape.

☆   ☆   ☆

On Malcolm's way back to the radio room, he stopped by police headquarters to talk to Daniel Lang.

"You didn't know Lípos was headed for Seuthopolis?" Daniel asked, clearly surprised. "I had a drunk in here four days ago telling the sergeant that. He was pissed that they weren't going to Abdera. I'm surprised that Eumenes figured out what was up in time to get reinforcements to Seuthopolis before Lípos got there."

"I'm not sure he did. All I know is that the radio team from Abdera is now at Seuthopolis."

"Well, why don't we go upstairs and ask Rico about it?"

☆   ☆   ☆

Rico and Sophronike were in the radio room. Rico was playing with the computer and Sophronike was reading a printout of something. Daniel Lang looked at Sophronike and considered whether to ask her to leave. Then he remembered that she was Thessalonike's maid and probably knew more about what was going on than he did. "Rico, how did you find out that Lípos was going to Seuthopolis?"

Rico, suave master spy that he was, immediately looked at Sophronike like they were kids in the process of being caught trying to rob a candy store.

"When did you tell him?" Daniel asked Sophronike.

Sophronike looked at Daniel, then back at Rico and rolled her eyes. Daniel figured Rico was going to hear about this later. Then she told him.

Daniel shook his head, trying to figure it out. He knew that Thessalonike was unhappy with Cassander, but helping Eumenes . . . that didn't make sense. "Why? You may have gotten Thessalonike killed. Cassander knows, thanks to Malcolm Tanada here. Well, at least suspects."

"Seuthopolis is a holy place. It's new, not entirely finished yet, but it is built on the ruins of a previous holy place and sanctified to Sabazios, and Cassander planned to desecrate it." Then she looked at Daniel. "You have to protect Thessalonike."

Daniel considered that. "Where is Eumenes' army?"

Rico turned back to the computer and called up a mapping program. He pointed. "He should be right about there."

Eumenes' camp, en route to Seuthopolis
November 20, 319 BCE

The camp was in a valley, and by the time they got set
up the sun was sinking below the hills to the west. By
now their radio wagon was a thing of practical beauty.
The Macedonian craftsmen made a rod in sections that
was held upright by a quadruped stand also made in
sections for easy set up. Each leg of the stand fit into
a corner of the wagon; together, once it was set up, it
sent their antenna wire forty feet up into the air. Erica
watched as the eight Macedonian soldiers pulled the
contraption upright and placed the front legs in the holes
in the wagon, then as Tacaran attached the antenna to
the connector cable. Then she climbed into the wagon.

Erica Mirzadeh pulled up the computer, fired up the
radio set, and set it searching for active radio sources. She
got Rico Gica at Pella and Alice Blevins at Seuthopolis.

Shouting back and forth as Tacaran used a crank
to shift the antenna, she got and recorded signal max
vectors for each station. Then she had Tacaran adjust
the antenna for both. Between the vectors and terrain
features from Google Maps, she placed them. They
were a bit east and well north of Pella, but actually a
bit west of Amphipolis now, having had to go around
the mountains. But they were behind Lípos.

Once she had their position she pulled up the messages and got the emails from Seuthopolis and Pella, as
well as Carthage and every place else relayed through
Pella. Like the internet back in the world, as long as
you had an active link, your message could be retrans-
mitted to anywhere.

"Let's see," Erica muttered as she worked. "A request

for our location from Seuthopolis." She would let Eumenes decide about that. "And another one from Pella."
That was from Rico Gica, who was mapping their
progress just for himself. She sent him the new cords.
There were also private messages for a merchant who
was accompanying the army and several of the soldiers.
The standard request for weather information, wind
speed, humidity, temperature, barometric pressure. She
fed that in, then pulled up the weather program. It was
a perfectly fine program, but there were less than fifty
weather stations on this side of the Atlantic. It could
predict the weather, but the level of confidence was
not much better than Sergeant Kopra's game leg. Still,
it was better than nothing.

The printer, a dot matrix job using lampblack and
oil for its ink, clattered as the messages came out. And
it took a while.

About half an hour later she collected up the sheets of
papyrus. She shut down and disconnected the antenna.
It was raining and though the weather prediction program didn't predict lightning, she didn't want to take
the chance.

☆   ☆   ☆

Eumenes read the decoded message from Seuthopolis, then handed it to Eurydice.

"Well, at least the radio made it," Eurydice said
as Eumenes started reading the next message, also
from Seuthopolis, then started to smile. "Someone in
Seuthopolis is clever." He passed it over.

Eurydice read it, then looked at him. "Do you think
the imitation rockets will work?"

He shrugged. "They might. For that matter, just
the presence of the ship people might give Lípos

pause. But it doesn't really change anything. Seuthes doesn't have the force to defeat Lípos in the field, not by himself. We still need to proceed to Seuthopolis."

He turned to Erica. "Please see that our position is sent to Seuthopolis and that goes for every stop we make until we get there. And let us know as soon as Seuthes reaches his capital."

Erica Mirzadeh nodded and left.

Seuthopolis
November 21, 319 BCE

The afternoon sun was getting close to the hilltops when the lookout on the south tower saw a flash from near the edge of the valley. He looked again and saw more flashes. It was a signal mirror. He noted the flashes with a charcoal stick and soon enough he got confirmation it was Seuthes. He would be here, at least at the walls, by midmorning tomorrow. Grinning, the guard turned toward the army to the northwest and made a rude gesture, then shouted for a runner.

Lípos' army camp, one mile northwest of Seuthopolis
November 21, 319 BCE

Lípos got the news not from the guard's rude gesture, but from his scouts. He turned to his commanders. Each of whom had their own opinion about what to do now, but all of whom—even those who had yesterday been insisting that he not attack—blamed him for failing to attack before Seuthes and his cavalry got here.

They were about evenly divided between "attack now" and "retreat."

The deciding factor was the rockets. He had seen them with his own eyes. They were real. They were there. And he noted that his one commander who had been with Lysimachus at the Bosphorus insisted that an attack against rockets was suicide and was firmly in the retreat camp.

Lípos gave the orders to break camp in the morning and move away from Seuthopolis. All the while wondering what Cassander would say when he brought his army home with its tail firmly between its legs, and without a battle.

Cassander's private chambers, Royal Palace, Pella
November 22, 319 BCE

The sun shone dimly through the translucent shutters. They were made from animal intestine on wood frames, painted with tree sap. But they let some of the light in and did a decent job of keeping the cold out. It gave the room a dim feel that Cassander fought with two of the ship people–designed oil lamps with blown-glass chimneys.

Cassander sat in a chair on a platform, the two lamps behind him and a table in front. Across the table and a step down stood the spy, Kallipos.

The spy was a small man and Cassander didn't like him, but he was reliable. "I have it from a serving woman who works for the ship people," said Kallipos. "Lípos has retreated from Seuthopolis without ever drawing his sword. Seuthes has his army in the city and will leave at least a thousand horsemen and *real* rockets there when he leaves to pursue Lípos."

"Real rockets?"

"The ones that scared Lípos away were fakes. Just painted wood."

There was, Cassander was sure, a sneer under that calm recital. But he needed this man. It had taken months for the agent in the ship people's kitchen to learn enough of their barbarous tongue to be of any use. In a way, this news was worse than Lípos' defeat would have been. He had been frightened away. Macedonians would put up with a lot, but not cowardice.

Cassander hadn't heard of the game of chess before The Event, but now he played it regularly, and he was quite good. He was a man who saw the board several moves ahead. And the next move on this board was clear.

Lípos would retreat ahead of Seuthes until he ran into Eumenes' army, then either surrender or be defeated in battle.

All of Cassander's credibility with the Macedonian nobility would be destroyed by Lípos' ignominious defeat.

And he would be deposed.

It would take several more days, perhaps even weeks. But he wouldn't be both king and alive by the end of the year.

He had to escape, but to where? Ptolemy was out. He would give Cassander to Eumenes without any hesitation. He doubted that he could reach Antigonus One-eye, or any of the eastern satraps. And even if he could, none of them would shelter him.

Nowhere in Alexander's empire was safe for him now.

Carthage was possible, but he didn't trust the slimy bastards. They would sell him to the queens and Olympias would have him flayed alive.

Rome . . . maybe. It wasn't much now but in a few hundred years . . . And maybe earlier. With enough silver, he could buy a seat in the senate, or at least a tribuneship. Marry a Roman noble's daughter, build a new life. But Romans had silly rules about only having one wife.

Thessalonike would have to go. But not now. Not until his son was born. Then he would have her killed and his son brought to Rome later. For now, all he would take was the treasury.

Cassander looked up from his brooding and considered the spy. An Athenian, and not of good family. Reasonably educated, but of the lowest classes. A man with few opportunities. "Kallipos, I need you to quietly start collecting gear for a long trip. A wagon . . . No, a ship. And food, clothing for you and for me. There will be several chests I will be bringing."

The little Greek got a calculating look in his eyes, and Cassander almost called the guards to have him killed. But he could trust Kallipos as much as he could trust anyone. "Go now."

Kallipos left.

Pella, police headquarters
November 23, 319 BCE

Pella is one long-running Spy vs. Spy *cartoon,* Daniel Lang thought as he read the report by one of his confidential informants—spies—while he sat in the lamplit room. The lamp was semi-modern and proof of international trade. The design was from Wikipedia, the wick from Egypt, the copper body made right here in Pella, the glass chimney from Carthage and the kerosene from the oil fields at Trinidad. That was, in a way, what the report was about. The ship people didn't introduce international trade to this world. Trade was here long before The Event. But the ship people added greatly to the product list and provided more trustworthy forms of currency. What Daniel was reading about was a silver coin smuggling operation. Cassander wanted his tariffs, and money from merchants here in Pella was finding its way to Amphipolis, where it was picked up by the *Reliance* and became ship people dollars that could be used from Tyre to Trinidad, to buy things like the glass chimney on his lamp.

He continued reading the CI's report.

A little after sunset yesterday, Cassander opened the door to the strong room and came out with a large heavy case.

Now, why would Cassander be stealing from his own strong room? Daniel wondered. The only reason he knew about it was because Daniel's beat cops had lots of CIs, most of them slaves. There were more slaves in Pella than free people. Most craftsmen were slaves, and most households had at least a couple of slaves. Many of the slaves were quite loyal to their masters, but a lot weren't. And while slaves couldn't buy their freedom without their owner's consent, it was legal for them to buy it if they could put together the money. So in a place as big as the palace, it was a safe bet that at least a few would sell information on their master's actions.

He made three more trips to the strong room.
Each time he carried away a heavy leather case.

Daniel still didn't know why, but it was pretty clear that Cassander was raiding the treasury. Whether that was legal, Daniel wasn't sure. But doing it by the dark of night didn't suggest it was aboveboard.

Daniel wrote out a note describing what the report said, then went upstairs to visit Rico Gica and Sophronike.

Royal Palace, Pella
Around midnight, November 23, 319 BCE

Sophronike handed Daniel's note to Thessalonike, who opened it and took it over to a lamp to read. Her face paled.

"He plans to abandon us! Me and our child. He will steal the silver from the strong room and run, if he hasn't already. I have to find out how much he has taken."

She dressed quickly, used the chamber pot and waddled out of the room, motioning Sophronike to silence.

Sophronike didn't wait more than a few minutes before she left at almost a run. She couldn't gainsay her mistress, but was afraid of what might happen if Thessalonike were to run into a guard. Daniel Lang would protect them all with his ship people magic.

Royal Palace, Pella
Around midnight, November 24, 319 BCE

Thessalonike moved through the halls of the palace as silent as a ghost. It was part of her training. She carried no light, and felt her way using the occasional dim lamps left burning overnight. It was a slow way to travel, but what was needed here was stealth, not speed.

Finally, after almost an hour, she reached the strong room. The bar was locked in place by a bronze lock of ship people design but made in Egypt. She, however, knew the three-letter combination. Cassander thought he was so smart. ICP wasn't that hard to figure out. Iollas, Cassander, and Plistarch, Antipater's three eldest sons, of whom only Cassander still lived.

Carefully, more by touch than sight, she rotated the three wheels into the proper position and removed the lock. Then, as quietly as she could, she shifted the heavy bar and pulled open the door. It didn't squeak at all.

Once in the room, she found the lamp that was located next to the door and tried to light it using a flint and steel. The flint and steel struck and produced sparks, but the angle was wrong and the wick didn't catch. She tried again and again. Sparks all around the wick and no flame. The flashes from the sparks had dazzled her night sight painfully, but she persisted. It was almost two minutes later that she finally got the small wick on the Aladdin-style lamp to catch. It gave her dim light in the dark room, and first she pulled the door closed. Then she went to a shelf on the right.

Her dower was stored in those chests. She opened the first. It was empty. Then the next. Again empty.

Macedonia had more money than a man could carry, but much of it was in forms other than coins. The money in this room was to cover day-to-day expenses, and when needed to do things like pay the army. That was still an enormous amount of money, but Cassander, over the last couple of nights, had managed to make quite a dent in it.

She heard a noise and turned to see the door opening.

☆   ☆   ☆

Cassander saw the lock missing from the bar and the bar pulled to the open position and knew he had not left it so. He readied the bronze copy of the cap-and-ball pistol that he now always carried. The caps were stolen and very hard to come by so he had very little practice with the thing. Gun in one hand, he pulled open the door.

There she was. The little harpy who loved only the gods, not her husband. Disloyal. He was surrounded by disloyalty. He pointed the pistol at her, mostly just to hold her there while he called the guards. But she didn't freeze into immobility. She pulled a dagger from her belt. He fired. The report was loud and the room was filled with smoke. When he could see again, she was on the floor with a hole in her shoulder and blood everywhere. For a moment he thought he'd killed her. Then she started to get up.

☆   ☆   ☆

Daniel Lang was already in the hall leading to the strong room when he heard the shot. He ran, followed by Demos and Sophronike. Surprisingly, Demos was turning into something approaching a good cop. He had fewer of the bad habits than the older city guards and didn't need the graft that was an ingrained part of their income. The door was half opened, and their running footsteps must have alerted the perp. He turned and Daniel saw the bronze copy of a ship person pistol in Cassander's hand. Daniel stopped and drew his own pistol.

The bronze gun came around and Daniel was looking down the shaking barrel. He brought his own gun up as Cassander pulled the trigger. The bullet whistled by his head and he was blinded by the smoke. Daniel fired blind and fired again. Cassander fired again. Daniel fired a third time, and barely over the ringing in his ears heard a body hit the floor. As the smoke cleared, he moved forward to see Cassander. One of his shots had hit the man in the right chest and turned him half around. Another hit him in the side of the head, and the .45 caliber bullet propelled by a black powder charge shattered the weak part of the skull just above and in front of the ear. Cassander was dead before he hit the ground.

☆　　☆　　☆

Daniel didn't wait. He reached down, grabbed Cassander's pistol from the floor and ran to the strong room, to see Thessalonike trying to sit up, tears coming from her eyes, but not a peep out of her. "Stay where you are," Daniel said to her. "Let me check it. Demos, where's the emergency kit?" All Daniel's cops carried emergency kits. They contained bandages and a small vial of wood alcohol. He'd started by using grain alcohols, but that didn't last more than a few days before it was drunk.

Demos handed him the kit. Daniel pulled it open,

hauled out the vial of alcohol and poured it on to the wound.

Thessalonike still didn't scream, but she apparently bit her lip. A little blood started seeping from her mouth. Daniel put a pressure bandage on the wound and tied it in place with twine.

☆   ☆   ☆

Fifteen minutes later, it was only his reloaded pistol and Thessalonike's insistence that kept Cassander's personal guards from trying to kill him. They were not happy that the new regent to the as-yet-unborn king of Macedonia was a young woman. This was complicated by the fact that said child might be a girl.

The politics of Macedonia had been reeling since the death of Philip II, Alexander the Great's father. Every time they got some nice, comfortable reactionary on the throne, he got himself killed. The last two times, Antipater and Cassander, indirectly by women. Roxane and Eurydice for Antipater, and Thessalonike for Cassander. Clearly, it was all due to the curse of Olympias and the ship people.

On the other hand, Macedonian kings getting killed was hardly a new phenomenon. Kingship in the here and now was not a safe occupation.

There, in the hallway in front of the relocked strong room, the nobles of Macedonia tried to work out what to do while looking at the bandaged and still-living Thessalonike and the very much still-armed Daniel Lang. He was backed up by Demos, who at least was one of their own.

Somewhere in the explanation for what had happened, the fact that Cassander was in the process of looting the treasury got out. Then the fact that neither Daniel nor Thessalonike knew where the money was. At that point, a lot of the nobles scattered to go find the treasure, leaving only a few to determine who would be the new government.

☆   ☆   ☆

Finally a litter arrived and Thessalonike was carried off to rest. Daniel retreated to police headquarters.

Radio section, Pella
2:00 A.M., November 24, 319 BCE

"Get up, Ricardo Gica! Get up now!" Sara was shaking Rico. He sat up, bleary and confused, but Sara would not be denied. In only a few minutes, Rico, still in his underwear and a robe, found himself in the radio room, firing up the system in spite of the fact that it was raining again.

Sara handed him a stack of messages. "Send these. Send them now."

All of the messages were marked "most urgent." There were two to the *Queen of the Sea*, one to Olympias, and one to Alexander IV in care of Roxane; two to Eumenes' army, one for Philip III in care of Eurydice and one for delivery to Philip Lípos, commander of the army of Macedonia in Thrace. That one to be delivered only if there was a positive response from Roxane and Eurydice. All of the letters were in clear, but also in Macedonian Greek. There was also a general announcement, again to be released only if the messages to the queens regent got a positive response.

Rico's curiosity got the better of him and he ran the messages to the queens through the translation app.

After explaining the events of the evening in the messages, Thessalonike made a proposal:

While I know that my nephew Alexander IV has the best blood claim on the throne of Macedonia, that throne has never passed strictly by blood. Alexander the Great received it, not Philip, then Philip and Alexander shared it, all by acclamation of the nobility of Macedonia in the form of the army. On that basis and because the child beneath my breast is here in Macedonia, I request that Philip III and Alexander IV yield to me, not the crown of the empire of Alexander, only the crown of Macedonia, which is now a part of that empire, but no longer its whole.

This was weird. Rico knew that there were irregularities in the way Alexander the Great got the crown, and even more when Philip III and Alexander IV got it. But this made it sound like that was standard. And how could Roxane and Eurydice be queens regent of the empire and not Macedonia? He wondered what Lípos would say about that. For that matter, he wondered what Ptolemy, Antigonus One-eye, and the rest of the satraps and kings of the empire would say.

Queen of the Sea, *off Amphipolis*
November 24, 319 BCE

The phone in Roxane's cabin rang and Dag reached over and grabbed it. "Yes, I'm up. I'll be there in twenty," he mumbled sleepily.

"What?" came over the phone. "Her Majesty has an urgent message."

"Huh? What time is it?"

"Two twenty-seven A.M. local. Now, will you get Her Nibs up? Cassander is dead. Shot by Daniel Lang."

Dag shook Roxane awake. "Babe, emergency. Wake up," he said before the meaning of the words had quite penetrated. "I think you might have just won the war."

☆   ☆   ☆

Fifteen minutes later, in a conference room with Marie Easley, Olympias, Lars Floden, and Amanda Miller representing New America, Roxane read the message. She then looked at her mother-in-law, half-wondering how Olympias managed to get to this meeting. Then she saw the message in Olympias' hand. "Well?" she asked.

"I think you should do it," Olympias said. "Thessalonike makes a number of good points. The nobility of Macedonia itself wasn't all that fond of my son. Most of those who loved him followed him on his campaigns. Those left will never trust you, or my grandson, for he is only half Macedonian. They might allow Eurydice's child"—Olympias couldn't keep the sneer completely out of her voice, but she tried—"should she ever manage to have one, and if they believe that Philip is actually the father. But Thessalonike's child will carry the blood of Philip II and Antipater."

Marie Easley spoke up. "Don't discount that the basis to your claims over Alexander's empire all start with Alexander the Great as king of Macedonia. If you give that up, what supports the rest of it?"

It was a good point, but so was Olympias', Roxane thought.

Then Amanda Miller spoke. "Don't forget the constitution. It established that Alexander and Philip were the co-rulers of the United Satrapies and States of the Empire, as well as the kings of Macedonia. Besides, if you don't go along with this, won't Lípos keep fighting?"

"He might well, even if you do," Marie said. "If Cassander had any legitimacy at all, Lípos is at least as good an heir as Thessalonike's child. In fact, that's a big part of what concerns me about this. It legitimizes Cassander after the fact. Won't it invite others to repeat his rebellion?"

Roxane considered. The only other real threat at the moment was Antigonus One-eye in Babylon, and the sooner Eumenes' army was free to deal with that, the better. Besides, Roxane would really prefer not to have to kill any more people than she already had. "Tell her I approve, but only if she can bring Lípos to heel. She must send him orders to stand down."

Olympias held out another message. "This is to Lípos, should you and Eurydice agree." The message was an order from Thessalonike as regent to Cassander's child to stand down his army and place himself and his army under Eumenes' orders.

"Very well," Roxane agreed. "But we need to word this right. Not as an abdication. As a grant. We give Macedonia to our vassal, Thessalonike and her child, as a kingdom within our empire."

Olympias laughed. "Now all we need to do is get Eurydice to agree to it."

Eumenes' field headquarters, Western Thrace
Sunrise, November 25, 319 BCE

Tacaran Bayot reconnected the antenna array to the radio and shouted to Erica Mirzadeh, "Ready! Fire it up!" Then he climbed down. The morning was cloudy, but thankfully not raining. But his boots squished in the mud as he walked around to the back of the wagon. He climbed up onto the running board and scraped his boots before climbing in.

Erica Mirzadeh already had the system up and was getting something. At first Tacaran thought that it was the morning weather report, but then he saw Erica's face. "What is it?"

"Cassander is dead. Don't get comfortable, Tacaran. You're going to be taking messages as soon as I get the printer going."

☆   ☆   ☆

"Good plan," Philip III said, looking at the tent post. "The Macedonians will accept it and we can live on the *Queen*."

"But we give up our home, our kingdom." Eurydice sounded more like a teenage girl than she ever had in Tacaran's hearing.

Eumenes looked back and forth between Eurydice and Philip, and Tacaran was almost sure he was hiding a smile. "No. You're simply granting a part of your empire in fief to a king of your choosing. Precedents work both ways. If you can grant it, you could someday revoke the grant, should it be needed. But if the nobles gathered in Pella do it without you, you have no say."

It took a while, but eventually Eurydice agreed. A rider carrying the message and a flag of truce was sent searching for Lípos' army.

Lípos' camp, Western Thrace
Late afternoon, November 26, 319 BCE

Philip Lípos sat in his tent with the afternoon sun breaking through the clouds to shine on the muddy ground and turn the sky purple and crimson. It was an afternoon both beautiful and ugly. Cassander was dead. The printed message from the ship people said so. He wasn't supposed to be dead. He was supposed to send Philip to Aetolia in a few years, where Philip would win two major battles and be remembered as a great general, great enough to still be remembered two thousand years later.

It was all the ship people's fault. How had history found out about the hoof and the poison it held? No one knew of the plot to kill Alexander the Great. No one but his father, his brothers, and him. Well, and the Cabeiri assassin who made the poison. It wasn't as if they'd had any choice. The maniac Alexander was going to have Antipater executed. They all knew it. What were they supposed to do? Let Alexander kill their father and disgrace their family? *No! It was an entirely justified act of family self-defense.*

But now everyone knew, or at least suspected. And Philip was personally sure that Olympias knew, which meant he was a dead man if he didn't manage to kill her first. But she was on the *Queen of the Sea*, which meant she was safe.

Safe. On the Queen of the Sea*! Could that be a way out?* If Philip couldn't get at her on the *Queen of the Sea*, she couldn't get at him either. He felt himself smile for the first time since he opened the message. To sit on the deck of the *Queen of the Sea* and look at the old harridan and know she couldn't get at him. Even better to have her know that she couldn't get at him.

That just left the question of how to arrange it. He would need money. Living on the *Queen of the Sea* wasn't cheap. He needed to make sure he had full control over the army. Because his plan was to, in effect, sell the army to Eurydice for enough money to live his life on the *Queen of the Sea*.

He called in his officers.

☆	☆	☆

The next morning, the messenger left. He didn't have nearly as far to go. Eumenes' army had not stopped to wait.

Eumenes' army, on the march
Late afternoon, November 27, 319 BCE

Eumenes was riding near the vanguard when he saw the messenger approaching at a trot. Eumenes waved, and the messenger brought his mount to the gallop. A few moments later the man pulled up and lifted the pouch over his shoulder to hand it to Eumenes. "He said you would need to discuss his counterproposal with Queen Roxane."

Eumenes felt his eyebrows lift. But he nodded and turned to an adjutant. "Have the radio wagon, Eurydice, Philip and their guards pull out of the march and set up. The rest of the army will proceed to tonight's camp. We'll catch up there."

☆	☆	☆

Eumenes waited to open the pouch until they were all there. The contents of the pouch were really quite close to what they wanted. Lípos would not surrender. Instead, he would turn over command of his army to Eumenes and the legitimate government, keeping both armies intact. In exchange, he wanted enough money to live out the rest of his life on the *Queen of the Sea*. It could be in the form of a job, or however they wanted to do it to make themselves look good, but it had to be guaranteed. Then Eumenes laughed as he read the line:

I want Lars Floden's confirmation that I will be allowed to stay safe on the Queen *and that my passage is fully paid.*

"Well, Cassander's little brother inherited at least some of Cassander's intelligence." Eumenes continued reading. Once he finished, he waited while Eurydice read the message, then handed it to Philip, who glanced at it and handed it back, then went back to looking at a branch he was examining. Eumenes suppressed a slight shudder. Philip often did that. It didn't mean he hadn't read the message. No, he read and memorized it at a glance. He could quote it now, or a year from now.

"Well?" Eumenes asked Eurydice. "What do you think?"

Eurydice said, "Philip?"

Philip, still looking at the branch, said, "Olympias."

Now, what the hell did that mean? Eumenes wondered.

"What about Olympias?" Eurydice asked patiently.

"He's afraid of Olympias," Philip said.

"And well he should be." Eurydice nodded. "Did he kill Alexander?"

"Don't know. Ask after he's on the *Queen*," Philip said.

"So you think we should take the deal?" Eumenes asked.

Philip only gave a minimal shrug, his eyes never leaving the branch. Eumenes looked at Eurydice.

She looked back. "What I want to do is catch him in a pincer, use our army and Seuthes' to crush him like the bug he is, and terrify the Macedonian nobility for the next five generations." She sighed deeply. "But what we should do is take the deal, move the army to the coast, ship them to Oea, and march them to Babylon. One-eye is the last of the truly powerful traitors."

214–216 12th Street, Fort Plymouth, Trinidad
Late afternoon, November 27, 319 BCE

The brass bell tinkled as the front door of the shop opened. Stella Matthews looked up and smiled as Lisa Hammonds came in with her baby in a carry bag. Lisa looked around and Stella followed her eyes.

This was strange. Stella herself was noticing the changes. The front room of the shop was a place of black-fabric-covered shelves with glasses and vases, lens blanks, bottles, including baby bottles, and glass-bead jewelry. It was a bit of a shock to see the place as Lisa must see it.

It had been so gradual. Here an addition, there a change. New fabric covers on the wood shelves. It happened a bit at a time, but now she was in an elegant little shop full of glasswares that sold for good prices. She was still in debt, but her debt was shrinking. After three changes of employees, Carthalo now had an apprentice who looked like he was going to stick around and learn the trade.

"You were right, Lisa," Stella said. "Glass was the way to go."

"I'm glad it worked out." Lisa smiled. "But there were a lot of things you could have done that would be producing by now."

Stella nodded agreement. Twelfth Street was full of shops making all sorts of things. All of them in small amounts, but many of them of quite good quality. "So what brings you all the way out here?"

Lisa lived on 4th Street, in a townhouse that was a bit bigger than Stella's double, and which had the indoor plumbing that Stella still didn't have. The main lines were in, but it was being installed a bit at a time as workers could be spared from other projects.

"Baby bottles and gossip," Lisa said. "Did you read about the Macedonian treasury going missing?"

"Yes, I read all about it. Why? Do you have anything new?"

"Just a rumor. Daniel Lang told Jane Carruthers, who told Congresswoman Davis, that a ship sailed out of Pella the morning that Cassander was killed, and at least two ships have gone after it. Who knows? They know how to cross the Atlantic now. We may see it here." Lisa grinned and Stella laughed. Then they talked baby bottles and latex nipples, and the various options that Lisa had, from breast pump to goat and cow milk. Soy milk was not a possibility, because the soybean was still local to the Far East: China, Japan, and Korea. At least according to Wikipedia. No one had made the trip to be sure yet.

Argos, *Mediterranean Sea*
November 27, 319 BCE

Kallipos leaned over the railing and launched his lunch. It was no great loss. The meal was rye porridge with a little bit of fish. And too long in the pot by half.

Down in the hold were several amphorae of good red wine and in those amphorae below the wine were gold and silver coins. It was Kallipos' idea. Something that would appear fairly valuable, but not so valuable as the true ingredients were.

Then Cassander got himself killed, and Kallipos had to run, and run now. He went to the ship, boarded with a chest of silver, and paid the captain half the silver to carry him and the other half of the silver and the wine to Port Berry on Formentera Island.

The captain knew what Kallipos was doing. The moment he set foot in Port Berry, he was, by treaty with the ship people, free. In Port Berry.

It was such a good plan, Kallipos thought, then heaved again. But there was nothing left to come up. He just hadn't counted on the storm. Slowly, hand by hand on the railing, he made his way back to the stern, where the captain and the steersman were guiding the *Argos* through the ten-foot seas.

"Where are we?" he asked, only to have the question swallowed up by the pounding rain.

The captain looked at him and shook his head.

Captain Barta of the *Argos*, a Sicilian merchant skipper, cursed his luck. He never should have picked up this Jonah. The term he used wasn't "Jonah." It was a Carthaginian word having to do with a Carthaginian legend that was closer to Jason and the Argonauts than anything biblical. But the meaning was just the same. A bad-luck charm that brings a ship to disaster just because the gods are angry with him.

Barta waved the Jonah away, and tried to figure where they were. The winds were blowing almost due west and in spite of the fact that he had shortened sail, they were moving swiftly and had been for the last twenty hours. He shook his head. For all he knew, he was about to run aground on Formentera Island. Or maybe the Pillars of Hercules.

He couldn't see anything. He couldn't even see the bow for the rain. There was a creaking and a grinding, and Barta looked at the main mast in horror as it bent in the wind. Then it snapped and he prayed to Neptune that it broke in time.

It hadn't.

In the bilge, two planks, already split from the strain of the mast, opened farther and the western Mediterranean Sea poured in. The *Argos* was fully loaded before the leak and it went down.

It took it almost an hour, plenty of time for the lifeboat to be lowered and the crew to get off. They even took Kallipos.

It was three days later when they reached the coast of what would someday be Spain.

CHAPTER 26

ATTACK

West Babylon, Radio Building
Late afternoon, November 28, 319 BCE

Susan Godlewski had the duty when the general announcement came in.

> *Philip Lípos, eldest surviving son of Antipater, has turned over command of the Macedonian army to Eumenes and will be taking a position as Assistant Consul to Queen Roxane. He has announced his support for the actions of queens Roxane and Eurydice in appointing Queen Thessalonike regent for the unborn child of Cassander who will be the king of Macedonia. Macedonia itself will become a state in the United Satrapies and States of the Empire.*

Susan took the message from the printer, called one of the assistants, then printed another copy to be sent across the river. She hoped it ruined Antigonus' day. Food was still getting through, but the blockade runners were as close to pirates as made little difference. They were charging a fortune to ship the food in. There had been two not-quite-epidemics in the last month. One was a typhus outbreak and the other was probably a variant of smallpox that was a bit less lethal than its cousin. Both outbreaks had crossed the river to hit both sides of Babylon and had struck the children and the hungry worse.

East Babylon
Evening, November 28, 319 BCE

Calix sat at the bench eating old bread and broth, wondering if coming to Babylon had been a good idea. He was working for Antigonus and that gave him some protection from the ship people, but old One-eye was a chancy master. Calix's knowledge of chemistry, both from the Cabeiri and from the ship people, meant that he was now in partial charge of the gunpowder shop, which was not a very safe job. He finished his dinner and went to check on the slaves who were making the gunpowder.

He walked between the long tables with slaves at each job, one group moistening the charcoal, then, using mortars and pestles, grinding the chunks into a fine paste. The paste was then spread onto a drying table to form a brittle black sheet that was easy to turn into powder. The next room held large pots of water with potassium nitrate from dung heaps and middens added after the pots were brought to a boil. After that, it was boiled until the yellow crystals dissolved and then allowed to slowly cool. Then the water was drained off, leaving crystals that were considerably less yellow. Using a small tong, Calix lifted a shard. It wasn't clear, but it was closer than the stuff they got from the bottom of dung heaps.

Then, he went to another room, where sulfur—brimstone—was being ground into yellow powder.

Finally, the mixing room, where all the ingredients and water were mixed to form a black paste that was dried, then carefully ground again into a coarse black powder.

The rooms, all of them, were filled with slaves in loincloths. Their bodies were coated in a patina of charcoal dust, sulfur and saltpeter.

He was in the middle of his rounds when the messenger reached him. He was to report to the palace immediately.

☆   ☆   ☆

Calix bowed deeply, and Antigonus said to the top of his head, "Where is my gunpowder? Where are my rockets?"

Calix stood. "Coming, Majesty. We have to be careful or it will be this half of Babylon that explodes."

"Be careful faster, you coward!" Antigonus roared. He shook a sheet of papyrus in the air. "That idiot Cassander is dead, and his fat toad of a brother has given his army to Eumenes. We are running out of time."

Calix groveled. He was good at it. It was a necessary skill to a man in his position. And as he groveled, he made his plans to escape Babylon with the money he had skimmed from the gunpowder production.

Over the next two weeks, while news of Eumenes' army traveling to the Aegean coast, then taking ship across the Med to the coast of Lydia reached them, Calix made his preparations.

East Babylon
After midnight, December 11, 319 BCE

Calix slipped out of his small room a little after midnight, taking all the silver he could manage and a bag of twenty gunpowder bombs with string fuses. They were, he thought, similar to the grenade that Dag Jakobsen had used to kill a Silver Shield two years ago. He made his way down to the docks.

The boatman was waiting. Calix reached into his pouch and handed him two of the reeded-edge silver coins made by the ship people.

The boatman looked at them carefully, lifting them close to his face and feeling the reeding with his fingertips, then grunted and nodded. He whispered, "Get in the bottom of the boat."

"Don't whisper," Calix said quietly. "It attracts attention."

"Get in the boat, you Greek ponce," the boatman hissed.

Calix got in the boat.

"Lie down," the boatman said quietly, and when Calix did, he tossed a reed rug over him. It stank of river water and piss. Calix waited, breathing shallowly, as more bags were loaded onto the boat.

Finally, they pushed off from the dock and floated gently downriver. Somewhere along the way, he fell asleep.

East Babylon
Midmorning, December 11, 319 BCE

It took time for the word to reach Antigonus One-eye. First, Calix's direct boss noted that he wasn't in his workroom at the gunpowder shop. Then it was discovered that he wasn't in his room. A more thorough check showed that much of his clothing was gone. Then a sum of money that was supposed to be in the shop was found to be missing. And finally, around midmorning, it was clear to everyone that Calix was missing and Antigonus was informed.

"When?" Antigonus didn't shout or grit his teeth, both clear danger signs.

"We don't know, Lord Antigonus. Sometime during the night."

Antigonus looked out his window at West Babylon. What if Calix was over there right now, warning them about his plans? What could they do? There had to be an answer to rockets.

Then he remembered something. It was something Calix told him about, in fact. They were called artillery duels. Each side would fire their rockets not at the enemy, but at the enemy's rockets. And the one who aimed best would win. Calix could tell them the location of all his rockets, down to the house they were on. He would lose before he began.

Ever since Cassander got himself killed, Antigonus knew that he was running out of time. Now the hourglass was empty. It was attack now, ready or not, or fail entirely. "Ready the troops. We attack as soon as we can."

The plan was long made. Rockets to soften the

enemy and keep their heads down while his infantry was stiffened with cavalry crossed the Euphrates. The cavalry on the west side of the Euphrates would attack as soon as they saw the rockets. He used mirror codes to warn them it was coming today.

☆　　☆　　☆

Karrel Agot was in an aid station near the river, giving home remedies to sick children. The placebo effect was doing as much good as the medicines, but Karrel would take what he could get. He heard a sound in the distance, like bottle rockets, but louder. He went to the door of the small building and looked up. There were rockets coming in. Falling into West Babylon. He saw one hit and shatter, splashing a liquid in a twenty-foot radius, then he smelled a smell like cooking. Another one came in closer, and exploded shortly before it hit the ground with a loud bang. Instinct honed by hundreds of war movies sent Karrel flat on his belly, but the people around him didn't have that experience to call on. They didn't know to duck and cover.

More explosions and shrapnel flying everywhere, ripping holes in the people on the streets. Then, as Karrel watched, a burning shard of something fell in the wetness that came from that first rocket and it began to burn. The fire spread quickly, consuming the alcohol and igniting the lard. The whole street was burning.

Karrel was crawling backward toward the door to the aid station when he saw a woman with her clothing afire run by him. She would die. He leapt up and ran, throwing his cloak around her to smother the fire. It was then that another missile with shrapnel went off. Three chunks of bronze scrap tore through him, one in his left arm, one in his belly, and one in his right foot. The belly wound was probably fatal, Karrel realized as he found himself sitting next to the body of the woman who had been hit in the head by a piece of shrapnel. Her brains were all over him.

The missile that caused the belly wound had probably also shredded his intestines. If he didn't bleed out, he would die in a week or so, of infection.

Slowly, with effort, he slid himself back to the wall and pulled his pistol out of his belt. He was in shock, thankfully. Thinking clearly, but not well. *No point in thinking well*, he thought. *I'm dead, anyway.*

☆   ☆   ☆

He was still sitting there, pistol in his lap, when the first of Antigonus' forces reached him. Sitting there, eyes open, but drying in the heat of the fires. The soldier saw the man and his clothing. He came over and looked closer. It was one of the ship people, he was almost sure. Then he saw the pistol. He'd heard about those, but never seen one until now. He looked around to be sure no one was looking, then took the pistol and went on.

In spite of the lack of preparedness, the rocket barrage did its job. By midafternoon Antigonus had three bridgeheads in West Babylon and was pouring troops into the battle.

But Attalus' troops, fully aware of Antigonus' reputation with captured enemies, were in no mood to yield. The fighting was bloody and the bloodier it got, the angrier Antigonus and his men got.

West Babylon, radio room
December 11, 319 BCE

Susan Godlewski was at the radio, reporting on the fighting. Antigonus wasn't the only one with rockets. After the initial attack, Attalus used his, firing into East Babylon, concentrating on Antigonus' palace. Antigonus wasn't there, but his wife of twenty years was. She and two of his younger children burned in the fire.

Susan reported the fire, but not the deaths. She could see the fire, but didn't know that Stratonice or the kids were caught in it. She probably wouldn't have cared even if she had known. She had never met Antigonus' wife and there were people she did know and care about dying all around her. Some burned to death, some were killed by shrapnel, but the majority were killed by hard men with sword and shield. She could see it out her window, and hear screams from elsewhere as well. Babylon was alight with fires.

It was 4:24 P.M. according to the clock in her computer when the fighting reached her part of the building. To keep the equipment safe, she shut down the system and pulled the double bar knife switch to disconnect the antenna and keep the equipment safe. Then she waited.

A few minutes later, a bunch of troops entered. By the nipples on the bronze breastplates, she figured they were Companion Cavalry who worked for Antigonus.

"I am Susan Godlewski of the *Queen of the Sea*. I have diplomatic immunity." The words were Greek and actually translated into something closer to "ship people protection," but immunity was how she thought of it.

The large, grizzled man in the lead took two steps

across to her and hit her in the face. It wasn't a
slap, either. He used a closed fist and came close to
breaking her jaw. "Fuck your ship people. The big
ship is far away."

Susan was shocked, in pain, and terrified. She had
a pistol in her belt. It was made on the *Queen of
the Sea*, a six-shot cap-and-ball black powder pistol
shooting a .45 caliber round with enough force to get
through standard bronze armor. She knew that, but
somehow, in the moment, she was unable to draw it.

She cowered in the corner next to the wooden file
cabinet. Then he reached down, picked her up by the
front of her shirt, and drew his fist back to hit her
again. She lifted her arms to protect her face and he
hit her in the stomach. She threw up all over him,
and he threw her onto the floor, dizzy and dazed.
One hand found her holster and, terrified, she drew
the pistol and pointed it up at him.

Cyniscus saw the weapon. He'd heard about them,
but never seen one. But the way she was holding it,
the way her hand shook, he wasn't very worried. Long
years of experience with Alexander and then Antigonus
had taught him well. In battle, don't hesitate. Go for
the attacker, hit them before they're ready.

He wasn't stopping. She jerked the trigger. There
was a loud bang. He was still there. She jerked again
and again and again. She kept pulling that trigger
until the hammer clicked on an empty chamber and
the room was full of smoke.

And still he was standing there. As the smoke
cleared, she saw the blood. It was leaking out of

two holes, one in his chest plate and the other in his arm. His face filled with rage and pain. Using his other arm he reached, picked her up, and threw her against the wall.

It was an eternity later when Antigonus One-eye arrived and brought the beating to a halt. Surprisingly, Susan's only broken bone was her nose.

The beating stopped for a time as they spoke, and the Macedonian words passed by her without leaving any meaning behind.

"I told you to be careful of the ship people," Antigonus said angrily, but not shouting. "This is the only one we have now. The other one died in the fighting."

Cyniscus was a captain in his own right and the son of a noble Macedonian house. He was of the Companion Cavalry and an experienced commander in the field. "I *was* gentle. The bitch shot me. By rights she should be dead." By now the pain was excruciating. Cyniscus' left arm was broken and bleeding. His right chest, just above the gut, burned like fire and he knew enough about arrow wounds in the same place to know that his chances weren't good.

Looking at him, Antigonus let it drop. "Have the healers bandage you up. We'll talk about this later."

Antigonus looked at the woman on the floor. This wasn't how he wanted to do it, but then he looked out the window across the Euphrates to the burning palace. It was possible that his wife and children were still alive, but not very likely. Killed by devices brought by the ship people in a place where they should have been safe. He looked at that fire, and didn't care about ship people protection. The man was dead anyway. So the death of the woman shouldn't matter.

But if he were to do it, he should make a point. A point for the ship people, and a point for the other satraps so they would know that ship people weren't gods to fear. They were just people who could be defeated and brought to heel like any others.

"Get her up." He gestured, and two of the Companion Cavalry lifted the woman and held her up. Her head lolled, and she was bleeding from her nose and mouth. Apparently, aside from the broken nose, she had lost some teeth. Well, that wouldn't matter, not for long.

He stepped forward, grabbed a handful of her hair, and lifted her head. "Listen to me, woman. You're going to do what I say, or I'm going to give you to Cyniscus and he will kill you slow."

"Ship people protection," she said.

At least that's what he thought she said. Between the missing teeth and the fact that she was only semiconscious, it was hard to be sure. "I don't care about ship people protection, woman. The ship cannot reach us here, and before I'm done the only protection the ship people will have is what I grant them. Now, you will turn on your radio and put me in touch with your Captain Floden."

☆   ☆   ☆

Susan Godlewski didn't argue. By now she didn't have any argument left in her. She couldn't take another beating like that, much less torture. Besides, if she had any hope of surviving, it would be because Floden convinced this crazy asshole that he had to fear the ship people.

It took a while. She managed to restore the double bar knife switch to connect the antenna. Her eyes were blurry and her fingers didn't want to do what she told them, but she got the password typed in and the system came up. The radio connection was established, and she called up the video conference protocol. She wanted Floden and the rest to see what they'd done to her. She got the radio tech. He took one look at her and put her through. A short time later, she had Lars Floden, Marie Easley, Dag Jakobsen and Roxane on screen in four squares.

That was when Antigonus One-eye pulled her away from the desk. He stood her up and spoke to them all. "You ship people are not gods that we should bow down to. You are sheep for the shearing. The only difference is the quality of the wool. That gives you a little extra value, but not so much."

The hand that was holding her up now drove her to her knees. Her head drooped forward.

☆   ☆   ☆

Lars Floden looked at the scene shot from the computer's screen camera. Susan Godlewski was on her knees, head bowed, and Antigonus One-eye was standing over her with his famous one-eyed helmet shiny and bright. But there were bloodstains on his armor as he drew the cavalry *kopis* from his belt. Lars barely had time to take in the scene and no time at all to react.

"I am no coward to bow before you. You will accept your place and deliver up your wool or you will be butchered."

Antigonus swung the *kopis* down, and in one mighty stroke took Susan's head from her shoulders. Blood gushed. Antigonus flung the corpse onto the floor.

Then he stepped to the desk and leaned forward so that his face was close to the screen, so close that Lars could see the scar tissue peeking out from the edge of his helmet.

"You will send me more ship people to replace these two, or I will butcher you all."

Lars was frozen by shock, horror, and growing rage. He just sat there, not hearing as Antigonus One-eye blathered on about his demands. But, thankfully, Lars wasn't the only one on the call.

Marie spoke from beside him. Her voice was calm and icy. "Antigonus One-eye is dead, and ship people don't talk to corpses."

Then Dag spoke from Roxane's suite. "Radio room, shut down communications with Station Babylon and disable the equipment."

Dag and Roxane's faces disappeared from their insert in his screen. Lars heard the radio tech say, "Captain?" And suddenly Lars was captain again. In careful Greek, he said, "Confirmed, radio tech. Antigonus One-eye is a dead man walking. Babylon Station is offline until further notice."

☆   ☆   ☆

Antigonus heard the ship people words, then the captain's face went from shocked to hard, and he said in Greek, "Confirmed, radio tech. Antigonus One-eye is dead. Babylon Station is offline until further notice."

A moment later the image on the screen went blank. The screen was now filled with little boxes of text, but they were in the strange, almost Latin, script of the ship people and Antigonus could not read them. Then a little box came up and writing appeared. Then the screen went completely blank.

Slowly it came to Antigonus that he might have made a mistake. He looked carefully at the device. There were still small glowing parts, but he didn't know what they meant. He stood and turned. "Find me someone who knows how this works."

He looked at the body and the blood and added, "And have this place cleaned up."

EPILOGUE

TO KILL A CORPSE

Queen of the Sea, *off Formentera Island*
Sunset, December 11, 319 BCE

As soon as they entered the captain's suite where Lars and Marie were waiting for them, Dag said, "Sir, we have to kill that bastard One-eye. Forget the *Queen's* usual neutrality."

"It has nothing to do with neutrality," said Roxane. "The *Queen* holds its position in the world not simply—not mostly, being honest—because of neutrality. You hold the position you do because everyone fears to anger you. And with good reason. They remember what happened to Gorgias' fleet and the men who seized the *Reliance*. If you let Antigonus live now, your authority will start slipping away. And Macedonia is no longer a hazard, now that Cassander is dead and Thessalonike will be ruling there."

"I quite agree," Lars Floden said. "Now please tell me how we are going to kill Antigonus—which, mind you, will require defeating his army as well. He's in

Babylon. That's three hundred miles from the Persian Gulf, twice that far from the Mediterranean coast."

"I don't know, sir, but we have to find a way." Dag sat down at the table. "We are going to need New America for this. They have some navy veterans in their navy and... Wait a minute... they converted that lifeboat they bought into a patrol boat. Could we do that?"

"Do we know if a lifeboat can get that far up the Euphrates?" asked Floden.

"I think so, sir. I think the reason Babylon is there is because it's about as far up the Euphrates as you can get before you have to start portaging your boats."

"But if we build them on the *Queen* every scholar on the ship is going to know what we're doing," said Marie.

"Yes, they will. We need to talk to New America," Dag said. "Have them build the platforms, then have the *Reliance* bring them to us somewhere out of sight of anyone."

"All right, Mr. Jakobsen. We have the start of a plan. It will need to be fleshed out, and it's going to take months, all while what that bastard did to our people leaks out. And some of the locals are going to flock to his banner over it." Captain Floden shook his head. "I never wanted to be a military man, Dag, but right now I would cheerfully trade the *Queen of the Sea* for an Abrams tank."

"We'll figure it out, sir. One way or another, we'll get the bastard."

Roxane sat next to Dag. "You will need Eumenes, also. And Attalus, if he's still alive. And most of all..."

She paused, as if steeling her will. "You will need Eurydice—and Philip."

Eumenes' army camp
Evening, December 11, 319 BCE

Philip was sitting up in their bed when Eurydice entered their tent. He was working on his notes. Something mathematical.

"You heard?" she asked.

He didn't look up. "Yes. Eumenes came in and told me."

Eurydice herself had been attending a childbirth. One of the camp followers had had a baby that afternoon. It was not the first time she'd ever been present at such an occasion, but she now had a much keener interest.

Normally, she would have discussed the new political situation with Philip. He still found politics mostly a puzzle, but he did have flashes of insight. Eurydice had come to understand, over time, that in his own way her husband was quite brilliant.

But that had to take second place this evening.

"I'm pregnant," she said. "I'm quite sure of it."

Philip said nothing. He didn't raise his gaze from the notes he was scribbling.

Eurydice wasn't offended or angry. This was just the way he was. She went over to the bed, sat down next to Philip, and squeezed him as tightly as she could.

After a few seconds, Philip asked, "Have you spoken to Roxane?"

"Yes."

"The empire has to survive. It has to prosper. That means you and Roxane have to keep getting along."

She smiled—and kept a tight squeeze. "Yes. Yes. Yes. She thinks all that is true also."

"Good." He went back to working on his notes.

Eurydice didn't release him. After a while, Philip spoke again.

"I have been reading about the ship people's history. Their great empire was Roman, not Greek like ours."

"*Macedonian*, not Greek," she said sternly.

"There's not really any difference. Not in the long run. But what's important about that history is that the Romans often had two rulers. They made it work. They *did*, Eurydice."

"I believe you."

"We're much smarter than Romans, too."

"That's true," she said. "Although they'll probably get smarter after..."

She decided not to finish the sentence the way she'd intended. *After we conquer them* might upset Philip. So she just said:

"After they spend more time with us."

Again, he surprised her. "After we conquer them, is what you really mean. That's all right. In the ship people's world, they conquered us so it's only fair we do it here. But first we have to deal with Antigonus."

"Antigonus is dead."

Philip shook his head. "That's a silly way to put it. You need to study calculus. Antigonus is *becoming* dead."

CAST OF CHARACTERS

Abial—Captain of *Nenet's Dream*

Agot, Karrel—Radio tech in Babylon

Alexander IV—Son of Alexander the Great and Roxane

Antigonus ("One-eye")—Satrap

Arrhidaeus—General for Alexander the Great

Attalus—Satrap

Banyous—Village headman in Thrace

Bayot, Tacaran—Radio tech with Eumenes' army

Beaulieu, Elise—First Officer, Navigation, *Queen of the Sea*

Bryant, Eric—Ship person, assistant and translator for Quitzko, the king of a Central American tribe

Calix—Member of the Cabeiri cult; poisoner

Capot Barca—Carthaginian envoy on the *Queen of the Sea*

Carruthers, Jane—Hotel manager, *Queen of the Sea*

Carthalo—Indentured servant; Carthaginian glassmaker

Cassander—Eldest son of Antipater

Cleopatra—Sister of Alexander the Great

Comfort, Anna—New America politician

Cotys—Son of Seuthes III

Dahl, Anders—Staff Captain (Executive officer), *Queen of the Sea*

Davis, Yolanda—New America politician

Easley, Marie—Historian; passenger on the *Queen of the Sea*

Eumenes—General of Alexander loyal to the royal family

Eurydice—Wife of Philip III

Floden, Lars—Captain of the *Queen of the Sea*

Gica, Rico—Radio tech in Pella

Godfrey, James—Envoy and radio tech to Carthage

Godlewski, Susan—Radio tech in Babylon

Howard, Paul—Military adviser in New America

Jakobsen, Dag—Environmental Compliance Officer, *Queen of the Sea*

Johnson, Tina—Chief of Station, Carthage

Kinney, Eleanor—Chief Purser, *Queen of the Sea*

Lang, Daniel—Chief Security Officer, *Queen of the Sea*

Lofdahl, Bruce—Radio tech in Alexandria, Egypt

Lysimachus—Macedonian general in Thrace

Matthews, Stella—Glassmaker in Fort Plymouth

Menander—Satrap

Menelaus—Ptolemy's brother, lives on the *Queen of the Sea*

Mirzadeh, Erica—Radio tech with Eumenes' army

Miles, Laura—Chief Medical Officer, *Queen of the Sea*

Miller, Amanda—Ambassador from New America

Newton, Sean—Cleopatra's boyfriend and financial adviser

Nike—Daughter of Seuthes III

Olympias—Mother of Alexander the Great

Palmer, Walter—Radio tech in Athens

Pharnabazus—Macedonian general in Eumenes' army

Philip III—Half-brother of Alexander the Great; husband of Eurydice

Ptolemy—Satrap of Egypt

Quitzko—Local, king and leading liberal light of Suthic tribe

Roxane—Widow of Alexander the Great; mother of Alexander IV

Scott, Adrian—Captain of the *Reliance*

Seuthes III—Priest-King of Thrace

Tanada, Malcolm—Radio tech in Pella

Thaïs—Hetaera; mother of Ptolemy's children

Thales—Soldier in Eumenes' army

Thessalonike—Foster daughter of Olympias; queen of Macedonia

Wai, TinTin—Radio tech in Alexandria, Egypt

Watanabe, Setsuichi—Chief Justice of New America

Wiley, Allen ("Al")—President of New America